The Bloodborn
by Jackson Salzman

THE BLOODBORN

First edition. March 15, 2024.

Copyright © 2024 Jackson Salzman.

ISBN: 979-8989821617

Written by Jackson Salzman.

Table of Contents

For my parents, who challenged me to write.

For the strong women that I've met.

And to the countless coffee shops along the way.

Kausha sat upright staring at the sheer face of the moon-lit wall. Her red and purple jumpsuit was stained with a mix of dirt, blood, and sweat, skewered through like pins in a cushion. Her sleeves were rolled up, feet bare for maneuverability. None of the blood was hers, of course, she wouldn't let that happen after hundreds of years of practice. She let herself collapse backwards for a moment, lingering puffs of clouds from the storm earlier in the night flying by overhead, blocking the stars momentarily. "Better get moving," she grumbled while struggling to her feet. She shifted her insides with a passing thought, tightened the knot in her crimson hair like she had done thousands of times since her childhood, dusted off what wasn't already dried and crusted from the night's activities, then set off towards The Forest.

Chapter 1: The warmth of a fire

Some time ago.

"Come on you Urt, show me what you've got already so we can settle this. It's not like Kausha over there is going to help you this time," a tall, burly Spearhead grumbled through sharp teeth. Playing cards littered a stone block placed on The Forest floor in the middle of a clearing in a small village called Lumber.

A dwindling fire crackled off to the side, warming and illuminating Kausha's brown and gray cloak from behind while casting a flickering light onto the other's faces around the block.

"Oh, 'ye moss off, Skirm and let tha Urt es turn - erryone knows they try ta bore ya ta death ta win," responded the second Spearhead in the circle. He was about a head smaller than the first, white with black spots covering his body with six fingers instead of three. Both hands cupped a jar filled with a pungent, sour smelling drink that was obviously alcohol in nature with the way he slurred his speech and rolled back and forth like he was constantly trying to keep himself from falling over.

"How many times I have to tell you, Shaum, to cool it off with that stuff - it's going to be the death of you," remarked Skirm with a wave of his hand, his small, perfectly circular black eyes focused on the Urt. Kausha sat cross legged on her stump, staring unblinkingly at the Urt, her tongue still dull from the Spearhead drink, mind foggy, awaiting the final play of the third and final match. The Urt's red eyes, sticking straight up out of its head like feelers, peeked up over his cards, and gazed over each player sitting around the stone block. Then, retracting his eyes behind his cards, he placed one card face-down on top of one of Skirm's cards and his final card face-up on top of Kausha's closest card to her body.

"Moss," Kausha cursed, knowing that that card was the one that did her in, nullifying her entire attack. "Should have known with those beady eyes of yours, Taulas."

"I could kiss yur tail, ya Urt!" yelled Shaum as he jumped up, throwing his hands up in celebration, spilling what was left of his drink on top of his head. Echoes of laughter erupted in the clearing as Shaum tripped over his stump backwards, landing in a thunk, his feet splayed out and in the air. Skirm was the loudest and most distinct out of all of them with his bellowing roar of a laugh, slapping his knee at the same time.

"Alright, alright, you had your game, now do as you promised and get out so I can clean up all this mess," squeaked the owner of Lumber, a three foot tall Marpet with bright yellow eyes, hundreds of small, sharp quills on its back, large, fluffy ears, a pointed nose, and surprisingly large hands for something that small.

"Just one more game, Yaula. Shaum will buy the next round," Skirm struggled, still laughing at Shaum on the ground who was struggling to right himself.

"Like ell I will!" barked Shaum in response from his back, attempting to roll over.

"You know as well as I do that these games last a good dragon's breath, so you aren't playing here! Now pay up and get on with it!" squeaked Yaula, this time a little louder, her quills visibly vibrating.

"Fine, fine," replied Skirm, pushing on his knees to stand, then proceeding to lumber over to Shaum to help him up.

No one even thinks of messing with Yaula, thought Kausha, as she herself uncrossed her legs, dusted herself off, and dropped two coppers on the stone to pay for her drinks.

Leaving the campfire, laughter, and berating behind, Kausha headed west through the beaten-down grass in between trees, which constituted a path of sorts after years of wanderers passing through the small village of Lumber. Three paths split from the main area, consisting of a few tree houses each, with the north one containing the businesses constant of a normal village, all dark at this time of night. Kausha would have to visit those come daylight before she continued her trek further west towards her birthplace of Purtghast to visit her great great grandmother, who was coming up on her final moons. Walking silently, albeit with a stumble on a root here or there, she could still hear Yaula scalding Shaum and Skirm over their protests, picturing her pointing her small fingers at them all the while. Everyone knew though that Yaula loved every second of these wanderers, and the gossip from further out in The Forests even more.

As Kausha rounded the corner of the largest tree nearby, one that signaled nearing the treehouses for visitors, her ears perked up at something else off to the left. She froze, one foot in the air, hand immediately jolting to the knife in her waistband. Much simpler to use than her special skills. Nothing. She felt silly standing in this position, but like fishing, once you move, it moves. *There.* She spun on one heel, maneuvering her insides towards the back of her body, away from who or what it was, and in one swooping motion, knife point faced outwards, she stopped.

"Eep," squealed Taulas, his eyes retreating into his head, nearly falling backwards over his own feet. Kausha stepped back, sliding her knife back into her waistband in one effortless movement as if the alcohol never had an effect on her.

"What was that, Kausha?! You could have took an eye off!" Taulas exclaimed.

"Sorry Taulas, thought I heard something," replied Kausha.

"You did! Me! Is this because of the card game?"

"No, it isn't, I heard something else, over there," Kausha pointed. They both went still, staring through the limbs and leaves into The Forest for a moment, as if they both wanted proof of a sound.

"You're just being paranoid like always - it *IS* The Forest afterall," Taulas ended as he let out a sigh, then strode past Kausha, his eyes returning back to their full height.

"That wasn't natural, I know it," whispered Kausha under her breath, but it was too dark and too late to do anything about it right now. The best she could hope for was for whatever it was to be scared of groups and fire. Following in Taulas' footsteps, Kausha walked to the end of the path where the three treehouses presided, each larger than anything she had slept in lately, consisting of twelve bedrooms on three levels wrapped around the tree itself. They were never filled - maybe three or four wanderers at any given time passing through, or staying longer in the case of Skirm and Shaum. Upon climbing the steps to reach her room, Kausha removed the knife from her waistband and placed it under the feathered pillow stuffed with feathers long fallen from their owner.

"You're being a little over worried, don't you think," she chided herself as she lay down to get comfortable. Little did she know that this would be the most comfortable she would be in a long, long time.

Chapter 2: The smell of death

Kausha awoke to a putrid smell assaulting her nostrils. Blinking groggily, it took her a few moments to recognize the smell. *Green acid!* Her eyes went wide, blood coursing into her head in order to think clearly. She had encountered this smell ages ago on her visit to the southern parts of Uradaria and where the smell lingered, nothing stood, not even the trees and shrubbery. She looked up and saw green acid eating through the tree-branch ceiling in multiple spots, confirming her suspicion. She scrambled out of bed and surveyed the ceiling and walls, attempting to find a safe way out of the room. *There!* She darted left, right, right, left, right, left - a straight shot now to the exit. Without worrying to fiddle with the handle, she slammed the wood-slatted door open with her shoulder and saw horror at her doorstep with three of the other rooms in her treehouse already away, only small slivers of branches remaining. She looked up and saw a massive green cloud, which looked exactly like a storm cloud, glowing in the deep red moonlight, dripping acid at what appeared to be at random places and random intervals.

"Moss!" she cursed as her heart continued to pound in her stomach, the safest place she could think to move it. Sweat dripped from her forehead. She looked down at The Forest floor, retracing the stairs leading to the various levels, and noticed that there was only a small gap that had melted away below and moved before thinking, running as quickly as she could down the stairs. All the while, sizzling sounds hissed around her as leaves, trees, branches, and anything else the acid touched melted away. Nearly to the ground, Kausha leaped the rest of the ten feet over already-melted parts of the stairs. She rolled upon impact, but couldn't stop in time.

"Moss!" she cursed, pain shooting through her body as she rolled right into a puddle she couldn't see from higher up, the acid eating through her cloak and skin at the same.

She ripped her sleeve off immediately to see steam coming off of a melted-off section of her flesh at her shoulder. No blood leaked from the wound due to Kausha's special blood movement, and no major organs were injured either. She tensed, and through watery eyes, she took the sleeve she ripped off and tightly wrapped the injured part of her arm off as if it would help. Being around other races had taught her about medical care, something her family had never needed to learn. Gathering her thoughts, Kausha looked up at the acid cloud, moving as if it had a mind of its own. Moving east, then stopping momentarily before turning north, acid slowed slightly - or was she just further from the center of the cloud. *The others*, Kausha panicked, peeling her eyes away from the cloud, turning to run back through the trees along the same path she took just hours ago, or minutes, Kausha wasn't sure. The path was now laid with large toffs of acid-severed tree branches with puddles of acid everywhere.

Turning at the enormous corner tree, she wasn't sure what she was going to see when she arrived at the center of the Lumber, but being more focused on the ground and acid cloud above, now looking like it was moving south again, kept her mind occupied.

What the moss is going on?! She burst into the clearing near the stone table in the middle of town.

Maybe being out in the open will be the safest spot to make sure I'm not hit. Standing next to the stone table, she crouched slightly to get ready to dodge the acid if needed.

"Child!" she heard, head spinning to the north in the direction of the voice. "Child, this way, come. Hurry!" She recognized that voice - it was Yaula.

Lowering her gaze, she saw Yaula waving from inside of a large dirt mound. Kausha glanced up and could hear the sizzle sound of acid falling harder to the north out of view, then bolted towards Yaula, dodging acid puddles, leftover cards and mugs from earlier.

TSSSSS. Kausha heard it before she felt it - this one on her calf - making her tumble into the place Yaula was beckoning. Kausha rolled head over heels over herself, ending on her back, sat up, then reached down, tearing the part of her pant leg off that had the acid on it to reveal steam coming off of an even larger melted-off section of her flesh than her arm.

"Moss!" Yaula exclaimed, wincing at the sight, sound, and smell of Kausha's flesh melting away. Eyes blurry from the pain in both her arm and leg, Kausha quickly wrapped her calf tight. Her head swam, pain taking over her every thought as she collapsed to her back, unable to move.

"Kausha!" she heard in a muffled tone, almost as if underwater. "Kausha, are you alright?!" Yaula asked. Kausha's eyes fluttered. The last thing she saw before passing out from the pain was Yaula and two other shadowed faces standing over her.

Chapter 3: Whispers

Olibtine, in his normal attire - a blue and white cloak with the Gbinti symbol of a scale over a book in the middle of his chest - had his hood hanging down his back. He sat at an ornate oak desk cluttered with parchment, scales, relics, and stacks of books that would give anyone an anxious feeling of being overwhelmed with work, but not Olibtine. He enjoyed the busy work - there was just something about diving into his research, puffing on his pipe, and complete silence that appealed to him. Today, under candlelight, Olibtine was focusing on the trade disputes between Gbinti and its sister city, Nortmund - a larger, more prosperous city due to its access to ujuntu deposits, the most rare of the metals found on Uradaria.

Knock knock knock, Olibtine heard at the study's door. He ignored it - maybe they will just go away. *Knock knock.* They didn't. With a sigh, Olibtine sat up straight in his high-back wooden chair made of the same ornate oak material that the desk was made of, and continued to puff on his pipe.

"What is it?" he asked towards the door.

"Sir, we have news of another attack."

Another attack? That seems highly unlikely. If so, that would mean the frequency is speeding up, Olibtine thought.

"Sir?" came the voice behind the door again, this time slightly louder than before.

"Yes, come in, come in."

The small, circle door began to swing inwards, casting flickering light from the hallway into the large, mostly dark study. In pops a small, slender man with indiscriminately features, dressed in a comfortable blue and white uniform with the same symbol of a scale over a book in the middle of his chest as Olibtine's.

"Hello Sorito, is this true?" asked Olibtine before Sorito could even cross the short distance to his desk.

"Yes sir, we just got word that just a few hours ago, a large, green mass was seen over The Forest to the west, unmistakably dropping acid over a swath of land. We do not have specifics on the location or why, but multiple scouts were able to pick this up at the same time," Sorito explained.

"And where is the cloud now?" Olibtine asked while clamping down on his pipe, even though he already knew the answer.

"It dissipated a mere five minutes after it began and there is no trace left in the sky," replied Sorito.

Olibtine wrinkled his nose. "Same as all of the other occurrences as well then."

Sorito nodded as Olibtine took another puff from his pipe, resting his head back against the chair, staring up at nothing in particular, but noticing the flickering light from the hallway dancing across the ceiling. His eyebrow rose above green eyes as he thought he saw something move in the shadows. He closed his eyes to right himself while taking another puff.

"Sir, there is one more thing," Sorito revealed with a quiver in his tone. Olibtine opened his eyes, lifted his head from the chair, then looked at Sorito. *Did he look more haggard than when he walked in mere moments ago?*

"What else?" prodded Olibtine, meeting his eyes.

Sorito shifted slightly, only noticeable due to his body being backlit by the candlelight from the hall. "One of... one of the Bloodborn's lives is ending," he spat out.

A jolt shot up Olibtine's spine as if his chair was hit in the back with a hammer. Sitting up even straighter than before, his eyes widened, white knuckles showing as he grasped his pipe harder at the news.

"How... How did we come about this? The Bloodborn are few and far between and are far outside of our city's reach," asked Olibtine, this question being one that he truly did not know the answer to.

Sorito licked his lips, clearly struggling with how to relay the information, then replied in one breath. "We received word from a merchant vessel that returned to port not days ago. Their vessel was in the area, not a few towns away, when word reached them. We believe that the word from the merchant can be relied upon. It has been hundreds of years since the last Bloodborn's passing and not a rumor since has crossed the people's lips."

"I see," Olibtine started, eyebrows narrowing, "Is that all that was heard - that one of their lives is ending?"

"Yes," responded Sorito, "there was nothing else that was said, but the ears that know what to do with this information will understand."

"Thank you, Sorito."

With that, Olibtine nodded while taking another pull of his pipe. Sorito turned heel and walked out without another word, shuttering the flickering light from the hall and leaving Olibtine with the single candle on his desk. He sat there for a long while puffing on his pipe, contemplating what this meant to Gbiniti, The Forest, and every living soul in Uradaria and decided that no more work was getting done tonight. He sighed before blowing out the candle, then put his hands on the table, pushed himself up, and slowly walked out of the study as if the weight of the Uradaria was just placed on his back.

Chapter 4: Natural Tendencies

Kausha was lounging with her mother, grandmother, great grandmother, and great great grandmother in an airy outdoor seating area that was covered with a tan cloth canopy draped cross-ways from corner to corner attached to four thick wooden pillars. They each had on the customary red and purple jumpsuits befitting the women of the Bloodborn, each embossed in the front with a single teardrop of blood to symbolize their heritage, the oldest in Uradaria.

Kausha could not remember how she had gotten here, but the salty breeze from the sea and heat from the intense sun above distracted her for the time being.

"... know that to be true," she caught at the end of her mother's sentence directed at her grandmother.

"That, I will admit, but that does not forgive their previous transgressions, no matter how many new rulers they go through," replied her grandmother, this time looking at her mother and her mother's mother, each nodding their heads in unison. "Plus," she went on, "why should we ease our standards and traditions for ones that are but an eyeblink to us? They have no need to think long-term because they cannot envision long-term. Doing so would not benefit us in the least bit - it would do the complete opposite and give the impression that *they* are the ones that should lead Uradaria. I fear that if this transgression is allowed to hover over the heads of everyone, the Bloodborn will fall to the timekeeper's clock."

Everyone casually nodded their heads at that while glancing at one another in order.

Kausha sat up straight and interjected, "What about their societal advancements? Sure, they have short lifespans, but my most recent trip to the east saw advancements in boating, fishing, trading, and even their leadership choices, which are no longer decided by bloodshed, but by brain. They are not the same as they were hundreds of years ago, that I can say for fact."

There was a long pause in the air as the women gathered their thoughts, examining the past, which between the five women, was substantial.

Great great grandmother tapped her cane to the ground, her purple eyes bright and youthful against wrinkled brown skin. "I have seen those from the east set one another on fire, tear one another limb for limb, and worst of all, rape their women, and all for the simple pleasures and appetites of a barbarian society."

She lifted her eyes, staring directly at Kausha. "Do you see none of these things anymore when you visit, child?" she asked, Kausha feeling a chill creep up her spine.

"While they may..."

A tap of wood on stone interrupted her. "Answer me, plainly, child," demanded great great grandmother, eyes intense.

Kausha hesitated for a moment, gathering her thoughts. "I have not personally seen these things, but they are still happening, but not in public view like old. They are advancing, just slowly. Maybe if we helped..." a knock this time rather than a tap as she was interrupted once again.

"You do not teach a bloodhound to suck blood, they must learn for themselves," great great grandmother responded in a finality tone that was not to be second guessed. "Now child, heal yourself up and get back here - I don't have much time left."

Kausha tilted her head, face tight with the look of confusion. *What?* She gazed around the space. Everything was beginning to fade, darkness enveloping the outside of the pillars around her, then from the sky. She blinked and when she opened her eyes, she saw a brown ceiling, curved near her left side and felt something soft beneath her. As she looked around in the dimly lit area, she saw faces she recognized, and one she didn't, sitting at a rectangle table on benches, cups in hand, chatting so quiet that she wasn't able to hear what was being said. One of them, a woman she did not recognize, glanced over, "She's up."

All eyes then turned on her.

Chapter 5: Curiosity

Kausha had always healed relatively quickly due to her bloodline, but this was something entirely new. She once even healed from a wound she received in training that nearly cut her arm clean off, but even that took an entire week.

How long have I been out? Kausha wondered, shifting her body in the soft bed.

Yaula stood up, nearly spilling her drink. She hurriedly sat it down, jumped off of her seat, and scrambled over to Kausha as she began to sit up. Yaula jumped up onto a stool, then put out her hand onto Kausha's shoulder, forcing her to stay put.

"There is no need for that, child, just lie back down. You're in no condition to be moving around right now - you nearly lost an arm and a leg earlier."

"Earlier? That was this morning then?" Kausha asked, rubbing her forehead.

"Yes, child, you were out for nearly an entire day. Expected you to be out longer, but this is much better. You actually don't look bad at all, but you sure were mumbling up a storm earlier," Yaula answered.

"I feel pretty good actually. Did I say anything?" Kausha asked as she rubbed her shoulder where the acid had dropped - now heavily wrapped with large green leaves with some sort of wet, almost sticky, paste.

"Didn't catch anything, really. How about you all?" Yaula turned her head towards the three others that were sitting at the table still. There was Skirm and Shaum, whom Kausha recognized, but the third, a female Catsnif with striking orange eyes that stood out from a striped furry face of brown and tan, she didn't know. They all shook their heads in unison, the large spearheads looking

14

goofy sitting at such a small table as if they had to squeeze their way in.

"Regardless, you had us worried there for a bit. That acid got you real bad, especially on your leg." Yaula glanced down, Kausha following her eyes to see a similar wrapping she had on as her shoulder.

Kausha began to sit up again, Yaula once again putting a hand on her shoulder attempting to force her back town. It was a good attempt, but Kausha was larger and easily stronger than her, even if she had been injured recently.

"Yaula, I'm fine," Kausha stated, continuing to sit up. Yaula pulled her hand back hesitantly. Kausa looked down at the bandage on her shoulder and began to peel at it from one end.

"Tsssst!" Yaula hissed, eyes wide, but she didn't move to stop her. Kausha continued to peel it off slowly. Her suspicions were confirmed when Yaula's mouth dropped open. There was no wound at all, not even a scar where the acid had eaten away at her brown skin.

"Moss! What in Arduinna's forest?! There is nothing there!" Yaula exclaimed as she placed both hands on the edge of the bed to support herself for a closer look.

The two Spearheads clanked their cups on the table and jolted up, nearly knocking the entire table over with their knees in the process. Once they crossed the entire span of the room in two strides, they looked at one another and smiled.

"Thas' mighty impressive thar, Kaush," Shaum eyed while scratching the top of his head with his six fingers.

"Mighty impressive indeed," agreed Skirm, nodding while bending over far too close to her shoulder, forcing Kausha to lean away from him slightly or else she would be hit by his large head. He then rubbed the spot where the leaf used to be. Kausha frowned, huffing, then rolling her shoulder away from him.

"How did you do that?" Skirm started, "No way anyone normal can heal up that quickly in less than a day's time. Moss, I was just getting my heart back to the normal pace myself." Kausha just shrugged.

"Oh, come off et, don't give us tha," Shaum crossed his arms in response, narrowing his eyes.

While Kausha knew it was her bloodline, she never went around telling anyone for fear of being treated like her ancestors of old. This, however, was entirely new to her too and so it was easy enough to feign a surprise towards the others.

"What about your leg?" Yaula asked from between the two Spearheads, barely coming up to their hips even while standing on the stool. "That wound was even worse than the one on your shoulder."

Kausha reached down to her calf and undid that leaf wrapping too. A high pitched whistle came from Yaula's lips accompanied by the sound of smiles crossing the spearhead faces.

"Well, that'll do it then," Yaula awed, completely taken aback, "You all ever seen anything like this before?" Yaula looked up at Shaum, then to Skirm. Once again, both simply shook their heads in unison. "You, Nalia?" Yaula turned to face the female with furry, pointed ears. Nalia shook her head as well. "Alright then, seeing as this is new to everyone, we should get to chatting about what happened here earlier this morning. Come now, I'll cook us up some stew while we do so."

Chapter 6: Reflections

Yaula stood not ten feet away in the kitchen, humming while stirring the concoction in a copper pot on a copper stove with a wooden fire underneath. A stone block for countertops flanked the stove to the left and the right, which were currently occupied with knives and forgotten food scraps. Kausha, Skirm, Shaum, and Nalia sat at the horizontal wooden kitchen table that had seen better days, eyes glued on their wooden mugs.

"Soooo anyone got any idea of wha' append this mornin?" asked Shaum, gripping his mug with both hands, six fingers overlapping one another completely engulfing it as if it wasn't even there. Yaula's humming stopped abruptly, but she didn't stop stirring the stew. No answer. Shaum rolled his eyes. "Ah, cmoff it, I know someone ere knows somethin."

"I've heard of something like this happening in the past all across Uradaria on random occurrences, but nothing in The Forest before." Everyone's eyes around the table shot up to look at Nalia, speaking in a soft, yet singing voice, at a much faster pace than the Spearheads. "Last year, north of Gbinti, a town called Eqout was practically wiped away from the acid and no one knows why. There was one more rumor that I heard of one that happened up north not too far from The Forest border, but I don't know the details of that one, but I would assume that the same thing happened there as well," she went on to say without so much as taking a breath between sentences.

"Really?" asked Skirm, eyes wide, "Did you see the one at Eqiut?"

"Eqout," corrected Nalia, "And no, I didn't see it at the time, but I had been through there a lot growing up, and seeing it after was something I couldn't even imagine before. Huge holes in the ground, practically the size of Skirm, from the acid eating it away.

Homes half leveled, crops ruined and completely unfarmable, and worst of all - hundreds of grave plots all along the road leading out of the village, some just entire families in one due to the fact that the acid ate them away and what was left of them indistinguishable from one another. It was the most horrific thing I had ever seen," she finished, hanging her head and closing her eyes as her ears drooped at the same time. A silent contemplation hung in the air, only broken up by the continued stirring of the stew coming from Yaula.

"Es a good thing tha Yaula ere had this undergroun ouse then!" roared Shaum in a jovial fashion, glancing between Kausha, Nalia, then Skirm while raising his mug at the same time. He frowned once he realized they were not going to do the same, then he took a large swig, his face returning to normal once putting down the mug.

"Hey Yaula, got anything stronger than this ale?" asked Skirm, turning around on the bench, bumping the table and nearly knocking over Kausha's drink, to face Yaula. She simply pointed to her left at the dark oat cabinet, continuing to stir. With that, Skirm looked back at the few at the table, shrugged, and got up, slowly this time as to not knock the table again, took a few steps to the cabinet, and grabbed a large oak cask layered with horizontal copper rings around it, and walked back over the the table, putting it in the middle of everyone. Shaum proceeded to chug his current mug and was the first to pour himself a helping of the stuff. Even with a Spearhead's tolerance, he sniffed and his eyes watered a little as he pulled back his chin and scoffed.

"Phew, tha stuff smells strong as our pop's swell from ome, Skirm!" Shaum grinned, revealing his sharp rows of jagged teeth. He took a swig and when his mug cleared his mouth, his face was in a grimace, eyes squeezed tight, mouth in a pucker.

"Ahh, that's tha stuff!" he sighs with a smile on his face. Skirm chuckled and poured his own while motioning towards Kausha and Nalia's to gauge if they wanted some. Kausha held out her mug while Nalia covered hers and shook her head.

"Still have some," she stated. Skirm shrugged, then placed the cask back in the middle of the table.

"Well?" Shaum asked as Skirm and Kausha took a sip together. Skirm cringed the same as Shaum, but came up and replied, "Yup, that's the same as dad's," while Kausha kept as straight a face as ever, not showing any sort of response to the liquor and even took a second, larger gulp right after. Shaum's eyes widened, his white and black spotted cheeks turning a shade of red as he stared. He felt himself staring too long and instead diverted his eyes away towards Yaula.

"How'd ya... How'd ya get tha Spearhead recipe? I never ad it outside o' my ome," Shaum asked.

Yaula turned half way around, still stirring, and had a smirk on her face this time. "Spearheads aren't the only ones that know how to make good liquor. That, plus I may have had a Spearhead or two come through this village before you two showed up." She then turned right back around to continue stirring. Shaum looked at Skirm, raising one eyebrow quizzically and then shrugged.

Tap tap tap tap came the familiar sound of wood clanking against a copper pot. Yaula heaved the pot, descended the stool she stood on, then heaved it over to the middle of the table where everyone was sitting. She turned around, grabbed five bowls, shooing Shaum over so she could get some seat, then lifted herself up so stood on the bench, immediately spooning servings out to every drooling mouth at the table.

"Enough with the idle chat, let's get to what we're all really thinking about," began Yaula, still spooning out the steaming stew, sliding filled bowls to each in turn, "which is the mossing acid that ruined The Forest and my village. Nalia, anything else you can tell us about what happened to those other towns besides what you told us?"

"Nope," Nalia mumbled in response with a mouth full of stew, "I only know what I said."

Yaula's head shifted towards Kausha, her yellow eyes boring into her. "And you, Kausha? I didn't hear you say anything about it. Where did you come into The Forest from anyways?"

Kausha hadn't taken a bite of the stew yet, unlike the others who were practically shoveling it in their mouths. "I heard much of the same as Nalia before I traveled here except that it was much worse than what she described, with bodies practically glued to the ground from being melted and fused with it, unable to tell where someone ended and began," she explained, even though she knew much, much more about the acid clouds than what she let on, and even where they came from. This, she knew, would give herself away to them, so she held her tongue.

Skirm pushed his bowl away, half eaten, face laid with disgust at that description while Shaum just kept on eating, even with eyes pinned on Kausha. He seemed to have either gotten to the point where the drink got to him or he simply didn't mind hearing about this sort of thing while eating. Nalia nodded slowly, squinting as she stared at Kausha, while Yaula sipped on her drink.

"And what happened here, it's the same as the other places?" Yaula asked between sips, glancing from Kausha to Nalia, who both nodded in agreement. "Moss. Well, at least we know that we aren't alone in this, but there are now more questions than answers. Why would it happen here? Is it going to happen again? If someone is behind this, who, and how can I rip their throats out? I just don't know, but what I do know is that while you were unconscious, Kausha, the Spearheads and I went out searching for survivors and only found Nalia here, and boy was she lucky."

Nalia stared into her bowl, stirring in small circles as if wanting to dodge their eyes.

"So what's next?" Skirm asked after clearing his throat.

"Well," Yaula started as she lowered her mug upon the table top, eyebrows narrowing down, face becoming serious as she glanced between those at the table, "I don't see much worth staying here with the village the way it is now. There are other villages in The Forest, most hidden with very few, if any, travelers, that would take at least a few days' trek to get there. We might be able to find some answers there, but who knows if they were hit by the same acid as we were, so that might be a lost cause. Kausha & Nalia, where were you two heading?"

Kausha stared into her stew, spoon fishing around for nothing, wanting Nalia to answer - anything to not have to disclose her intentions. Nalia took the hint after glancing at Kausha who didn't acknowledge the question. "I was traveling to conduct some business in Nortmund, taking the quickest way through The Forest. This village was the stop where I had planned on gathering provisions and continuing at daybreak, but alas," she finished, shrugging, "you know." Everyone nodded their heads. Shaum went in for seconds on the stew while Skirm watched over a grasped mug that hovered at his lips. A subtle shaking of his head accompanied the stare focused on his brother.

Yaula turned her head towards Kausha. "What about you, child?"

I can't tell them. Kausha looked up from her stew, letting her spoon slide into the bowl as she sat straight up. "I was heading to Nortmund as well, but for family reasons," which wasn't completely a lie - she *was* going for family, just not to Nortmund. Everyone seemed to accept it - why wouldn't they? They had only met each other recently and had no reason to think she was a liar.

"Well, it seems like we have at least a general direction in mind. I want to see if the central village has fared better than this one, which is a general northwest direction. Both of you two seem to be heading that way as well," Yaula stated with two nods, one towards Kausha and one towards Nalia. "And you two mossing oafs have nothing better to do after hanging around this village for many moons now, right?" she mocked the Spearheads.

Skirm shrugged once again while Shaum came up for air from shoveling stew in his mouth. "Gonna bring tha liquor and make more o tis stew?" he asked with a grin, even more jumbled than usual with a mouthful of stew.

"Sure, Shaum, sure. Just stop talking with your mouth full like that, you oaf."

Shaum nodded enthusiastically, then went back to devouring his meal, shoveling a large spoonful between sharp teeth.

"That settles it, at daybreak we will gather up supplies and head towards Nortmund. Who knows what we will find. Now, eat up and don't drink too much more." Yaula stared daggers into Shaum until he raised his eyes to meet hers, spoon half-way to his mouth with a smile.

Chapter 7: Old Minds

The Council of Minds sat in a perfectly circular room with plain white walls where three tiers of seats, cut directly from one complete block of white granite stone. Hanging from the dome ceiling were four enormous silver chandeliers, each containing dozens of candles to illuminate the room when the light filtering in through the thin, nearly translucent granite ceiling, failed.

Gbinti's form of governance is that of a Noocracy, which is to say it is ruled by the intelligent - each passing a number of intellectual and problem solving tests to become a member of the Council of Minds. Olibtine was seated in the lowest tier in a high-backed, uncomfortable wooden chair. The only one seated at the bottom, in fact, in order for him to hear all of the voiced thoughts filtering down from the other levels. With each Mind in the traditional blue and white Gbinti robes, all were allowed to give voice to grievances or support on topics discussed on any given day.

His ears perked at a slow and gentle, yet confident voice coming from the second tier. "There is no other way around it, we must accept these agreements if we are to continue to expand. Our citizens are becoming restless in their overcrowded conditions," Guane, the oldest Mind with a bald head and shaved face, stark white eyebrows and prominent wrinkles on his face showing his age, plainly stated as everyone listened intently. Being the eldest of the Minds, when Guane spoke, one listened. "On occasion, it is preferable to lose one's shirt in order to gain new shoes."

Plainly put, old man. He doesn't seem such a waste afterall. Olibtine shifted his focus around the room, landing on each Mind in turn. Some nodded in agreement while others didn't reveal a hint of their thoughts as they stared expressionless at Guane.

"Thissss ssshall move to a vote if no one elssse hasss more to sssay on the sssubject. Right hand for yesss, left for no," remarked a cold, but firm voice from the second row. Bjorgene, a man with mostly gray hair littered with black spots, equally graying thick eyebrows, cheek bones visible, brown eyes seemingly popping out of his head, and a robe far too large for his body, stood addressing them all. This moon, he was the orator in the Council of Minds, providing the guardrails for topics and decisions throughout the moon's passing.

No one spoke up, and as customary, Bjorgene began the vote by raising his right hand to display "yes" and others followed, including Olibtine, each voting with their right hand in turn.

"The motion of agreeing to the new condisssions has passssed and the sssmartest among usss will finalize the ressspossssse," he finished, glancing at Olibtine with a nod.

Finally we can move on from this trade discussion. Olibtine squirmed in the uncomfortable chair to sit up straight. It wasn't that Olibtine hated talking about trade, he actually relished it, it's just that everything being said was a mere repeat of what had been said dozens of times before, albeit in varying ways. What he truly wanted to discuss was coming next.

"Thisss concludesss this day'sss Council of Mindsss," announced Bjorgene, tapping wood against granite, signifying the end of the meeting. Robes began to flutter and hushed chit chat enveloped the chamber as the Minds filed out.

Wait, what?! Olibtine panicked, standing quickly. *What about the attacks or the Bloodborn? We have too much to discuss.* Frowning, he watched the chamber slowly empty through the only exit on the third tier, then started striding across the bottom level, kicking up his robe along the way, to approach Bjorgene.

Maybe if I can get to him right now, we call back the Minds immediately. As he approached Bjorgene from behind, Bjorgene was ending a thought with Gaune "...a sssour mind during this time, unfortunately with all going on." Both shook their heads, eyes turned down.

Now is as a good as time as ever. Olibtine dry rubbed his hands.

"Minds, we must call back the others and discuss the two other topics plaguing our continent," Olibtine pleaded frantically, looking up at the two. Guane turned to his right, Bjorgene to his left, and acknowledged Olibtine.

"Do you ssssimply propossse that we hold the Mindsssss in here all day, Olibtine?" responded Bjorgene in a mocking tone. "We have accomplisssshed the mossst pressssing matter, and asss you know from your own resssearch, undoubtedly, everything elssse can wait until the next meeting," Bjorgene finished. He began turning back towards Guane.

"Say that to the faces of citizens constantly looking to the sky, wondering when the next acid rain is going to level their homes and melt them alive!" Olibtine exclaimed, his voice echoing throughout the chamber causing Bjorgene to fully turn to face him, providing all of his attention now. "They've heard the stories of human flesh fusing with the ground, unrecognizable after the acid rain sweeps through. When will the next attack occur?! By my calculations, the frequency is picking up and these are becoming more and more sporadic as time goes by." Olibtine's voice became louder as he went on. "What would you have us tell the citizens while we are held up in our fortified palace away from the danger?!" Olibtine felt his face reddening, heart racing now, passion driving his thoughts over intelligence.

"Lad," Bjorgene started, "you've been here, what, ssssix moonsssss now?" It wasn't a question, Olibtine realized, as Bjorgene continued without pause, "And you sssshould know by now that the Mindsssss move methodically, ensssssuring proper disssscusssion is had around one topic at a time, not sssssome town hall meeting where all thoughtssss under the ssssstarsssss. The citizensss will ssstay patient asss long asss we provide proper, continued guidanccce."

Olibtine's eyes darted to meet Guane's, trying to gauge where he stood on the subjects. He saw nothing, not even an eyebrow twitch, causing his hands to turn to tight fists. *So passive.* He released a breath he didn't realize he was holding, then relaxed his hands. Olibtine knew that he wasn't going to move either's opinion of this right now, so he abruptly changed the subject.

"And what of the Bloodborn?" This time, he saw Guane's hand grab his robe. "We have records of what happened the last time a Bloodborn's life ended, we must prepare for the worst case possibilities."

"Lad -" Bjorgene began, but was abruptly interrupted by Olibtine.

"Please, call me Olibtine."

Bjorgene raised his eyebrow, then smirked, "Olibtine, my apologiessss, the older I get, the more informal I get asss well. Olibtine, ssseeing asss you've read thosssse accountsssss, as old asss they are, you will noticcce that a Bloodborn's life comesssss to an end very sssslowly, taking many, many moonsssss to do sssso. We do not know how ssssoon we heard word of thissss, how much time hasss passssed sssince the processsss began, nor the meanssss to find thisss out quickly. Sssshould we worry about a rock falling from the asssstralsss, even though we cannot predict when and where that will happen? The here and now are what we on the Council sssshould be contemplating, not sssssome bloodline beyond The Foresssst far to the Wessssst," he finished, shooing absentmindedly to the west with his left hand like he was dismissing a helper.

Olibtine, cooled off at the rebuttal, looked at Guane, and almost pleadingly asked, "And you, Guane? After all you've seen on the Council, the longest tenured, do you think this is a matter to be left to the wayside until we have more information?"

Guane closed his eyes in thought for a few seconds, opened them slowly, his deep, thoughtful blue eyes focusing on Olibtine.

"It is in my experience that the more the Council focuses on the ifs and inevitables, they will lose sight of the immediate needs of the citizens. One cannot focus on their fate and expect the present to unravel into said fate, but rather, should plow the path in order to make a clear way into it. One comes before another." He paused, ensuring Olibtine understood. "That being said, the accounts of the last Bloodborn passing are... disturbing, to say the least. Which of these accounts are true or false, we are unsure of, but I don't see why anyone on the Council of Minds would hinder you from trying to find more information on your own in regards to the Bloodborn, Olibtine. If history should indeed repeat itself, even if not for many moons, we would be better off knowing something." Guane turned his head slightly to look at Bjorgene, awaiting his response on the subject.

"Yesss, I agree," Bjorgene begrudgingly agreed after a sigh, "But we will not be bringing this ssssubject up at the next meeting. Do assss you will alone, then report back to the ssssecond tierssss when you can corroborate ssssomething ussssseful." He raised a single finger. "But firsssst, you mussst finalize the resssponsse to Nortmund to end thissss dissspute."

Olibtine nodded, a hidden smirk appearing at the corner of his mouth. *Good enough for me - seems that Guane is holding back more than he's letting on.*

"It shall be done," he replied, turning towards the stairs, leaving the old Minds to themselves.

Chapter 8: The Sorcerers Atop the Tower

A droplet of water splashes into a shallow pool inside of an ujuntu basin placed on a circular wooden platform not a foot off of the stone floor in a circular, stone room at the peak of a large, pointed tower. Surrounding the room at eyeball height is a single slit in the stone, providing the only light in the room, save a dim, red glow resonating from the water basin. Kneeling next to the basin are three sorcerers, faces hidden under deep black robes. A darkness resonates from their bodies, engulfing the center of the room and the ujuntu basin almost as if it wanted to snuff out the light. A human face, appearance shadowed from the other side, appears from ripples in the water basin.

"We seem to have some interference beginning to look into the Bloodborn alongside questions sprouting up about the acid," the voice, a sharp, matter-of-fact tone spoke. "Was she taken care of?"

There was a pause for a few seconds as the sorcerers communed with one another without speaking a word.

"She was not," the middle sorcerer with a deep, rumbling voice started while the left one spoke in second with a high-pitched, quick follow-up, "She was not, she was not."

"Complications," The third spoke immediately after, a monotone response, "Complications... of an expected nature."

"Expected?" asked the face in the basin in an exasperated tone, "If it was expected, why didn't you account for it then?"

Another pause while the sorcerers communed - this time, the third spoke first. "It is of no consequence - everything is according to plan - the Bloodborn will not complete her journey."

"Not complete, not complete," the high-pitched sorcerer followed.

"Fine," the face in the basin huffed, "but the interference is a Mind and they are not easily handled alone - do as you will with him, but leave the city alone." And with that, the face in the basin was gone along with the faint red emanating as well, leaving the sorcerers with their own thoughts in the dimming evening light squeezing through the slit in the stone.

Chapter 9: Leaving Lumber Behind

Upon opening the door from the underground home, a horrible stench assaulted Kausha's nostrils, forcing her to cringe, eyes watering from the fumes in the air. Through watery eyes, she glanced back at the others to watch the wave hitting each in turn forcing them to cover their mouths and noses while practically gagging at the smell.

"It will help if you get a cloth wet and cover your mouth with it," Kausha directed.

Kausha turned back around while readjusting her pack, which was really just a bedsheet with items in it strapped to a branch, and took a deep breath to acclimate herself with the stench, causing her to hold back a cough. Once that was done, she looked around one last time to get her bearings. *Off to the north end of the clearing, which grew larger due the acid melting trees to their stumps, there are four potential paths to take, each leading to a separate part of The Forest for who knows how long. Yaula said the north one doesn't go very far, so we are heading west first and then north to Nortmund.*

Kausha took the first step, ensuring to begin on a path that had the least amount of acid pools still eating away at the ground, and the others followed. Clanking items distributed between the five of them and grumbling complaints followed her along the winding path she created. Shaum and Skirm carried the heavier items while Yaula carried the lightest.

The journey began in a somber state, no one speaking a word except for the occasional phrase heard underbreathe from Yaula, who was leaving her home, for what she realized might be the last time. While gathering supplies for the journey, they hadn't stepped outside for fear of lingering acid continuing to eat through anything it touched and so this was the first chance Yaula had to see what had turned of her little village. Each step brought forth more and more agony and anger, heating her skin to a deep shade of red, fists squeezed tight showing white knuckles, something none of her companions had seen before, not even Skirm or Shaum no matter how mad they made her in the past. It was clear that while Yaula was keeping her composure while inside tending to everyone and prepping for what lies ahead, she clearly had something else in mind for the journey.

Passing by the turning tree on the way to the tree that Kausha slept in not two nights ago, they found nothing but felled and melted remains mixed with beds, chairs, half-burned candles, and flat, partially melted floorboards. *That's odd.* Kausha slowed their progress into the open area - one that was much larger than she remembered from before.

"What is it?" asked Skirm, eyes darting throughout the clearing.

"I was just thinking about that night. I ran into Taulus while I was heading here. Does anyone know what happened to him?" she asked, glancing over the rubble. Each looked at one another and shook their heads in turn.

"I don't even remember him leaving the main camp that night," replied Skirm.

"He must have gotten caught in the acid - it seems like there was more here than there was in the rest of the village," Kausha explained without going into too much detail.

"Mustuve..." replied Shaum, a frown crossing his face as he looked up and down the acid laden trees. "Noone survivin tha."

"And nothing here worth taking with," Skirm grunted, kicking a part of what looked like a bedpost while shaking his head.

Kausha caught Yaula staring at her out of the corner of her eye, even while Shaum and Skirm spoke. *I wonder if she's thinking the same thing as I am.* Kausha turned back the way they were headed. *She has to know that this section was smaller and more overlaid with trees before, right? No way she couldn't know. Why didn't she say anything either?* A bead of sweat dribbled down her brow.

With a final, hesitant glance at what was and what could have been, they stepped into the shade of The Forest, hearing something they didn't realize was missing - nature.

Chapter 10: Discoveries

By candlelight, Olibtine finalized the trade agreement, placed his quill down, basking in the feeling of completion. While the Council can get a little drab at times, he always kept the thought that it is always for the betterment of Gbinti as a whole. He read over the trade agreement one last time to ensure all of the pieces fit into their unique place, and upon a satisfactory nod, he placed it in the top right drawer of the desk, the place he designated for only the final products of documents. He picked up his pipe, filled it with flower, and lit it using a stray string lit by the candle, then leaned back to enjoy the feeling. *Now that I've finished that, I can begin.* He glanced to the left-hand side of the desk, stacks of parchment, drawings, books, and more, piled as high as the candles' light reached. *This is going to be fun.* Puffing out smoke, a smile crept to his face.

Olibtine never wanted to be on the Council, not really, and certainly didn't strive to be the smartest of the Minds. What really excited him was the idea of solving mysteries. Before the tests, he was a modest city guard that advanced a few ranks into a Problem Solver, those that take the tough problems, or mysteries, plaguing the citizens, and solve them. He wasn't just a Problem Solver, but he was the top Problem Solver in the city, piecing together everything himself on many occasions. The last thing he wanted to do was to give that up, but he had no choice in the matter - the smartest got put on the Council whether they wanted to be or not.

He studied the first few items in a stack - an artist's rendering of an old cave painting that was deep red with black outlines of something, a written and rewritten account of the Bloodborn's home, Purtghast, that described massive square slab stones along a sheer cliff jutting out over the ocean, and a parchment with a blurb about the female-headed society where men had no say in governing. Writing at the bottom corner of the parchment caught his eye - *35v50 BL, meaning the 35th moon in the 50th bloodline where each bloodline is 100 years and each year has 8 moons.*

Now that was a long time ago. He puffed out a large plume of smoke. *If the Bloodborn had societies with clear governing styles back then while the rest of the continent was scrambling around and just beginning to have societal bands, how far have they advanced in these last few BLs? The cave painting doesn't have a date on it, but seeing as it came from a population predating those from the parchment, I would assume dozens of bloodlines ago.* Olibtine felt his hair stand on end at the realization. His breath caught mid-smoke, making him cough until his eyes watered. *Who knows how far back the Bloodborn go besides themselves? Is there anyone I might be able to talk to in regards to their true age? Getting side-tracked Olib, that's not important,* he scolded himself.

These cave paintings point to a horrendous event, showing explicit red paint all over the black outlines of themselves? Has to be. What happened back then? As Olibtine continued to dig through books, notes, and more drawings, he picked up a small book, almost the size of his hand, with a red and black leather cover, cracks throughout from age or poor handling, about as skinny as a thumb. Olibtine's eyebrows perked up as he removed the pipe from his mouth and placed it down on the table next to the pile of items he'd already gone through, a sliver of smoke rising unimpeded into the air. He moved the candle closer to the book to look at the cover - it was faint, but he could see the Bloodborn's symbol of a single droplet embossed under the red and black of the book.

He began to slowly open it, but three loud bangs hit the door making him jump in his chair, causing his knee to hit the desk, nearly knocking over the candle while doing so.

"Sir," came a female voice from the hall, "Sir, the guests have arrived."

Moss, how long has it been since I finished the agreement? He glanced towards it, snug in the desk.

"Sir, are you there?" came the female voice again.

"Yes, I am. I will be right out," replied Olibtine as he stood up, book still in hand. He outlined the symbol with his finger, then placed the small book in the middle of his desk. He opened the drawer, grabbed the agreement, then snatched up his pipe before blowing out the candle in one puff. *Might need this tonight.* He pocketed the pipe, then walked towards the door outlined by candlelight in the hall.

Chapter 11: Inner Thoughts

The Forest lies directly in the heart of Uradaria, enveloping half of the entire land mass. Even though there are small villages throughout, with its sheer size, no one truly knows what lies therein throughout its entirety. It has an extremely diverse collection of trees, shrubbery, and fauna with the northern parts containing heartier trees due to the occasional cooler weather. The south is filled with lucious, wide trees with branches hunched over as if attempting to touch the ground. The central parts are filled with the tallest and thickest of all, forever fighting for sunshine, becoming so thick that they block that very thing they need from reaching the ground.

Yaula didn't grow up in The Forest, but it's the place she's lived nearly a third of her long life. She's made a life for herself in that little village of Lumber, practically starting it all by herself, working hard to create a little clearing of trees, moving heavy boulders around in order to create a decent seating area for travelers, cutting paths through the wood by hand, and recycling the wood in order to make a few rooms for travelers to rest their weary feet. All of that is behind her now and she decided that she would more than likely never return, at least not until she figured out what exactly happened with that acid. Her gut told her that there was something more to the acid than what they all knew.

Why, out of how mossing massive The Forest is, were the clouds only above Lumber? Was it just sheer unlucky that it happened? There were other incidents of it happening in other towns across Uradaria, but I haven't heard of anything in The Forest, itself. Moss. Whatever it is, I will get to the bottom of it, Yaula thought, jaw clenched, fists in tight balls, heart racing.

"Yaula, 'ey Yaula!" Shaum exclaimed, causing Yaula to shake herself from her thoughts.

"Ya wanta take a break?" he asked, sweat dripping down the tip of his head.

"You okay, Yaula? Seemed out of it just then," Skirm asked, his eyes soft.

Yaula felt her firsts still in a ball and forced herself to relax, a smirk coming to her mouth while looking up at Shaum.

"Buzz off you big oaf, why are you so sweaty? Is that pack too heavy for you?"

Shaum smirked back, putting his pack down, then immediately pulled out a jug of liquor and took a large swig, some dribbling from the side of his mouth. He wiped it away, making eye contact with Yaula again. "Na, jus wanta drink some more." He took another swig before offering it up to his brother, who shook his head.

"Shaum, that's not helping anything right now. Put it away."

"Elpin me it is. I feel like I can go again for a distance," he replied, similarly offering the jug to the others, only Kausha accepting. Shaum's cheeks grew hot after feeling himself staring for too long.

"So when's the next village?" Skirm asked, leaning against a tree twice his size around. "This place is giving me the creeps the further we go."

"We still have a ways to go - won't be getting there today, maybe not tomorrow either. The Forest is extremely vast and it's impossible to truly say why villages prop up where they do, but the spacing between them has never made much sense," replied Yaula, brushing a fallen log of dirt and taking a seat. "As soon as we begin to see the trees changing, that's when you'll know that we are getting close."

Skirm nodded his head in reply. "We might as well just camp here for the night since that oaf Shaum is already drunk."

"I'm nah drunk, jus feelin like I can ride a sky eel!" slurred Shaum in a failed attempt to look sober as he pointed a wobbly arm at Yaula, spilling liquor and nearly dropping the jug all in one go. "Okay, maybe I'm a lil bit drunk, but I can keep goin if needed," he followed up, face grimacing, but sounding sincere.

Yaula stood from the log she was on and started walking towards Shaum, eyebrows narrowed as she stared him in the eye. Shaum shrunk back, his eyes wide watching her come right at him. "No, we'll stop here and start early." She then snatched the jug away from Shaum, putting the cork back in. "I don't want you oversleeping and complaining about us leaving."

Shaum's mouth opened to rebuttal, but Yaula glanced back at him while walking away, eyes narrow and sharp teeth showing, a clear sign not to test her right now, so he closed his mouth and accepted his current drunken state with a huff.

"With the sun going down, we should prep for the night. Skirm, go get some firewood. Kausha, see if you can find some water. Nalia, scout the area to see if there are any signs of travelers or anything. Shaum..." Yaula started as she looked over to him only to find him lying down with his eyes shut, "...oh nevermind you big oaf."

Skirm never really liked The Forest - way too many things for his head to get caught on and far too many tight gaps between trees to fit through. There was a majesty to them, he'd admit, but the way things were going, he'd be stomping through here for days, weeks maybe. *Why do I always have to keep Shaum out of trouble? It's always his impulses that we follow, never mine. If it were up to me, we'd be back home swimming in Circle Lake with only the sky lake above our heads. The only reason we are here in the first place is because of him wanting to go and drink unencumbered away from the townsfolk. Yaula said that some other of my people passed through her village, I wonder if we knew them. She DID know how to make the liquor afterall.* Skirm proceeded to find a few fire starters and logs for the fire and headed back to camp.

Nalia had always been a good tracker, as is her entire family - her ears allowed her to hear things that others didn't and her nose was as sensitive as any axehound's, so this was an easy task for her. *Did Yaula know this or was it just sheer luck that she told me to scout the area? My ears might be a dead giveaway, but she has to know, right? Doesn't matter anyways, I need to get to my sister - who knows what is happening to her in that hellish place.* She insisted that her sister not go to Nortmund, especially after hearing all of the stories about it - the rich and powerful throwing all they can into slavery to mine for their precious ujuntu in order to keep the power they've gained over centuries of mining. Once you've gotten too old to work the mines, they force you into another slavery duty whether it be polishing, counting, transportation, or just another menial task. Her sister disregarded all of the stories as hearsay, always stating that they were overblown for one reason or another, maybe even concocted by the rich in order to stop travelers from going and taking their ujuntu. All Nalia knew was that she hadn't heard from her sister in six moons, three times as many as usual, and needed to find her and see if she was okay. *This group slows me down a bit, but this forest is just too expansive to walk alone. Best to stick with the group, at least for now.* Nalia continued her circle around the camp, looking for traces of animal or traveler alike and came up empty handed. *Odd,* she frowned, *figured there would be at least some animal tracks around.* With a shrug, she headed back into camp.

Kausha couldn't hear any running water and they certainly didn't cross any streams coming through, so she'd probably have to work one of the trees. *Why did I agree to leave with this group again? They are only slowing me down. I have time with great great grandmother only beginning the end of her light, though, and this is much safer than traveling alone. At least those Spearheads are decent company. Their kind is always ready for a drink or card game. What to make of Nalia though. She's awfully quiet and it's hard to trust the furry eared* Catsnifs *that are always looking out for themselves and only themselves. At least they have amazing senses that'll make this trip easier.* Kausha looked around to make sure no one was around, turned to a healthy looking tree, then used her ability to first push her blood through one of the pores below her fingernail, creating a three inch long, sharp point, similar to a nail, and jabbed it into the tree trunk. Once it was in, she forced the blood into a circle creating a faint sawing noise, cutting the inside to cover more area for the water to seep out. Once that was done, she simply pulled the blood back into her, a chill entering her body, leaving no trace that that had happened outside of the hole in the wood, but any bird could do that. She grabbed her empty jug and placed it underneath the spittle of water leaking out, filling it up. Once that was done, she put the cork back in and began walking back to the clearing.

A distant *snap* made her freeze in place, breath catching, her insides shifting as blood flowed into her arms. She turned her head where she thought the noise came from and stared. *Maybe it's Nalia - she was supposed to check the surrounding area. No, that was too far away for that and not a small branch either.* Kausha stood there until her body fought against her for the will to breathe. She exhaled, hearing only her heartbeat. *This sure is an odd place. The Forest is beginning to live up to the stories.* She continued towards the clearing, ears open, focusing on her surroundings just in case.

Chapter 12: A Children's Story

Nalia was entering on the opposite end of the clearing from Kausha while Yaula squatted in the middle next to a small fire. Shaum leaned against a log next to Skirm, watching Yaula intently, jug in hand again, undoubtedly faking his earlier "nap" until everyone got back from their tasks.

"Ave ya ever eard abut the Bloodborn tribe's last passing? It's a Spearhead legend tha our pops told us when we were minnows," Shaum asked Yaula in slurred speech, sloshing the liquid around in the jug while using exasperated movements with his hands. Yaula tossed in another small log, stoking the flame, ignoring him. Shaum noticed Kausha approaching out of the corner of his eye and set his focus on her. "Ave ya ever eard bout the Bloodborn tribe's last passing?" he asked again as if she didn't hear it the first time.

Nothing I don't know already. "Nope," she answered while shaking her head and taking a seat on a patch of dirt, back leaning against her pack.

"Oh, yer in for a treat then!" Shaum took a huge swig from the jug, wiped his mouth, then passed it off to Skirm. He sat up straight, crossed his legs in front of him, then with one motion of his big hand, brushed away the rocks and loose objects in front of him so only dirt remained. He cleared his throat, then raised his finger expectantly, looking over at Skirm, who rolled his eyes.

"Ready brutha?" Shaum asked. Kausha raised an eyebrow. *He isn't going to tell it?*

Skirm shrugged, then took a swig, his face cringing when swallowing. He looked at Kausha, then Yaula, who had the same expression on her face that Kausha had. "He thinks I tell it better. But he draws better," Skirm explained, leaning the jug against the log, then nodding to Shaum.

"It was a night like tonight hundreds of years ago in their city called Purtghast far to the west past the edge of The Forest." Kausha's eyebrows narrowed at Shaum, who was scribbling something into the dirt. She stood, then walked over to see what he was doing and she nearly jumped at what she saw. Drawn in the dirt illuminated by the fire was Purtghast. It wasn't a very good depiction of it, more wrong than right, but it was unmistakably her home. *How,* she gawked, completely transfixed.

"A land where beasts roam, not a single soul wants, and bloodlines last thousands of years. Long before Spearheads, humans, Catsnif, Marpet, or anything else lived on Uradaria, there were the Bloodborn," Skirm continued.

Shaum followed, drawing each in turn, wiping away each drawing after finishing, quickening his pace, then ending with the droplet symbol of the Bloodborn. The fire caught it just right to make it glow with red - with blood.

"Everything outside of the Bloodborn is inferior in their eyes, and why wouldn't they see it that way? They've been around for thousands of years before everything else. They typically leave themselves out of the rest of the world's problems, never placing themselves in the inferior's evolution from an uncivilized, wandering hunter-gatherer society to one with cities and governments. Until the last passing, that is." Shaum wiped the dirt clean, starting fresh, drawing a young woman on a hill, fire behind her enveloping trees and huts. "During one of their passings, a Bloodborn went mad. Till this day, no one knows why, but a young Bloodborn wrought havoc on what is now Gbinti, burning crops and huts alike, killing everything she saw in sight."

His drawing turned frantic, using all six of his fingers in tandem. "This is said to have lasted for an entire moon, leaving nothing but flat, charred land behind. Those that ran were hunted down like they were wild animals." Shaum drew a woman with a spear raised towards a child, bodies littered on the ground around her. "She disappeared back into Purtghast. No human, Spearhead, or anything else, wished to find who was behind all of the destruction for fear of tempting the Bloodborn once again. No one knows why it happened, but let's hope it doesn't happen again while we're alive."

Shaum wiped away the final drawing, then looked up at Skirm. "But ow did anyone know wha appened if they all died?"

Skirm looked up in contemplation. "Moss, I don't know, why didn't you ask pops that?" he replied, absently reaching for the jug and taking a swig.

Shaum, with rosy cheeks and a big smile, looked up at Kausha. "Whatcha think?"

Kausha was still transfixed at the drawings that Shaum just erased, an after-image burnt into her vision of her ancestor. *Well, not at all true, but I see why so many are afraid of us.* She felt Shaum staring at her, then shifted her gaze to look at him.

"A little childish, don't you think? How can anyone believe that someone would ruthlessly hunt for a full moon, wiping out an entire town? Seems like an excuse for parents to sway their kids to never leave," she teased, crossing her arms.

Shaum shrugged, his mouth frowning as he leaned back against the log. "Thare was a passin though, and Gbinti really was ruined."

"Pops may have exaggerated a little - don't all parents?" Skirm replied, handing Shaum the jug.

Nalia, who was standing on the other side of Skirm, spoke up. "Wonder why she did it."

Kausha nearly jumped at the voice. *How long was she standing there?*

Shaum had to turn his body to look up at her. "Thas tha true mystery, int it?" He shrugged again, raising the jug to his lips. "Alls I know is tha ya don't wanna be around if it appens again." Then, he took a swig, offering it to Nalia between clenched teeth. She shook her head, then found a seat around the fire.

Yaula, squatting on the opposite end of the fire, the frown on her face looking deeper than it was due to the dancing flames, spoke up, "It's true that no one knows, but I've heard similar tales from travelers moving through Lumber. Some say that she was mad while others say she was taken control of by a sorcerer while even others say it was a way to ensure the Bloodborn would actively hold down the other races of the world. I've heard it every mossing way from this way to that and I've come to the conclusion that no one will ever know until the next passing, if that is even a thing. By Arduinna's forest, I hope that it doesn't happen again," she finished, poking the fire with a stick, creating wisps of embers that floated into the sky.

Everyone nodded at Yaula's last statement, but only one knew that a passing was actually happening as they spoke.

I'm coming, Kausha thought, staring into the fire.

Chapter 13: Confirmation

Olibtine disliked this the most of his duties. He could research and read for days, getting lost in thoughts and scenarios, oftentimes forgetting to eat and drink. He'd done the hard work of finalizing the agreement and producing the document for trade, now he just needed to play the role of the face of the Minds and leave his personal bias behind. *Detestable, really.* He gritted his teeth. *Rather than helping the citizens, the Nortmuder's richest would rather continue to enslave them in order to keep their power and riches. STOP! This is just a means to an end that will help our citizens prosper, even if it is in the name of Nortmund greed.*

Olibtine sat in the largest of the ornate wooden chairs in the large, horizontal dining hall. Its gray stone walls were broken up by stained glass of light blue and whites befitting Gbinti that gave the hall a feeling of being outside when the sun shone through. Right now though, dozens of candles placed upon three giant chandeliers hanging from the ceiling's cross-beams, ones similar to those inside of the Chamber of Minds, gave ample light throughout. Three chairs, currently unoccupied, sat on each side of Olibtine for the older Minds to sit at. The slightly raised platform he sat upon was a subtle way of showing the difference in power, which Olibtine hated, but it allowed for a nice vantage point to read the room and everyone in it. Currently there were only four large tables in the room, including the one Olibtine sat at, the rest being removed for more room to walk around. The tables were arranged in a square with an open space in the middle, allowing each Nortmunder full view of the Mind's seats, no matter where they were. At the time being, everyone except Olibtine was in the area in the middle of these tables. Groups formed for hushed conversations about one thing or another that most likely didn't have anything to do with the agreement they were all here for. He knew the Council's faces by heart, but even without that there was a stark contrast in appearance between the two groups. While the Council's clothing was always a simple robe in Gbinti colors of blue and white, the Nortmunders all wore brightly colored robes that coincided with their house showcasing numerous ujuntu rings on each hand and a thick ujuntu necklace hanging from their necks that showed the rank of their houses, ranging from one to six. The only physical trait about them that differed was the fact that they were all dwarves, about half the height of the Minds, but almost twice as thick, with pale skin and thick, brown or black braided beards - their mountain mining lineage passed down through generations.

Just one of those rings could feed a village for an entire month. Olibtine cringed, recollecting the countless faces he'd met during hit time as a Problem Solver. *And all gained on the backs of others, working their entire population to death. We're the ones conducting business with them, what does that say about us?* In an attempt to get out of his own head, Olibtine focused on their nearest group.

"...rumblings of further destruction and chaos from these acid clouds, that luckily have not hit any of our mines," the Nortmunder with the bright yellow robe with a 4 around his neck said to a small group of one Mind, another Nortmunder with bright blue and the number 6 around his neck, and two others, one in bright yellow, one in bright blue, neither wearer rings or necklaces, meaning they were the assistants. Number 4 had a pretentious tone to his voice at all times where he elongated the ends of words every so often.

"Doing so might take me down a numberrrr or twoooo. On ujuntu's luck I'll never drop thaaaaat far," he scoffed, turning his nose up with a sideways look at number 6.

I don't get it, is going from 4 to 6 that much of a difference? Olibtine was baffled at the disrespect shown.

"And the loss of life would be disastrous as well knowing how large those mines are," responded Poreme in a flat tone, one of the Minds chosen for today's meeting. The number 4 stared at Poreme like he had been insulted to the deepest degree possible. "But they are your lives to treat, my lord," Poreme followed as quickly as he could. Number 4 smiled as if he was just paid the kindest compliment. Moving his arms and twirling his hands in a presumptuous manner, he followed with, "That they aaaare. The loss of life means noooothing to the richest - we will take and give when we choose, whether that be a life, a task to perform, or freeeeedom. They know their place in Nortmund and we know ours - without both, the entire ciiiity would fall, taking the entiiiire continent with us."

Not very subtle, Poreme.

Poreme nodded slowly, showing he didn't agree with what was said, only that he knew that number 4 meant every word and that in his mind, nothing else mattered.

"Have you heard anything concrete about the acid clouds? Where they might come from, how they continue to pop up, seemingly random. The Council of Minds has begun our research recently and see no correlation to the locations of the acid clouds at this time," Poreme finished in a relaxed tone.

Ah, so you're giving him something he can use to try to blow over the insult. Smart, Olibtine smirked at the subtle shift, something he'd used a time or two in his life.

Number 4 rubbed his chin under a thick, brown beard with cross-cross patterns throughout, looking up in contemplation as if in thought. "We haaaad also thought of looking into the location of these clouds and found no tie to any of them recently. We are currently looking at the freeeeequency as well but there is no pattern we can see except that the frequency continues to pick up, especially with the recent one in The Forrrrest."

So you know about that one too, then? Olibtine raised an eyebrow.

"Ah, yes, location was our next step. That should save us some time and effort," replied Poreme, nodding, this time showing true appreciation.

"...Bloodborn," Olibtine heard off to his left, ears perking, head jerking to a new group of three. "While we do not know of her whereabouts, we do now know that it is a female and was last seen entering The Forest near this city."

Wait, what? Olibtine's eyes widened as he clenched the arm of his chair. *She was near Gbinti before she went into The Forest. If that is true, then that means the one that is currently passing is happening sooner than we thought. It isn't going to be moons from now, it's going to be much, much sooner.*

The implication made Olibtine's entire body tensed up, feeling the weight of it all behind a seemingly normal sentence. As little research as he'd done tonight, he knew something disastrous was on the horizon and this confirmed that it was going to happen sooner, not later. From his understanding, it takes nearly a moon to get from one end of The Forest to the other, nearly double that if one were to go around it. That means that at the least they have one moon, possibly two, to answer what, how, who, why, and a dozen of other questions as soon as possible. Olibtine missed the rest of the conversation, too focused on the implications that this revealed. For the first time the entire evening, he stood, conversations continuing unabated without him, and proceeded to make his way towards the back right doorway, ensuring he didn't pass the others. *I must find the answers immediately. We don't have any time to waste.* His pace quickened upon entering the hall, candles flickering as his robe fluttered behind him, beads of sweat accumulating on his forehead.

By the time he got to the end of the long hallway, Olibtine's mind was spinning in circles. He reached for the knob to the study and pushed the heavy door open, his silhouette outlined by candlelight from the hall. His excitement to begin that which he loves pushed him forward, except this time it was to find something he dreaded to think about. Upon closing the door, his eyes incapable of working in the lack of light, his other senses improved, and with a sniff, he smelt smoke but no source of the smoke. *Odd.* He retraced the path he always took to the desk, the smell getting stronger the closer he got.

This can't be from earlier, can it? It has been hours since I put it out. He felt for the matches near the candle where he always kept them, grabbed one, then lit the candle in one fell swoop. Once the light began to steady itself he looked down at the middle of the desk and only saw wood. His heart skipped a beat, recognizing something was missing. *The book, it's gone!* He scrambled around the other stacks on his desk, frantically throwing papers on the floor in every which way. *Where is it, where is it?* He had been known to forget where he put things at times, but was he that gone that he forgot where he put this book?

The only thing left on the desk was the candle now. Two palms placed on the desk, back slumped over, head down, eyes shut, Olibtine accepted defeat.

"It's not here," he confirmed aloud, "I know it was right here." He tapped the middle of the desk. "Someone MUST have taken it, but who and why?"

He pulled his chair up and slumped down into it, elbow on armrest, hand balled into a fist under his chin. Curiosity and confusion fought within him. *I need a smoke.* He removed the pipe from his pocket and the leftovers from earlier in the day, lit the wound up string on the candle to prepare the light for the bowl and froze. Flame flickering in front of his eyes, a thought shot into his mind like a blast of cold wind. *Could it be them? They should have all been at the discussion all evening, but I can't keep an eye on them all - not that I had a reason to in the first place. Moss. I have no reason at all to suspect them. This could just be a coincidence.*

With a deep sigh, he blew out the lit string, placed the unlit pipe back in his pocket, and sat back in his chair. *I have a new case to solve.* Excitement overshadowed the disappointment he endured just moments ago. *Time to get to work.*

Chapter 14: Hunters Appear

The acid pools leftover from the rain in Lumber begin to bubble, green steam emanating from dozens scattered throughout the village. With every pop, the acid slides towards a central point in the village square as if drawn by some unseen force, leaving a trail of barren soil in their wake. Overhead, a cloud begins forming from the steam, churning together as if the wind was circulating. The acid creates a single, large, churning mass, formless and ever changing, then suddenly splits into three distinct pools. From each pool, a shape begins to form, seemingly growing out and up to form a head, four arms, and a large base with no visible legs. The acid cloud above splits into three, moving directly over each of the pools, catching the constant green steam rising from the creatures. The clouds split open, raining down acid on the forms, replenishing their bodies after every popped bubble, a constant cycle of growth and decay. The forms seem to look around, attempting to gather their orientation. Settling their sights northwest, they begin to crawl away out of the village center in the same direction Kausha and the others headed.

Chapter 15: The village in The Forest

The moon faded away as the sun cut through the tops of trees, shedding light on the little clearing that Kausha and the others slept in. *What a restless night that was. Just couldn't get over that feeling of being watched.* Kausha glanced around at the edges of the clearing as Skirm, Shaum, Nalia, and Yaula began rolling up their bags, silently prepping for the day's journey through heavy eyes. The only sounds in the camp were ones of feet shuffling, bags being packed, and Skirm constantly yawning through large, sharp teeth. *I wonder if they feel the same as I do,* Kausha continued to wonder.

Yaula interrupted Kausha's thoughts. "Another long day ahead of us in the same direction as yesterday. We might be able to make it to the next village today if we hurry. It's one called Soplnet that is supposed to be directly in the middle of The Forest. A long way yet to the west north edge nearing Nortmund."

Shaum audibly groaned at the thought, but perked up as if remembering something important.

"They got any gud liquor?" he asked in an excited tone.

"Get off it, you big oaf. As if you haven't had enough these last two days," Yaula protested with a shooing hand as if batting away a bug.

"A Spear'ead can drink es weight in liquor in a day an be fine tha next," Shaum responded while standing up straight and pounding his chest with one fist.

"I've seen him do it before, Yaula, not something I'd bet against," Skirm butt in.

"Moss, you big oaf, that's not something to brag about," Yaula responded, buttoning up her pack.

Shaum shrugged. "I know two females tha like it quite a bit," he retorted with a smirk coming to his mouth. Skirm audibly let out a moan, eyes rolling as if he'd heard that a million times.

"Also something you shouldn't brag about," Yaula responded dryly. Shaum deflated a little at that, shoulders sagging, smirk disappearing from his face.

Skirm finished his pack, stood up, and looked up to the sky. "Anyways, Yaula, you said that the next village is supposed to be in the middle of The Forest which means we aren't even half-way to the edge of The Forest, are we?"

"As close to the middle as adventurers could do back hundreds of years ago, but no, we aren't even half-way to the edge. You sound like you know some about The Forest," Yaula responded, just as matter of factly as Skirm had.

"I've heard stories and read books on The Forest back when I was a minnow."

"Oh, don let em fool ya. Es read all tha books we 'ad around about The Forest," Shaum butt in, smiling, and throwing his arm around Skirm. "E's tha smart on in tha family, no wonder why he forced me to come out ere with em."

"Oh bug off," Skirm began, throwing Shaum's arm off his shoulder, "I didn't force you into anything, you practically followed me!"

Shaum took a step back, hand to his chest, eyes wide. "Ya lyin through yur teeth, Skirm. I only wanted to know what yer up to. Couldn't let me little brother just wander off."

"Yeah, yeah," Skirm began, rolling his eyes, "more like wanted to get away from the rules of home."

Shaum opened his mouth in rebuttal, then decided to close it and shrug. "I guess thas a little right," he agreed, slinging his pack over his shoulder. "Welp, we eaden off or jus stickin round ere all moon?"

Later that evening

Yaula, leading from the front of the group, short legs moving as quickly as they could, halted the group behind her in the dimming light. "We're not too far off from Soplnet now - either we keep pace and get there when the moon is high in the sky or we stop here and camp for the night. I'd rather get there tonight. Opinions?"

Shaum, who was second in line, looked back at Skirm, who was last, Kausha and Nalia in between. Skirm shrugged uncaringly. Shaum looked down at Kausha and Nalia, who both shrugged as well prompting Shaum to speak up to Yaula.

"Seems like the lot want to jus get there."

"Okay then, let's prep here then," instructed Yaula. She proceeded to grab a few short branches that were lying on the ground nearby and set them into a pile. She stood up, walked over to a tree behind Skirm, pulled off some moss, then walked back over to the pile of branches. With everyone watching silently, she grabbed a branch and wrapped one end of it with moss, spit on it a few times, then placed it down next to her as she proceeded to repeat the steps four more times. Once finished, she handed one to Shaum.

"Here, we'll be walking with torches tonight once I finish a starter fire. We don't want to be caught around here without it." She distributed the remaining unlit torches to the rest.

Yaula proceeded to get a small fire going, her larger-than-should-be hands working away. Within breaths, she had it spreading shadows around the small space they were in. She lit her torch first, then the others. Once everyone had theirs lit, she covered the fire with dirt nearby. She looked up past the group. "Just in time." Kausha followed her eyes above the treetops. *Dark already?* She frowned.

"This part of The Forest is denser and unexpected. Even during the peak sun, there is very little, if any, sunlight that bleeds through. Keep your guard up, but your eyes down," Yaula instructed in a stern voice while looking North into The Forest. She took a step and disappeared into the darkness, torch out in front to illuminate her path.

Kausha stepped into the darkness from the small clearing they were in and into something she was not expecting - noise. A cacophony of bugs, birds, wind, trees, insects, and leaves seemingly yelling at the top of their lungs. It was near deafening. *What is happening!?* she yelled to herself, glancing around for the source of the noise all around her.

"YAULA!" she yelled, wanting to ask her what this was, but Yaula just kept walking, showing no signs that she heard Kausha. *Can she even hear me?!*

"SHAUM!" she yelled to the Horneater, who was just ahead of her. No response. She started to panic, heart racing, eyes darting between the two ahead, the torch held out to her side, unsure of what to do. She spun, turning to Nalia and Skirm behind her, torches lighting their faces, both in a scrunch as if in pain. She waved her torch into the air over her head towards the two to get their attention. She motions to her ears, mouthing, "Can you hear that?" Both nod, returning a similar motion back to her. *Well at least now I know that I'm not crazy hearing nothing back there and everything here.* Kausha turned back towards Shaum and Yaula, their torches growing dim at the distance. Eyes darting between the ground and the two ahead, she marched off towards them in a hurry.

There wasn't a word spoken on their march into the middle of The Forest - mainly because every word spoken would be lost to the myriad of sounds surrounding them, all distinct, but blending into a single, unrelenting assault.

Yaula stopped before a gigantic felled tree in their path, three times as wide as Shaum was tall. Yaula turned towards the others, placed her dwindling torch on some dirt, then motioned the others to do the same. Once they had done so, they could clearly make out Yaula's face and hands motioning that they would need to walk around the tree to the west. She then put her thumb and finger close together, mouthing "close", which seemed to lift the spirits of the entire group. Once everyone nodded, she picked up her torch, waited for the others to do the same, then walked up to the tree, placed a hand on it for guidance, then proceeded west. Shaum followed, then Kausha, Nalia, and Skirm, each doing exactly as Yaula had just seconds ago.

They proceeded along the felled tree's trunk for some time, Kausha feeling like they were somehow retracing their steps from earlier. *This is one massive tree,* she focused through the noise, wondering if they were truly as close as Yaula said they were. *And this torch is about to go out.* She glanced behind, then in front. *So are theirs.*

Yaula's torchlight disappeared in an instant in front of her, causing Kausha to freeze. *Did hers already go out?* Kausha's heartbeat in her ears blended in with the sounds of The Forest. Shaum's went out next. *No. Both of theirs now?* Thinking hers was next, she spun, removing her hand from the felled tree to look back at Nalia and Skirm who were gone. Not a shred of torchlight or outline of where their bodies were. *Moss!* Panic tightened in her throat as she frantically waved her torchlight in front of her, hoping to catch a glimpse of anyone.

"YAULA? SHAUM? ANYONE?" she yelled, knowing that it was useless in this part of The Forest - her voice would be snuffed out.

She felt something on her free arm, causing her to drop the torchlight in the other, Bloodborn reflexes subconsciously taking action before she could even think. She felt her blood retreating away from the spot she was being grabbed while pushing blood into the hand the torchlight was just in. Blood daggers glistened in the light from beneath each fingernail. She raised her hand in preparation to strike, looked at her assailant and saw large yellow eyes staring at her in the fading torchlight.

Yaula! Kausha recognized, eyes wide, retracting the blood daggers in an instant. *Yaula!* Her body relaxed, relieved. Yaula had a grip on Kausha's arm, guiding her into the darkness ahead. Kausha scooped up the dying torch, put it over her head in front of her, and let herself be pulled in Yaula's direction, still unsure of where the others were.

After taking a few steps the way Yaula was guiding, the felled tree appeared again in the torchlight. *How far had I gone?* Kausha wondered, eyebrows narrowing. Yaula pulled her closer to it and disappeared. Kausha looked closely, putting the torchlight right over the spot where Yaula was a moment ago, but it was still just as dark as if she didn't have the fire. She proceeded to put her hand up to it and it vanished. *Ohhh.* A lightbulb sparked inside. *This is just like the secret library in Purtghast.* She pulled her hand back out of the darkness to make sure. *All fingers still accounted for.* Then proceeded to step into the void.

Yaula, Skirm, Shaum, and Nalia were there to greet Kausha, each clearly visible and smiling at her as if they knew all along. The deafening sound of The Forest was gone, too, Kausha noticed.

"Wait, did you all know?" Kausha asked, putting on the air of surprise, which it was, but not as much as they thought.

"I knew from the books I had read and Shaum should know from me telling him." Skirm slapped Shaum on the back.

"And I always knew, child," Yaula responded, glancing at Nalia, "and judging by Nalia's expressions, she knew as well." Nalia nodded in confirmation.

"No one thought to tell me? Just like the loud noises we had to wade through to get here?" Kausha asked with a frown on her face.

They each looked at one another, Skirm responding with a shrug and a soft tone, as if explaining to a child. "We assumed you knew, sorry Kaush."

"Don't get mad child, we didn't mean any harm by it, but we're here now," Yaula smiled, nodding back behind her towards the town. "Soplnet," she announced with a wave of her hand.

Kausha's eyes bulged and her mouth threatened to drop open while taking it all in - a stark contrast to the pitch black dark outside. Over the other's heads she saw a large clearing surrounded by six massive trees, each with winding staircases wrapped around their trunks leading to thick, expanding branches overhead. Limbs and branches intertwined, making it impossible to see where one ended and the other began. On the thicker parts high above held a maze of walkways, bridges, and what seemed like homes. Each walkway held glowing bugs attached to strings on ropes, giving them ample room to fly around. Brilliant, flickering colors of green, purple, white, yellow, and blue lighted the clearing down below. On the ground level, there was a felled tree right in the middle of the clearing with a flat top, clearly cut by tools, with smaller logs to either side for seating. Settled between the six trees finishing off the circle shape of the clearing were mounds of raised dirt, similar to Yaula's back in Lumber. Some sat with doors open, light spilling out from the inside from candlelight and bugs alike. Sounds of bugs fluttering around, fires crackling, travelers carrying on their conversations, and an instrument being played in one of the raised dirt mounds nearby, created a comfortable village feel throughout. *This is nothing like Purtghast,* Kausha gawked, catching a glimpse of the others doing the same - all except Yaula, who was already walking towards the closest raised mound to her left. They all must have seen her walking away as well, for each started walking nearly at the same time in her stead even if their heads kept jerking upwards to look at the odd lights dancing above.

Yaula led them to what was clearly the location of the most noise, a tavern bursting with laughter, music, smoke, and the occasional mug hitting a table. The closer Kausha got, the more clearly she heard the music, a single voice louder than the rest to the tune of a stringed instrument, slow and deliberate.

Through The Forest
Into the noise
She rushed herself to make it home
Called upon the wind that swept
Straight towards those who wept
To naught there save
But taught the same
She did learn a thing or two
But not before the memories flew
Off she went to prove herself
What she found was someone else
She slew and slew and slew some more
Only to realize she know not what for
Turning away from one or the other
To shed the life or set the world asunder

As they entered the tavern mound, the music, voices, and clatter abruptly stopped. The only things heard were chairs creaking and clothing fluttering as each patron turned in unison towards the door to get a view of the newcomers. Kausha entered first followed by Nalia, Shaum, then Skirm, who both had to hunch down to get through the doorway. After a brief second of them standing just inside the entrance, a deep, raspy, but playful voice rang out from the raised platform on the opposite side of where the entrance was.

"You four, welcome to The Smitty, come come, sit over here," he said while pointing to a few haphazard logs on the dirt off to the right of him. "Just move the seats where you want and I'll be right with yous all in a jiff."

As soon as the group began walking, the tavern noises picked up again. The patrons were chatting, laughing, slamming their wooden mugs against wooden tables, and puffing smoke into the air. The bard, a slender human with bright red hair, a large nose, and freckles all over his face, was beginning to pluck his instrument once again as if to prep for another song. Once everyone got to the area the barman told them to, they arranged their logs in a circle and sat without saying a word to one another, each glancing out of the corner of their eyes at the existing patrons.

Kausha looked up at the raised platform to find the barman, but he wasn't there. A raspy voice appeared next to her, making her jump. "We've got white liquor harvested from local trees nearby and smoke from the same trees. Best in these parts of The Forest haha. Oh, just a little joke because, well, we're the only ones around."

She searched in the direction of the voice, back and to her left, and saw him. A short, four foot tall, brown furry creature with a long pointed snout, two huge brown eyes, wearing a dark green tunic with light brown embroidery. *Fitting*, Kausha smirked.

"I'll ave tha liquor, and make it a double," Shaum ordered excitedly through a toothy smile that gave the barman a start.

Skirm gave his brother a side-eye before saying, "I'll have one liquor." He looked at Nalia next.

"I'll take both the liquor and the smoke," she responded flatly, which gave both Skirm and Shaum a start with Shaum giving a long, drawn out whistle.

"And I will go with both as well," Kausha requested without prompt.

"Wait, I wan tha smoke too!" Shaum spat out hurriedly before the barman began to retreat back behind the raised platform.

"Ya lasses tryin to out-do me?" Shaum smirked, leaning forward with one arm on his knee. He sat back up and pounded a first on his chest. "I can drink AND smoke yas unda tha tree! You'll see!" Skirm, Nalia, and Kausha each rolled their eyes knowing he would do something like this.

Skirm knew exactly what to do. "Shaum, just drink, smoke, and enjoy the break for the night. Here," he nodded to the strangers, "the other patrons seem like they've been at it for a while. Try beating them." Shaum looked over at the others to gauge his interest.

"Fine. Jus know tha I could do it," he huffed, looking at Nalia and Kausha in return.

"Where's Yaula at anyway?" Shaum asked, pursuing the room again.

"Over by the bard," Nalia pointed to the opposite side of the room. Kausha turned around, while Shaum and Skirm had to crane their necks to see her in between the larger of the patrons. Curiously, Yaula, with a mug already in hand, spoke out of the corner of her mouth towards the bard.

"Anotha tune, Skip. And this time, make it a bit more fun than your last one," came a deep, throaty request from one of the groups off on the other side of the room. The bard's head popped up to look over the group.

"You request all night and I haven't seen a hint of an offering from you nor your group, Blogy. At least buy me some liquor or smoke if you're going to be pushy," the bard mocked in a high-pitched, mocking tone.

"Fine. Ey Smitty, give Skip a drink so he can play us another," yelled Blogy from across the room, pulling all of the eyes of the room to their conversation. "Better be a good one, slick."

"Your mom seemed to think it was good last night," teased Skip, loud enough for the whole place to burst out laughing and those at Blogy's table to bang their jugs against it as he turned redder by the second. "Oh calm down Blogy, you know I'm only kidding," replied Skip in a playful tone, grabbing the drink that Smitty just dropped off and taking a swig.

Yaula and the bard shared a few words before she left his side to disappear behind the rest of the patrons. As the bard began playing his stringed instrument, Kausha saw Smitty walking over with a large wooden block that seemed far too large for him to carry alone, let alone have four jugs and pipes balanced on top of it. He got to the group, then proceeded to shift his hands a few inches over as legs popped out from the bottom of the block. Once they were straight and solidly on the ground, he adjusted it to sit in the middle of the group to complete the typical table and chair feel, then walked back to the platform.

Shaum was the first one to grab a jug, not worrying about formalities in the least bit, then chugged three huge gulps as if he hadn't drank in days. After letting out a gasp of air, he slammed the jug on the table, shaking it and causing some of the other jugs to spill a little. "Ahhh, now thas' refreshing. Even if it isn't as good as Yaula's stuff!" Shaum wiped his mouth with the back of his hand, a smile covering his face upon reveal.

Each grabbed their jugs in unison, took a sip, and nodded their heads in agreement.

"The local trees really did the liquor justice," Skirm smiled, eyeing the liquor inside of the jug as he twirled it in one hand.

Kausha's head perked up hearing a faint crash outside of the tavern that sounded like a tree hitting the ground. She glanced around the room, first towards Shaum and Skirm, then darting her eyes around to Nalia, who had her ears perked up, unlit pipe in hand half-way to her mouth. They made eye contact, scrunching their eyebrows slightly. Neither moved, focusing their ears to anything abnormal outside, but nothing came. *I know I heard something out there. Is that normal for this deep into The Forest? No one else seems to have heard it, or if they did, they clearly didn't care.* Kausha took a gulp, keeping eye contact with Nalia, then moved her head in a motion that insisted they go check it out. After setting the unlit pipe back on the table, Nalia took a quick gulp from her jug, then nodded in agreement, both placing their jugs on the table and standing up.

Shaum saw them first, already on his second round of liquor, and blurted out, "Where ya two goin? Lady stuff?"

Skirm shook his head, his eyes drooping as he mouthed "Sorry" to them.

"No, actually we're just going outside for a minute. Keep killing yourself slowly, but don't get too sloppy." Kausha smirked before proceeding to walk towards the exit ahead of Nalia.

Shaum chuckled, calling out in her stead, clear over the ruckus from the other tables. "Oh, I will! Don be mad if yur jug is in my belly when ye get back."

Once Kausha and Nalia breached the doorway outside, the air was quiet, only the sound from the tavern mound spilling out into the dark. *It's late, maybe this is just how it is.* Kausha glanced at Nalia, who must have had a similar thought with no signs of worry on her face.

"Where do you think that came from?" Kausha asked, glancing around.

Nalia shrugged. "Not sure, hard to pinpoint it with all the noise inside."

After what seemed like minutes listening intently and staring off, no sound of movement seen save for the combined fluttering of the bug's wings above, Kausha broke the silence.

"So... what is the business you have in Nortmund?"

"Huh?" Nalia responded, sounding like she was in her own world at the moment.

"You said you had some business in Nortmund, what is it?" Kausha repeated, looking at her.

"Well, um, it isn't really business," fumbled Nalia, no hint of following up with more information.

The two began walking clockwise around the main clearing without a word, starting by the second tree, just right of the tavern.

"What type of business?" pried Kausha.

"Just some family stuff," Nalia replied, sounding far away.

"So we're doing the same thing then, meeting up with family. Nortmund can be a scary place for some. What is she doing up there - clearly you aren't from there, correct?" *Was that too far?*

The questions hung in the air for a long while, leaves crunching below their feet as the two passed by the second mound between the second and third tree. Nothing moved inside of the dark interior. On the outside by the door was a hung sign with a loaf of bread on it.

"I'm not from there, no. She was going there to find work. She was always reading about the culture and architecture and had to see for herself. I kept telling her it was a bad idea, but she wouldn't let it go and eventually just up and left with only a word's notice."

Kausha could hear the angst in Nalia's voice and understood. *Nortmund is not for the faint of heart and her sister is probably a slave by now.* Kausha knew that the six are ruthless and care about one thing.

Continuing past the third tree, Kausha spoke up again, "Do you know what she is doing up there?"

Nalia stutter stepped at the question, clearly upset about something, but attempting to mask that with confidence in her voice. "No, I don't - haven't heard from her in a few moons now, but I intend to find out."

Kausha couldn't help but to feel for her, but knew that it'll take a little more than confidence to find her. *You're going to need more than intent to accomplish that.* Kausha thought it best to leave the rest unsaid, and continued walking.

As they passed by the fourth tree nearing the third mound, Kausha smelled something familiar that made her arm hair stand on end.

"Moss," she froze, "do you smell that?" Kausha turned to Nalia, noticing her whole body was tense, her ears and orange eyes flickering back and forth as if hunting for something specific.

"Yes, it's the acid," Nalia whispered through clenched teeth.

Kausha searched for the source of the smell, first down around her feet, then sweeping out towards the trees and nearby mound. Nothing. She kept sweeping with her eyes, less adept in the faint bug light shining down on her. Out of the corner of her eye, she saw Nalia crouch, then slowly creep forward, eyes fixated on something. Kausha attempted to follow where she was focused.

There! Her body began moving without thinking in the same way Nalia was towards the hand-sized puddle on the ground. Eyes focused on the puddle for fear she would lose its location in the dark and then she remembered Lumber. *Above.* She shot her eyes to the tree walk. *No cloud, that's good. But then where did this come from?*

As the two crept towards the puddle, making no sound even with dead leaves underfoot, they could see a light puff of steam emanating from it as it ate into the leaves and dirt, clearly fresh.

"What the..." whispered Nalia as they crouched mere feet from it, unwilling to get closer after what they've seen recently.

"Yeah, this isn't right." Kausha wiped her nose, attempting to get the stench out. "We need to tell the oth..." but cut herself off as she saw something move. A slight back and forth movement like water being sloshed around inside of a bucket, except there was no bucket and this wasn't water. It slid around the end of the seating log in the center of the village, then kept moving towards the spot where they first entered. The ground melted to the dirt as it passed over. Kausha's insides began to churn as she peeked over the log, following its path. *Is there a cloud outside of this clearing? I've never seen the acid do something like that before.*

It disappeared from the clearing, which seemed to shake both Kausha and Nalia from the stupor they were in. They looked at one another, both seeming to have the same thought as they nodded at one another, Kausha voicing it. "Let's go tell the others."

Together, they crept towards the front of the felled log to peek around the edge towards the tavern. Kausha's eyes grew wide at the sight, her insides churning even faster than before.

"Do you see that?" Kausha whispered to Nalia.

"I do. Are those what I think they are - acid blobs?"

"That's what it looks like to me." Kausha watched the blobs churn in the colorful bug lights from above as steam released from their bodies to be caught in a cloud above, dropping back down to replenish them in the form of acid rain. *Had they seen us? We're all the way across the clearing. Can they even see?* Sweat began to fall from Kausha's forehead, fists clenched in anticipation. She moved, body practically making the decision for her, not wanting to find out. She began circling back around the central felled log counter clockwise, hearing Nalia following her closely. *Seems like she thought the same. There is more to her than meets the eye.*

They reached the tip of the felled log, crouched, and glanced around the corner towards the blobs. *Still there.*

"They aren't moving." Nalia's confidence in her voice from earlier wavering.

Kausha nodded. "Why aren't they though? And what are they doing?" Nalia shook her head, silent.

What do we do? It's closer to the tavern than us so if it can see, it'll see us for sure. If it moves towards the tavern though, everyone in there will be trapped. An idea sparked in her head. "We need to warn the others. If those things can see, they will certainly see us, so we need to plan for that and split up."

Nalia's eyebrows narrowed, worry and fear clearly visible on her face. She glanced at Kausha, but nodded in agreement all the same. "I'll be the decoy and make a bunch of noise over at the other end of the log, opposite the tavern." Nalia pointed near the fifth tree in the circle.

Kausha nodded. "Once you make the first noise and I see them moving towards you, I will run to the tavern. Ready?"

"Ready," Nalia nodded, then began to creep back the way they came, but quicker this time, Kausha watching all the while. Once she saw Nalia at the far end of the log, she readied herself to run. But before Nalia could make her move, the two acid blobs started moving towards the light of the tavern. *Moss, not good.* Kausha's heart raced frantically. She darted her head back towards Nalia, who was still crouched at the end of the log, unmoving. *What are you doing?! Move. Move!*

The blobs, accompanied by their clouds, moved closer and closer to the tavern, practically folding over into themselves with every inch. *Moss moss moss!* Kausha panicked, glancing back to Nalia, who still hadn't moved. *It's now or nothing!*

Fighting against the churning in her stomach, Kausha leapt out of her hiding place, jumped into the air a few times, hands waving over her head and yelled, "Hey! Over here! Over here!"

The blobs stopped, then shifted towards her. *Well, that answers that.* She took two steps back, glancing at Nalia who had turned towards her, eyes wide and mouth open in shock. With a quick hand movement, Kausha shooed Nalia away in an attempt to get her to move. *Moss, Nalia, get it together.* Kausha hopped, forcing herself to look back towards the blobs. "I know what you want, come get it!" she yelled again, louder this time.

The blobs didn't move though, they just stayed in the same spot, shifting in place, acid rain slowly falling into them and the surrounding area. Faint sizzling sounds reached Kausha. She shivered. *Something isn't right. Maybe they can't see me?* She took two steps forward in an attempt to keep their attention. Nothing. Two more steps, now ahead of the felled log. *That did it.* She froze as the blobs crossed into the light spilling out of the tavern, providing her a better view of what they were.

Moss, they almost look human! Kausha noticed, taking a step back, recognizing a constantly shifting head, base, and four arms on each. The blobs moved slowly and deliberately from the tavern lights back into the multicolored bug lights, ominous intent radiating from each fold.

Out of the corner of her eyes, Kausha caught Nalia sneaking from her hiding spot, passing by the sixth tree, creating a wide loop clockwise around the clearing. *Thank you Nalia.* Kausha let out a deep breath, relieved to see her move again.

Those things are hideous! Nalia thought to herself, a full body chill washing over her as she continued to creep slowly towards the tavern like she had when playing in the fields with her sister. *Sorry Kausha, I was too weak to do anything. How am I supposed to help my sister if I'm such a coward? Don't let those things catch you.* While still creeping along, nearing the entrance they first came in, she watched Kausha jump up and down again, arms flailing over her head in an attempt to keep the blobs focused on her. She took two steps back, keeping her distance, but still baiting them away from the tavern where light and music continued unperturbed.

Nearly there. Nalia dodged the melted ground, nearing the light spilling into the clearing. She approached the edge of the door and squeezed inside as quickly and quietly as possible, all of the tavern sounds smacking her in the face at the same time, disorienting her momentarily. She stood upright, glancing over at the spot she and Kausha left the others just minutes before and saw only their packs, empty jugs, and empty seats. Her eyes darted around trying to find the large Spearheads and Yaula, landing on Shaum and Skirm near the bard, arm in arm, rocking side to side to the beat of the music.

From the back of the tavern near the platform, Yaula saw Nalia immediately and knew something was wrong. Not only did she enter crouched, but she was breathing heavily, sweat showing on her fur like she had just ran from one edge of The Forest to the next. Yaula immediately put down her jug and started scurrying over Nalia, who at the same time seemed to notice Shaum and Skirm near the bard. Nalia began working her way through the groups of patrons as quickly as she could without bumping into them, but felt a tug at her sleeve that made her jump back a foot, readying her feet to move quickly if needed.

"Yaula!" she exclaimed, "Yaula, we need to get out of here. Now!"

Yaula could clearly see the fright in her eyes. She glanced at the entryway, then back to Nalia. "Where Kausha?"

Nalia cringed, looked towards the door, and whispered, "Out there with acid blobs."

"Acid blobs?" Yaula asked with a raised eyebrow.

"No time, we need to get out of here!" Nalia yelled without realizing that the music had stopped and everyone was staring at her and Yaula now, unsure or incapable to comprehend what was happening so quickly.

Skirm stood up first, grabbed Shaum's arm bringing him to his feet as well, and practically dragged him back over to their packs.

"Ey, whuts gives, Skirm?" Shaum protested, the liquor and smoke clearly impacting his ability to comprehend and move with haste. Shaum picked up two packs and shoved them into Shaum's chest. "Carry these."

"Hey, what's going on there Yaula?" Smitty asked from the platform. The entire tavern had gone quiet, eyes darting from the Spearheads to Yaula to Smitty, then back to Yaula awaiting an answer. Yaula looked up at Nalia, forwarding the question to her without actually saying it. Nalia eyes darted around, finally landing on Smitty.

"There are acid blobs outside going after Kausha. We need to get out of here."

Chairs creaked and wooden legs grinded against the wooden floor as the groups turned, mumbling to themselves while Shaum and Skirm picked up the rest of the packs in haste. Shaum eyed the liquor Nalia left behind earlier, and deciding they had time, he chugged the liquid in two quick gulps before burping and dropping the mug. Yaula tugged on Nalia's sleeve again, this time forcing her over to the Spearheads.

"Got everything?" she asked the two in a hurried tone. They both nodded. "Let's go," she commanded as she looked up at Nalia with a final nod. She turned quickly to leave, but bumped into someone that wasn't there seconds ago. "Moss! Watch where you're going, you..." she exclaimed before looking up. She raised her eyebrow while making eye contact with the bard who stood between them and the exit. Loot in one hand, a small pack slung over his shoulder in the other, it looked like he had been prepared for a hasty exit.

"I'm coming with," he stated, blue eyes unblinking above a smirk without even a hint of it being a question. Yaula could hear that he wasn't going to take no for an answer. "Moss. Fine, then move!"

One of the groups near the door must have taken Nalia seriously for they scrambled out the door first, scattering this way and that in the dim light upon exiting. Yaula exited the tavern followed by Nalia, the bard, Shaum, then finally Skirm. Nalia pointed towards the opposite end of the clearing at the log.

"There's Kausha and the blobs can't be far from her." It took a second for the others to get their eyes right in the dim light coming from the bugs, first only seeing the seating log in the middle of the clearing.

"Where?" asked Yaula, squinting.

"On the closer side of the seating log near the end. She's moving clockwise," Nalia pointed.

Each followed her finger as Kausha emerged from the edge of the log walking backwards towards them, glancing over her shoulder every so often. "Where are these blobs, I don't see them," asked Yaula, trying to see what Kausha was moving away from.

Before anyone could answer, the first blob came into view around the log, moving at a slow, deliberate pace, churning over and over into itself, green steam rising, acid rain falling from a small cloud above it.

"Moss!" cursed Yaula, "What is Kausha doing?!"

"She's distracting them away from the tavern, but it looks like space is running out." Nalia wanted to run away as fast as she could as Kausha and the acid blobs inched closer and closer.

"The entrance to the village is over here," the bard interjected, pointing to the right of where they were.

More began flowing out of the tavern, running towards various stairs around the trees lining the clearing, none knowing what exactly was happening. Doors began opening, candlelight brightening the upper parts of the trees with onlookers above looking below to see what the ruckus was about. What used to be a quiet clearing with only bug sounds was slowly turning into chatter mixed with screams and footsteps slamming against wood as the villagers ran about after seeing the two blobs below, uncertainty forcing them to act.

Smitty finally exited the tavern. "What is going on out here?!" He answered his own question before anyone else could. "Moss!" he exclaimed as he ran back inside and slammed the door behind himself, snuffing the tavern light that Yaula and the others were standing in.

"Welp, there goes that option if it ever was one," the bard sighed, shaking his head. "Innkeepers are all the same."

We need to help Kausha. Nalia's hands twitched, fighting the urge to run in the opposite direction.

"Child!" Yaula called out to Kausha through cupped hands, who turned to look back in the direction it came. "We're here, let's get out of the village!"

Kausha decided long ago that in order to save the village she would have to guide these things out the way they came. *We can outrun them, they are slow.* She looked back at the others once more, noticing that they were still a ways away from the entrance and shooed them to leave first. They understood it seemed, and started jogging their way towards the hidden entrance, dodging small acid pools in the process. *Now that there's no chance they will see...* She forced blood out beneath her thumbnail, creating a blood dagger like she had done thousands of times and broke it off with a snap. She held the three inch blood dagger in her hand knowing that it would stay solid as a rock, even when separated from her body, and readied herself. *Just need to find out where... There, where the eyes should be.* She stopped, which shockingly stopped the acid blobs too. *Interesting.* Right foot in front, left foot back, dagger held back by her ear between her thumb and index finger, she waited for the blob's undulating form to create a larger "head". She felt her bloodborn blood coursing through her arm, strengthening it as she waited for... Before she knew it, the blood dagger was flying through the air, her weight shifted forwards following her arm. It struck its mark, disappearing into the blob with the similar hiss sound that the blobs make when burning the ground. Nothing happened. *Moss, so much for that.* Kausha recovered her feet, but right before she was about to turn to follow the others out of the village, the hissing grew louder. Kausha covered her ears at the intense hiss. The blob began writhing faster, the cloud above it expanding and contrasting nonstop. Kausha took two steps back but they didn't follow. She kept moving backwards, watching the first blob expanding faster and faster, arms flailing, its body churning into itself. Kausha cringed as the hissing grew louder by the second, drowning out everything in the clearing. It went still and silent. Kausha tensed, expecting more noise. But without warning, it collapsed into a puddle. The cloud above burst, causing all of the acid within to fall to the ground at once until it and the blob were no more. *Well, that answers that.* She continued to walk backwards, measuring the second blob, which hadn't moved from where it was. The acid puddle from the first one began to churn.

"Moss!" she cursed, not wanting to be here if the blob came back. This time, she turned and ran towards the darkest spot she could make out. Upon reaching it, she put her hands out to brace herself, wincing for impact. But none came.

Emerging from the village's hidden entrance, her eyes watered, forcing her to squint as light from the sun streaked through the canopy above. *Daytime already?* She threw her hand up to block the light in an attempt to gain her bearings. *Wait, I can hear myself think.* She focused on her surroundings, blinking the tears away.

No sound whatsoever, just like Lumber. Glancing around, she saw the damage the acid blobs had done creating a path through The Forest as downed trees, melted grass and ground alike surrounded her. *That is what must have been the sound we heard,* she guessed through a frown while looking at a large felled tree off to her right. Glancing around again, she wondered where the others were.

"Kausha!" she heard nearby, "Kausha, over here!" She glanced back to her left where the guiding tree was. Yaula, Nalia, Shaum, Skirm, and the bard were standing there waving her over, faces worried as their eyes kept darting from the entrance to the village back to The Forest surrounding them, clearly wanting to get away from this place. *The bard?* She noticed curiously, willing her legs to move over to the group.

"Glad to see you. Where are the blobs?" Yaula asked, glancing around her towards the entrance where they just left.

"Inside still. Not sure if they will follow me, but let's not wait to find out. Is there a way to the other side of this tree?"

Yaula pointed west. "Of course, just a ways that way." Each in the group looked where her hand was pointed.

Kausha nodded, "Right, let's get moving." She grabbed her pack from Shaum, then turned the way Yaula indicated and began to run, each in the group following closely, footsteps and packs echoing together through the silent forest.

Chapter 16: Backlash

The three sorcerers knelt around the ujuntu water basin in their high tower, incapacitated in their current state, focused solely on the hunt. A soft, red light enveloped their hoods from the glowing water below. One of the sorcerers fell backwards as if being pushed by some unseen force. *That was... unexpected*, the sorcerer thought. *We should have just torn the whole place down, not waited for her to be separated.* The sorcerer blinked, looking at the sorcerer to the right. *Should have listened to me.*

The sorcerer stood, brushed its robe, then stepped over to the crack circling the room. Looking northwest, the sun began to spill its golden light onto the tree tops. *These others she is with are becoming irksome. We will simply have to take them out as well.*

Chapter 17: A different path

Olibtine found himself walking west down Gbinti's main street, just outside the Palace of the Minds. The street was made of large, square and flat boulders surrounded by a thin layer of sand, each roughly the size of a human. This, combined with the wooden and brick homes and shops lining the street, jam packed butting against one another with no room to spare in between, created a cacophony of sounds that only a city could produce. Constant tings rang through the air from the blacksmiths nearby. Creeks of wooden wheels rolled over the stone from the carts moving goods and people back and forth, humans and non humans alike haggling for the best prices. The city watch jogged up the street, feet stomping in unison, as they yelled for citizens to part way. A smile grew to his face, realizing this was what he did it all for.

"...why we must continue to allocate the resources we receive from Nortmund... Olibtine, are you even listening to me?" came the familiar voice of Poreme next to him.

Olibtine shook himself, "Yes, sorry, momentary distraction. What do you think Gbinti would look like if it wasn't destroyed in the last passing? Would we have become a Noocracy like we are today, or something akin to the Nortmund's brutal slavery society? Would we even be able to recognize ourselves if the passing never happened?"

Poreme's eyebrow rose at the questions. "Burying yourself in your research again I see."

Olibtine shrugged. "I feel there is something I am missing - like an itch that is under your skin and you can't hit, no matter how much you scratch. Something WAS in that book, Poreme, I know it."

"Perhaps, but the book is gone, Olibtine, and all of the searches we conducted were fruitless," Poreme replied, shaking his head.

It's true, not even I was capable of finding the book. Moss. Olibtine let out a sigh, his eyes drooping. "Yes, yes, I know. A man can wonder though."

"It's what we do."

They entered the main intersection of the city, a large square with various merchant booths surrounding the outsides ranging from food, jewelry, weaponry, clothing, and everything in between, decorated with all of the colors one could think of. A number of seating logs dragged from The Forest occupied the middle of the square where dozens of citizens sat chatting. Leading from the center were five roads branching off into other parts of the city, including the one they just came down. Olibtine and Poreme walked silently, dozens of thoughts passing through their heads as they glanced from one thing to the next.

Poreme broke the silence while looking towards two children playing tag around one of the seating logs. "I don't think we would be like them, no. Maybe that's simply wishful thinking, but we're different from the Normtunders. They can never have enough wealth, which may be true for citizens here, but maybe it's better that we aren't as rich as they are with their ujuntu deposits underneath their beards. While the environment we have grown up in is a trying one, I feel that it brings out the best in everyone when you know the citizen next to you has been through similar experiences. Our city may not be as old as others, and while we still have a ways to go, we have the right groundwork in place to continue growing."

Olibtine smiled at the children as one caught the other and they started to run the opposite way around the seating log. "Thank you, Poreme," he smiled earnestly, patting him on the shoulder even though his head was filled with what if's and how come's.

"Shall we head back, then?" Poreme asked, "The next meeting is soon and I was hoping to see where your head was at on allocating the resources we received from Nortmund."

Olibtine nodded, taking in the citizens around the intersection once more before turning back the way they came.

The meeting started as it always did, with the announcement of the discussion topic for the day. Today's topic was the allocation of resources, as Olibtine and Poreme had just finished discussing. Providing the citizens with shelter, nourishment, and clothing was all Olibtine cared about, which seemed to be a general consensus between all of the Minds, but formalities are needed in any form of government. Sitting on the bottom row, as customary, Olibtine was lost in thought, paying little attention to what was being said in the room.

I just need a few more pieces of evidence to bring forth to the second tiers. He glanced from left to right at the older faces in front of him. *The few dated accounts that I have aren't good enough, I even know that - I need something substantial.* He thought of the book on his desk one moment, gone the next, gripping the arms of his chair while clenching his jaw. *That could have been the final piece! But you don't know that,* he scolded himself. *It could have been just another of the same old manuscript of stories everyone already knew.* He forced himself to take a few deep breaths, calming his mind.

Once the meeting had concluded, a relatively swift one compared to the previous few, Olibtine simply sat in the ornate, wooden chair, unmoving. It's not that it was comfortable. On the contrary in fact, it was extremely uncomfortable, but he found that it allowed him to think more clearly. *Comfort is the crutch of civilization. Allow a man to sit comfortably all day and he will not seek movement or growth.*

Lost in thought, he realized all but one had left the room - Guane, the eldest of the Minds. With a raised eyebrow, Olibtine wondered what he was still doing here.

Olibtine stood up, stretched his back by twisting his body left and right, then took the few steps distance towards Guane, his slippers slapping against the granite floor. "You're still here?" Olibtine asked as he approached.

Guane jumped, his eyes widening momentarily at hearing his voice. "Oh, hello Olibtine, I didn't see you there." Olibtine looked back at his seat, smack dab in the middle of the room. *Well, I guess I didn't see him here either until after everyone left.* He shrugged, looking back to Guane.

"And I, you. Do you mind?" Olibtine asked, nodding at the place next to Guane.

"Not at all," Guane replied, turning to watch him approach.

Olibtine sat, staring at his seat in the middle of the room, one level down.

"Something on your mind?" Guane asked in a slow, gentle voice.

Without looking over, Olibtine answered, "The passing."

Guane nodded, "I see."

"I've read over all of the manuscripts, studied the drawings, even picked the brains of other Minds, but I can't help but to feel that I am missing something. How is it that we don't have anything but hearsay from the last passing?"

Guane scratched his chin as if in deep thought. "It is puzzling until you remember that we, as a city, and as a continent for that matter, are but newborn pups, still new to this world. You wouldn't ask a pup if they recalled the womb, would you?"

Olibtine shook his head, finally turning to look Guane in his eyes. "No, but the Minds have been around long enough to have compiled some sort of truth to the passing, right?"

"And who would they get this information from? The Nortmunders? The citizens that fled into The Forest? There simply was no one left to provide a true account of the why behind it all," Guane shook his head softly.

Olibtine let that sink in. Sure, he had thought of that before, but having it said out loud really drove it home.

"But..." Guane started, "there may be something you can do to fill in the gaps. Rather, somewhere you can go to do this."

Olibtine perked up, sitting up straighter. "Where?" he asked.

Guane shifted in his seat, his eyebrows ruffling in thought as he fiddled with his hands.

"Oh, come on, you can't do that," Olibtine protested.

Guane glanced up, his blue eyes intense, squinting, as he met Olibtines. "The sorcerer's tower." Olibtine visibly shivered, only hearing about the sorcerers of Baugroun through readings and stories. A vile group that cared only about obtaining ujuntu at any cost.

"The sorcerer's tower? Why would that help me?" Olibtine asked, forehead scrunched.

"The sorcerer's tower is older than recorded history, and to my knowledge, has never been destroyed. It may even be as old as the Bloodborn themselves. There are no promises that I can provide you that there will be answers that you seek, but if they are not here, they are most likely there. Unless you want to go ask the Bloodborn themselves in Purtghast," he finished with a chuckle, slapping his knee as if telling a joke.

Olibtine smiled and shook his head in return. "No, I do not think that is wise in our current circumstances. Would I even have the time to make that journey? Won't the council need me?"

"The council has gotten by with less. Plus," Guane continued through a frown, shaking his head softly, "you aren't going to win over the second tier with what you have currently. We've all read through the same manuscripts and looked over the same drawings that you have and if you do not have more information to provide, your attempt at persuasion will be in vain."

"If what I fear is correct, we may not have the time for that, Guane!" Olibtine exclaimed, narrowing his eyebrows, the fear for his people bubbling up to the surface.

"Ah, but as it stands now, we are ill prepared anyways, as you stated yourself. Correct?"

Olibtine nodded, then stood. *Moss, he's right.* "Thank you, Guane. I will be off as soon as I can."

Guane looked up at him, raising one of his gray eyebrows. "By yourself?"

"Well, yes."

Guane nodded. "If that is what you feel is best. Stay safe, Olibtine, and do return before the passing."

Olibtine nodded. "I will. Thank you again, Guane." And with that, he turned towards the stairs leading up and out of the room, leaving Guane to his thoughts.

Olibtine hurried down the maze of halls, past dozens of wooden doors and stained glass windows, slippered footsteps echoing with every stride. Time was of the essence and he'd already wasted enough of it scouring the libraries and picking the brains of the other Minds. *I should have gone straight to Guane from the start. Moss. I could have been half-way to the tower by now,* he scolded himself for not thinking of it sooner.

Upon entering his chamber, a modest room with a nondescript bed, desk, wardrobe, and chair placed at a window sill, similar to all of the other Mind's chamber rooms, he began to fervently throw what he needed on his bed. Cloaks, undergarments, a pipe with some smoke, some string, and a knife he had carried with him since childhood that had come in handy a time or two when he was a Problem Solver. *I'll need to get some food and a book or two on the sorcerer's tower.* A list had formed in his head that he was checking off.

He jumped as a knock came at his door, instinctively preparing his knife in his right hand, blade up. *What am I doing?* he scolded himself as he glanced at the knife in his hand. Setting it back with the other items, he steadied himself and walked the few steps to the door, and slowly pulled it open a few inches to see who it was.

Leaning against the far wall with arms crossed in the blue and white cloaked attire of Gbinti was a dark brown Foxlet. A face full of short, shiny fur and big, pointed ears that were constantly twitching above a pointed nose with a black tip and deep, black eyes, she stood there staring. Working a long piece of straw in her mouth, a bow string across her chest, the wooden parts sticking up behind her shoulder and near her hip, she looked itching to move. Olibtine looked down to notice a small gray pack on the ground next to her foot, which made his eyebrows narrow in thought.

"Um, hello...?" Olibtine called out, as he opened his door the rest of the way, letting the light from inside spill out onto her face. Her eyes became a deeper black, but her face stayed just as expressionless.

"Daria. Guane sent me," she replied in a high, squeaky tone that fit her appearance. She smiled, sharp teeth visible. "By the look on your face, you weren't expecting me. Guane does that. One time when I was a kid he sent me to go get some fresh bread from the baker down the street. I showed up when I was told, but the baker wasn't expecting me even though Guane told me he was." The straw in her mouth bounced up and down as she went on. "Well, we can probably agree that this is a little different than that, but Guane does things without others knowing all the time. No doubt his old age thinks he can do what he wants." She smirked. "So, you ready to go then?"

"Go?" Olibtine asked, tilting his head, looking her up and down again, landing on the pack, the dots connecting. *You sneaky old man.* He sighed while rubbing his forehead.

"I'm sorry, but I cannot allow you to accompany me. I told Guane that I was going alone and that's what I intend to do," Olibtine clenched his jaw, reaching for the door to close it, "Please give Guane my regards."

Before he could get the door shut, Daria spoke up, "What, you're going to fend off anything that comes near with that little pocket knife of yours?"

Olibtine paused, glancing at the items on his bed. *How did she know? You can't even see it from here.* He looked back at her, opening the door again all the way. *She's something else, isn't she?* He met her deep black eyes once again.

"I've had my fair share of run-ins," he reveals, *but they haven't been outside of the city.*

"You're a smart man, the smartest in fact from what I'm told. You've probably read what is out there outside of the city, right? Maybe even experienced it a time or two. Whatever you've read about is only the tip of the tree. I hope you never have to witness them first-hand, but if you do, you'll need something a bit bigger than that little dagger," she finished, bending over and grabbing her pack, slinging it over her shoulder, and walking away down the hall. Olibtine had read plenty of books and seen more drawings than he could of the creatures outside of the city. From goblins that bore underground to human-sized bugs that suck the life out of everything they find, leaving only skin and bones in their paths, he knew that going alone was a fool's errand. *The mind can only take one so far. Admitting that you can't do it alone and relying on others to help you takes more strength than being stubborn.*

"Wait!" Olibtine yelled after her. She froze, her ears twitching back towards him, but not looking back. "Okay, you can come with."

Daria smiled to herself and turned back towards Olibtine. "Well, when do we leave?"

"As soon as I get some food and a book or two regarding the sorcerer's tower," Olibtine replied, turning back into his room to finish packing his supplies.

"I've got the food," Daria calls from down the hall. "No books though - too heavy for my liking. Do you really need those to get along?"

"We can cross food off the list then, but I need to make final preparations for the tower the way I know best. It won't take long to grab them and I will carry them, so no burden to you."

Daria stood inside the doorframe now and gave a shrug. "No hair off my back."

Shoving everything on the bed into his pack, Olibtine heaved it over his shoulder, then led Daria into the library, grabbed two books, *Baugroun's Topography* and *Plants and The Sorcerer's Play Things*, and headed west, out over the Binti river and through the main gates of the city.

Chapter 18: Introductions

Kausha doubled over in a clearing attempting to catch her breath. The sun, directly above, barely filtered through the thick canopy. She turned to see the rest of the group panting, similarly hunched over, except for Shaum and Skirm who were on all fours, seemingly on the verge of collapse from carrying the majority of the weight on their speedy haste from Soplnet.

"Think.... Think we lost em?" Shaum panted, struggling to find his breath, glancing back the way they came.

"Not likely," Yaula responded, "but from the sound of this part of The Forest, we have for now. If those are what I think they are, they aren't likely to give up either. If you noticed, there was no sound in Lumber when we were around the acid, but as soon as we got far enough away, the sound started again. It repeated outside of Soplnet - it can't be a coincidence."

"And what exactly... are they?" Skirm gasped between shallow breaths, wiping his forehead with the back of his forearm, now sitting with his back against a tree holding a jug.

"Sorcerers," Yaula responded between clenched teeth. Each in the group shifted at hearing that, their heads darting between one another questioningly.

"Sorcerers? Like...?" the bard asked, his right hand moving as if casting a spell with a wand.

"Not quite, but close enough," Yaula replied. "It's now obvious that sorcerers are the ones creating those acid clouds, so it's only right to tie them to those acid blobs too."

Skirm froze, the jug nearly at his mouth as his eyes went wide. "Wait, what? Why are there sorcerers and why are they creating acid clouds?"

"Rumor is that sorcerers have been around for thousands of years, performing nefarious deeds like assassinations, poisoning of crops, and more. I wasn't sure at first, but with the acid blobs in Soplnet, I'm fairly certain of it now. As to why they are doing this, you'd have to ask them," she finished, shrugging while everyone listened intently, eagerly awaiting more answers with lumps in their throats, but none came.

Kausha knew that sorcerers were alive. She knew that sorcerers took jobs from anyone that had enough ujuntu. She even knew why the acid rain and blobs were here. She squeezed her hands into a fist. *It's because of me,* she admitted, lowering her gaze to the ground.

"I need a drink," Shaum grunted, wiping sweat from his brow as he turned over from his back, sat up, then dug into the pack in front of him, pulling out a jug with liquor, then taking a swig.

"So if these are indeed sorcerers, are they after us?" Skirm asked, glancing at each in the group in turn.

Kausha caught Nalia looking at her, holding her gaze a little too long. *She knows.* Kausha looked around as well in an attempt to throw Nalia off.

Yaula shook her head, "I'm not sure, but I find it hardly coincidental that Lumber was ruined by acid rain and then as soon as we arrive in Soplnet, those acid blobs came around."

"Moss. What did I get myself into?" the bard cursed, pushing his hair back and making his way over to Shaum, sitting down next to him while motioning for the jug. Shaum took another swig before handing it over, only then noticing Kausha's eyes on the bard with a curious look on her face.

"Oh, Kaush, this es Skip, es tha bard from tha tavern," Shaum introduced, then nodded to Nalia. "And thas Nalia over there."

"Pleased to meet you, Kaush," Skip nodded towards Kausha, a smirk crossing his face, then turning his gaze towards Nalia. "You as well, Nalia."

"Kausha will do. Why are you with us?"

After swallowing a mouthful, Skip glanced around at each in the group, then returned his eyes to Kausha. "Well, I'm a bard and bards need adventure. Something to sing about. I wasn't about to get that in that dinky old tavern now was I? You lot seemed absolutely brimming with fun. And so diverse too!"

"Es a good lad, Kaush, we can trust em," Shaum frowned, roughly taking the jug back from Skip before he could take another gulp.

"At least we know he won't slow us down," Skirm added, shrugging.

"Fine, but you just heard what Yaula said, so don't come crying to me when you get burnt by some acid," Kausha replied, stomping over to a felled log opposite the two, then taking a seat while wiping her forehead with her rolled up brown sleeve.

"You positively won't hear any complaints from me," Skip nodded with a smile on his face.

After each had time to rest and catch their breath, Skirm broke to silence. "Well, what are we going to do now? If those things can track us, how are we going to make it out of The Forest?"

The question hung thick in the air. Each was thinking it, but Skirm was the one to put voice to it.

"We'll just have to stay ahead of them," Yaula answered while glancing over their faces, "I don't know if there is a way to stop them. Anyone have any ideas?"

They all looked at each other in turn, lips tight.

"Then running away seems to be the only option currently," Yaula nodded curtly. "Let's rest up while the sound is still around us. No fire and be ready to move at a moment's notice. Nalia, can you use your ears to warn us if you hear anything or nothing?"

Nalia nodded, mouth downturned, arms crossed in front of her chest as she stood leaning against a tree twice as thick as she was.

"And Shaum you big oaf, you better not keep drinking that or else I'm going to leave you behind," she scolded, staring darts into Shaum as he was raising the jug to his lips again, deciding to lower it once she set her sights on him. He knew when to not challenge Yaula on his drinking.

Yaula went on, "We are getting deeper into The Forest and while up until now there was an expectation of things we would run across, outside of Soplnet though, it gets much less so. The vast majority of travelers stop there, rarely ever going west for fear of the Bloodborn, and those that go in the direction of Nortmund don't exactly make it back to spread the word about the northwest part of The Forest. From this point forward, we need to move quickly, yet carefully, always being at the ready in case we run across anything."

An unexpected chill ran up Kausha's spine. She had been through training and traveled enough to keep her head on a swivel, but something about the northwest part of The Forest gave her the creeps. She knows that others like to exaggerate about the unknown, letting their imagination get the better of them, but from her mother's serious nature when talking about that part of The Forest, that it should not be taken lightly. *I could sneak off and head west like I had initially planned… Great great grandmother isn't going to pass for a while, giving me plenty of time to get back even if I head to Nortmund with this group, though.* She looked over at Nalia, who was standing against one of the large trees in the clearing, foot propped up, eyes closed, arms crossed at her chest, and ears constantly darting back and forth listening as Yaula asked her to. *Plus, I can't help but to feel for her and her sister. If I truly cared though, I'd steer the acid blobs away from them… but what if they go after their trail vs mine - I know I can beat them with my blood. Moss.* She clenched her fist and closed her eyes, repeating the options in her head in case she missed something.

"Kausha," she heard next to her. It was Yaula, eyebrow raised while looking at her clenched fists, which she promptly relaxed. "Something on your mind, child? I mean, besides all of this," she motioned with her hand while looking up and around.

Kausha leaned her head back, looking up into the canopy to see light green, back-lit leaves here and there, the only sign that the sun was up above. "No, I'm fine," she answered with a deep exhale that said more than the words she spoke.

"You know..." Yaula started, turning away from the clearing so that the others wouldn't hear, "back when my spines were much shorter than they are today, a traveler that looked like you visited my Lumber." Kausha stiffened, throwing a glance down at Yaula who didn't seem to notice. "She kept to herself for the most part, but we did have a talk about her daughter, a young girl named Kausha. I had forgotten all about her visit until your wounds healed and that sparked my memory." She looked up at Kausha, whose eyes were wide. Yaula returned her gaze forward, looking into the trees, continuing. "The reason it sparked my memory was because she said she needed some time to heal from her journey through the eastern Forest. I offered my help, as I do with every traveler, but she refused saying that it wouldn't take long and that normal remedies would only slow her down. I don't think she meant to say that last part because we didn't talk again in the few days she was there. I'll never forget the look in her eyes when she left though, the same look that I saw in you in Soplnet - confidence and unwavering determination that I have not seen in Uradaria since."

Yaula let that hang in the air, hoping Kausha would fill in the blanks, but she received nothing in return. She sighed. "Everyone chooses their own path and with those eyes, you won't stop at anything to follow yours. I just hope for Uradaria's sake that it's the right one for us as well as you. Well, rest up while you can, we'll be off sooner rather than later."

Yaula made her way back to the others on the other side of the clearing, leaving Kausha to her thoughts, an image of her mother popping into her head. *Mother?*

Chapter 19: A new task

"We require an update on your progress," the disjointed face in the glowing red ujuntu basin demanded. Only one of the sorcerers was hunched over the basin placed on top of a small, wooden table flush against the wall at the top of the tower.

"We are currently on her trail," came a monotone response, providing no further explanation. The face in the basin disappeared for a second, leaving the red water still. Returning in a ripple, the face responded, "Time is of the essence. We cannot afford any further delay. If we need to find someone else to handle this, we will."

The sorcerer regarded the threat. "If you wish to do so. The Bloodborn is more... resourceful... than we assumed," *and deadly*. "We drove them out of Soplnet into the dense Forest. It won't be long now."

"This is acceptable," the face in the basin replied. "Furthermore, you will have two visitors very soon. Take care of them as you see fit, but no acid. We cannot have this being traced back to us."

"It will be done," the sorcerer responded as the face in the basin disappeared, the red water going still.

The sorcerer stayed hunched over in contemplation regarding the current predicament they were in. *Two visitors will not be an issue*, the sorcerer thought, turning to glance across the room at the two sorcerer companions, their deep black robes fighting against the red glow of the water. A thought blossomed in the sorcerer's mind as it stood straight, then began making its way down the winding staircase to a landing two floors below the top of the tower. A thick, wooden door slid open with the wave of a hand and in stepped the sorcerer. *No matter, we have more than one way of handling this sort of thing.*

Chapter 20: A Detour

Olibtine wasn't nearly as used to walking as he used to be before becoming a Mind. Especially in sturdy boots. He spent more time nowadays sitting in various places, whether that be his desk, the Council's Chamber, the great hall, or the libraries. *Good thing I have my smoke*, he smiled while taking a puff, attempting to alleviate the pain in his feet from walking on the cobblestone path leading from the city. Staring ahead at Daria's back, he couldn't help but be jealous of her. She clearly had been used to walking long distances, or at least didn't show her pains like he did. *Who is she anyways, and why would Guane send her to accompany me?* He looked her up and down again like he'd done a dozen times before already. *The bow looks rather worn and her shoes are well broken in.* He turned his head and listened. *And I can't hear her footsteps either. Impressive.* He took another puff.

"Hey Daria, you want some?" he asked, exhaling, holding his pipe out ahead of him. She looked back at him with her black eyes that seemed to somehow seem deeper in the sunlight, then the pipe.

"Sure," she shrugged, turning around while still walking backwards in the same direction and grabbing the pipe. "You know, I once stole a bag full of smoke from a farmer at a local village to sell it on the streets of Gbinti. Allowed me to eat for a month after as well as buy Shooter here," she tapped her bow sting. "Yup, Shooter and me go back a long ways, practically family now. Guane told me I'm the best he's seen with a bow. Who knows if that's true," she shrugged, moving the wheat in her mouth to the side in order to fit the pipe in the mouth, "he is suuuper old," she smirked, taking a puff and holding it in.

She sure likes to talk. That does explain the wear from the bow though.

Blowing the smoke out in one big puff, she nodded and handed the pipe back to Olibtine. Turning back around the way they were headed, she spoke up again.

"The road didn't used to be like this, you know? Seems more are going this way these days for some reason or another. I've heard rumors that there is a town somewhere outside of Gbinti where you can buy anything your heart's desire. I've seen some of the things brought back, like slugs with legs as long as a finger, rocks with slushy goo on the inside, and vials of blood from the Bloodborn themselves! Imagine that, Bloodborn blood that is thousands of years old! I haven't been there yet, but it sure would be cool to have one of those vials - I could find a use or two for those. There's another town that..."

"Wait," Olibtine interrupted after digesting what was just said, senses a little dulled from the smoke, "what about the Bloodborn blood? How did they get that?" he asked, scurrying up next to her.

She looked sideways at him. "Oh, that? I don't know, they didn't say. Not sure they even asked the shop owner either. You don't ask a baker how he gets his ingredients, you just buy it."

"Wait, what?" he frowned. "A baker gets his ingredients from farmers who have fields and animals. Bloodborn blood is something completely different." Daria only shrugged as if both were the same concept, only different objects.

"Are you sure it was Bloodborn blood and not just made up?"

"Eh, it sure wasn't any blood that I had seen before."

Olibtine's eyebrows narrowed. *I'll have to come back to that.* "Do you know where this town is?"

Daria nodded. "Kind of. Told ya I haven't been, but I can get there." She turned her head towards him. "Why?"

"I'd like to stop there to see for myself," he replied, tucking his pipe away. "If there truly is, or was, Bloodborn blood there,

I want to see it and find out how they got it. It could help us tremendously."

Daria shrugged. "You're the boss. It's not on the road to the tower, but it won't take long to get there, just a little south through the marsh."

"Lead the way," Olibtine motioned with his hands, a smile on his face, the new discovery giving his legs and feet new life. *Guane is one crafty old man.*

The cobblestone faded into dirt the further from Gbinti they traveled. Tall grass lined the road, wide enough to walk side by side with room to spare, void of the abundant trees that one would find near the city. Cresting a small hill, Daria paused and squinted west, catching Olibtine off guard as he stuttered to a stop.

"What is it?" he asked, looking at her, then realizing she could be looking at something. He pivoted on his toes as quickly as he could to look back the direction they were headed. His eyes darted up the path, then off to the sides of the dirt road. "I don't see anything," he whispered out of the corner of his mouth. Turning back to Daria, he noticed she was now looking south. *What the.* He looked off in the same direction, noticing the sun sparkling off of the ground.

"Is that the marsh?"

Daria nodded, but shifted her gaze towards the ground as if searching for something. Olibtine tried to follow her gaze, but didn't know what they were supposed to be looking for. "Should we be looking for something?" he finally asked.

She squinted while moving back and forth on the dirt road, eyes darting in search for something all the while. "There is supposed to be a wooden path somewhere around here. There!" She stopped, pointing towards the bottom of the embankment off to her right, then scampering side to side down towards it.

"Where? I don't..." Before he could finish his sentence, he saw it - a single sapling-sized path, nearly the same color as the surrounding grass, practically buried in the dirt.

"Not far now!" she yelled back at him. "Hope you aren't afraid of getting those pretty robes dirty," she laughed, stepping on to the path.

The start of the path was easy enough to walk upon, even if they had to walk one behind the other. With every step, they moved further into the marsh, grass growing taller than their heads, bugs and animals deafening, all while the path sank deeper into the mud and water from their weight. Apart from the wet feet, Olibtine thought he might like this place. Light waning, the only thing to do was to follow Daria's darker outline between the grass. Something at the top of the grass caught his attention. *Is that a light?* Squinting and refocusing his eyes directly forward again, he froze.

"Daria?!" He turned around frantically. "Daria?!" Turning back the way they were headed, he took a few steps, the path leading around a grass bend. Slivers of light snuck through the stems again. He crept forward, trying to hide his footsteps with little avail. "Daira?" he struggled to get out, the bugs around louder than his voice was, taking a few more steps.

"You coming already?" Daria asked ahead of him out of sight at normal volume. Olibtine sped up, water splashing from either side of the wooden path with each step, attempting to catch up to her voice.

Turning around another small grass bend, he finally noticed where the light was coming from, making his jaw drop at the sight. An opening in the grass revealed a single wooden path with dark pools of water on either side leading up to a wide, flat, central structure on massive, glowing red and green mushrooms, acting as both the stilts that kept it suspended off of the marsh's water as well as the light source. The structure itself was actually a number of thick, wooden planks with lumps of small, square hardened mud buildings on top. None of the buildings were exactly the same size, but each was pivotal in holding up every building next to it. Tight alleyways provided the only walkways throughout the structure for citizens to make their way around, but judging by the place, there wasn't much of that happening.

"What's this place called?" Olibtine asked, unable to take his eyes off of the glowing mushrooms.

"They call it Shroomsgrove. Fitting don't ya think?"

Olibtine nodded, still staring at the mushrooms. He shook himself after seeing Daria halfway across the walkway and hurried to follow. The closer he got, the more impressive the structure was. "I've never even read about mushrooms getting this large before."

"These?" Daria scoffed, looking over at one. "These are actually small compared to the ones deeper in the marsh. Some say they rival even the largest of trees in the middle of The Forest. Who knows though, can't trust a Muddy for anything."

Olibtine raised his eyebrows. "You sure know a lot about this place without ever being here."

Daria looked at him shrugging with a smile on her face.

As they made their way up the wooden steps to the buildings, Olibtine noticed that the square structures were simple mud and stick buildings that must have been built using the surrounding area, maybe even the mud directly beneath the structure. *Clever*, he smiled, as they approached the left alleyway with Daria. The alleys looked substantially skinnier than Gbinti's, and upon approach, they certainly were. The two could barely walk side by side. Olibtine's shoulder rubbed against the mud buildings, which, he found out after a jagged piece tugged on his robe, were hard as rock. Making their way through the alleys, Olibtine realized that he hadn't seen a single "Muddy", as Daria called them.

"Where are the townsfolk?" Olibtine asked, looking down an alleyway to the left in an intersection.

"They're probably closer to the middle. That, or in a tavern," Daira replied over her shoulder, not breaking stride.

They approached a T section of an alley and Daria led them left. Then another and Daria turned right, then left, then right again. *I thought she said she hadn't been here before.*

"Is this the right way?" he asked after a few more turns without seeing any sign of life.

Daria shrugged. "I'm just trying to go to the lights and sounds."

"Wait..." Olibtine halted, his eyebrows narrowing. "So we're just wandering aimlessly through this place? What if we go down a wrong alley and run into something we don't want to?"

Daria shrugged again, taking a second to stop and look him in the face, a smirk visible in the mushroom light far behind. "It's a hunch. You're welcome to stay here if you like." She turned, confident as always, and kept moving down the current alley. Olibtine hurried to catch up, looking around at the new area they were in. *Looks exactly like the buildings before. Are we going in circles?*

A few more turns and Olibtine thought he could hear voices nearby just around the next turn. Daria walked into the square first, stopping so Olibtine could stand beside her. What he saw was not something he had expected walking through that maze of alleyways.

An open square surrounded by mud buildings met his eyes. Running along the outside were tables packed with all diversities of food, hats, animals, and oddities, most of which he had never seen the likes of before. Behind each table, and throughout the square, sat little rat humanoids chatting away, barely as tall as his hip. The only clothing they wore were hats, not one the same throughout the square, their pointy ears sticking out through holes on each side. The color of their fur is what truly stood out, though - from purple to white to green and all shades in between. Olibtine was transfixed, his eyes darting from one to another. *I wonder if that is their natural color*, his scholar mind thought, mouth agape. Staring at one that was larger than the rest with bright blue fur and a hat that resembled a book, he couldn't help but to smile. A mix of voices traveled through the air to him, similar to what you'd hear in any central square in a city, indistinguishable without getting closer.

"Are these the Muddies?" he asked Daria, unable to take his eyes off of the square.

"They are. My first time seeing them too, but I've heard them described as being much scarier than this," she replied with a smile. "What do you say we join them? I see a table with mugs over there," she pointed off to their left.

Olibtine nodded. "Yes, let's."

As they approached the table with the mugs, a bright red Muddy with a large poofy purple and gold hat and deep brown eyes that seemed too large for its body, sat in its chair, rocking back and forth.

"Well helllllo there strangers. Ya'lls first time to Shroomsgrove I take it the way you're staring at me?" The Muddy's voice was a higher pitch than even Daria's. Olibtine and Daria nodded slowly. "Let me give ya'll the quick run-down. Here is where ya'll can get a drink or some food, but there are others as well. The one over there with the animals hanging from sticks has all sorts of things you'd find in the marsh, from toads to bugs and everything in between. Over there..." she pointed behind them with her sharp claws, "is where ya'll can find a place to sleep if you're wanting. And ya'll will just have to walk around a bit to see what other goods are available. Can I get ya'll a drink? It's Shroomsgrove's finest psychedelic that'll make yer inners glow. Don't worry, even for ya'll outsiders, it won't hurt ya, but you'll be feeling extra good tonight," she finished with a wink, already ladling out the glowing concoction into mugs, uncaring that she spilled some over the brim.

To Olibtine's shock, Daria went right for it without hesitation, grabbing one of the mugs and taking a deep gulp. Upon lowering the drink beneath wide eyes, her lips had a blue glow to them.

"That's gooooood!" she exclaimed, showing her sharp teeth through a huge smile before taking another gulp.

Olibtine looked back at the Muddy smiling with large, pointed teeth. He looked down, grabbed the one left, watched the ripples settle, then hesitantly took a sip.

"It tastes like, like..." he took a few gulps, "delicious!" He exclaimed, unable to put words to what his mouth was feeling.

"Ah, so you're blue for calm," the Muddy observed while looking at Daira. "And you're yellow, the color of curiosity. A fine combo."

So it isn't natural, Olibtine deduced, looking at the Muddy's red fur again, as it swirled slightly. He blinked hard. *What the...* He turned to look at Daria, his eyes slow to catch up to his head, who was rubbing her eyes with her free hand, blinking hard between each rub.

"That's the shroom," the Muddy warned. "Don't worry though, ya'll will get used to it - everyone here has, including me." She took a swig from her own mug. "Try taking a seat over there and let it take your mind off things for a bit."

Before Olibtine and Daria realized, they were sitting at one of the tables in the center of the square, surrounded by bright colors everywhere. *How...* Olibtine started, but couldn't quite finish his thought. He looked over to Daria, a huge smile on her face, her head detached from her neck and spinning slowly. *What the?!* He grabbed his head to make sure it was still on straight. "Phew," he breathed out.

"What?" Daria asked, her head back on straight.

"Your head," Olibtine forced out of his dry mouth. "Your head," he repeated as she grabbed her head in both hands.

"What?" Daria asked again, blinking hard in an attempt to focus on Olibtine.

Olibtine began laughing uncontrollably. Daria joined in.

The next thing Olibtine knew he was chewing on something, holding a stick with a snake on it. Cocking his head to the side, a frown on his face, he looked over to Daria and she was chewing as well, snake on a stick in her hand. *How did we?*

Olibtine found himself laughing again, Daria next to him laughing as well, surrounded by Muddy's of all colors at their table laughing too, a mug in every hand.

Light forced Olibtine's eyes open, the blue sky above causing his head to spin. With a groan, he looked around. He was outside on a bench, Daria next to him, Muddys sprawled out everywhere he could see. *What the?* He rubbed his eyes. Reaching over to Daria, he tapped her on the shoulder.

"Daria." She groaned, turning to the other side. "Daira," he said louder, shaking her. She groaned again, turning back over to her back.

"What?" she asked softly.

"Daria, what happened?"

"What?" she asked, lifting her head and finally opening her eyes to a sliver as she looked around. "Wait, what?"

"That drink..." Olibtine stumbled, unable to finish a proper thought. "That drink must have done this to us."

Daria closed her eyes, leaning her head back down, a smile appearing on her face. "Yup. Awesome."

"Moss. We didn't even find the vial yet."

Daria rubbed her eyes, scooted off of the table, and began stretching. "We will, don't worry. I think I remember seeing a table with vials on it last night, we should be able to find him today."

"How can you do that right now? Isn't your head swimming?" Olibtine asked incredulously, rubbing his temple.

"Sure, but that doesn't mean my body is. I feel pretty great otherwise."

As the Muddys started to stir, Olibtine glanced around looking for their packs - still in the same spot they left them before drinking. *That's a relief.* He forced himself to get up and stumbled over to his pack, removed the canteen and took a few chugs before taking Daria hers.

"Do you know where the man that sells the vials is right now?" Olibtine asked, sitting down next to her.

"Nope, but I'm sure one of these Muddys knows." Daria glanced around at the Muddys stirring, noticing the red one that sold them the drinks last night on the table close by. She walked over to her and shook her awake. With a stretch, the Muddy sat up, locked eyes with Daira, and in muted voices too far for Olibtine to hear, pointed towards a table not far off from where Olibtine was at the moment. With a parting laugh and a hug, Daria walked back over to Olibtine. "His house is on the other side of the table he was at. Seems like all of the Muddys behind tables also lived right behind those tables. Convenient."

Olibtine nodded. "Let's go see him then."

The two walked over to the door of the building, Muddys throughout the central square coming to their senses and meandering off to do whatever it is they did, and knocked. No response. Olibtine had his arm outstretched to knock again.

"Whatdya want, it's early," a gruff, deep voice came from behind them, completely different from the other Muddys they had heard. Olibtine and Daria turned to see a dark green Muddy with a boiler hat on stepping towards the door. They made room for him as he opened the door and then disappeared into darkness. "Well, you're here already, come in," he called out through the open door, his voice sounding far off.

They set their packs down outside of the door and Olibtine entered first, then Daira, both having to duck down due to the small door frame. Daria shut the door behind her, putting the place in pitch black darkness. *No windows,* Olibtine blinked forcing his eyes to adjust to the dark. The sound of water sloshing jerked his head to the right, unable to see what it was until a light yellow glow started to appear, moving back and forth at blurrying speeds. It slowly grew brighter with every move until Olibtine could see that it was the Muddy that was shaking a bottle of some sort, first his hands visible and then his face. A few more shakes and the entire room was lit up by a pleasant yellow glow resonating from the bottle. He placed it down on a table near him, then grabbed another one and shook it the same as the first, this one emitting blue light.

"Mushroom light," the Muddy started, "It's what we use here, but if you pluck them from the ground, they need water and movement to glow again. Now, what is it you two want?" he asked gruffly, walking across the room towards them and placing the bottle on a low wooden side table near the doorway leading to the outside. As he walked off, Olibtine bent over to get a better look at the vial and sure enough, it had a small mushroom with a full stem and cap floating in liquid. *Ingenious. I wonder how long these last and how movement plays into it. Is it a defense mechanism like the Lunper fish where it flashes a bright light from its antenna?*

"Well?" the muddy interrupted his thoughts, sending him upright and turning to see the muddy had taken a seat on an uncomfortable looking armless, backless wooden chair.

"We are looking for something specific that we've heard that you've had before," Olibtine began, taking in the room. There was nothing on the walls, a few mismatched chairs across the room near a circular table with various bottles, vials, and objects atop it that he had no clue what they were. He brought his eyes back to the Muddy. "To be specific, it's Bloodborn blood."

The Muddy stared at him, not a single emotion on his face. "Rare, that is. I've had some, but don't have any right now. Last few I had were bought by some other tall human with black robes and hoods covering their faces. I've got some other blood though." He stood, then walked into another room that Olibtine hadn't noticed before. "I've got Spindlebock, Horfstun, Lurnda, Nargocki," he called from the other room. "Need any of those?"

Daria, getting bored, started to walk around, footsteps silent as usual, glancing over the items on the desk, moving things around, then picking up the shroom vial that was emitting light giving it a few shakes.

"Don't touch anything!" the Muddy scolded from the other room. Daria looked back at Olibtine with a raised eyebrow. She lifted the vial menacingly, then shook the vial a few more times with a smirk on her face.

Olibtine shook his head at her. "No, that's alright, we simply came for the Bloodborn blood. Seeing as you don't have any, do you have any information about it?" Olibtine asked. The Muddy placed something down with a clink, then appeared in the doorway.

"Information? What do you mean?" the Muddy asked.

"Where did you get it, first off."

The Muddy crossed his arms before responding, looking at Daria first, then Olibtine, a deep frown on his face, his eyebrows narrowing. "I'm an honest tradesman. I come by my wares through traveling, trading, and by completely legitimate means. I think you two better..."

Olibtine interrupted because he had dealt with enough shady traders to know where the conversation was going. "Oh, no, sorry sir, I didn't mean it like that. I am a simple researcher from Gbinti that is just looking for any information about the Bloodborn and their passing. I meant no offense and wasn't implying anything of the sorts."

The Muddy looked them up and down again, shrugged his shoulders, then straightened his hat before unfolded his arms, clearly happy with Olibtine's response. "Okay then. A traveler came through a number of moons ago and traded them to me for shroom vials, a place to stay, and a map of the grove. Simple as that, really. Nice girl she was."

Girl, Olibtine's forehead wrinkled. "Girl you say? How many vials was it?"

"Yup, a girl. She was by herself and heading to Gbinti from what I recall. She had five vials with her - would have taken more if I had them."

A girl traveling by herself in the marsh AND had Bloodborn blood with her, one of the rarest things in all of Uradaria. It's rare for women to travel around by themselves in the first place, but to have vials as well makes this a highly unlikely scenario. Olibtine scrunched his face and scratched his chin.

A loud *tink* made the Muddy and Olibtine jump and look the way it came. Daria was bent over the yellow glass, cringing as it rolled in a circle, hands interlaced at hip level as if she tried desperately to catch it. She looked up at Olibtine and then at the Muddy, her eyes wide, mouth in a line. "Sorry," she shrunk into herself.

"Moss! I told you not to touch anything! Move, move!" the Muddy yelled, rushing over and scooping up the vial gently with both hands. "Do you know what would have happened if this would have broken?! We'd be dead, that's what! Just get out of here, I told you everything already!" he yelled.

"Did she give her name?" Olibtine asked, staring at Daria with a frown on his face.

"Kausha. Now get out!"

"Terribly sorry, sir. And thank you for everything," Olibtine finished, then turned and opened the door, motioning for Daria to leave first, following in her steps and closing the door behind them. He looked at Daira with raised eyebrows and she only shrugged, picking up her pack in the process, then began walking away.

Kausha, huh? Olibtine committed to memory. He picked his pack up and followed in Daria's footsteps.

Chapter 21: Hidden Threats

The further they trekked through The Forest, the denser the tree trunks and canopy became, blocking out every glimmer of sunlight from above until they had to use torches even at mid-day when the sun was at its peak. The Forest constantly groaned as if it were breathing in and out. Above, the leaves and branches fluttered about as if an unseen force was playing with them. At ground level, the air was completely still, wrapping the group in warm, wet air. Unknown, glowing eyes followed at every twist and turn around massive tree trunks while thick roots sprang out of the ground creating bridges overhead and obstacles underfoot, threatening to trip anyone passing without proper light. The Forest was alive.

"Es no wonder nobody goes tis way, ye can barely take two steps in a straight line without fallin oer a Mossin log," Shaum grumbled, small black eyes wide while waving his torch around trying to get a better look at his surroundings.

"How do we even know we are going the right direction with no sun or stars to guide us?" Skirm asked, ducking under a thick vine.

"You big oafs, don't you know anything about The Forest? Look here," Yaula chided, putting her torch close to one of the trees and walking around, searching for something. She stopped and pointed at something. "See these red spotted bugs? They only land on the north side of trees. Moss, you would think you two had never been into The Forest before. I expected this much from Shaum, but from you Skirm?" Yaula shook her head at the Spearhead.

Skirm walked over to where Yaula was pointing and bent over, squinting. "Those things?! Those are tiny! We're big. How were we supposed to know that - we're from the Circle Lake, not The Forest.

Ask us about finding your way under water and I bet we'll know more than you," he huffed.

Yaula eyed Skirm under narrow eyebrows while mumbling something under her breath, causing him to shrink up and retreat back to Shaum.

"Ye shouldn't av said anything. Ye know how she gets," Shaum chuckled.

"Yeah, yeah," Skirm replied, staring at his feet and kicking dirt on the ground.

Kausha knew all of this already and was making sure they were all heading the right direction. After living so long, you tend to know a lot more than the average traveler. She looked back the way they came, pitch black outside of the puddles of torchlight. *They're back there somewhere.* She caught Nalia staring in the same direction, ears forward, focused on something.

"What is it, Nalia?" Kausha asked, drawing the attention of the others.

"I'm not sure if it's anything out of the norm of this place, but I can feel more and more eyes on us the deeper we go."

Each nodded their heads slowly, understanding what she was saying, but afraid to voice it for fear of giving it life, whatever *it* was.

"We best keep moving," Yaula led from the front, turning back north. The others agreed and followed in silence, ears open, sweat on their foreheads glistening in the torchlight from the stillness of the air, packs clanking every so often as they stepped over and under roots.

The familiar tree groans were growing unfamiliar now, seemingly yelling at them as a warning to turn back. Twigs snapping off in the distant dark caused torches to fly back and forth attempting to locate the source with no avail. Labored breathing accompanied a quickening pace as they constantly dodged shrubs, fallen logs, vines, and roots in the underbrush. Something darker than the dark ahead crossed Yaula's path causing her to skid to an abrupt stop, nearly being burnt by Shaum's torch from behind.

"Stop, Stop!" she exclaimed as loud as she dared while still breaking through The Forest sounds.

"What is it?" came Skirm's anxious voice from the back.

A ruffling in the bushes to the right made everyone turn abruptly, then one to the back, then to the front, then above, a swaying vine a sign that something real was there.

"What is it?!" Skirm asked again, his voice quivering.

"Nalia?" asked Yaula.

Nalia shook her head, ears darting as if responding to every sound nearby. "I can't see anything."

Kausha happened to look up in time to see it - or part of it. It looked like a skinny tree trunk moving over their heads from one side of them to the other. She raised her torch to get a better look and saw it again followed by a snapping sound in the same direction the thing moved. *What is that?* She squinted as if it would help. An answer slumped down and stared her right in the face, just on the edge of the torchlight. Her breath caught as her insides shifted sporadically, her blood moving instinctively into her arms and hands at the sight.

What little she could see of the thing was the size of Kausha herself. Countless eyes staring at her, reflecting her wide eyes and gaping mouth in the torchlight. Long gray hairs drooped off of it, swaying like grass on a wind-swept plain with three separate, circular mouths in a line, each with rows of teeth bare as sharp as a Spearhead's, lining the inside. The sight made Kausha shiver, but her torch thrust towards the creature without thought. It retreated back up into the darkness above, away from the light, then continued to move its legs from one side of the group to the other.

"It's a Trender!" Kausha yelled. Everyone immediately tensed, staring at her, eyes wide in fright.

"Moss! I thought those were fairy tales!" Yaula exclaimed, waving her torch over her head and in front of her.

"Is tha bad?" Shaum asked, looking around. "I dunno wha a Trender is."

"Oh, they're bad," Skip hopped in. "At least in the stories they are. I haven't even heard of any interactions with them in my travels. This must be one of the last ones in existence."

"Okay, so whadawe do?" asked Shaum frantically, jerking his head whichever direction a leg landed.

They all looked at Kausha. "We run," she said cooly, much cooler than she'd expected. "It's too big to squeeze under the roots or around them, so stick to smaller spaces if you can. And hold your torch above your heads so it doesn't come down on you from above."

Each held their torches above their heads while looking up, eyes wide and darting everywhere with mouths agape sucking in air as if they just ran miles, seeing nothing but darkness. Each sound made them jerk in unison, torches held towards it.

"Go!" Kausha ordered, pointing north, shaking them out of their stupor.

They started to run, hard as it was in the thick underbrush, towards no place in particular as long as it was away from the monster. Light illuminated the group in a shifting puddle. They ducked under and around roots, long-dead carcasses and leaves crunching underfoot. Loose, untouched dirt flew up from beneath with each step as they skirted around a long dead tree.

Shaum, out in front of everyone, came to a sudden halt looking around frantically, then turned left around a tree, followed by Yaula, Skip, and Skirm. Before Nalia could reach the tree, the monster's giant, wood-like hairy leg slammed down right where she would have been not two steps later. She dodged with a yelp, dropping her torch in the process, forced to divert around the tree to the right, followed closely by Kausha.

Moss! Kausha cursed in her head, watching the leg retreat into the darkness above, sparing a moment to hope the others were okay.

"Wait!" Kausha wheezed, listening for sounds nearby. "I don't hear or see it anymore... It must have followed them instead! Follow me!"

Nalia nodded in agreement, not a moment's hesitation in following Kausha. The two rushed west, the large trees and roots proving difficult to set a direct route.

"Any ideas?" Kausha asked Nalia between breaths, stopping to look around while holding the torch off to the side in a futile attempt to acclimate their eyes to the dark. Nalia focused her ears, listening for something - anything.

They heard a scream northwest, both glancing at one another for confirmation, then ran towards it without saying a word. Hopping over decomposing logs and roots, rounding one tree, then another, they stopped, breathing heavily while glancing around for another sign. None came. *Moss, Moss Moss!* Kausha's blood coursed through her legs urging her to move.

"There! A light!" Nalia pointed off to the west. She started running into the darkness, Kausha following, unable to see what she was referring to. Rounding one more tree, Kausha saw the familiar glow of torchlight, three figures in a small circle, backs towards each other, frantically swinging the torches back and forth in the air as if fending something off.

Should I do it? Kausha contemplated, coming to grips that she might have to fight to save them. *Yes, I have to! They saved my life once and have stuck with me since Lumber and through Soplnet.* She watched as a giant leg came slamming down close to Shaum, forcing him to jump back for fear of being impaled. Through gritted teeth, he forced his way back to the others. Kausha dropped her torch, trusting her training. She needed to free up her hands to do this. She pushed blood from underneath her right index fingernail, creating a sharp point not an inch long and stabbed her left palm, controlling the blood within so none escaped, but leaving a hole to push it out through. She retracted the blood from underneath her fingernail while at the same time pushing blood out of the hole in her hand, hardening it as it left her body, a thick blood spear growing longer and longer. She grabbed it with her right hand, pulling on it to speed the process up, the group only a few dozen feet away. She cut off the blood flow, breaking off the four-foot spear with a snap, repositioning it in her right hand, ready to throw. Just a few steps later, she finally noticed why the three fought for their positions - Yaula was lying face-down, motionless on the ground in the middle of them, torch beside her head, illuminating her bright yellow eyes.

Moss! Kausha clenched her teeth, shifted her insides towards the back of her body, then held her breath over the final few steps towards the group. Nalia's eyes shot wide open, finally noticing the blood spear in Kausha's hand.

Noooo! Kausha yelled to herself while watching the Trender's dozens of glossy eyes glistening from the torchlight, lowering itself towards Yaula. She reared back, using all of her momentum from the run strengthened by blood-filled legs and slung the spear with all she had, aimed directly in the middle of its eyes. Tumbling forward from the momentum, she didn't see it hit, but a high-pitched scream told her enough. Skitting to a dusty stop in a crouch, she watched as green liquid gushed from the broken eyes pieced by the spear. With one final, ear-splitting scream, its legs buckled under its enormous head, crashing straight down next to Yaula, green ooze seeping out, long, tree-like legs twitching. Shaum, Skirm, and Skip stared at its lifeless corpse, each falling to their knees panting and drenched in sweat. Shaum grimaced, holding a bloodied left arm after dropping his torch. Nalia stared at Kausha with narrowed eyes for a moment, then shifted her focus towards Yaula and the others. Kausha, drained from using so much blood, shuffled over to Yaula, then fell to her knees as well.

No. She glanced over the motionless, blood-covered body through watery eyes. Three circular holes spanning from hip to shoulder void of quills, something Kausha herself would even have trouble healing, made it clear what caused it. *No, this can't be. Yaula.* The others crawled over, exhausted, and huddled silently around Yaula. Tears began rolling down Shaum and Skirm's faces, each grabbing the other in an embrace.

"She... she tripped behind us and it..." Skip started, looking over at the Trender, "...it came down right on top of her before we could stop and turn to help," Skip finished, looking over to Kausha, who glanced at the Trender, dozens of reflections staring back at her, only now noticing it had a number of quills stuck in its mouths, green ooze seeping from those as well. Kausha blinked tears away, returning her eyes to Yaula.

Rest peacefully in Arduinna's embrace. Kausha reached towards Yaula, shutting her eyes for the last time.

Kausha forced herself to stand on wobbly legs, body sore and fatigued from the blood she'd used to spear the Trender. She glanced at the others one by one, Shaum and Skirm still holding each other, Skip sitting in the dirt on the edge of the torchlight, and finally Nalia, who was staring at her with her large orange eyes. *It has to come out now.* Kausha shifted her focus to the hole in the Trender's head, her blood spear no longer there after it melted away. *After we take care of Yaula.*

"We should bury Yaula." Kausha knelt and softly turned Yaula face-up. "Shaum and Skirm, can you dig a hole next to her here?" she asked, pointing next to Yaula.

Through sobs, Shaum and Skirm silently did as Kausha asked, tears still falling from their faces, then placed Yaula in the grave before standing up, forming a circle with the others, then bowing their heads in remembrance before replacing the dirt to create a mound, the dead Trender almost like a headstone.

"I'm Bloodborn," Kausha admitted in a flat tone after a moment. "I'm heading home to Purtghast because my great great grandmother is passing." She closed her eyes, clenching her fists. "And I believe the sorcerers Yaula spoke of are after me. Yaula…" she opened her eyes, looking through blurry vision at Yaula's grave, fists relaxing, "…thought so too."

She let that weight hang in the air for a while, only The Forest sounds and crackling torchlight to fill the space. She looked around at each of them in turn. "I understand if you no longer wish to travel with me - they are after me after all. It's safer that way."

Shaum and Skirm glanced at one another. "I knew it," Skirm stuck out his chest. "I knew you were different when you healed up from the acid in just one night."

"No ye dint," Shaum replied in a mocking tone. "Don lie."

Skirm simply rolled his eyes at his brother. "Anyways, after seeing what you just did, I'd feel safer with you around. Right, Shaum?"

"Right," Shaum answered with a nod, wiping his face and eyes with huge hands.

Kausha looked at Nalia for a response, but none came, simply a flat stare, eyes glowing bright in the torchlight.

"I'd like you around too," Skip agreed on the opposite side of Nalia. Kausha's head turned towards him, nodding. She got a small smile in return.

All four turned towards Nalia, expecting an answer, but only got a nod in return.

"Then that handles it," Skirm started, "we're going through this together no matter what is behind us, or why. Yaula... would have wanted it this way," he finished, looking down at the mound that was Yaula's grave. Each nodded, gathered their bags and torches, then spared one last glance towards Yaula's resting place before continuing north in silence through the pitch black unknown of The Forest.

Chapter 22: The slow approach

Kausha. Kausha. Kausha. Kausha. Olibtine repeated in his head, never wanting to forget that name after putting the pieces together while walking. *She was in Gbinti not long ago - could have been right under our noses and we would never know. What does she look like? Does she mean ill intent? If she did, she could have done something when she was there, but the last moon has been normal. What was she even doing in the marsh?*

The more Olibtine thought, the more confused and frustrated he became. Normally, he'd be able to hunt down answers the way he'd always had, but moving the opposite way of the answers left a sour taste in his mouth. *You're looking for answers now, stop beating yourself up.* He forced it out of his mind for the time being as they continued their journey west towards the tower. Cobblestone and packed dirt far behind them, the road wasn't much of a road anymore with this part of Uradaria being nearly completely uninhabited due to the dry and desert climate. That, combined with the sorcerer's tower, made it an easy choice to live anywhere else.

Daria paused at the top of a sand dune ahead of him, shielding her eyes from the sun above while looking out in the distance. "Look," she pointed before he could get to the top.

Olibtine crested the dune. A sharp, black spire came into view, slicing the clear blue sky in the distance, expanding with every step until he stood next to Daria, chills creeping up his spine. It was the tower, or what he could see of it. An ominous pitch black blight on an otherwise tan landscape.

"We're in Baugroun, now," Daria announced, staring ahead.

Olibtine waited for more from her, knowing she had a story to go along with it, but none came. *She must feel it too.* Chills cutting through the heat forced his arm hair to stand on end.

"How long?"

She shrugged. "Maybe one more day's hike. Not sure though, I've never been this close to it before. You know, there are rumors that say that if you set eyes on the tower, you will always feel like you're being watched no matter where you are. Heard it from an untrustworthy source though, so I wouldn't think about it too much."

There she is, Olibtine smiled, relieved and yet spooked all at the same time. "Well thanks for that," he replied sarcastically. "Let's keep going while we have light."

"You're the boss," Daria shrugged. She then began the small descent from the dune, Olibtine following close behind.

On a dune downslope, Olibtine and Daria sat around a campfire cross legged, eating a part of their food rations, staring off in the distance towards the oppressive tower. It stood there, darker than the darkness of night, a constant distraction in an otherwise silent landscape. Nothing stirred outside of the crackling of the fire as if only Olibtine and Daria were the only living things around. *Only a little further now.* Olibtine found that the best thing to do when faced with uncertainty is to go over plans in his head, so that's what he did. *The book said that sorcerers are old, resourceful, and ruthless when they want to be. They don't simply act on their own accord, preferring to be paid for everything they do, even assassinations. They will expect a trade of some sort from me, whether that be money, knowledge, or something else. Knowledge is all I have and so I will need to share something I have that they don't, but what? I should have known this before leaving and known what to trade. Think. Something they don't know...* he perked up, stopping mid chew. *The Bloodborn's name?! Would that do? What if they already know it?* He shook his head. *There isn't enough known of them to know for sure, but it's worth a try.*

He looked across the fire at Daria laying on her side staring towards the tower. *Her too, huh?* She sat up abruptly, squinting as if looking at something. *What?* Olibtine froze mid-chew, attempting to look in the same spot she was, finding it impossible to see anything in the dark. He glanced back over at her, her bow now in one hand, a vial in the other. *What the?*

"What is it?" he whispered, his beating heart racing loud in his ears. "What do you see?"

She didn't answer, only continued focusing on something in the distance, then shook the vial in her hand, a faint yellow emanating from it, growing brighter with every shake. Olibtine's eyebrows rose. *When did she get that?*

She stood up, reared back, and tossed it in the distance - much further than her body should have been capable of. Olibtine followed it with his eyes until it landed on the upslope of the dune opposite from them, illuminating a good portion of it. He stared at it until dry eyes forced him to blink. Opening his mouth to ask another question, he saw movement - the sand rising up behind it as if it was being lifted from below. His eyes grew wide and he jolted upright as well, unsure of what to make of it. The creature flew out of the sand, wings expanding to its side, a long, sharp beak in the shape of a curved sword the size of a man opening wide, ready to engulf its prey from above. Before Olibtine could take it all in, there was a wizzing sound cutting through the silent air to his right. *Are there others?!* He nervously looked over at Daria, her bow arm extended, right arm cocked back next to her head, empty, still focused on the creature. He looked back to it, wanting to gauge how long they had until it got to them. As soon as he did, the arrow struck the creature straight through its open mouth. A quick shriek passed through the air to his ears before the creature went limp. Olibtine's jaw went slack, staring at the lifeless thing next to the vial, dimming with every breath.

In awe, he fixed his eyes on Daria, who was relaxing her bow arm and beginning to sit in the same spot she was just seconds ago. "Did you..." he stuttered, gulping. "What just happened?" he asked, still standing, dumbstruck.

Daria shrugged. "Looked like it wanted a snack and I don't see anything else around here to eat, do you?" she asked casually, picking apart some bread and taking a bite.

"How did you even see that thing? I couldn't see it until it got to the vial you threw."

Daria met his eyes across the campfire, an unnatural glistening to them in the light. "It's kind of like focusing on something without focusing on it. Sometimes the corners of your eyes are better at catching movement and light. I'm not smart enough to know the why behind it, but I learned that when playing hide and seek as a kid in the streets. I was looking at the tower and saw it from below going over that dune. Got lucky with the throw though," she chuckled.

There's more to it than that. Olibtine scoffed, shaking his head. "I see. Seems like you've got some tricks up your sleeves then, once again proving Guane to be correct."

Lowering himself to the sand, he looked over to the creature once more, the vial's light blinking out. *Going to have to check that out tomorrow.* "Think that was the only one?"

Daria shrugged. "Got me. I've seen birds like it before, but nothing that travels through the sand like that."

Olibtine turned back towards Daria. "Should we take turns keeping watch then?"

"That might be best," she replied, scooping up sand and smothering the fire. "I'll take first watch."

Chapter 23: Let them come

The sorcerer cursed, watching the pet being skewered through from the vantage point of the tower. From here, wherever anyone or anything can see the tower, the tower can see them. They made sure nothing could approach them without at least a day's notice, melting all of the trees and shrubbery, creating a barren landscape for miles around.

The sorcerer huffed up the stairs. "How did they kill my pet so quickly? She is a perfect hunter of the night. Who are these visitors?!" Reaching the fireplace-lit room of the book-lined study, the floor directly below where the other two were still transfixed in their ujuntu basins, the sorcerer looked up, "And what is taking them so long?!"

The sorcerer glanced around at the countless books stacked haphazardly around the room on the floor, then up the book-filled shelves, thinking what to do next to take care of these visitors. *Another pet? No, if they killed Saphtira, they will kill the others. Acid is not to be used. A tearing of the earth?*

Browsing the titles of a stack, eyes wandering to the vaulted stone ceiling, the sorcerer remembered the tower in all its glory. Floors and false passages, poisons to spread, creatures to let loose. Grinning deviously under the deep, black hooded robe, an idea popped to mind. *Let them come.*

Chapter 24: The Tower of Baugroun's Welcome

After a restless night on the sand dunes, Olibtine and Daria set their sights on the tower, front lit by the sun's first light, still as deep black as ever, almost as if it soaked up the night's darkness and stored it for the following day. Upon reaching the dune where they expected the creature to lie, all they found was the vial Daria had thrown. The sand didn't even look disturbed, which felt ominous to Olibtine. *Had I dreamt it?* He searched the sand again, then looked up at the tower. A chill creeped down his spine in response. *No, it WAS here. The vial Daria threw is here.*

Daria knelt down to pick the vial up, squinting ahead of it in the spot where the creature should have been.

She is thinking the same thing, Olibtine realized, looking down at her.

She stood up, looked to Olibtine with a nod, and handed him the vial.

"I've got another," she revealed, then led the two to the top of the dune. Still a half a day's trek, the enormity of the tower hit them both, looming over them like the tallest peaks of the Uhlbrar Mountains to the far north.

The sun was high in the sky when they reached the base of the tower. The sand was completely flat and hard as rock all around the tower, spreading hundreds of feet from the base as if it was all melted and then frozen again in a flash. Decades of stray, windswept sand created embankments against the base, interrupting the intended perfection of compacted sand. Even with the sun high overhead, the area around the tower felt cold, a stark contrast to the surrounding desert and deep black of the tower itself, almost as if it were sucking the warmth out of the air. It was even taller than Olibtine could imagine. If there were clouds in the sky, it would have undoubtedly cut through them like an arrow through paper. The levels of the tower were easily discernible from the outside, each level alternating in size, one slightly skinnier, one larger, one skinnier, one larger, never truly getting smaller the higher it went until the very top floor where it was fatter than the rest, jutting out like a canopy of a tree. *That is where the sorcerers spend their time performing rituals,* Olibtine remembered from the book The Sorcerer's Play Things. Even reading about it did not prepare him for what he was staring up at. *How does it not topple over? Does it have some sort of counterbalance in the middle to hold it steady, or...* he trailed off, remembering what he was there for. *This is not the time.*

He glanced over to Daria, similarly transfixed on the top of the tower, maybe even thinking the same thing he was just a second ago.

"Daria, are you ready?" he asked.

She nodded and pointed to the top. "Are we going up there?"

Olibtine shrugged. "Not sure. We might not have to if we can find the answers below. You never know, they may be at the bottom floor and ready to welcome us with a nice cup of tea..." *If they even accept my little piece of knowledge,* he finished in his head.

She nodded again, her hands in tight fists, her eyes darting around, looking nervous for the first time since Olibtine had met her. He faced towards what looked like the door to the tower and forced himself to begin walking forward, each step sending the grating sound of sand on top of a hard surface to his ears.

The door was even more ominous up close with each side depicting a giant, faceless, hooded figure, their eyes, even if unseen, staring directly at the two. The doors themselves looked as if they had been clawed at, giant scars giving way to even more black stone. *How do we open this?* Olibtine measured the door up and down. He approached it to get a closer look, putting his hand up to it, hesitating momentarily, then touched the stone, feeling the warmth emanating from it. Upon opening his eyes from a blink he was surrounded by pitch black. His heart raced, blinking over and over to try to return to the light, but it never came. He looked around, struggling to digest what just happened. Closing his eyes, he forced himself to think. "The vial!" An echo met his ear as he reached into his pocket, pulling the vial out and shaking it, making it glow softly, a yellow pool expanding around him.

POP he heard nearby, making him jump. He thrust the vial out ahead of himself towards the source.

"Daria?!" he asked, slack jawed seeing the woman standing there with a dumbfounded expression on her face. "Daria, how did you.."

She shook her head, blinking hard either to adjust to the pitch black around or find out if it was all a dream, Olibtine couldn't say. "Where... where are we?"

"I'm not sure. I was touching the door and before I could open my eyes, I was here," he replied. "Did you touch the door too?"

She nodded looking around. "You just disappeared in a flash. I had to do something, so I did what you did, and poof. I'm here. Wherever here is."

"Then it was some sort of transportation spell?" Olibtine began, shaking the vial again to make it brighter, examining the stone next to them, noticing a similar looking stone door as the one on the outside. "I think this is the front door. Look..." he pointed to the scratches on the door. "These look like the ones outside."

Daria nodded, reached into her pack and grabbed another vial similar to the one Olibtine had and began to shake it, a dim blue light starting.

They turned around.

"So that means... we're in the tower?" Daria asked, raising her vial in an attempt to lighten the room.

"Seems like it," Olibtine nodded, doing the same to illuminate the space, or what the vial's light could reach anyway.

The light barely reached a dozen or so feet from them towards the center of the room, showing no trace of another wall. Unable to know the sheer vastness of the room itself, Olibtine had a plan.

"Daria, you walk that way following the wall and I'll walk this way," he nodded to his left, "That way, we can get a clear picture of where we are. If you see anything, tell me."

Daria began walking without a word, hand outstretched nearly to the wall for guidance, but never touching it for fear of being teleported again while Olibtine walked the opposite way, turning back to glance at her every few steps. At opposite ends of the tower, all they could see of one another was a dim light from their vials - the room much more vast than they ever imagined. With each step muffled by the stone below and on the walls, the only thing audible was their breath and heartbeat, a constant thumping in their ears. Upon closing in on one another again at the opposite side from the entry, they came across a wall jutting out from a near-perfectly circle surrounding wall. Following the wall up with extended vials to light the way, they noticed that it extended upwards.

"Must be a staircase," Olibtine guessed, looking for the entry into it. "Here!" He pointed his vial to a small alcove off to his left, noticing steps leading up. He looked back at Daria, nodded, grabbed his knife from his hidden pocket, Daria following suit, palming something she pulled from the inside of her cloak, and the two slowly began climbing the stone steps.

***

The sorcerer stood with fingers placed inside of a small ujuntu basin filled with water set on top of a chest-high podium. A soft, red glow illuminated a book placed next to the basin as the sorcerer mumbled incoherent lines.

***

One by one they climbed the steps for what seemed like hours - each the exact same as the one before. Legs sore, pack straps digging into their shoulders, and breath labored as if they were reaching the summit of the world. *How much longer can this go on for?* Olibtine thought as the vial became slippery in his hand from sweat, already pocketing the knife long ago. He stopped, doubling over with his hands on his knees and glancing back down at Daria with her mouth agape and eyes down focused on the steps he just finished. "How.... far... have we climbed?" he asked, heaving as he spoke.

Leaning against the wall two steps down, she waited to catch her breath before responding. "Not sure. It feels like we've been climbing for hours. Even with how tall the tower looked from the outside, surely it wasn't this high was it?"

Olibtine shook his head, unsure. Standing back up straight and wiping his brow, he moved his hand towards the inner wall, illuminating the near perfect solid stone to get a closer look. *It's stone sure enough.* To give himself something to do, he moved up two steps, examining the wall all the same, Daria following. He took another slow step, then another, studying the wall for something, anything.

He froze, eyes bulging. *What the...* He rubbed a small crack in the stone, remembering something oddly familiar a dozen or so steps before. He looked back at Daria, who lifted an eyebrow at him. "What?" she asked.

Without a word, Olibtine retraced his steps, moving slowly but deliberately. *Am I going mad in here?* He frantically searched with each step, hand gliding over the stone back and forth.

"What is it?!" Daria asked again, "Why are we going down?"

"I.. I think this is some kind of a trick. I felt a crack above that felt exactly the same as one below," he stated, continuing down the steps, eyes darting everywhere along the wall as the fingertips of his free hand searched the stone. "It should be right around here if my memory isn't fooling me."

"So," Daria questioned, "Stones have cracks, a lot similar. I've seen lots of stone in my day that has similar footholds, handholds, lines, whatever. How does that help us?"

How does it? Olibtine paused and wiped the sweat from his hand on his pants before returning it to the wall. He closed his eyes, resting his forehead on the stone, free hand sliding to drop to his hip, then he paused it from going further, breath catching and eyes opening.

"Here!" he shouted, pointing. "It's the same as above! Look."

Daria's eyebrow rose, but walked to where Olibtine was pointing. She rubbed her hand on it. "Okay, so? If it is the same as above, what does that mean for us?"

"If the books I have read are right and the sorcerers have immense power that we can only dream of, it means this is one of them. Maybe..." Olibtine searched the area near the crack, squatting to get a closer look at the bottom near the stairs. "Maybe we can find something around here." *Wait, what's that?* The exhaustion from moments before seemed to be swept away at the excitement of a possible puzzle. He shook the vial a few times to brighten it and placed it near the spot he was looking. *It... It isn't connected,* he felt, moving down a step. *Here neither.* He moved down one more step, his eyes narrowing. *But here it is.*

"Daria, stand here please." He pointed at the current step he was on. She sighed, doing as he asked. He moved back up the stairs, counting how many steps weren't connected. *Five,* he counted, looking back to Daria below. *Looks to be about the size of a door. Coincidence?*

He took out his knife, gripping it tightly in sweaty palms, then attempted to shove it into the tiny gap. The grating sound of metal on stone made him clench his jaw, but he was only able to get the sharp tip inside. With it still inside, he began sliding it down the steps towards Daria, creating a high-pitched grating sound that made them both cringe this time. With each step he retraced, the knife slid further and further in until he reached the one Daria was at, the knife devoured up to the hilt. Grunting, he attempted to slide it further down the next step, but it wouldn't budge. He looked up at Daria, eyebrows raised. Since it wouldn't budge, he tried something new - turning it like a key. A faint click followed by stone on stone grinding could be heard to the left of them. He jolted upright, staring at the source of the sound, which was the same spot he first put his knife in and saw something new - a vertical break in the stone. He yanked the knife out and crept up the few steps, vial ahead of him to provide light, and a shadow deepened at the crack, straight up and down like a...

"Door!" Olibtine exclaimed, "It's a door!" Daria's mouth fell open, catching herself on the wall next to her.

He felt at the crack with his free hand attempting to pull it open. It didn't budge. Pocketing his vial, he called over to Daira. "Come give me a light." He tried to pull it open with both hands, the crack so small only the ends of his fingers were able to fit along the edge. It didn't budge. He took a step back and examined the outline of the door while wiping his hands on his pants again. *It's massive! How are we going to get this open?*

"Let's try together," Olibtine instructed, having Daria place her vial on the steps above the two. With the two of them straining, pulling as hard as they could, the jarring stone on stone sound echoed up the stairs. A ray of yellow light spilled out into the stairway, filling them with new energy. They pulled harder, groaning, sweat dropping to the stone, fingers cramping. Inch by inch the door moved until Olibtine's fingers slipped causing him to nearly fall backwards down the stairs. He crumpled to his butt, breathing heavily, Daria doing the same a step down. Wiping the sweat from his eyebrows, he looked at the opening. *Can we squeeze through there?* He forced himself to get up. He peeked into the light behind the door, eyes squinting until they became accustomed to the stark difference from the stairwell to whatever it was on the other side of the door. *Another stairway*, he saw, heart wrenching inside of his chest. *Moss! What is going on?!*

He turned sideways in an attempt to see if he could fit, putting his arm and leg in first. "I think we can fit. Toss me the packs when I get inside and then follow me through." Sucking in his breath with clothes scraping and tugging against the stone, he forced himself through. He reached a hand back out of the opening. "Okay, toss me the packs." She handed him the packs one by one, then slid in herself, eyes squinting from the light. Olibtine waited for her eyes to adjust expecting a similar reaction as his. "Moss," she cursed with a groan, finally seeing the stairs.

***

Fingers removed from the basin, chant halting, the red glow subsiding, a smile crept to the sorcerer's mouth. *Now the fun begins.*

***

The sorcerers crept through the silent Forest in their acid forms, melting the underbrush as they went, a constant sizzling sound left in their wake. They approach a dead Trender, skewered through directly in the middle of its dozens of glassy eyes.

This is her doing, one sorcerer thought in a deep voice to the other.

Her doing. Her doing, the other agreed with the first in a high-pitched tone.

We are not far. We will reach her before The Forest ends.

Not far. Not far. Death awaits.

The two blobs continued their hunt north, forever on the blood trail.

Chapter 25: The Final Stretch

Kausha and the others sat huddled on the ground around a campfire in a small clearing beneath a pair of roots that crisscrossed overhead. The Forest was still alive all around, but the heinous sound of twigs snapping and bushes rustling nearby that previously signaled the Trender were no longer. Exhausted from what felt like days of walking - impossible to say just how long it had been though with the thick tree canopy hiding every trace of light - they sat in a silent mourning. They knew they couldn't stay still long with the acid still on their trail, but the idea of continuing without Yaula felt wrong.

Staring into the fire, Kausha broke the silence. "We really shouldn't be sitting here with the acid blobs on our trail."

"We been at et fer ow long now?" Shaum replied, resting his cloth-wrapped injured arm across his lap while taking a swig from a jug with his other hand. "Mah stumps are killin me. We can afford a break, right Skirm?"

Skirm shrugged, eyes glossed over with the fire's reflection in his eyes.

"Yaula would say we need to keep moving," Kausha replied, looking at Skirm then the others to gauge where their minds were at, landing on Skip who was the only one staring back at her.

"While I didn't know Yaula very well..." Skip started, moving his eyes over the others "...I'd imagine she would push us to keep moving and call you, Shaum, an oaf or something and tell you not to drink too much." A smirk crossed his mouth.

Shaum held the jug to his mouth, staring at Skip, hesitating from taking a swig, then ultimately taking one and then smirking back at him after a large gulp.

Skirm chuckled. "That sounds about right to me."

129

Skip spoke again, face somber. "I have something before we depart the rest of the way... or at least I hope it's the rest of the way out of The Forest. Do you mind?" he asked, looking at Kausha, "Won't take long."

Kausha shook her head, curious at what he meant.

He pulled his lute from his pack, testing each string before readjusting and crossing his legs. The first pluck reverberated around the fire, the deep, sad note setting the tone.

"One will stay and five will go,
Fate may take, but she will grow
Time won't slow, so they'll have to go
Due to her spirit insisting so
From Lumber she came with eyes set forth
To help the five travel north
On the hunt to find loved ones
Whether mother, daughter, or even son
She eventually became what they sought
Without realizing she's the one that taught
That whatever your goal, whatever your strife,
Fight for something or fight for another
Life is meant to be a bother
So don't you fret and wipe those tears
She'll be here and here and here"

On the final line, Skip motioned up in a sweeping loop, then pointed at his head, then to his heart. With a final pluck of his lute, one that reverberated around the campfire, he paused, eyes shut, head down, letting the words sink in. Tears dripped down Shaum and Skirm's chins, Kausha deep in thought of waking up to Yaula's worried face in Lumber all that time ago, Nalia steady as always, transfixed on the fire.

"Tha," Shaum started, wiping his eyes, "tha was perfect."

Skirm nodded, wiping his eyes as well.

Skip placed his instrument back into his pack, stood, stretched his arms across his chest, and smiled. "What do you think, should we get moving now?"

They all nodded in turn, standing to feel their muscles no longer ached and their heads clear, a renewed feeling having washed over them like a cool breeze.

Before they smothered the fire, they lit their torches, picked up their packs and started north again, this time with renewed focus and reason.

***

The acid blobs approach a still smoldering fire, acid dropping from the clouds above. They stop for only a moment, having no need to discuss what is in front of them. They notice a fresh path in front of them heading north and continue their pursuit.

***

Way lit by torchlight, they continued on, Shaum at the head of the group followed by Skip, Kausha, Nalia, then Skirm. While the undergrowth and roots were getting less of a hazard the further north they got, the canopy did not provide any hints of giving way to the sunlight - or did it? It was impossible to tell if it was day or night in this part of The Forest, whichever that was.

How much further is it until we get out of this place? Kausha glanced at the others, noticing that it wasn't just her that had begun wiping sweat from her brow and breathing heavily. Their pace had picked up noticeably after their break. She thought of the bard and his song, glancing at him ahead of her. *Was that some sort of magic or just Shaum with his long legs?*

Curious, Kausha squinted out past the glowing of the torches into the darkness. Instead of pitch black, she started to see faint objects - the occasional outline of trees nearby, trees half the size of their brethren they had to weave around further back into The Forest. *We MUST be getting close to the edge then!* Only then did she notice that the only sounds she heard were that of the groups - footfalls, breath heavy, packs bouncing around. A tingle shot up her spine. *Now?* She frantically glanced around outside of the torchlight again to little avail. She shot a look back at Nalia whose eyes were darting back and forth with her ears, the same expression as when they when the Trender struck.

Kausha abruptly stopped in place causing Nalia to run into her back. Skirm narrowly dodged them with a surprisingly graceful twirl.

"What.. what are you doing, Kaush?!" Skirm exclaimed between breaths. Shaum and Skip came to a halt ahead of them.

She turned south sure that they would come that way. "Go ahead. The edge can't be far."

"What?" Skirm exclaimed, throwing his hands into the air looking at Shaum.

"Ya, whatru talkin bout, Kaush?" Shaum asked frantically after jogging back over to them to create one large pool of light.

"Don't you hear it?" Kausha asked, looking around. Each listened for what she was talking about.

"Hear what?" Skirm asked, eyes wide immediately after he said it, recognizing that The Forest had gone quiet once again.

They all felt it, the too familiar deafening silence signaling that the acid pools were near. They turned south, holding their torches over their heads to get a better look, but the hissing sound of acid melting the underbrush was all they needed to hear to know that they were close.

"Go!" Kausha yelled, looking right at Nalia and Skirm, then left at Skip and Shaum, "I can handle them myself!"

She forced the blood from under her fingernail like she had done thousands of times before, creating a sharp blood knife the size of her hand, then snapping it off. She repeated this one more time to have two ready to throw. *I can't get close and this worked last time, so I'll try it.*

"No."

She looked right. *Nalia?*

"No," Nalia started with narrowed eyebrows, "You could have left us at Lumber or Soplnet or at Yaura's grave, but you didn't. You promised we'd find my sister and I'm holding you to it." A smile crept to her face. "Plus, you're the best chance we've got, miss Bloodborn."

Kausha looked at Shaum, who nodded, then at Skip and Skirm, who also nodded. *Alright,* she nodded, mouth in a line. Who was she to deny the will of others?

"First, each of you needs to run north like you're running away. Nalia and Skirm, put your torches in a tree ahead to make it seem like you're standing at a distance watching, then go around to the right side of them. Grab a large limb, a large rock, whatever, and as soon as you see them move towards me, toss it a little behind them. Don't try to hit them, just distract them. Skip and Shaum, you two go to the left, but take your torches with you and see what they do. If either come after you, run back to me. If they don't and focus on me like I believe they will, throw the torches right by them to try to light the underbrush. If you toss it too close to them, their acid will just put it out right away. I'll take care of the rest. Got it?" she asked, gripping the knives. Each nodded in their understanding, the hissing sound from the acid pools growing louder.

"Good, now go!" she yelled, not for them, but for the acid pools to hear. Without hesitation, they ran north. *Now, to bide time.*

Kausha tossed the torch a ways ahead of her, wanting to put something in between her and the acid pools in order to give light to the creatures. She waited, flipping the knives over in her hand, calming her breath, relaxing her muscles, feeling her blood course throughout her body like she had been trained all those moons ago. The hissing approached, growing louder and louder until... *There.* She squinted, seeing a faint outline of the two acid blobs beyond the firelight. They crept into the light, one nearly two times the size of the other with twice as many arms, dark green forms in a constant state of movement, acid dripping and hissing on them from their unseen clouds above.

"I know who you are," she stated, wanting to give the others time to get into position, but also wanting them out of ear shot as well, "And I know that you know that I can kill you." She wanted that one to hang in the air for a second to let them think. "So why? Why still come after me all this way? Who sent you?"

A long silence hung in the air, only the hissing sound of the acid falling into their bodies audible.

A deep, sinister response that sounded like two overlapping voices, rumbled through the air as if it had traveled a vast distance to get there. "We are impressed."

What? Kausha's eyebrows narrowed at the response. Regardless of the words, her insides shifted around as if they were trying to find a place to run and hide. *Wasn't expecting that.*

"You would do well in our ranks, Bloodborn. Join us and shatter apart your destiny."

Destiny? What are they talking about?

"You're murderers! You melt villages with no regard for life and will do anything your masters say! Why should *I* join you monsters?" Kausha replied, grasp tightening on her knives enough for her blood to retract into her arm away from her hand on instinct.

"We have no masters. We choose to serve those that buy our services with ujuntu. We have no allegiances and are above this petty squabbling that humanoids and the like do. Nothing matters to us because we can do anything we wish," the deep voice replied matter of factly.

Kausha felt a chill as how simply they put it - no regard for lives, only doing what they wanted as if everything were a toy to them, free to discard whenever they wanted. "You have no remorse, no care, no feelings - what *are* you then? And why do you want me?"

"We are but three that shattered our destiny. You can too."

Kausha's forehead scrunched in confusion. "What destiny did you shatter?"

"Our family."

Kausha went stiff, eyebrows narrowing, frowning, unsure of what to make of it. *Family?* A picture of her mother, grandmother, great grandmother, and great great grandmother popping to her head.

"Join us and we will not kill you," the deep voice came again, interrupting her thoughts.

"I would never join you murderers!" she snapped, coming back to the world around her. "Now tell me who sent you!"

A long pause hung in the air as if they were deciding what to say. The torch she threw was losing its light with every breath. *I must know.*

The deep voice rumbled through The Forest, crashing into her. "Weren't you listening? The ujuntu holds the key."

The Nortmunders? But why would they want me killed? My family and the six don't butt heads, at least we didn't when I was last home.

"The Nortmunders? Why would the Nortmunders want me killed?" Kausha took the chance asking.

"We do not ask questions, only demand payment."

"Then how can I trust what you're saying?" Kausha asked, regaining her composure.

"That is your decision to make," the deep voice replied, no further explanation given.

None of this matters right now anyways. They are here to kill me and my friends. Feeling like that was all the answers she was going to get, Kausha raised her blood knives to her shoulder. "Now!" she yelled.

A large boom rang out in front of her, further away than the acid blobs stood while a fire sprung up off to their backside. The acid blobs seemed to turn in place, confused at what was happening around them all at once. Kausha took the chance, body acting without thought, and flung the first of the two blood knives at the smaller of the two blobs, hitting it directly in the middle of its body. The familiar hiss grew louder and the blob began writhing faster as if in pain. Its body churned into itself, hiss growing louder like a blood-curdling scream, then acid rain held in the cloud splashed down all at once to the ground, melting everything around it signaling the blob was no more.

Back-lit by the torch thrown behind it, the final acid blob seemed to turn back towards Kausha after realizing it was just a ruse. As expected, the melted blob began to churn, sliding towards the remaining one, feeding on it, growing to nearly twice the size it was before, towering over Kausha.

Moss! Kausha cursed, throwing her remaining blood knife at its middle. Acid shot out from the blob, hitting the knife in mid air and slowing it enough to stop it short. Sizzling, it skidded along the ground short of its target.

Well that's new. She began pushing blood from under her fingernail again, wanting to try again in case it was a coincidence. She snapped off the blood, the familiar knife in her hand, ran a few steps to her right, then flung it at the blob's middle again. The blob, churning wildly, acid rain falling like a heavy rain storm, once again shot acid from its body at the incoming blood knife, slowing it to a stop.

Kausha shuffled back a few steps to ensure she kept her distance with it shooting acid. *Moss. New plan.*

The blob's churning slowed, eight arms now clearly visible. Acid rain continued to pummel it from above, a loud hiss emanating around it as it melted trees and undergrowth alike.

Kausha thought back at her previous encounters with the acid, both rain and blobs. *The town outside of Gbinti. Lumber. Soplnet. They can be defeated with my blood, but that rain is far too heavy to get close. Maybe if I created a spear again - my blood is running low though, it would be the last blood weapon I create today. Think!*

The blob shot a sizzling ball of acid at Kausha. She dodged, just barely getting out of the way of it as it splashed to the ground next to her, melting the undergrowth where she stood not a second before. The torchlight had dwindled to a faint glow. The hulking, undulating mass churned, preparing its next move. Without warning, another acid ball flew out from one of those numerous popping bubbles, which she easily dodged this time now that she was watching for it. She hopped behind a tree next to where she was standing, hoping to get more time to think.

Okay, small objects won't work, which means I have to create something larger and will only get one shot at it. If I can... A rustle nearby forced her body to move to a crouch immediately, blood expanding from below her fingernail. "Kaush?" she heard, the familiar voice of Skirm whispering close by.

"Skirm?" she replied.

"Kaush!" Skirm replied, appearing from behind a tree with Nalia close behind. "The log worked! But that big blob is still here. Why didn't you kill it, too?"

"I tried but it shot an acid blob at my knives and stopped them short."

A splash nearby followed by a hiss forced Kausha to move away from the tree. Its trunk was melting through near the base.

"Moss, Kaush..." Skirm started, eyes wide at the tree, imagining what that would do to himself, "...what should we do?"

Nalia spoke up, eyes soaking up the dim light left from the torch. "I have an idea. Kausha, can you climb that tree?" she asked, nodding to the one that was just hit with the acid.

"Um, sure, I guess. But it's melting."

"Skirm, can you knock the tree over in that state?"

He looked it up and down. "Sure, I've knocked over..." he started, but was interrupted by Nalia.

"Good. Now Kausha, throwing something at it might not work straight on, but if we distract it with a tree falling into it, that should give you the time to hit it from above."

Kausha looked the tree up and down, then over to Skirm next to her and nodded. "I'll try it. I've only got enough blood left today for one more spear, but it's now or never." She focused her sights on the part above where the acid was burning through the tree, pushing blood down into her legs for strength while at the same time pushing blood below her fingernails to stab the bark. Focusing, jaw clenched, she ran, then leapt off the ground with both feet, easily clearing the acid and stabbing into the tree for support. She looked back at Skirm and Nalia, their mouths open as they stared at her.

"Moss," Skirm cursed in awe.

Kausha scurried up the tree, reaching the limbs with ease, steadied herself, and refocused her blood into a similar spear that she had used with the Trender. She snapped it off, her vision swimming from loss of blood. She looked down, now unable to see the two on The Forest floor. Darkness enveloped her as the torchlight blinked out - from acid or fuel, she didn't know. Her eyes darted across the darkness as she clutched the tree beneath her with one hand, the other tight around the spear. *Focus,* she told herself, closing her eyes and opening her ears. The constant hiss of the acid raining from the cloud above the blob gave it away. A smile crept to Kausha's mouth, not due to the current situation, but from the countless years of training she endured that seemed to prepare her for this very moment. Staring down into the darkness, she readied herself for what was needed.

Then, she felt the tree shake. Grip tight on a branch next to the one she was standing on, it rocked forward, then back, then forward again, then back, each sway larger than the last, the tree groaning under the movement. The hissing grew closer and closer to Kausha's left as the tree rocked from Skirm pushing on it from below. A final rocking forward sent a loud *snap* through the air. The tree lurched beneath her, the trunk finally giving way, sending her falling directly towards the acid blob.

Kausha readied her legs, not wanting to jump on to the blob or over it, but to the side to ensure she didn't get caught up in the acid. The tree branches in front of her started to hiss loudly as soon as it entered the acid cloud, getting closer and closer.

Almoooost, Kausha tensed, holding her breath and shifting her insides. Time seemed to slow for a moment, allowing her to squat down to get into the perfect position. Her eyes burned from the putrid acid causing tears to stream down her face. She squeezed them tight, trusting her other senses to take over. *Almost.* The sizzling grew louder as branches were gobbled up. *Now!* She let go of the breath while leaping from the tree at an angle away from the hissing sound, twisting her body and aiming the blood spear towards the middle of the hissing, then threw it as hard as she could while falling through the air towards darkness. She slammed into The Forest floor on her side, pain shooting through her shoulder, ribs, hip, and leg. Her head swam, the darkness swallowing her vision. She heard the hissing grow louder, then nothing.

***

A comfortable breeze carrying the familiar smells of the ocean enveloped Kausha as she stared up at the cloth canopy overhead. She knew immediately that this was another vision like she had in Lumber. *This is all too real*, she winced, rubbing her chest. She glanced down at her clothing, the customary purple and red jumpsuit with the Bloodborn's teardrop of blood symbol embossed on the front. Outlining the tear with her finger, she felt every fiber possible. *So real.*

"Kausha, were you listening?" she heard her mother ask from her seat on the other side of the canopy. Kausha glanced over between her mother, grandmother, great grandmother, and great great grandmother sitting in a circle focusing on her.

"Sorry mother, I was thinking about something else," she replied, pulling herself upright to get a level view of them. They all looked the same as when she last saw them in person - the real in person, not these visions.

Her mother rolled her eyes, then sipped on the iced drink in her hand. "Your journey must really be taking a toll on you if you're on your second vision already."

So it IS a vision. Kausha was happy to get an answer to at least one thing she'd been wondering.

She nodded her head. "It has become more complicated as well. The sorcerers..." she started, noticing her mother's eyes momentarily widen at the reference, but only for a second before returning to her steely composure, "... seem to have orders and payment from someone that wants me dead. They hinted at the Nortmunders, but I am not sure whether I can trust what they say."

I'll leave the family part out now. She waited for a response from her mother.

Her grandmother chimed in. "You can never trust a sorcerer. Their greed has tainted them and the magic they use is unmeant for this world. They will do anything for payment, and have been doing so for a long, long time. They dare not move against Purtghast, but it seems there are others that think they can," she ended with a glance towards great great grandmother, who had her hands interlaced on top of her cane with her chin resting on top of her hands, eyes glazed over deep in thought.

"The Nortmunders, you say?" her mother asked.

"Well, they didn't explicitly say the Nortmunders are behind it, but they mentioned ujuntu and that it was the key to it all. The Nortmunders have the ujuntu mines, and so I assumed it was them. Are there others?" Kausha asked.

Her mother took another drink, glancing over to her mother and her mother's mother, neither showing any sign of refute.

"It sounds right..." her mother agreed after placing the drink down on the table next to her, "... but we have no quarrel with the Nortmunders and haven't in hundreds of moons. Having you killed would only set them back in terms of diplomacy."

Kausha felt that something wasn't being said. Usually great great grandmother has something to say whenever we talk in a group like this, but she's being subdued. *Should I?* She struggled, not expecting much more from the current line of discussion. Before asking, she focused on her mother and grandmother, who were most likely to give something away through their expressions.

"Has any Bloodborn ever abandoned our family?" she asked plainly, keeping a close eye on the two. Her mother was reaching for her glass again when she asked and nearly knocked it over when she heard the question. Kausha saw her grandmother shift in her seat at the question, and even her great great grandmother shifted her cane under her chin, her eyes becoming bright and fully aware again for the first time all day. *Well, that's a response,* Kausha narrowed her eyebrows.

The question hung in the air, a tension appearing that wasn't there before. Kausha had never recalled a tension like this in the canopy - a place where plenty of serious conversations happened throughout her lifetime.

A single tap echoed through the air - great great grandmother's cane. Kausha shifted her focus away from her mother to notice the usual soft and calm purple eyes of her great great grandmother replaced with something intense and angry as she lifted her head. Kausha's breath caught in her throat, her body going stiff at the sight.

"Where did you hear this?" she asked, her tone clear in wanting a straight answer and nothing else.

"Um..." Kausha started, finding her breath again, "... I didn't exactly hear it, the sorcerer said something about families and shattering destiny."

Her great great grandmother's eyes glossed over again, seemingly deep in thought at Kausha's answer. *What is going on?* Kausha attempted to sift through her years of study when she was a child to see if she had missed something, anything.

A sigh came from her great great grandmother that drew her eye. *What's that look?* Kausha hadn't recalled seeing it before. The typically strong and intense eyes of her great great grandmother shifted, replaced with something else - pain, maybe.

"When I was a child..." she started, sitting up straight, "... there was a Bloodborn family that lived here in Purtghast that was a friend of ours. There were three sisters that were older than I was, but still very friendly to me. They would take me with them on adventures outside of the city, show me new ways of using my blood, and even tell me stories that they'd read while in school.

They were like my older sisters." Her chin dropped as her mouth drew to a straight line, her eyes shutting for a moment. She shook her head, opened her eyes, and raised her head, eyes intense once again, staring straight at Kausha.

"And then one day, they told me about a dark magic they read about in an old tomb, one that had been lost in time. The ujuntu-based magic. Dark magic that uses our blood and ujuntu together for nefarious purposes. You've come to witness these first hand. The three sisters played with this magic for a while, hiding it from everyone at first, but the tomb only held deeper and darker magics within, and so they themselves delved deeper into the darkness, until one full moon they delved too far, shattering their family and destiny in one fell swoop. The darkness enveloped them as if it were a part of them, their family line evaporated, unable to pass down their blood." She began to cough, Kausha's mother hurrying over to hand her her drink. She took a sip, shoulders slumping, hands resting on her cane again.

Kausha looked at her elders in turn, each showing sorrow in their faces. *They all knew. They knew, but didn't tell me anything.* The revelation of it all hit Kausha square in the face. She had thought maybe the sorcerers were talking about the Bloodborn families, but it didn't feel real until just now. *The sorcerers are Bloodborn,* she repeated in her head, hands sweating, a heavy weight seemingly dropping out of thin air onto her shoulders.

"Why hasn't anyone told me this before?!" Kausha exclaimed, annoyed at this seemingly hidden, massive secret.

Her mother shot her a look that could stop anyone in their tracks - eyes narrow, mouth in a line while still bent over her great grandmother.

Her great grandmother spoke in a soft tone, eyes filled with sorrow as she looked up to meet Kausha's. "We had hoped to leave it in the past. We had not envisioned the sorcerers - the sisters -

would come after you. Neither I nor your mother have had a single encounter with them in our entire lives and we assumed it would be the same for you."

She's being truthful. Kausha could see it in her face and tone.

"So how do I stop them?" Kausha asked.

"Their magic surpasses ours by leaps and bounds. They have had generations to learn, practice, and grow. These acid tricks are just the tip of their power. The only thing to do is to find those buying their services and stop them."

Kausha pictured the acid blobs, writhing in front of her. *Only the tip of their power...* She visibly shivered at the thought.

Kausha didn't notice it when her mother walked over to her and grabbed her head softly with both hands, turning her head up to face hers. "Heal yourself now, Kausha, and come home."

"Wait!" Kausha exclaimed, darkness spreading from the corners of her vision, the light fading. "Not yet! I have more questions!" The background behind her mother faded into black, leaving her alone in her vision. A breeze whisked her mother away, leaving only pitch black in her vision. She blinked, a blue and pink sky appearing above her.

"She's up!" came the familiar voice of Skirm, his face looming over her a second later. Then Shaum and Skip followed, staring down at her smiling.

"Eh Kaush, nice ta see ya 'gain." Shaum smiled with his sharp teeth.

Kausha sat upright on one elbow, rubbed her head and saw Nalia sitting on the opposite side of a fire, staring at the embers within.

"Don let er fool ya, Kaush, Nalia oer thar was tha most worried o all of us!" Shaum slapped her back causing Kausha to grunt. "Oops, sorry."

Even under her brown and tan fur, Nalia's cheeks turned a light shade of red as she stared over the fire at Shaum. "Oh, shut up you oaf."

"Where are we?" Kausha asked, finally noticing the line of dark trees with sparse leaves a ways behind Nalia.

"We made it out of The Forest!" Skirm exclaimed, moving over to the log near the fire. "Thanks to you, that is. We've been camped out here for two days resting. We all needed it after that," he finished, nodding his head towards The Forest.

"The acid blobs? Is everyone okay?"

"Everyone but you," Skip answered next to her. "We found you on the ground unconscious with acid burns on your side." He nodded at her bandages. She looked down and noticed that her midsection and shoulder were wrapped in leaves and clothing. "It's the best we could do," he frowned, shrugging.

"She's probly fine now. Las time she was asleep like dat, she woke up with nothin wrong," Shaum chuckled, walking over to the fire, opposite his brother, grabbing a jug that was sitting on a stump and taking a swig.

Skip looked down at her, eyebrow raised.

Kausha felt around her side and shoulder before unwrapping the shoulder from its bandage. Skip audibly cringed, but didn't try to stop her. He'd definitely seen what acid does to flesh. After fully unwrapping it, she turned it towards Skip whose mouth dropped open, then bent over to get a better look in the fading evening light.

"Moss. That's down right amazing. There was a hole there two days ago."

"Told ya," Shaum scoffed.

Kausha placed the bandage aside, stood, gauging her blood content, moving it around inside of her, happy with the progress her body made, then walked over to Shaum, sat down next to him, grabbing the jug from his hand, and took a few swigs of the liquor.

"Well," she took a swig, looking at everyone around the fire, smiles on every face except Nalia's, "tell me what happened while I was out."

Chapter 26: New Plans

The two sorcerers fell backwards from their ujuntu basin as if being shoved by strong hands. They both groaned, bodies sore from being hunched over for so long in the hunt.

A monotone voice spoke up behind them, "I see that we were unsuccessful."

The two sorcerers on the ground raised their heads, looking up and over at the third who was enveloped in the orange and pink light of the fading sun sneaking through the long slit around the tower.

"You are correct," a rumbling voice responded.

"Correct, correct," the third sorcerer repeated in a high-pitched voice. They both stood slowly, stretching, then walked over to the slit to look out over their domain towards The Forest to the north.

"They have escaped The Forest and are nearing Nortmund," started the monotone voice. "Our employers are becoming impatient and will not like us exposing ourselves in the city. We will need to be subtle from now on. There is also another job they have given us."

The two sorcerers recently out of their trance glanced at one another under their black hoods, and even though their faces were hidden, they understood one another all the same.

"There are two in the tower that need to be disposed of however we seem fit. The young Head of the Minds and his companion."

"Who bought this contract?" the deep, rumbling voice asked.

"The same with the Bloodborn contract. We will need to carry out both of these at the same time. The Mind has only gotten to the ujuntu store rooms. We will take care of the Bloodborn, and you..." the monotone voice turned to the sorcerer with the high-pitched voice "... will handle these intruders."

"Intruders. Handle Intruders," the high-pitched voice responded, hooded head nodding.

"And do not use acid on them - a direct request from the contract."

The high-pitched voiced sorcerer scampered away out the door and down the stairs while the two remaining watched the moon rise once again, contemplating what to do next.

Chapter 27: The Yellow Room

Olibtine and Daria sat resting against the wall near the door they just entered, drinking from cantines and staring up at the staircase. *At least this one looks real.* Olibtine fixated on light filtering down from a few steps up.

"Well," he smirked, "at least now we have some idea of what they are capable of."

She shrugged her shoulders. "It doesn't seem like they want us here. It's like a time when I was little and I entered an alleyway - there were little traps set everywhere, from strings attached to crates overhead that fell if you walked into them to holes in the ground deeper than a man is tall. If you make it to the end of that, what's waiting for you is often more dangerous than the traps themselves." She took another swig from her cantine, then tucked it away again.

"It could just be something that is always here though," Olibtine replied, putting his cantine away too. "I read that these sorcerers prefer being cut off from the world and maybe they just don't like visitors." He shrugged, standing up, reaching for Nalia's hand and helping her up. "Regardless, we're here and made it this far. However far this far really is..." he trailed off looking back at the thick stone door they squeezed through.

He grabbed his pack, which Daria took as a sign to grab hers as well.

"Shall we?" he asked.

Nalia shrugged. "Following you."

Please be shorter, Olibtine hoped, squeezing his jaw tight as they started the climb up the stone staircase. The steps were shorter, but roughly the same width as the last staircase. The wall texture and black color were the same as the last too, which matched the stone doorway they seemingly teleported through. His legs felt like they were going to collapse, having to support himself with his hands on his legs with every step. To his relief, it didn't take long to get to the next floor, this one open to the staircase itself, which continued up out of sight. *Should we keep going or search this floor? They could be anywhere in the tower, so might as well.*

He stared into the floor, a long, black stone hallway from floor to ceiling lined with six wooden doors and six red-glowing objects next to their handles, three on each side, capped with a large glass window at the end that let in ample light. It was something that belonged in a basement of a castle, not a floor up in a tower. Beautiful and yet ominous all at the same time. His eyes fell upon the frosted, plain glass window that stretched from floor to ceiling in the shape of a full moon rising that was halfway above the horizon. *Odd.* Glancing around, he noticed all of the dust built up on the red glowing objects. *What are those anyway?* He walked over to the closest one to get a better look. His eyebrows narrowed as he noticed that it was just a globe with water in it attached to a metal object resting on the wall. *Even more odd.* He tapped it with his finger and was answered with a light tink vibrating back to him. His eyes wandered to the wooden door next to the globe, noticing a normal handle similar to what they had in Gbinti, and tried it. A quiet click sounded at his fingertips. He glanced back to Nalia with raised eyebrows, her face hard, hands already filled with her bow and arrow, ready for something.

Olibtine slowly began opening the door, a creek in the hinges from old wood and metal filling the air. He squinted as a bright red light assaulted his eyes through the crack in the door. He blinked, clearing his watery eyes while sliding the door open further. His jaw dropped, his hand pushing the door open falling limp to his side as he realized what it was. *Ujuntu.* All shapes and sizes of the roughly cut mineral.

"Olibtine?" Daria asked worriedly, seeing a bright red light wash over him and spill into the hall. With bow and arrow cocked and pointed at the opening in the door, she crept over to him, looking over his shoulder into the room. Her jaw dropped similarly to her arms, followed by a "Whoah."

"It's... it's ujuntu," Olibtine externalized in awe. "In all my time as a Mind, I've never seen this much wealth in one place. Does this mean..." he started, turning around to look at the door opposite of him. He strode over to the opposite wooden door, clicked the handle without hesitation and swung the door open in one push, red light spilling out. He turned, running down the hall to the last door on the left, clicked the handle, pushed the door open, and once again, red light spilled from the room, just as full of ujuntu as the last two.

"How?" Olibtine's jaw dropped wide while staring into the room. "How can there be so much of it? This much wealth could feed our people for many moons and it's just sitting here. Did they amass this from all of the nefarious contracts taken? It's just... so much." He put his back to the doorway, shivering and gasping for air while bending over to place his hands on his knees as the realization overcame him. Tears welled up in his eyes thinking of Gbinti and its citizens as the red lights from within casted their harsh glow on his face.

He heard clanking in the first room where Daria had been standing a few seconds ago and forced himself upright, shoving the meaning of the wealth away from his thoughts. "Daria?"

He walked over to the first room to see her kneeling down and piling ujuntu into her pack. "What are you doing?" he asked with a raised eyebrow.

"Isn't it obvious? I'm taking some," she responded without looking back at him while picking up a large chunk off to her right and placing it softly in her pack, which was bulging already.

"Can you even carry that much? We don't even know how much further we have to go up this tower."

"Yeah, I got it," she assured, picking up one more piece, tossing it in her hand, then putting it away as well. She stood, facing Olibtine with a huge smile on her face. "Plus, it's probably blood ujuntu and they..." she looked up, "..don't deserve it if it's just going to sit here in these rooms."

Olibtine shook his head. "Fine, but I'm not carrying your pack when it gets too heavy for you." He looked around her towards the wealth, thinking *I could take some now too, it isn't that heavy.* He skirted around her, noticing a large chunk at the base of a pile, bent over and picked it up, tossing it into the air.

"I knew you couldn't resist!" Daria chuckled, slapping him on his shoulder. "It's like I always say 'someone else will get plenty of use from trash'. Well, this isn't trash, but it sure seems like they are treating it like that. Sitting on a mound of wealth, not locked up, easy for the taking. Yeah, I'd say they have far too much of it and we're being kind enough to help them get rid of a little of it," she explained with a smirk as if it should have been common knowledge. "That all you going to take?"

Olibtine shrugged, staring at the shallow gashes in the large piece as he turned it over, a sign on how it was mined. "You realize how much this is worth in food, right?" he asked as he lifted the chunk. "This will feed a village for a moon! If we can find this place when we leave, I will grab more, but this will do for now." He gently placed the ujuntu in his pack.

"Well, I'm officially stumped at all of this," Olibtine started, walking out of the room. "First, we are teleported in, then we are thrown into an unending staircase, and now, the first real floor we get to, we find wealth beyond our imagination. What is this place?"

Daria shrugged. "You're the Mind here. I'm just the muscle."

Olibtine raised his eyebrow at her. "Okay then, shall we continue?" he asked, looking forward to the stairwell landing.

"Ready when you are," Daria answered behind him, adjusting her pack with a grunt.

With Olibtine leading, they reentered the stone stairwell, unable to see anything above with the harsh, red lighting enveloping the landing. *Oh yeah,* Olibtine winced, feeling his legs again, just as sore as before. They began ascending the staircase slowly, feeling the extra weight to their packs from the ujuntu. Olibtine heard something up above, pausing his climb and turning his head back to Daria, motioning her to stop.

"What is it?" she whispered, glancing up the stairs then quickly back to him.

I don't know. Olibtine's eyebrows narrowed, focusing on the sound above. He heard it again - a grinding sound of stone on stone. He took one step up, trying to make as little sound as possible. Then another. Only silence answered. Exhaling, he took another step, another landing coming into view with no more steps leading above, with a wooden door on the inner wall, similar to the ones in the floor below.

"I thought I heard a grinding sound on the stone, but I don't hear it anymore. There's a door up ahead," he whispered, ascending the final few steps. They stood on the landing of the floor with a wooden door ahead of them, a soft yellow light coming from under the wide crack at the bottom. They glanced at each other, then back at the door. Olibtine reached out for the handle, a familiar clicking sound coming from within. He slowly pushed it open, the soft yellow light hitting his face and arms, unexpectedly providing no warmth as he peeked inside. All he could see were flat, gray stone walls to his left and front, connected to create a corner, each going up half-way to the ceiling, about twice his height.

He opened the door the rest of the way revealing the rest of the wall in front of him expanding to his right, ending not too far away. Where that wall ended, another wall stood flush against the entrance wall, creating a turn like a hallway. *It might be a maze. An entire floor that's a maze?*

"Well then. This looks... fun." He walked to the first corner, looked left, then confirmed it. He glanced back at Daria who was still in the doorway staring up at the source of the yellow light - a globe similar to the ones on the floor below, except much larger.

"It's a maze."

She closed her eyes, shaking her head, then sighed. "Yeah, so what now?"

"Well," Olibtine looked back in the direction the maze was leading. "Only one direction to go. The good thing is that if the floor is the same size as the one below, which it should be, the maze can't be very large - only a few twists and turns here or there."

An uncertain frown appeared on Daria's face as she stood beside Olibtine, looking around the corner. "I've never been good at mazes. I prefer straight alleyways like we have in Gbinti. I got lost going to Guane's office more times than once even."

"That's okay, stay close and I can guide us through." Olibtine deepened his voice to sound confident, thinking back at the times he used to crack mazes his parents made for him as a child. Daria gave him a deeper frown, no doubt hearing the difference. He ignored her look, putting his hand to the outer wall. Cold shot through his fingertips sending a shiver throughout his body. *As long as we follow this until it breaks, we will have a clear understanding of what the maze looks like.*

Following the wall, it took a turn left, then ended while the other wall continued straight for a ways while at the same time it looked as if a new wall started on his left and in front of him - almost like it was split - to reveal another way. He paused to take the open area in. *Three different ways to go.* He looked up at the light in the middle of the room straight ahead. *If I can keep in mind that the entrance is straight south of the light, we should be able to get back if needed.* Rounding the wall his hand held, it was only a few steps later and then it turned left, a straight hallway ahead of him with a turn further down. Half-way to the turn, the wall cut off on the right, creating a small hall leading to another hall with left and right options. He stood for a second, looking back at the light above. *Behind and to the left. Looks like...*

He jumped, spinning after hearing the grinding sound again like before, this time not far behind him. Daria seemed to have heard it too, her back turned away from him looking the way they just came.

"What was that?" she whispered over her shoulder, her fingers twitching as if wanting to draw her bow.

"That's the sound I heard on the stairs," Olibtine replied, releasing his hand from the wall, moving back in front of Daria, replacing his hand on the wall once again. "It sounds like it came from up here to the left." He started retracing his steps, turning left, then right again expecting an intersection near the first big branch-off, but was met with a dead-end.

"What?" He felt at the wall ahead of him that shouldn't be there, noticeably warmer than the others. His eyebrows drew down as his head tilted to the side. *Odd.* "This shouldn't be here."

Daria nodded her head, gulping. "I'm not even good at these things and I know that."

Olibtine looked the stone up and down, then attempted to push and pull it out of his way. *No use, it's not budging one bit.*

"It looks like we aren't going back the way we came," he huffed, a faint grinding sound reaching his ears as soon as he finished. *Great. This isn't going to be like the mazes I'm used to.* He repositioned back to the other side of Daria, who was glancing around at the walls all around.

He held the right wall again, following it right down the small hall again, then right again. Three turns later they were faced with what seemed to be an endless straight hallway with half of it cast in a shadow from the left wall. Olibtine glanced at the light again envisioning where they were at. *The entrance can't be far off to our left.*

He glanced back at Daria, noticing her mouth in a line, eyebrows drooping. *Odd for her.*

"It's going to be okay," he comforted in his gentlest voice, recalling a tactic he used before becoming a Mind. "You know..." he began, walking again, hand on the right wall, "...I'm curious. Out there on the sand dune, I'm not sure I've seen such amazing work with the bow. How did you learn?"

"I taught myself, shooting smudgins for food," Daria replied after a few seconds.

Smudgins? Olibtine envisioned the small, purple, slow-moving, slimy creatures that lived in the alleyways and sewers of Gbinti. "For... food?" he asked.

Daria shrugged.

That's more like her.

"I had to eat something. Not like anyone was just going to give a street kid like me their food, were they? There were tons of us down there living off of whatever we could find. 'There is no trash, only treasure.' Guane used to tell me. That old man obviously never spent time in the sewers or else he would realize he was wrong," Daria finished with a smirk.

"How did you and Gaune meet?" Olibtine asked, finally glimpsing what looked like the end of the hall, not too far ahead of them. He glanced at the light, making a mental note that it was behind and to the left, before continuing.

"He caught me trying to steal bread from a bakery. Gave me two options - go with him or go to jail. Pretty easy choice. Probably would have ran into you if I decided on the latter. He did me right though. Fed me, helped hone my skills with a bow, taught me a lot about Uradaria, the Minds, and other old people things."

Wait, she knew I was a Problem Solver? What else did Guane tell her. "I'd say that was a pretty easy choice," he replied, pausing at the end of the long hallway, the outer wall turning left.

The familiar grinding sound echoed closer this time, close enough for Olibtine to feel it on his hand. He glanced at the light again in the middle of the room, hanging in front and slightly to the left. They went straight a few steps, then turned right, then right again, doubling back on the short hall.

Daria grabbed Olibtine's robe, nearly yanking him back. Olibtine yelped, turning on Daria with a frown on his face. Her face was flat, bow out and knocked, facing the way they were supposed to be headed. *How did she...* Olibtine frowned, glancing back down the hall where she was transfixed.

The wall... is moving? He blinked, taking a step back, a loud grinding sound echoing off the walls towards them.

"What is that?!" Olibtine exclaimed as quietly as he could, refusing to take his eyes off of it, even though it was nearly impossible to see if it wasn't moving.

"I don't know," she replied through a clenched jaw, bow tense in her arms. "Is it still there?"

Olibtine squinted again, trying to make its form out against the stone wall. *Useless. It's the same exact color and texture... if it even is a thing. Maybe it's the sorcerers playing another trick on us.* He took a small step forward. A grinding sound came from it again and he thought he could see the turn at the end of the hallway shrinking, the light shifting ever so slightly against it.

Against his better judgment, he took another step forward, focusing intently on the corner and light. Another grinding sound greeted him in return.

"There!" he whispered. "It's the entire wall straight ahead."

"How do you know?" Daria responded from behind him.

"The light and depth of the corner is shrinking with every sound. Here, watch." He took a step back, the thing following his step and inched closer, showing no sign on arms, legs, eyes, or anything that could be mistaken as a creature.

"Moss. Don't do that again," Daria replied through her teeth. "So what do we do now?"

"It seems to move closer no matter what we do, so we won't be able to make it through that way. We're going to have to go back the way we came. Maybe it will only move when we..." a grinding came from it again, causing Olibtine to flinch.

Or not, Olibtine, eyes wide, immediately knew what they needed to do.

"Run!" he exclaimed. "Back down the way we came!"

By the time he turned to run, Daria already had her bow placed across her back, running as he said. They turned right back down the long hall, the loud grinding of stone on stone echoing behind them in pursuit. Olibtine retraced the maze in his head in case they needed to leave the room completely, but what was in front of him ruined the retracement entirely. They both skidded to a halt, placing their hand on the cool stone barring their path.

"This wasn't here earlier, right?" Daria asked, the words flying from her lips. Olibtine shook his head as a response. He noticed something right then, though. Glancing back the way they came, the grinding didn't stop even though they had. *Moss!* he cursed, only seeing one option.

"Just go!" he yelled, the constant grinding right on his heels causing the ground to rumble. Daria turned right into the new opening, closely followed by Olibtine, then stopped at a three way intersection. Olibtine looked left, then right, then forward, noticing two more openings at the end of a short hall. *Is this?* He moved forward without a word.

A loud crash behind made them jump. They spun on their heels in unison to see dust and stone flakes rolling along the ground in the now nearly-closed opening in the long hall. Only now did they see that it really was a creature, powerful looking stone legs sticking out the back of it, attempting to drive itself further down the hall. It paused. The grinding halted momentarily as it lifted its massive body of a stone slab up in the air a few inches, then began turning itself towards the opening directly at them.

"Moss!" Daria cursed. Olibtine thought the same thing, but nothing came from his mouth. He grabbed her forearm, then pulled her right down the new hall.

The halls guided them right, left, left, straight. They stopped at a four-way intersection, the grinding sound distant, but growing louder.

"Which way?" Daria asked between breaths, looking left then right.

Olibtine looked up. *We're almost right under the light. If this were any normal maze, the exit would most likely be at the opposite end of the entrance.*

He glanced down each hall, each with the same grey stone hall, heart racing as the grinding grew louder, almost frantic.

"Right!" he yelled, heading away from the light above. They turned right and were met with another right down a straight hall. Then a left that doubled back. A right, then straight again, then left. He looked right down a hall, then again straight ahead, noticing something.

"Moss!" he cursed, realizing they were back at the same four way intersection. He looked at the hall the way they came, feeling the vibrations through the floor, the grinding sounding as if it were nearly upon them again, then it appeared, grinding towards the intersection. *I guess that decides for us.*

He grabbed Daria again, who was staring at the thing creeping into the intersection, and took off the opposite way down a hall, hitting a two-way intersection. *Left or right?* His mind frantic, realizing this might be their last chance to get away from the thing. He hesitated, eyes darting both ways, feet unwilling to make the snap decision, feeling the ground shaking with the thing right behind them.

Too late. Daria grabbed him this time and ran right. Packs clanking, feet stomping on solid stone, breathing haggard, they ran a short distance and could only turn left, then another left, a long hall standing in front of them. They ran as fast as they could, the grinding at a fever pitch, seemingly right next to them. Then *BOOM.* Stone exploded behind them, the thing ramming through the left wall where they were not two steps ago. Dust enveloped them, impeding their vision. The impact sent rubble flying everywhere. Large chunks and small rubble alike rolled along the ground and flew past their heads. Olibtine lost his balance, still arm and arm with Daria, bringing her down with him. Shaking his head to clear his mind, the dust created a yellow-brown atmosphere, impossible to see anything past his hands. "Dar.." he started to say from his knees, but a strong hand grabbed his arm and yanked him up to his feet, tugging him a few more steps before coming to a halt. A two-way intersection greeted them, the dust lighter, but still making it impossible to see anything down either hall. Left or straight.

Without thinking, Daria scrambled to the left hallway. Olibtine looked up for the light. *It's at our left. That means...* he looked forward. "Daria, WAIT!" he yelled as loud as he could over the scraping sound and rubble moving around. "This way!" he pointed. Daria hesitated, looking the way she was initially headed, then ran back to Olibtine, who was already heading down the hall.

"Here!" Olibtine exclaimed, noticing a wooden door off to the right that was identical to the one they first entered. He rammed it open with his shoulder to reveal a dark stone landing on the other side. Wincing, he encouraged Daria to run faster, waving one arm frantically while using the other to point into the landing. The thing, towering over her and closing fast, churned the stone rubble it created from slamming through the wall. Daria strode towards him, pack slapping against her back, eyes wide, focusing on the doorway he pointed towards. She leapt from the stone hallway into the landing, Olibtine following closely behind right before a chunk of wall churned end over end where he was standing a second before. He slammed the door behind them. The ground vibrated from the impact as a loud boom sounded from the other side as the thing slammed into the stone wall that barred their path, no doubt bursting through that one too, cutting off all light into the landing.

Chapter 28: Nortmund

Kausha was the first one awake the following morning, watching the sun rise over the horizon unimpeded for the first time in what felt like many moons. Her mind kept going back to her last vision with her family. *The sorcerers are Bloodborn*, she repeated over and over again, each time sounding more strange. *The sorcerers are Bloodborn that betrayed us. Does that mean that 'shattering their destiny' meant they didn't go through the ritual, breaking their line?* It was all so confusing. She looked northwest, the expansive mountain peaks of Uhlbrar cutting through the morning sunshine in the distance. *What I do know is that I need more answers and Nortmund holds them.*

She heard stirring nearby and noticed Nalia had awoken and was sitting up on her elbow, gazing towards the mountains as well. Kausha knew that Nalia only had one thing on her mind right now - finding her sister - and let the silence be.

Shortly after, the others began awaking from their slumber, Shaum being the last, but the loudest, groaning and rubbing his head. He reached for the jug nearby his head, tipped it up, but nothing came out.

"Moss," he cursed, placing the jug down on top of his pack. "Who drank all tha liquor?"

Everyone just stared at him, knowing very well who drank it all.

"Ey, well I guess I was a bit thirsty las nigh," he smirked.

Finishing her packing, Kausha prepped everyone for the journey ahead, "Nortmund is at the base of the Uhlbrar mountains on the southern slope. Leave the excess weight - we can restock whatever supplies we need in town." She glanced over at Nalia, her stance tense, mouth in a line, eyes narrowed as she stared towards Nortmund. *We WILL find your sister, Nalia. And hopefully some answers.*

"Everyone ready?" Kausha asked, throwing her lightened pack over her shoulder.

They each nodded in turn, turning their backs on The Forest, the Trender, the dead acid blobs, and Yaula's resting place, then took off on a jog towards Nortmund, the richest city in Uradaria.

***

Nortmund was nothing like Purtghast or Gbinti. For one, it hugged the Uhlbrar mountains, the most majestic part of the city closest to the entrance, with the countless caves in the mountainside deeper in on the slopes. From a distance, the city looked like something the Bloodborn would have built - tall, grandiose spiraling white towers mirroring the mountain peaks behind, practically blending in with the sheer white snow on the tallest peaks, making the city look even more grand than first imagined. The towers were where the six richest presided, overlooking the inner, dirtier parts, cut off from the noise and dust yet still inside the layers of massive, white-washed city walls, each wall taller than the last. The land outside of the city had long been hollowed out in search for ujuntu deposits, creating a half-moon moat around the outside of the wall that was refilled every spring during the snow melt.

That is where the facade ended though. Once past the riches of the city wall and six richest, the city opens up to dirt, dust, decrepit shacks, down-faced eyes, and slave masters driving those unfortunate enough to find themselves in gambling debt, caught stealing, murdering, or any other countless act that the Plutocracy deemed punishable. All of this in the name of riches that the ujuntu deposits, native to only this part of Uradaria, held.

Kausha and the others stood on the precipice of the moat, looking across to the city that adventurers far and wide came to admire, most of whom never leave. The bridge leading across the still water could fit an entire army on top of it, sturdy as anything Kausha had seen before. *These must have been cut from The Forest.* Kausha pictured the roots and trees she dodged over and under while running from the Trender.

"Now this is a bridge," Skirm awed, smacking the rail. "I've read about this, but seeing it is something else entirely."

"Don't let the opulence fool you. Other bards have sung that it took over ten moons to pull the trees from deep within The Forest to here. Countless slaves died in the process. The songs of this place are misleading - meant to lure travelers and adventurers alike into a sense of wonderment," Skip warned in a flat tone, something Kausha had not heard from the bard before. "I say this with every ounce of seriousness in my heart," he continued, "we need to stick together in this city or else we will become yet another slave to the six."

With that, the group grew quiet, an intense, dark feeling enveloping them, almost like a cloud had settled over the city, casting it in its true light.

"Well, what's the plan?" Skirm asked, turning towards Nalia. "Any idea where your sister might have gone when she first got into the city?"

Nalia shook her head slowly, eyes afire while staring at the towers. "The only thing I know is that she came up here to see the culture and architecture."

"Then we'll have to start on the outer parts and work our way in," Skirm forced out in a cheerful tone, putting his large hand on Nalia's shoulder, nearly enveloping her entire arm in the process. Skirm began walking across the bridge ahead of the others. *Why is he so gung ho?* Kausha raised her eyebrow and followed him like the others. Her eyes drifted up again. *The only ones capable of hiring a sorcerer would be someone with plenty of wealth, so they would have to be on the outer parts of the city. But what of the motive? Why would someone want me dead?*

They approached the first wall's gate, the smallest of them all, roughly two times the size of Skirm, no doubt looking like an odd group of travelers with two large Spearheads, one human bard, one Bloodborn, though that's impossible to tell on the outside, and one Catsnif. The two dwarven guards on each side of the entry, one in a bright blue cloak and the other in a bright yellow cloak over the top of heavy metal armor from toes to head, both brandishing a long pike in both hands, readjusted to stand side by side, blocking the width of the gate. Their dark eyes narrowed beneath thick, brown eyebrows that matched braided brown beards that hung down to their stomachs, both stark against their pale skin.

"Stop!" the one in blue exclaimed in a deep voice, holding out a meaty hand forcing Kausha and the others to come to a halt fifteen feet away.

"What is your business in the great six city of Nortmund, the jewel of the north?" he asked, brandishing his pike with two hands again, tip now pointed towards them. Taking in his stance, Kausha thought it firm, a sureness about the way he held his pike.

Skip took a small step forward and cleared his throat. "We are but a traveling group of bards, academics, and lovers of fine architecture who have come to partake in all three. Stories of the great six city of Nortmund, the jewel of the north, have reached far and wide, even to the shores of Circle Lake far south of The Forest." The dwarf glanced up at Skirm and Shaum, expressionless, then back to Skip. "If you will allow it, we would ask for permission to enter your fine city." And with a bow, Skip let his lute's neck slip forward in his bag to show the dwarf that he was serious, at least about one thing.

The dwarf in blue looked over at the one in yellow, as if wanting confirmation - a nod following.

"The great six city of Nortmund, the jewel of the north, welcomes you, travelers!" the one in blue exclaimed, standing straight and moving his pike back to one hand, then sliding to the side to let them pass. The one in yellow did the same, undoubtedly a practiced move.

That's it? Kausha followed Skip through the gate. *Does everyone just get accepted in like that?*

The next level city wall loomed over the space they entered, casting a shadow throughout, a full two times the size of the most outer wall. The area in between the outer wall and the next inner wall was a lot larger and more inhabited than Kausha expected. The ground was paved with large, white stone blocks, creating a perfectly flat surface that the citizens walked on. Everything was so clean, too - not a trace of dirt anywhere on the stone, the city wall, nor the square homes that presided in this section. Each home, a stark white, looked to be a large, single block of stone with multiple levels seemingly flush against the inner wall, each level containing six windows of paned glass fitted in a carved out section of the stone.

How did they find so many large stones, not to mention how they carved these out? Kausha looked left, then right, and as far as the curved wall allowed her to see, she saw that every home was exactly the same. *Amazing.*

The others were just as transfixed as she, gawking up and down each road that hugged the outer wall and the inner homes. She shook herself, glancing back at the two dwarves at the entry gate, who were staring at Kausha and her group with what seemed to be smiles beneath their beards. *At least we are looking the part. Wait, how do we get into the next layer?*

"I don't see the next gate," she revealed to the others, knocking them back into reality.

"Oh, um," Skirm replied, looking left and right down the roads, "I don't either."

Kausha glanced back at the dwarves again, the one in yellow pointing to the right as if expecting them to not know where to go. She looked the way the dwarf pointed, then nodded back in thanks.

"This way," she instructed, snapping the others from their trance.

"Es too clean," Shaum whispered, gazing at the white houses as they walked. "Ow es et tis clean?"

No one answered, but everyone was thinking the same thing. Slaves.

Where are the slaves anyways? Kausha observed the citizens as she passed, all wearing a cloak colored a different variety than the last, no doubt to match whichever six they held allegiance to. There were dwarves and humans roaming around without a care in the world, ignoring the group in their worn, tattered clothes. *And where are the other races?*

The outer layer felt all the same to Kausha after a while, even the variety of cloak colors standing out against the stark white of the stone homes got to be tiresome. She looked back the way they came in an attempt to see how far they'd walked from the first gate, but it was already out of sight - just the seemingly endless outer wall on the horizon.

"Oy!" Kausha heard Shaum say behind her, causing her to stop. She turned to see him waving at someone in a bright purple cloak trying to get their attention.

"Oy! Ow much further to tha inner gate?" he asked. Skirm palmed his spear shaped head with both hands, letting out an audible sigh.

The dwarf in bright purple stopped, looking him up and down, eyes narrowing above a long, braided brown beard with shiny stones throughout. "Not far that way," a feminine voice responded, pointing the way they were headed. Shaum didn't hide his shock hearing that voice come from under a beard, practically jumping back at the combination.

"Yer a woman?!" he exclaimed, leaning closer and squinting to get a better look.

"Shaum!" Skirm growled, striding over to his brother and grabbing his arm to pull him in. "Apologies my lady. My brother isn't quite right in his head after such a long journey." He bowed deep to the dwarven woman, who turned on her heel with a huff, her cloak whipping to her side with a flurry, then stormed off the opposite way they were headed.

"Wha?" Shaum asked, pulling away from Skirm. "Eh was jus curious - didn't know women had beards! Ers was betta than most men!"

Skirm glared at his brother. "If you would have listened to me when we were kids, you would have known that. Though..." he turned around to look at the other dwarves walking the street noticing they all had beards and the same clothing, "...it IS different to see with your own eyes."

Skip chuckled to the side, reaching up and slapping Shaum on his back. "It's okay, I've heard many bards sing of this and it still can't prepare you for the truth.

Nalia shrugged. "My race all have fur on their faces, men and women alike. It's not that strange."

Shaum's mouth dropped open at that, looking at Nalia as if he hadn't seen her in a while. "Eh ave ta see tha!" he smirked.

"Anyways," Kausha interjected, "should we finally get into the second level gate?"

They nodded their heads in unison, following Kausha's lead down the street. Not too far ahead, Kausha could see the outer wall closing in on the inner one, the white stones beneath their feet growing smaller as the street narrowed. Just as she noticed that, she saw the next gate on the inner wall. This one looked nearly identical to the first one, except it was easily twice the size, probably to match the wall's size. Standing on either side of it were two dwarven guards apiece, all in different colored cloaks - bright purple, bright orange, bright green, and white. *These are different colors than the first gate. Must be to give each a chance at showing force.* The dwarves gripped their pikes tighter upon seeing Kausha and the others, their knuckles turning red against pale skin. Their eyes followed each step, but none moved to stop them from entering the gated tunnel.

Their feet echoed upon entering the shadowed corridor, eyes squinting at the bright sun bouncing off of the smooth floor and walls alike from the other end. As they entered the light, their eyes adjusted to see a mix of colors and calmness greeting them. Straight ahead, roughly the same distance from the first wall to the second wall, stood the next inner wall, which was twice again the size of the one they just went through. *How many more are there?* Kausha followed the walls up to the line of stark white towers against the blue sky, the first sighting since entering the city. The towers loomed over them, casting shadows periodically on the ground. *Those must be on the next layer.* Looking down, she was taken aback by the simplistic beauty of a stone walkway equidistant from both walls following their curves, perfectly manicured green grass to each side that stretched from the walkway to the base of the walls. There were no stone homes on this level, only sheer walls covered from top to bottom in green vines with small red, purple, and yellow flowers jutting out.

Nalia started walking down the path, set upon her goal of finding her sister, which spurred the others into following, even when gawking at the towers.

"There's no one here," Skirm's voice echoed as he looked over the tops of the others heads down the walkway. "Where is everyone?"

"Maybe in the next layer?" Kausha guessed as they walked through the first tower's shadow, footsteps echoing between the walls.

"It's easy to see how travelers can succumb to the beauty of this place, though. It's such a picturesque facade in these first two layers." Skirm waved around with his hands as if to point out the obvious. "But..." he continued, looking around, softening his voice so it wouldn't echo, "I can't help but feel like we're being watched."

Kausha nodded, understanding what he meant. She looked up at the spiraling white towers again trying to imagine what they were going to encounter on the other side. *The security feels lax considering how close we are to the six. Maybe this is their way of setting one's mind at ease before they enslave them. They probably have watchers in the tower right now looking at us. This area would be a perfect spot for an ambush of opposing forces.* That thought made her skin crawl, her blood instinctively moving down to her hands. *If the Nortmunders wanted me dead, this would be their chance to do it themselves.*

They passed through the second shadow, the quiet stillness between the walls creating a tense feeling that grew between them, feeding off of Nalia's and Kausha's goals. They passed through the third shadow - the half-way point of the layer. Two more shadows passed without a word from anyone as they followed the stone walkway towards the opposite end of the half-moon layer. Entering the final shadow, Kausha thought she could see the gate on the inner wall, causing her to exhale audibly, Shaum looking down at her with his eyebrow raised.

There were six dwarven guards at the entrance to the next gate, one that looked similarly to the previous two except smaller. Each dwarf had a pike in hand, and wore different colored cloaks to represent the six rulers over their typical metal armor. Standing on opposite ends of the gate, they crossed their pikes as soon as Nalia drew the group near, cutting off further advancement.

"Halt!" The one in the bright orange yelled in a deep, reverberating voice, holding up a meaty, gauntleted hand. "What is your business in the great six city of Nortmund, the jewel of the north?"

Kausha looked over at Skip, raising her eyebrow. *Didn't we do this already?*

Before Skip could step up, Nalia spoke up first, sounding annoyed, "We already told the other guards."

The dwarf in the bright orange placed his hand back on his pike, lowering the tip towards Nalia with the others behind him following his move, shifting their feet with a quick, precise squat that sent an echo both behind them through the gate as well as in front of them, their movement ending long before the echo did. Nalia stepped back while Skirm stepped forward putting his hand in front of her, a full body taller than the dwarves, who all looked up at him, their faces growing harder at his size.

Skip cleared his throat, stepping around Nalia to get next to Skirm, and bowed, his red hair flopping around. "My good sirs, please, there is no need for this. We have had a long journey through The Forest and as we told your fellows at the first gate, we are but a traveling group of bards, academics, and lovers of fine architecture who have come to partake in all three. Stories of the great six city of Nortmund, the jewel of the north, have reached far and wide, even to the shores of Circle Lake far south of The Forest." This seemed to calm the dwarf in the bright orange. He stood up straight, his pike returning to one hand with the butt resting on the ground. The other dwarves followed as well, stepping aside to make a path for them to walk through.

"See as it your friends there..." the dwarf started, nodding up at Skirm and then to Nalia, "... show the same respect as you have just now or else you'll be in the mines by nightfall."

Skip nodded with arms splayed in a sort of feigned reverence. "Thank you, and they will."

Straightening himself, Skip started towards the gate's threshold between the dwarves, the others following, each staring at either Skirm or Nalia, white knuckles visibly flexed around their pikes. Kausha held her breath beneath a fake smile, hoping nothing would set them off. Each dwarf's face held a trained resentment with eyebrows drawn down above tense jaws beneath thick beards. She looked ahead again, noticing for the first time that there was no light at the end of the wall underpass - there was only darkness lit by a few candles placed some distance apart on either wall. *The wall can't be this large, can it?* Glancing back at the entrance, her breath caught, causing her to freeze. The light from the way they came was gone. Shaum nearly bumped into her from behind.

"Whoah," Shaum looked down at her with worried eyes, "whas tha matter, Kaush?" She didn't answer, just stared. "Kaush?" he repeated, this time following her eyes, looking back the way they came. "Wut tha moss?!" he cursed. "Hey, Skip!"

"What?" he called back.

"Um, ye might wanta look at tis," Shaum answered, trying to make sense of it all.

Skirm, Skip, and Nalia didn't even need to walk back to where Kausha and Shaum were standing to see what they were looking at. They saw it too - nothing where there should at least be some light coming from the entrance they passed through. Skirm turned around to look the way they were headed, seeing only darkness, then turned back towards where they just came, seeing only darkness. "Moss," he cursed, striding with Nalia and Skip in tow towards Kausha and Shaum.

"Whatdya make of et, Kaush?" Shaum asked.

"Not sure," Kausha replied, eyebrows narrowed, looking left, then right, only seeing darkness with the occasional candle lit on the walls. "Whatever it is, it can't be good."

The others nodded slowly in agreement in the dim yellow candlelight.

Before anyone could say another word, there was a stone on stone grinding sound echoing through the corridor, indistinct in the direction it was coming from. Then, there was a clanking of armored feet hitting stone echoing throughout. Kausha looked left to see a group of dwarven soldiers in full plate armor passing through the puddle of light from one of the candles. She looked right, seeing the same thing, the noise growing louder as they approached.

"Moss!" Shaum cursed as they huddled closer together, each looking a different way. "What do we do?!"

"Nothing," Kausha blurted out in a hurried, quiet voice. "There are too many of them and we're unarmed. Try to stick together if you can."

Kausha glanced over at Nalia, her orange eyes narrow and intense under the dim yellow light. *Looks like we know what happened to your sister.*

The group of dwarves on each side slowed, coming to a stop ten feet away, grasped their pikes in both hands, and leveled them into their familiar battle stance, one that looked like it had been practiced until perfected. The cloaks they wore were a variety of colors, one of each of the six houses as far as Kausha could tell. She glanced over each in turn, their eyes hidden in shadows, their stances true under stocky legs. Her insides churned causing her to slowly push blood into her arms and fingers, readying herself if needed.

"Wha es goin on?" Shaum whispered out of the corner of his mouth. Movement from the right towards the back of the group of soldiers made Kausha and the others turn to see what it was. Shuffling of the soldiers sounding through the air showed that they were parting down the middle, creating an opening for... someone.

It glided into the candlelight, as tall as Skirm was, but as skinny as a sapling tree, wearing a multicolored patched robe with squares of bright green, yellow, orange, blue, purple, and white. Its hood was pulled back revealing an angular, pure white face with high cheekbones that jutted out like rocks on a beach. Its skinny arms were wrapped around a thick, black tomb, one that looked far too heavy for the thing to carry. It looked the group over with its bright green, piercing eyes, ending on Kausha, and then it spoke.

"Hel-lo tra-vel-ers," it greeted in a soft, melodic tone that felt alien - almost as if it were forcing the native language of Uradaria. "You have passed through the six's do-main. You will for-feit your be-long-ings and serve the six as they please. Do not re-sist or you will be killed on the spot."

Kausha squeezed her jaw tight while slowly moving blood out of her fingertips to prepare blood daggers. *I could fight and probably take out all of these soldiers myself, but how could we escape the city? Take this thing hostage? It seems higher ranking.*

The others turned towards Kausha, eyes wide, foreheads glistening from sweat in the candlelight.

Kausha locked eyes with Nalia. *I promised.* She retracted her blood, hoping no one saw her do it. *And if I run, there will be no way to find out why I am being hunted. They can't know it's me. Could they?*

Kausha relaxed her body, standing up straight, the others taking her lead. "Alright." She met the thing's bright green eyes and dropped her pack. She felt Nalia's eyes grow intense on the side of her face from a sideways stare. "We won't resist. What now?"

The thing tilted its head sideways as if expecting something else. Kausha nodded to the others in turn, motioning for them to drop their packs, ending at Nalia, nodding again. *We will find her.* Hesitantly, they dropped their packs, then turned to the thing. It nodded, then finally said "Fol-low." It turned, gliding out of the candlelight between the soldiers. Kausha followed it, staring at each stalworth dwarf she passed, the others following in her stead. As she cleared the last dwarf in line, two of them broke off and followed in right behind her, pikes relaxed, but ready to be used should Kausha try anything. The others were similarly followed, each separated by two guards apiece.

I could take out this... thing... and the two guards easily, she imagined, instinctively moving her organs around. *No! Stop. I can't do that with the others surrounded. Where are they taking us? To the mines already? Is this what they do with all travelers to the city?*

The thing entered the hidden hallway before Kausha, its cloak flapping in an unseen wind coming from the direction it headed. Kausha crossed the entryway to the tunnel and was immediately thrown back to a time of sitting in Purtghast, cool wind blowing through her hair. But this wasn't Purtghast and she needed to be on guard. Looking ahead through the skinny stone tunnel around the thing, she could see a bright light at the end. *The exit?* Boots and armor echoing off walls and ceiling alike cut through her thoughts. Anxiety crept into her throat, expecting everything that Skip had told her before entering the city. She began preparing her body for the worst - a fight to the death, and it wasn't about to be her death. Her stride length increased slightly, just enough to get closer to the hovering thing in front of her, its colorful cloak nearly smacking into her as the wind buffeted it. The exit was steps away. The bright light made her eyes water as she was forced to squint and shield them with her arm. The thing exited, then turned left revealing what lay beyond the tunnel to Kausha. She had prepared herself for the worst, but this was something entirely different.

Chapter 29: The Sorting

Kausha exited the tunnel and found herself staring out over a large, shallow pool of water, split directly down the middle by a white stone walkway. The crystal clear water allowed a clear view of the bottom, which is what shocked Kausha the most. It was pure ujuntu. The substance that the entirety of Uradaria traded under. The substance that now seemed to be so plentiful that the entire floor of the body of water was covered in it. *What the,* Kausha froze, so transfixed on what was below her she forgot to look up. The stone walkway in the middle of the water went straight as far as she could see with t-shaped connections periodically where soldiers stood in the shade off to either side, under what seemed like bridges over top. *No, not bridges,* she realized, gazing up and noticing that the first of the six stark white towers spiraled above, looming over her and everything around. She was so close to the tower that she had to crane her neck up as far as it would go, and still could not see the top of it. *Well, we made it to the towers.* She was shoved from behind to the area off to the right, opposite the thing that guided them there where a wall stood behind as well as to the left while the right was flanked by the water, providing nowhere to run. After shoving her, the dwarves turned the opposite way to stand in a mirrored area on the opposite side of the tunnel.

The others were ferried in similarly, each with the same expression of awe when they entered the area. *Even evil can create beauty.* Kausha regained her composure as Skip, the final one through the exit, was shoved into the little section where the others stood together. The remainder of the soldiers lined the walkway that split the water, facing them with pikes pointed forward. The thing stood behind them, writing in its book and periodically looking towards Kausha and the others.

They stood there for some time, the sun growing hot in the reflection of the white tower into the still pool, even if it wasn't directly touching them.

"What is going on?" Skirm whispered out of the corner of his mouth.

"I think it's weighing us now that we're in the light," Kausha replied, unsure of what exactly was going on, but it seemed like a good guess.

"'*For them to do as they please.*' That's what it said? That means..." Skirm trailed off, looking at Kausha with wide eyes.

No one responded because they all knew the answer. *Yes,* Kausha's hands balled into fists, *that probably means the mines.*

"Ow are we getn out of this?" Shaum whispered from the back of the group, a slight quiver in his voice.

Before anyone could answer, a plump dwarf in the similarly colorful cloak as the thing hurried down the walkway, cloak flapping behind from the small, quick steps, brown beard thrown over his or her shoulder, writing in a book similar to the one the thing had.

"Ah, Parjune, you're accepting this lot in, I see," spoke the dwarf in a deep, bassy male voice that echoed around the enclosure. Without glancing up from his writing, he hurried towards the thing, the soldiers shuffling forward to make room.

"You are late." The thing named Parjune glanced over to the approaching dwarf.

The dwarf looked up from his writing for the first time acknowledging Parjune. "And what do we have with this lot?" he asked, motioning towards Kausha and the others with his quill.

"Have a lo-ok for your-self," Parjune replied calmly, glancing towards Kausha with a smirk on her face.

The dwarf let out an audible groan, moving towards the soldiers blocking his view. "Move it, move it," he demanded, forcing them to part ways. The soldiers made a gap for the dwarf, who stepped forward, eyeing each of them up and down, ending his sights on Shaum.

He tapped the quill against his chin. "Interesting lot here. Interesting indeed. Where did they come from?"

"The For-est," Parjune replied.

The dwarf visibly flinched at hearing that, turning a page in his book and furiously writing something down. "They certainly look like it, don't they?" he laughed to himself, glancing up at Shaum again, then scribbling something else down. He retreated back towards Parjune, the soldiers closing their gap again.

"Spread out! I can't see them when you're side by side like that!" the dwarf yelled. The soldiers flinched, armor clanking while quickly parted ways again.

"We don't have too many Spearheads here and that one.." he pointed to Nalia, ".. looks familiar. The red head looks far too kempt to have traveled through The Forest, and the human looks... fierce."

Kausha attempted to relax her face and fists upon hearing that.

"She is the one they look to-wards for gui-dance," Parjune replied, nodding its head.

"You've obviously written what you feel, let me see," the dwarf reached his hand up for her book.

"Ah, a bard, a scientist, and lovers of architecture? And a Catsnif - that's the word. I see, I see. And you're confident in your initial assessment?"

"I am. The gu-ards have re-layed ex-act-ly what the red ha-ired, the bard, sa-id ver-ba-tum," Parjune answered, staring straight at Kausha again.

"Was appenin?!" Shaum yelled over to Parjune and the dwarf, causing Kausha and the others to flinch unexpectedly. The soldiers shuffled their feet, armor clanking, grip audibly tightening on their pikes at the ready. Parjune continued to stare at Kausha causing her to shiver. *Does it know what I am?*

The dwarf looked up from his reading and turned towards Shaum. "Why, you're being placed."

"Placed?! Wudya mean, placed?" Shaum demanded. Skirm turned back to Shaum giving him a 'shut it' face.

The dwarf sighed, closed the book, handed it back to Parjune, then walked forward in front of the soldiers again, causing them to shuffle forward slightly to ensure protection at the unexpected move.

"You will each have a duty to the six. There is no refuting this, it is inevitable. You will perform your duties as taught without complaint. Those that complain, fight back, or any other type of malfeasance, shall be punishable by *death*." He emphasized the final word, pausing for a second and sweeping his eyes over them. "Now, Parjune has so kindly compiled notes and put each of you, based on what we know from word of mouth and of body, in one of these duties. They are final and irrefutable. Now, each set of soldiers will escort you to where your duty lies. Parjune," he beckoned, the thing gliding forward and opening its book.

"You, bard," Parjune started. Kausha and the others glanced at him, "...are bl-essed at be-ing one of the six's per-so-nal bards. This is a cov-e-ted po-si-tion that you sh-ould feel priv-liged to have." The dwarf next to her nodded his head and smiled at Skip.

Parjune continued. "You, Cats-nif, and you, hu-man..." it locked eyes with Kausha again, "...will be head-ed to the first's tow-er to per-form an-y-thing nee-ded of you."

Kausha turned her head to Nalia, Nalia turning hers as well, locking eyes, Nalia's narrow, her eyebrows drawn down. *Good,* Kausha thought, *I need that from her. Whatever it is, as long as we stick together, we can get out of this. Skip should be nearby if he's a personal bard.* She glanced at Skip, who was showing no sign of stress or worry. Kausha tilted her head slightly at that, wondering how he could stay so calm. Her attention was forced back to Parjune as it spoke again.

"And fi-na-lly, the two Spear-heads..." It glanced down at the dwarf next to her, who was now grinning with excitement. "You two will be sent to the mines," she finished, closing her book softly, but with a finality that said they were done here.

Kausha's throat caught as she looked back at Shaum behind her. *No, not the mines.* She imagined him deep inside a cave hammering the rocks day in and day out. The others must have thought the same, for Kausha heard them shuffling and turning towards one another. *Can we stop this?* She glanced at Skirm, his eyes filled with fear. He was a scholar, not a laborer, no matter how big he was. She forced her eyes away, turning to stare at Parjune. But before she could get a word out, Parjune's bright green eyes bulged momentarily, shaking its head ever so slightly. *What was that?* Kausha raised an eyebrow, but ultimately held her tongue. *It doesn't want me to say anything, but its eyes. Its eyes say something different.*

The dwarf's voice shook her from her stare. "That will be all, Parjune. Let us be on with it," he spat with a wave of his hand. "Guards," he called, turning away and walking back between the soldiers, who moved in on the Kausha and the others.

Kausha grabbed Shaum and Skirm at their wrists, pulling them closer so the approaching dwarves couldn't hear. "We'll come for you," Kausha whispered, locking determined, purple eyes with Skip, then Shaum, then Skirm. "Nalia and I will come for you. I promise to Yaula, we will come." This seemed to strengthen the group, especially Skirm, whose eyes were no longer wide and filled with fear, but narrowed with vigor, jaw clenched tight. She noticed the soldiers approaching from the corner of her eye. "Wait for us and stay strong."

The soldiers reached them and two by two guided them away, Kausha and Nalia the last to go. Kausha glanced at Parjune one last time, attempting to understand more of what she hinted at just moments ago, but Parjune continued staring right into Kausha's eyes, giving nothing more. *I know that was something. But for now, I have other things to worry about.* Scenarios and plans began swirling in her head while being escorted with Nalia by four dwarves over the stone walkway to the first's tower.

Chapter 30: The Council's Decision

"It ssssemessss that young Olibtine has better thingssss to do with hissss time than to help lead Gbinti into a brighter future. Either that, or ssssomething more sssssinissster hasss occurred. Either way, he hassss been abssssent for five meetingssss now, and we musssst ssssiece hope that he will return in pressssently. Thissss being sssssaid, I move for vote to replaccce him with another in our current Councccil while we ssssearch for a new head," echoed Bjorgene's cold voice from the second row of the Mind's circular meeting chamber. The chamber was occupied by all of the residing Minds, save Olibtine and Guane, the latter currently ill and bedridden.

A murmur began between the Minds following Bjorgene's speech. This sort of thing had been done before, but only when the smartest had fallen deathly ill, unable to perform his duties, or passed away. They all knew that he was headed to the Tower in an attempt to discover new details of the Bloodborn passing, but no one had heard word from him since he left. That was nearly an entire moon ago. The meetings had gone on without a hitch, but going without a smartest for so long was rather unprecedented in recent memory.

A tap of wood on granite, the sign that someone wished to say something to the group, echoed from the third row. A shuffling of cloth followed as each Mind turned, attempting to find where the noise originated.

"Yessss, Poreme. You have our earssss," Bjorgene acknowledged, looking up at him.

Poreme stood, fixed his robe, cleared his throat, then spoke in a strong, respectful tone.

"The Minds are only as good and as strong as we are intelligent. While Olibtine is indeed off on a journey it is one that is of the utmost importance to Gbinti, its people, and of Uradaria as a whole. We, the Council, should know that anything worth pursuing takes time, and should not expect immediate results, even with something that is immediately at our fingertips. This journey that Olibtine is on is one of danger and of an unknown ending. Not one of us here," he moved his eyes over each Mind and splayed his hands, palms faced up, out in front of himself for emphasis, "...has dealt with a sorcerer face to face. Olibtine is risking his very life and limb to unearth answers that just might save all of us and the solution that is brought up right now is to replace him with another? Does that sit right with any of you?" He looked around once again, meeting the eyes of his fellow Minds.

"I will counter propose that we continue as we are, accepting Olibtine back as the head upon his return," Poreme ended, nodding, then taking his seat once again.

A louder murmur arose this time than the first. Actual arguments, respectful as they were, arose throughout the chamber between the Minds. Bjorgene stared at Poreme, old eyes like daggers, causing Poreme's hands to clench into fists in his lap, his eyes diverting to browse the Minds throughout the chamber.

Bjorgene tapped his block of wood on the granite to calm the Minds. A silence engulfed the chamber.

"Thank you, Poreme. Would anyone elssse wissssh to ssspeak on thisss isssue?" Bjorgene asked, spinning in a slow circle to ensure he didn't miss anything. "No?" he repeated, gray, bushy eyebrows raised. "Then we ssshall call for a two votesss. The firssst one being that of two coursssessss. On one hand, we have the firssst courssse, replacccing Olibtine with another Mind. The sssecond coursse being the one Poreme put forth - leaving thingssss asss they are currently with no head Mind, where as Olibtine resssumes hissss role upon returning. The sssssecond vote, if needed, would be to choossse who to replaccce Olibtine with. Any objectionssss?" Bjorgene spun in a slow circle again, awaiting a response.

A tap of wood against granite echoed. This one from the second row near Bjorgene himself. A middle-aged Mind named Joran with deep black hair that hung down to his chin, a well-kempt beard, and striking blue eyes, began to stand. He didn't so much as glance at Bjorgene when he spoke in a deep, sultry voice.

"As we well know, Guane is bedridden. This vote would be a travesty if he were not here to both lend his voice and vote."

He sat down immediately after he spoke, only then glancing at Bjorgene for a second before looking out among the Minds with a straight face.

Bjorgene nodded at the Mind respectively and responded in his normal calm voice. "Guane is an important part of thisss body, but thissss is a matter of great importanccce. Ssssimilarly as Olibtine, we are unsssure of when he might be cleared to join usss again." He rubbed his chin in thought. "I propossse that if the voting is even one vote differenccce, we will take thisss to Guane and he can be the deccciding vote. Will thissss sssuit your objeccction, Joran?"

Joran nodded towards Bjorgene in acceptance, Bjorgene nodding back.

"Sssshall we begin then?" he asked the entire chamber. "Right hand raisssed is in favor of the firsssst plan. Left hand raisssed is in favor of Porome'ssss plan."

A ruffling of clothing spread through the chamber as hands began to pop up in quick unison. Bjorgene spun slowly, a slight grin appearing in the corner of his mouth, if only for a second, before returning to a flat-mouthed stare.

"The right'sss have it in favor of the firsssst plan. Olibtine is to be replaccced as the head of the Mindsss. With that, a ssssecond vote is required: A vote for who we wissssh to replaccce him with until we can perform the tesssts to find the next ssssmartest of our cccitizensss. Does any Mind wissssh to sssubmit a name, be it their own or another?"

The question was met with shuffled clothing and slippers, each Mind glancing around at one another and weighing their own. Not one of them would dare submit their own name, opening them up for ridicule for being selfish when the only goal for a Mind should be helping others. A light murmur began to grow as Minds leaned into their neighbor, weighing options. Each one of the Minds were the smartest in the city, but each has an opinion of their own in how everything from fund allocation and foreign relationships should be handled.

A tap of wood on marble cut through the murmurs causing the voices to go silent. Joran stood once again, clearing his throat before speaking. "I submit Bjorgene."

The room exploded in discussions. Some Minds bolted up, their faces red in finally realizing what was brewing under the surface for so long.

Bjorgene let the Minds debate unimpeded for a spell, glancing around the room at the different groups. Some used wild hand gestures while debating with those on different levels, while others simply sat in silence. He tapped the wood on the granite, silencing everyone.

"I accccept thisss sssubmisssion. I know it is of utmossst importanccce and I will do all I can to continue the tradisssion. Who elsssse will be ssssubmitted?" The Minds were visibly caught off guard, their heads darting left and right to one another. They assumed he would simply take it without opposition.

The Minds, half standing, half sitting, glanced around as the question hung thick in the air. Bjorgene spun slowly, glancing over each Mind in turn, some turning their faces down in disappointment while others shot a smile his way.

"No one then?" he asked once more. "Then I humbly accccept the possssition of interim Head of the Mindssss until we perform the tessssstsss and locate a new smartesssst." His gaze moved down to the chair in the bottom row, the centerpiece of the chamber. He took a few slow, deliberate steps to the stairs, then strode down the three wide steps to the bottom, visibly showing his position in the Minds. He approached the chair, softly placing a hand on one of the wooden armrests while taking it in, then spun, facing half of the Minds.

"The meeting issss adjourned," he proclaimed with a wave of a hand.

The Minds began to shuffle, filing out of the chamber leaving Bjorgene standing alone on the bottom row, smiling to himself as he stroked the wooden arm of the chair.

Chapter 31: Seeing Red and Green

Olibtine and Daria lay face-up on the stone floor, deep, panting breaths coming from both. Dust covered them from head to toe, but save for a few scrapes on their hands, knees, and elbows, they made it through unscathed. A soft yellow light filtered through the cracks around the wooden door, illuminating the dust in the air, creating a feeling of lingering fog.

"That... was close," Olibtine gasped through a heavy breath. Propping himself up while unstrapping the pack from his back, he dug out a canteen of water and the mushroom vial again for light, shaking it a few times in order to cast a soft, yellow light in the landing.

"Yeah," Daira agreed, eyes shut, attempting to slow her breathing, "a little too close for comfort."

Olibtine finished taking a few gulps from the canteen then tapped Daria on her leg, offering it to her. She opened her eyes, sat up, and accepted the canteen with a nod.

Olibtine stared up at the door they had just bolted through. *If we were just a hair slower,* he contemplated, a brief flash of Daria and himself lying bloodied upon a heap of rubble. He squeezed his eyes shut, shaking him from the thought.

"Hey," he heard behind him. Eyebrows raised, he turned to face Daria again who was looking at him with soft, defeated eyes above a frown. She rubbed her hands together, breaking eye contact before saying, "thanks for saving me back there. If we would have done what I wanted, we'd be..." she trailed off.

"Hey, you're the one that pushed us in the right direction the first time back there. I should be thanking you!" he replied, wanting her to go back to her fun, over-sharing self.

She took another gulp from the canteen, then handed it back to Olibtine with a forced smile on her face.

"Well," he started putting the canteen away and looking around through squinting eyes, "looks like we're in another stairwell. Let's hope there aren't any more mazes up above." He stretched the vial out while measuring the stairway to a darkness beyond the light that his eyes couldn't pierce. He stood while re-shouldering his pack and moved to the wall opposite the wooden door to get a better view. Daria collected herself and did the same, grunting with her pack from the weight.

"Looks like we have another climb," he grunted, staring up at the gray stone stairway, the same kind from the floors below. After glancing over to Daria with a nod, he began. It wasn't long until they both were breathing heavily, labored from the maze and the endless stairway below. With every step, the air grew warmer and wetter than the rest - as if standing in a swamp on a hot, windless day. Sweat began dropping from his forehead and face, splashing on the stone with every step. He felt his hands sweating too, having to switch the vial between each in order to wipe them on his robe every few steps. He paused, leaning against the outside wall, closing his eyes to catch a breath. Daria did the same on the opposite wall, wiping the fur on her forehead with her sleeve, which she had rolled up already. She leaned her hand against the wall and pulled back as soon as it came in contact, eyebrows raised and gripping her wrist as if burned.

"Feel this," Daria told Olibtine, placing her hand back on the stone wall. "It's cold to the touch and yet the air is boiling in here." Olibtine's eyebrows tilted down and hesitated before placing the back of his hand on the wall he was leaning on. The shock of the cold sent a shiver down his arm. The sweat on his forehead suddenly felt cold, sending another shiver down his spine.

"It's cold?!" he questioned, eyes wide, placing both hands on the wall after the second shiver subsided. "This has to be another of the sorcerer's tricks."

"At least we know how to cool off in this heat," Daria shrugged, turning her hand over in order to place the back of her forearm on the wall.

They alternated their hands, arms, and cheeks to touch the stone wall, cooling themselves considerably even though the air was just as warm as before. It seemed to help their lungs too, for Olibtine noticed that both of them were breathing normally again.

"Let's keep on," he pushed, keeping one hand to the wall in an attempt to stifle off the heat.

A few steps later, he saw another wooden door up ahead causing his heart to skip a beat, whether from pain or excitement, he couldn't tell. *Alright, what's next?*

They stood on the landing examining the door, which was an exact replica of the ones below, except this one was outlined by a red light filtering through the cracks on the bottom, top, and sides. They locked eyes, each noticing the other had their jaw set tight below furrowed eyebrows, exasperated by the red light filling the landing, but they nodded to one another all the same, then turned to face the door once again. Olibtine reached for the handle, the familiar click of the lock sounding through the landing, then he slowly pushed the door open, its hinges creaking as if it had rusted over.

A dull red light covered them from head to toe - the same kind as the ones from the ujuntu rooms below. Directly in front of them, and everywhere they looked, were plants. Plants with large leaves, ones with small, sharp leaves, ones that didn't even come to their ankles even - all, highlighted by the dull red lights from above, creating an eerie, shadowed room that made it impossible to see more than a dozen feet ahead. Olibtine knelt down, trying to get a look at the floor and noticed that it was dirt. *Makes sense as to why the air is so hot and wet. A greenhouse of sorts.*

He stood, pocketing the mushroom vial and looking at Daira who was moving her head left and right as she stared into the room, attempting to see through the thick plants and shadowed underbrush. "Seems like we've found the greenhouse," Olibtine announced.

"Yup. You know, Guane has a greenhouse?" she asked, squatting and squinting into the room.

"I didn't," he replied, still searching within the red light, "but it makes sense."

"He used to have me take care of them all the time. Plants I had never seen before his greenhouse. Odd things, plants. Some think that plants all want the same thing - food, water, and sunlight. But that isn't the case at all. Guane used to say that plants need love and affection just like everything else in the Uradaria. You can feed them the most nutritious food, give them the cleanest water, and give them the best sunlight, but if you don't give them love and affection, they'll wilt. I didn't believe him at first and tried a little experiment on my own. I had two of the same plants and gave them both the same food, water, and sunlight, but took one to the side and stroked its leaves, talked to it, and told it I liked it the best." Olibtine's eyebrows went up, trying to picture Daria, this hardened woman, doing such a thing. "And you know what? It grew faster, stronger, and was more colorful than the one I didn't do that with. Sure, the other one did fine, but I had come to the realization that living things need more than just the basic necessities to flourish."

It's true. I was simply getting by before I became a Problem Solver and then a Mind. While not quite love and affection, it gave me a purpose, which is what love and affection are - a purpose.

Guane flashed into his head, the man he respected more than any other, which made his resolve strengthen. *I will save you and everyone in Gbinti.*

Daria stood, adjusting her pack. "So, we have to go through this, huh? It's hard to tell with the red light, but I think I see some poisonous plants in there. That pointy short one right there," she pointed bending over to guide Olibtine's eyes, "is definitely poisonous. Guane has it in his greenhouse."

Why did I bring the Topography and Plants book if she already knows this? Olibtine attempted to recall the plant she called out, but nothing matched what he read. *Not like I'll need it now.*

"Okay, so we have poisonous plants this close to the door so it's a good bet that there are more inside. Who knows what else is in there as well."

Daria shrugged. "If we make sure our skin is covered and don't rub on the plants or get poked by them, we should be good. I've been poked by tons of plants and most just make the body part it hits go numb for a little bit. Kind of fun."

Olibtine shook his head, a smirk appearing on his lips. *That's it?*

Daria removed her pack and pulled out a dozen items of clothing, placed it all into a haphazard pile, then covered the exposed skin up to her eyeballs with what she had. Realizing what she was doing, Olibtine followed suit, feeling like he was already sweating through the clothing he had on - adding more just made it worse. They shouldered their packs looking at one another draped from eyeballs to fingertips to shoes in layers of cloth, Daria holding a knocked bow and arrow just in case, and Olibtine holding his knife. Daria looked back into the overgrown room, searching for the perfect entrance, then stepped inside, lifting her knees high to minimize the potential of plants rubbing on her. Olibtine stepped in behind her, mimicking her every step. The ground felt squishy under his feet with every step, like a field full of grass where it had just rained. He glanced around while they crept, red lights from above casting eerie shadows in all directions due to the taller plants nearby. Some had gigantic leaves that were the size of his own body while others looked like swords sticking out of the ground in clusters. The stillness of it all gave him an impossible chill on the back of his neck causing his body to shiver.

Daria stopped in front of a thick-trunked plant that looked like it belonged to a much larger tree like ones in The Forest. She leaned in and noticed something strange.

"Look at this," she pointed, "but be careful of those two knee-high purple and yellow plants to the right there - you don't want to touch those or else you'll be asleep in minutes."

Olibtine froze before slowly turning his head, his eyeballs straining towards the ground. *Wish she would have told me before.* He crept forward with eyes locked on the plants, giving them plenty of birth. In doing so, he accidentally scrapes his calf against a one behind him. He looked down and back, his heart racing, body stiffening to see a plant with broad leaves with fluorescent purple veins running through it. *Caught a thick part of my pant,* he hoped, not wanting to bend over to see if it somehow made it through the layers to his skin. Eyes wide, he found Daria looking at him with her eyebrow raised.

"You okay?" she asked, standing with legs slightly spread, a tiny green plant beneath her.

"Yeah, I just... Oh, nothing. What is it?" Olibtine replied, shuffling a few half-steps until he stood right behind her.

"This. It looks like... something scratched it, like a marking you would see in The Forest from a large animal."

He leaned around her, seeing two deep gashes in the trunk the size of his torso. "What could have done that?" he asked.

"Not sure, but keep your eyes open," she shrugged, her voice level, but the grip on her bow tightened.

***

"Kill! Kill," a high-pitched voice came from under the deep-black robe. The sorcerer paced back and forth along the stone floor, fidgeting her hands in the room with cages, each housing a different type of creature, both natural and unnatural. She stopped abruptly, hands going still, the hood of her cloak shifting to her right as she quickly turned, examining the creatures in the cage. She stepped forward, the small creatures stirring in unison, their finger-length yellow and blue spines vibrating as their black eyes watched the sorcerer close in on them. She stopped short of their cage, knowing that even her magic could not stop them from killing her if even one of the spines touched her. Movement in the larger cage to the right caught her eye while she was contemplating sending the small, spiny creatures down below. She shuffled to stand in front of the larger cage, her eyes studying the unnatural creature's two foot long scythes in place of arms that were as long as its entire, green body, which in of itself was one section, no discernable head or eyes, with a dozen small tentacles sticking out the bottom for movement.

The sorcerer's hands began fidgeting again as she glanced back to the small, spiny creatures, then back to the one she was standing in front of. With a flourish, she turned, moving to stand behind the ujuntu basin in the middle of the room, uncovering her hands in the process. She closed her eyes, placing the fingertips of one hand inside of the basin and mumbling something incoherent, picturing the plant room. Once she had the image perfectly in her head, she opened her eyes, fixating on the small, spiny creatures, the black of her robe growing darker, expanding beyond its normal bounds. A deep red emanates from the ujuntu basin, fighting against the black. Then, a black and red mist in the shape of a disjointed hand appears out of nowhere inside of the cage, engulfing the creatures from above, then slams down on them in an instant, the creatures vanishing without a trace. The mist shoots out of the sides of the cage between the bars, slowly falling to the stone ground, evaporating as if it were never there. She held her concentration, placing her other hand into the basin next to the first, mumbling, the plant room still in her head, and stared at the creature with the scythe arms. The ujuntu basin's red glow pulsates as the dark mist hand forms again, slamming down on to the creature, completely disappearing while the mist falls to the floor. The sorcerer's legs shake beneath her weight, her hands slide from the basin, her eyelids become heavy as the red glow fades. She crumples to the stone floor, too weak to climb the stairs to the library to rest. A smile creeps to her face, hidden by the dark robe.

"Kill. Kill."

***

Daria stood ahead of Olibtine, her eyes darting to find a clear path ahead, but no matter where she looked, she could not find anything. After ensuring nothing would touch his head nearby, Olibtine cautiously leaned around her through the red-tinted shadows and understood why she wasn't moving anywhere. *Those spikes coming off of the trees look like they could pierce the thickest of armor.* He shivered thinking about what they would do to the cloth he was wearing. *And that looks like a giant, open mouth with teeth, each as long as a man's arm.*

"Do you see a way through?" he asked, already knowing the answer.

Daria shook her head. "We're going to have to find another way. Let's turn around and retrace our steps to see if we can find another way."

Olibtine slowly turned, making sure to not rub against any of the plants below, keeping an eye out for the tree they looked at before. A rustling of leaves nearby caused him to pause mid-step. "What was that?" he whispered. They stood with baited breath for a moment, then the sound of plants rustling off to the left caught his attention making him cough. His head shot towards it, trying to judge how far off it was, leaning forward and nearly losing his balance.

"We're not alone," Daria whispered from behind.

Olibtine slowly craned his neck towards her, only able to see her with one eye from the position he was standing, but enough to see that she was staring down an arrow, bow fully taught to her ear. He instinctively reached for his knife, pulling it out at the ready looking the same direction she was, the shadows from the taller plants providing very little visibility, the red lights above playing tricks on his eyes. He saw one of the large leaves move in the same place he thought he heard the movement from earlier, and within a breath, he heard the familiar whizzing sound of an arrow followed by a soft screeching sound. He glanced at Daria again, the arrow gone from her grip, bow relaxed ahead of her. *How...* Olibtine awed. Before he could get a word out, Daria started to creep towards him, keeping an eye on the area where the screeching sound came from. She passed by him carefully and rounded the tree with the two gashes in it, then picked her foot up high, stamping down a plant ahead of her, then another. Once in a spot near where her arrow landed where she could squat, she reached out slowly, then stood up holding the arrow's shaft, a small creature punctured through with what looked like little spines on its back. Olibtine followed in Daria's footsteps, wanting to get a closer look at it. Daria moved the arrow closer to him as he arrived while still making sure to keep it at a safe distance. That's when he noticed how colorful it was. In any other context he would have thought it beautiful, but the spikes said it was just as deadly as it was beautiful.

"What is it?" he asked with narrowed eyebrows. "It has spines like a Marpet's quills, but is too small to be one of them, and I've only seen colors like that on creatures in the seas." *I still have so much to learn about this world.* That excited and disappointed him at the same time.

"This, I don't know," Daria answered, turning the arrow over to look at the other side of it. "Guane always said that the more colorful things are, the more a warning they are giving to potential predators, and so it's best to guess that this is something incredibly poisonous. Best leave it here," she finished, placing the arrow and animal safely behind the tree with the gashes in it.

"This way looks more open." she nodded towards what looked like a path off to the right. Without waiting for a response, she knocked another arrow before beginning forward slowly, one careful step at a time, her feet silent even in the squishy dirt.

Olibtine followed in her steps, knife still in hand. *How come we didn't hear that thing until just now? Was it waiting for us to get closer?* He glanced around into the deep, red shadows, sweat sliding down his forehead threatening his vision. He saw another plant move off in the distance, one that easily came up to his chest, but Daria kept moving and so he followed. A rustling off to the right made his head jolt, his body freezing, his knife hand gripping tighter. "Daira," he whispered, squinting towards the sound. "Daria," he repeated.

"I know," she whispered back, "just keep moving." She took another calculated step forward.

Olibtine was fully aware of his clothes sticking to his skin as a bead of sweat slid down his forehead, down his cheek, dropping to the moist soil, the knife becoming slippery in his hand. He wiped his left hand on the outside layer of his clothing, accomplishing nothing with how wet his clothes were. The air was thick, forcing him to breathe heavier, but with each breath he felt like he was breathing in just as much moisture as air. Another rustling sound from behind him caused his ears to twitch, almost making him jump and turn if it wasn't for him watching Daria continuing her steady pace forward. She slinkied around a tall, fat plant with huge leaves hovering above that looked like it was surrounded in cotton. He followed her footsteps all the while the rustling behind was getting closer and closer. A loud scratching noise off to their left, like that of something digging into a tree trunk, finally made Daria stop, and in one motion, she spun pulling the arrow she had knocked back to her ear, preparing to fire.

We're being hunted, Olibtine realized, turning to cover their rear where he heard the plants moving, his eyes darting between plants, trees, and undergrowth trying to find the source. They stood back to back, each taking deep, mouthy breaths as if they had just ran from Gbinti to the tower itself. The silence in that moment was deafening, blood pumping through their ears, sweat threatening their vision forcing them to blink hard in an attempt to wipe it away, not wanting to give their positions away.

"Moss!" Olibtine heard Daria curse under her breath. He could feel her back relax as if dropping the tension on her bow. He turned his head towards her, keeping his ears open and focused on everything else, and saw she had indeed dropped her bow to her side, the arrow gone from her hand, whether shot or put away, he didn't know.

"What are you doing?!" he asked frantically, licking the salty sweat from his lip.

She didn't answer, only dug into her coat pocket and pulled out two small vials.

The mushrooms for light? He scrunched his eyebrows. *What is that going to do?* "You don't think those are going to help us now do you?!" he protested.

She shot him a glance that made him flinch, her black eyes squinting with eyebrows and mouth narrow. *Moss!* he cursed to himself, biting his lips, instincts telling him to hold his tongue. Without a word, she turned back the opposite way of him, shook one of the vials vigorously, then threw it in the direction of the scraping noise they heard earlier. He watched the vial fly, blue appearing inside of it, first soft, then expanding, overtaking the reds from above and illuminating the plants it flew past. He didn't hear or see it land, but a second after it disappeared behind a group of thicker brushes, it exploded in the most brilliant blue - like that of a sky on a cloudless day. The intensity forced him to close his eyes and shield them with his arm, but even then the blue snuck through it all. As soon as it began, it ended. He felt it before he opened his eyes - an intense heat, that which put the heat of the room itself to shame. A bright blue fire had engulfed the area where the vile landed, sending everything up in flame from the ground itself to the highest plants, the red glow from above being swallowed up. The crackling of leaves and branches overpowered the blood pumping through his ears, making him forget what he was doing.

Daria put her arm around Olibtine, pushing his head down, shaking him out of his trance. Another bright blue flash appeared against the fire ahead of him, coming from... *Behind*, he realized, wanting to glance back, but Daria's hand held him forward.

"What is that?!" he yelled over the roar of the fire.

"Plan B," she replied. A number of pained, high-pitched squeals similar to the one before cut through to them, the combination of which overshadowed the crackling and roar of the expanding fire.

"We have to run!" Daria yelled. Olibtine nodded in response, pocketing his knife, but unable to find his words. "That way!" she pointed off to the opposite direction they came - the only area not currently engulfed in flames.

She took off running, high-stepping, leaping, jumping to the left and right, trying to dodge all the plants she could. Olibtine struggled to replicate her steps, falling behind.

He felt a stab of pain in his leg as they ran by another one of those plants with sharp spines the size of a man's arm sticking out, overcompensating and brushing his hand against a slimy plant on the opposite side. He caught movement in the corner of his eye to the left, but kept his eyes forward, refusing to tear his eyes away from Daria and the plants ahead. She swatted a large leaf towards the ground rather than going around it, Olibtine following suit. He noticed her head turn to the left for a moment. *She sees it too!* He jumped over a circular plant that Daria had, landing with a squish on the soggy floor. They ran, dodging as many plants as they could, but with how bunched and numerous they were, it was impossible. All they could do is rely on the thickness of their layers, feeling that the thing hunting them was much more of a threat than plants.

Olibtine saw it again from the corner of his eye, only this time something reflected the red light from above. Curiosity overwhelmed his mind, and with a quick glance, he finally saw it. An outline of two, massive claws that looked like gigantic, curved swords, backlit by fire. His eyes bulged at the sight, which caused him to forget what he was doing. He stumbled over something, barely catching himself on a plant's trunk with his left hand, a sharp pain immediately shooting through his hand, up his arm. He screamed, removing his hand from the trunk and holding his wrist tight with the other. Tears of pain filled his eyes as he looked down at his hand, skin and blood bubbling in the red light. He felt Daria's hand on his forearm, pulling him towards her. He looked up, and through tears, saw her mouth moving, but only heard the fire raging behind and his hand throbbing in pain. He blinked the tears away as others filled their place. He nodded without knowing what for, and let her pull him away, stumbling through the dense plants underfoot, unable to focus on anything but the pain.

Daria paused before a pair of thick trunks in a small clearing surrounded by dense plants on all sides. The firelight cast a low shadow half-way into the clearing. She looked back at Olibtine, still holding his forearm. *Moss.* She realized they could no longer outrun the creature chasing them. She measured Olibtine's condition, his face scrunched in agony, then glanced at his hand, bubbled up like he had placed it in a furnace, then decided now was their only chance. She guided Olibtine to the opposite side of the clearing where the firelight reflected his glossy, far away eyes, then helped him to the ground. After the second time of telling him to wait without a response, she knelt beside him, one foot forward, knee on the ground beneath her, pulled out an arrow, then readied her bow. *It will be coming from that direction,* she stared, attempting to slow her breath like she had done hundreds of times when hunting in The Forest. The flames, no longer blue, but growing hotter by the second, flickered to her left, engulfing more plants as it crawled forward, searching for more kindling to fuel itself. Her eyes darted across the short clearing, not even ten feet wide. *Only one chance for this.* She held her breath, pulled the string back to her ear, then watched it leap through the plants on the other side - a hideous, other-worldly creature with two massive claws extended above its body ready to strike. It moved forward as if gliding over the ground, straight towards her.

She let the arrow loose, connecting with the center of its body, imbedding itself half-way through the thing. It faltered at the hit, but kept moving, only a few feet from them. She pulled another arrow as quick as she could, but by the time she had it knocked, the claws were slicing through the air towards her. She pushed hard off her front foot, standing while taking a step back, her arms spreading to ensure she wasn't hit with the claws that slammed down into the ground where her foot was just seconds earlier. The thing jerked, trying to free its claws. Daria knocked the arrow, elevating her angle over it where she thought its head might be, then loosed it, embedding the arrow through the top of the thing, the force of the hit puncturing clean through, the tip sticking out the back of it. It went still, sharp claws still embedded into the ground.

Daria breathed out, staring at the thing leak thick, black blood from its wounds. *Moss, that's ugly.* She felt the heat from the fire grow closer still. She put her bow away, moved over to Olibtine, who was still conscious, yet blind to what had just occurred. *If you only knew.* She grabbed his right arm and threw it over her shoulder with a grunt. Giving the thing one more look, she glanced around trying to find an exit from the room, giving the fire a momentary glance. *Only one thing to do.* She set off the opposite way of the fire, Olibtine surprisingly moving his feet with her steps, even if labored. *Impossible to dodge the plants now with him in tow - we'll have to hope these aren't that bad.* They slowly made their way forward while keeping her eyes down just in case she should see something deadly.

"There!" she announced, noticing a red tinted wall in front of them not far off. "But where is the..." she started, looking for a door. *If each level is similar, the staircase should be on the back left.* She turned left along the back wall, remembering the previous floor. *Wooden door. Wooden door.* Her eyes darted along the wall, attempting to wish it into existence, the fire gaining on them, overtaking the deep red lights above as the primary source of light. She strained to speed up their pace following the wall, Olibtine speechlessly following her lead, and then she saw it - a shiny spot reflecting the firelight. *A door handle!* She glimpsed with eyes wide, realizing there was an outline of a wooden door in the furthest corner of the room possible.

"We're almost there!" she assured Olibtine over the roar of the fire, as if he could comprehend. They stumbled forward through large and small plants alike, ignoring the pains shooting up her legs from the needles they were moving through, eyes set on their goal. She reached the door, grabbed the handle, an inaudible click sounding in her ears, remembering the doors below, then threw it open. A cool, dry wind swept over her, chilling her to the bone and causing a shiver to creep up her spine. They stumbled through the doorway feeling the familiar stone beneath their feet. Daria placed Olibtine down gently against the opposite wall, then strode back to the doorway, watching momentarily as the fire continued to expand throughout the room, a slight pain in her heart seeing what she had to do. She slammed the door shut, a darkness engulfing them, then shivered once again.

Chapter 32: The Next Attempt

The pair of sorcerers knelt around the large ujuntu basin at the top of the tower preparing for their next spell.

"Are you sure of this? Doing so might upset our employers," the rumbling voice asked, while positioning herself on her knees.

"They have waited long enough," replied the monotone voice to her right.

"Even if this..."

"Enough!" interrupted the monotone voiced sorcerer, snapping her head under her hood to face the other as the darkness beneath coiled out like a dense fog. "This WILL be done now!"

Without another word, both sorcerers placed their fingers into the water, glanced at the book in between them and began chanting under their breath, darkness spilling from their bodies, a dark red light emanating from the basin, until the two fought for supremacy in the room atop tower.

The sorcerers' chanting went silent, bodies hunched over, completely oblivious to the world around their mortal bodies, minds elsewhere.

Chapter 33: Knowledge

The only light spilling into the stairwell that Daria and Olibtine sat in was through the small cracks below the door, the fire they escaped burning itself out on the other side. Daria could hear Olibtine breathing normally, which was a good sign, but every so often she'd hear a guttural grunt escape his lips from the pain in his hand. She felt drowsy, but she wasn't sure if that was from the life-threatening levels of the tower itself or the scratches she received from the plants. After drinking a few gulps of water, she started to dispel the extra layers that were thoroughly soaked through from sweat.

"Can you take your extra layers off, too?" she asked in the dark. A grunt followed, but she wasn't sure if that was a normal one from pain or a yes, but after hearing rustling of clothes come from the spot she laid Olibtine, she assumed that was a yes.

After getting down to her normal clothing and putting the extras away in her bag, she almost forgot that the mushroom vials were still in there. *Moss,* she cursed to herself for not thinking of it earlier. She pulled one out, shook it, and it started to glow a soft blue, illuminating the small landing they were in. She placed it between the two of them to give equal lighting, then proceeded to check the wounds on her body. A few scratches on her leg were long, but shallow, not showing any sign or swelling or discoloration out of the norm like she'd seen back home from experimenting with Guane's plants. Her hands were a little swollen and her fingertips were numb. *Probably from moving those leaves around, but this might cause problems with my bow if I can't feel it. Not bad overall though.* Hesitatingly, she looked over at Olibtine.

"Olibtine!" she gasped, her throat catching before scurrying his way, snatching up the vial as she went. Shining the light on his hand made her cringe, the putrid smell of burnt hair and flesh just as bad as the sight of it. "That looks like you put your hand in a fire and just held it there!" she exclaimed, looking into his droopy eyes to see that he was lucid, but barely, crust on the sides of his mouth showing he was severely dehydrated. She pulled a canteen from his pack, tilting his head back and forcing him to take a few gulps of water, his eyes shutting tight. After it started to flow, he grabbed the canteen for himself and gulped even more down. *He seems to just be in a lot of pain.* She glanced at his hand again. *I have never seen any kind of plant do this before.*

"Okay, we have to take care of your hand. I'm going to pour some water on it, which is going to hurt. A lot. I'm then going to rub some numbing solution from this vial..." she held up a green vial she grabbed from her pack just moments ago, "... and put it on your hand, then wrap it up tight. It's something Guane used to give me when I was training to speed my recovery. It numbs the area, but also has healing properties. Funny thing with plants, they can harm as well as cure - I'll need to see what other injuries you have as well from those plants. You ready?" she asked, popping the top of the vial.

Olibtine nodded slowly, biting on some cloth on his sleeve.

Daria put both vials down within close reach, then grabbed Olibtine's forearm along with the canteen of water. After a quick glance and a nod, she tilted the canteen, pouring water on his hand. A muffled yell escaped through the cloth as he tried to jerk away, but Daria held on tight. Quickly, Daira set the canteen down, then picked the vial up, shook a glob of the thick green substance on her fingertips, placed the vial back down, then without hesitation rubbed the substance deep into Olibtine's hand. He screamed into the cloth again, the visceral cry echoing up the stone stairway into forever. Tears were forced from his eyes as he squeezed them tight through the pain, free hand clenched into a white-knuckled fist as he pushed against the stone floor. Satisfied that the substance was applied thoroughly enough, she placed his hand gently on his lap before grabbing one of her extra shirts and ripping a sleeve off, wrapping it tightly around his entire hand, only his fingertips open to the air.

"Done," she huffed out, sitting back and wiping sweat from the fur on her forehead. *At least he has his other hand.* She watched his fist loosen as the numbing agent set in. His eyes opened, sweat mixing with tears as his body slouched, sleeve dropping from his mouth.

"Thank... You," Olibtine forced out, his throat still dry. He took a swig of water. "Thank you for that. And that," he finished, nodding to the door.

"We're even now," Daria shrugged with a smirk. "Here, now let me check your cuts. Where are your wounds?"

"My right calf," he answered, rolling his body over with a grunt. Daria held the vial up to his calf. Through a slice in his pants, she could see a bloody gash surrounded by green puss. She bit her lips in order to hold back any comments that might squeeze out from her lips.

She kept her voice flat, not wanting to raise suspicion. "I need your knife." Olibtine dug it out of his pocket and handed it to her. She cut the pants more for a better view, noticing the green puss was only around the edges. "I have to scrape this off." She glanced up at him, her jaw tight. "It might hurt."

Olibtine nodded, biting his sleeve again in anticipation. Daria set the vial down, grabbed his leg above the wound, turned the knife so the dull side was down, and attempted to scrape the pus off of the corners of the wound, Olibtine twitching at every touch. It wasn't coming off. She hesitantly turned the knife over so the sharp side was down, then, starting from one side, she dug the knife in, drawing blood, then scraped, pushing the skin down, but removing the pus in return. Olibtine writhed with pain, nearly as much as his hand, but held his leg in place, fearing what would happen if he twitched even an inch. Scraping the last bits away, along with some skin she accidentally went too deep on, and flinging it into the dark, she grabbed more of the green substance from the vial nearby and rubbed it into the wound. His body stiffened as she did. She tore another strip from her shirt and wrapped the wound as tight as she could, forcing the bleeding she created to stop.

"Done," she breathed out, wiping the knife off, then the sweat from the fur on her brow.

Olibtine breathed heavily, dropping the sleeve from his mouth, then sat back up, back resting against one of the steps.

"Ow," he grimaced, leaning his head back to wait for the numbing agent to enact.

"Ow indeed," she replied, shrugging, "who knew that plants were more dangerous than rocks?"

Olibtine forced his head upright, a smile crossing his face, which made Daria smile in return until she realized that they weren't out of this yet. She glanced above his head into the dark stairway, smile fading almost as soon as it appeared. Olibtine noticed her eyes leaving his and without looking in the same direction she was, knew what she was thinking. *How much more is there?* he asked himself. *Is this worth it?*

He shook himself, clenching his uninjured hand into a fist. *Of course it is! This is for an entire city - maybe even life as we know it. I have to find answers.*

He took one more swig of water, no longer sweating from the plant room, then placed the canteen back into his pack. "We aren't there yet," he groaned, propping himself against the stairs to stand, forcing himself up and grabbing his pack in one fluid motion. Standing over Daira, he held out his hand. She glanced at it, then locked eyes. The glossy look from minutes ago only a distant memory. She reached up and took his hand, allowing him to pull her up, standing face to face, noticing an intensity in his eyes she recognized from the first time they met from what seemed like many moons ago. She removed her hand, replacing it with the knife she held. He squeezed it, then pocketed it once again, nodding. She picked up the vials and her pack in turn, then walked up beside him facing the stairway, lighting the way.

Olibtine took the steps one at a time, a slow, methodical one foot and then the other, laboring his injured leg. It wasn't after but a few steps that his breathing became ragged again, nearly panting, as they climbed, but their progress proceeded. The silence of the starway was oddly comforting to him. He'd always enjoyed his dark study room back in Gbinti - only a single candle to light his desk and his smoke billowing from his pipe. He suddenly missed smoking, knowing that if he were to smoke any right now, it would make his mind and body protest at all the movements he had been doing in the tower. *This mossing tower.. These mossing sorcerers.* He paused on a step to lean on the outer wall facing Daria, needing a break, and pulled out his canteen to take a swig.

He looked at his wrapped hand amazed that he didn't feel the pain anymore. "How long does the numbing agent last?" he asked, looking up and meeting Daria's eyes.

She shrugged. "It varies. The few times I needed it, it lasted for quite a while, but the times that I've seen Guane use it, he reapplied it after every meal we had. There is more of it in the vial, so if you need more, just tell me."

He nodded, looking down at his hand again. *It's better than any medicine we have in the Council - how did I not know about it?*

"I think we're getting close to the top," Daria hoped, holding up the mushroom vial to light the stairs above. She shrugged, "Just a hunch though."

Olibtine frowned, eyebrows rising as he followed her eyes. *Sure would be nice.*

"Well, let's keep moving." He placed the canteen back in his pack. Settling himself, he began climbing again, Daria step in step to his right. A few steps later, he noticed the light hitting a flat wall on the back of a landing while the stairs continued on. *Another room?* He craned his neck to get a glance at the opposite side. Two more steps confirmed his suspicions, but the door was different from the ones below - it was solid stone. He stopped, legs protesting, his heart racing quicker, subconsciously reaching for his knife, feeling... something. Something different than anything he had ever felt in his life. He glanced at Daria, who already had her bow out with an arrow knocked in one hand, the other with the glowing vial in it still.

"You feel it too?" he whispered, fidgeting with his knife.

Daria nodded, whispering back, "I do. What is it?"

"Not sure, but it's different from what's below."

They tensed, hearing a sound come from the room that resembled a crow. They glanced at one another, lips curled in under their teeth. Olibtine nodded to her, then took the rest of the slow, silent steps to the door's landing. With each step, they felt as if the air around them were getting darker, trying to snuff out the vial Daria held before her. *What do we do now?* He wracked his brain. *And what if something is on the other side?* He glanced up the stairway. *Maybe we see what is up there first?*

He looked back at Daria who seemed to be thinking the same thing he was, for she pushed the vial at arms length towards the stairs, lighting as much as she could. She met his eyes with downturned eyebrows, nodding. They turned slowly towards the stairs, not wanting to make a sound, then proceeded to climb, fear driving their ascent faster than before. After the landing was out of sight, the dark feeling faded to almost nothing, just a lingering feeling in the back of their heads. Only a dozen or so silent steps later, another landing appeared ahead of them, a sliver of yellowish red light spilling out down the steps through a crack in a large, ornate wooden door that sat ajar. Olibtine stepped into the sliver of light to see if he could glimpse anything inside, but all he saw was a fire burning in a fireplace that held what he thought were books on top of it. He crept to the door, focused on the opening, noticing that he didn't feel the presence below any longer. *That's at least a good sign,* he hoped, peering into the room. After adjusting to the light, his eyes grew wide as he noticed that those were indeed books on a fireplace, but also there were books everywhere. The walls were filled from top to bottom with all shapes and sizes of books and the floors had stacks upon stacks of books as well. *This library puts the Mind's to shame,* he gaped, unconsciously pushing the door open slowly to see more. He heard Daria rush at him from behind, squeezing his shoulder and pulling him back, halting his entrance.

She looked down at him with eyes wide in horror as if asking what he was doing. Olibtine didn't say anything in return, just nodded towards the entrance to the room, guiding her eyes. She looked into the sliver of light, squinting and noticing the same thing he did. Daria looked back down at Olibtine and shrugged as if to say 'So?'. He looked back into the room. *This could be it. We have to go in.* He ignored Daria's hand of protest and pushed the door open inch by inch until his head could stick through. This one, unlike the one leading into the plant room, was well greased, giving no hint as to what was happening. He got on his hands and knees, wincing at the pain in his hand that was creeping through the medicine, then poked his entire head into the room. It was just what he expected - more books than he could count lined every wall next to which stacks of books were haphazardly piled high, lit by a single fireplace towards the front of the room. In the middle of the room, completely out of place, was a standalone black pedestal with a basin and book sitting on top of it. *No one.* He released a breath he held, removing his head from the door.

Olibtine looked back at Daria, her eyebrows raised with curiosity. "No one is in there," he whispered as he stood, pushing the door open slowly until he could fit through the opening. It was warmer in the room than the stairway, but pleasantly so - nothing like the plant room below. He awed up at the vaulted ceiling, then down a corner of the room at the stacks of books. "There might be some answers in here," he whispered to Daria, who was gazing around the room, eyes wide with amazement. Her eyes fell on the pedestal in the center of the room. Glancing momentarily at Olibtine with narrowed eyebrows above a questioning frown, she moved slowly over to see what was on it. Olibtine followed, noticing upon first glance that the basin was made of ujuntu like they had found in the rooms below, and that it was filled with what looked like plain water. The book is what caught his eye, though - it was turned to a page with text he couldn't read with an image of a winding staircase that seemed to vanish into nothing. *The staircase!* Eyes wide, he recalled the painful climb they had endured upon entering the tower. *They really did do that. And with this.* His eyes glided over the text next to the drawing, unable to make anything of it. He'd never seen anything like it in the library of the Minds. His hand trembled as he reached up to turn the page, whether from excitement or fear, he couldn't have said. *No, focus.* He pulled back his hand.

"Okay, let's search the room for anything about the Bloodborn - specifically their passing," he whispered. "You take the far side, I'll take the side near the door. Good?" he asked.

Daria nodded. "Good."

They proceeded to opposite ends of the library, Olibtine deciding to shut the door they entered through most of the way just in case, then scoured the spines of the books, noticing that none had titles on them. *Moss,* he cursed, realizing that the only way to do this would be to open each one and begin flipping through. He looked back at Daria, who already had a book in hand and was flipping through the pages. He turned back, grabbing the one at the top of the nearest pile.

The proper ingredients to... he turned a few pages. *A common side effect of the blastvine...* He closed the book, putting it to the side, grabbing the second book in the stack, flipping to a random page. *Time and time again, the native plant species in The Forest...* he flipped later in the book. *The near-extinct Trender, a giant creature with legs like...* He closed the book, putting it on top of the other he set aside, reaching for the third book, then paused. His hand trembled in mid-air, arm hair standing on end. Instinctively, his head darted to the left to stare at the door wide-eyed. *That feeling.* His breath caught, unable to move. *It's getting heavier, like below.*

Chapter 34: Truth

Olibtine felt two hands under his armpits lifting him, forcing him to stand, then dragging him backwards to the back side of the door. Stumbling to keep his feet beneath his body, he looked back and saw Daria holding one finger over her mouth to hush him. *She must feel it too.* He stared at the door, the presence enveloping him. He blinked hard, thinking his imagination was playing tricks on him with the firelight, but it wasn't and the fire was dimming as if being pushed back by some unseen force.

Daria knocked her bow, pulled the arrow back and lifted it to her cheek in one movement. They stood motionless, only the sound of the fire crackling and the quick, quiet exhales from one another filling the air.

Olibtine's eyes grew wide as the door began to swing open slowly, darkness creeping in through the opening like tendrils reaching for prey. He tensed as the door stopped. *The books! It noticed the books!*

"Visitors. Visitors," a high-pitched voice shot through the room, causing a shiver to creep down Olibtine and Daria's bodies. *It's one of the sorcerers!* Olibtine panicked, realizing his knife was still in his pocket. He fumbled pulling it out, palmed it, knuckles white gripping it tight, then noticed his hand was shaking uncontrollably. *Get ahold of yourself!*

The door moved again, snapping him out of it. He searched nearby to see if there was anything of use around him. *Only books.* He pulled a smaller one from the shelf on the wall next to him, pain shooting through his hand as he gripped it. *Moss!* he cursed, jaw clenching, feeling his heartbeat through his hand. He must have made a sound for Daria shot him a wide-eyed look, then glanced down at the book, then back to him. She motioned her head towards the fireplace, which Olibtine understood right away.

He changed the knife and book hand, reared back, and tossed the book through the air as hard as he could towards the fire. It fell short, sending a thunk through the air as it hit solid stone, sliding. Something red shot from the opening of the door and speared the book through, stopping its progress and sticking it to the floor.

Olibtine couldn't think, only stare dumbfounded at the book sitting there, red spear sticking out of it. His eyes shifted back to the door that continued to open slowly causing him to instinctively take a step back, not wanting to be anywhere near the sorcerer. Daria stood fixed in place, bow string taught, focused on the door.

The door, halfway open and perpendicular with where Daria and Olibtine stood, oozed darkness, swallowing the fire in the fireplace to a dim glow, but the sorcerer was still not visible.

"Give up. Give up," the high-pitched voice screeched into the room, sending chills down Olibtine's spine.

"And if we don't?!" Olibtine found himself yelling, taken aback by his own voice.

"Die! Die!" the sorcerer replied.

Before he realized what he was doing, Olibtine had a mushroom vial in hand. He pocketed the knife, enclosing the vial into his palm, then slid both the vial and his hand into his sleeve to hide the light in order to shake it roughly. He reached over and grabbed the biggest book he could carry, pain causing him to grimace. Daria turned and stared at him as if he were crazy, the bow still focused on the door.

"What are you doing?!" she whispered between clenched teeth, a slight tremble in her voice.

"Be ready," he whispered back, shaking the vial that glowed through the gaps in his fingers out the sleeve.

Then, as if being chased by the rock creature, he bolted by Daria, running towards the door as fast as his injured body could carry him, acting before thinking. *Guane would not approve.* He flexed his body before lowering his shoulder, plowing into the door, pain jolting through both shoulder and hand. The door hit something on the other side, whatever it was giving way slightly, a high-pitched grunt sounding on the other side. He gathered himself while pulling the vial out of his sleeve, closed his eyes, then slammed it on the stone floor on the opposite side of the door, bright yellow light engulfing the darkness for a split second.

"Ahhhh!" he heard from the other side - a visceral scream that made him shiver from head to toe. He opened his eyes and the bright light was gone leaving specs in his vision, but the darkness felt less, the firelight filling more of the room than before. He didn't see her move, but Daria was standing closer to the center now, within view of the other side of the door. He flinched as an arrow flew not a foot before his eyes, the whizzing of it cutting through the air, finding its mark in the sorcerer.

"Ahhhh!" the sorcerer howled, causing Olibtine's arm hair to stand on end.

Olibtine willed himself forward and shot out from behind the door, book held in both hands over his head, then slammed it into the first object he saw that looked like a body in the darkness. It connected with a loud *THUNK* as the book vibrated, falling from his hands, pain shooting up his arms, shaking his entire body.

"Move!" he heard from behind.

Olibtine fell to the side towards the fireplace as another whizzing sound flew by his head followed by silence.

The firelight grew, filling the room as it did before, unimpeded, crackling through heavy breathing.

Olibtine stared at the lump on the ground, a near pitch-black lump that didn't move. He scampered up to stand, then made his way around the pedestal to Daria's side.

"Is it..." he trailed off.

"I think so," Daria replied, eyes squinted. "You're dumb for a smart guy I hope you know." Daria's smirk made Olibtine smirk back.

He moved slowly, Daria following step by step, until they were over the black lump that was the sorcerer. He squatted, reached down to turn it over, but before he could do so, the black robe fell flat against the ground, a dark gray cloud of dust escaping the hood and sleeves.

Wide-eyed, he snatched back his hand as if it were a creature baring its teeth.

"Guess that proves it," Daria relaxed. "Moss, that was creepy," she finished, moving the robe around with her bow. "Think there are others in here?"

Olibtine nodded, looking out the open doorway into the dark landing. "Two more. Let's hope they didn't hear this."

He stood, kicked the robe to the side, which caused dust to fall out and float into the air, then shut the door again to leave it cracked open. "Let's get back to work."

The two searched, glancing at the doorway every so often until they felt that enough time had passed that nothing or no one heard what had just happened. The discarded stacks that Olibtine scoured through had a wealth of knowledge, some he'd accidentally gotten lost in, having to shake himself from reading entire pages on spells, creatures, and oddities that didn't fit into the world.

"Olibtine," caught his attention, turning to see that Daria had even more discarded books than he, "I think I found something."

Could this be it? He stood with a grunt, legs stiff from sitting for so long, then hobbled over to Daria. She glanced up as he approached, eyes wide and illuminated from the fire, which never seemed to lose its light no matter how long it burned.

"What is it?" he asked, heart beginning to race. She turned the book around, pointing at the middle of a page.

A Recreation of the Bloodborn Ritual, he read.

His breath caught, reading the line again. He looked up at Daria and was met with a smirk on her face. He hurried over to the fireplace, wanting as much light on the letters as possible, illuminating both pages as he turned his back to it, then began to read it aloud.

"The Bloodborn ritual of the passing has occurred for countless millennia, wasting not a drop of blood as time passes. The first occurrence of the ritual is not known, for the Bloodborn are older than any written histories. There may be oral stories passed down through generations, but I was not privy to any sort. Instead, I was welcomed to one of their rituals as I just so happened to be in their city of Purtghast as a diplomatic duty."

Olibtine paused, flipping back through pages to search for the author. On the first page, he found it. *Natalie Marnuchen.* His eyebrows narrowed, thinking, *Do I know that name?*

He shook his head, decided he didn't want to waste anymore time, so he flipped back to the page and continued reading aloud.

"I will not get into the details of the city itself, which is, and most likely will continue to be, the most beautiful, serene place I had ever stepped foot into. The ritual itself was rather subdued - no lavish parties, parades, or fanfare like they do in the other cities of Uradaria. The one thing that stood out to me the most though was the fact that only women were in attendance. I rarely saw men in the city, in fact. The ritual took place during a full moon and in a large, domed room that was bare of anything but two central beds - not plush beds, but still soft enough looking ones that gave way slightly when the Bloodborn lay. The beds sat off of the ground a ways, side by side, with one enormous ujuntu basin positioned below to catch the excess blood. Surrounding the beds placed on the ground were a number of smaller basins as well. The basin beneath the beds was shaped oddly - almost like a funnel, connected to a smaller, ujuntu basin as a liquid catch. There were two Bloodborn, one very old from the looks of it - wrinkled skin, white hair, barely keeping her eyes open, and having to use a crutch as she walked, and the other young from the looks of it, bright crimson hair splayed out around her shoulders. She could have been hundreds of years old for all I knew with how the Bloodborn aged."

"The two lay on the beds side by side, looking as if they didn't have a care in the world, surrounded by Bloodborn women of all ages, but all dressed in the Bloodborn red and purple robes with the single blood teardrop symbol on the front. The full moon shined bright overhead through the glass roof, the room alight as if it were the sun that was above us. The old and young Bloodborn connected hands, interlacing fingers, and stared at one another while the Bloodborn surrounding them dropped to their knees, faces hidden underneath hoods, then placed their hands into the smaller basins, which were filled with water, in front of them."

"Then, they began to chant. To this day, I do not know what was said, but it was one that I wish I never have to hear again. The chants started as a slow, quiet harmony - something you would hear in a group of bards rattling off, except somber and serious. The water in their basins began glowing red, illuminating their faces, and it was then that I could see that their eyes were shut, but their faces were as calm as a newborn in a deep sleep. The red glow enveloped the beds in the middle. The tempo of the chants began to rise together, filling the room with a mixture of voices, and then suddenly there was a break in the harmony where each Bloodborn was chanting something different, but keep in mind that I didn't understand what was being said in the first place, so it could have fooled me. Once the mis-harmony started, the air in the room itself changed. Gone, the calm, cool air - replaced with something heavy and dense with the moon at its peak directly above the two Bloodborn lying on the beds."

"This is where the ritual truly began. Blood began releasing from every pore of the old Bloodborn, seemingly defying gravity by floating in small droplets right above her. Her complexion changed almost immediately, the color of her skin turning whiter by the second from lack of blood, nearly glowing in the moonlight. Her blood - all of her blood - hovered over her creating an outline of her body. The chanting came to a fever pitch, a cacophony of seemingly random sounds echoing off of the walls and through my body causing my heart to race as if wanting to beat through my chest. The young Bloodborn's hand tightened around the old, and then the blood began to rush down the old Bloodborn's arm and into the young one's fingertips. The young Bloodborn convulsed, her back arching, legs flailing, her mouth opening and shutting as if saying something, but no words reached me. The blood moved in a wave towards, and into, the young Bloodborn while the old one lay motionless next to her, sheet white in the moonlight. It must have only been a minute, but it felt like much longer watching this ritual unfold. Once the last droplet had entered the young Bloodborn, she stilled, the chanting ceased, the red glow slowly fading away, moonlight engulfing the room once again. Suddenly, the young Bloodborn released her grip on the old one, and shot up into a sitting position, a blood curdling scream escaping her mouth, eyes wide with fear, holding the sides of her head as if in agony. That sight sent chills down my spine - the typically subdued Bloodborn, screaming in agony, cutting right through to my bones. I fell back, barely catching myself on the wall behind, frightened of the unexpected."

"The young Bloodborn slowly worked herself into silence, never taking her hands from her head. The moon's shadows elongated as the Bloodborn surrounding the beds began rising, almost laboring as if finishing a strenuous trek. They then slowly made their way to the old Bloodborn lying motionless on the bed, touching her hands, feet, head, arms, whatever they were closest to, and then repeated the same to the young Bloodborn, speaking something softly under their breaths. One of the Bloodborn calmly walked over to me, saying the ritual was finished, and then guided me out of the room. Leaving, I glanced back at the young Bloodborn, her head still in her hands, knees to her chest, now rocking back and forth with tears in her eyes."

"I did not hear of the attack until after I returned to Rulnart, and by then, I witnessed it myself. Fires, since extinguished, had seemingly engulfed the entire city, leveling anything that was vulnerable, but that wasn't the worst part. No, the worst part of it all was the massacre of countless Rulnarts, a peaceful people built on trade and commerce. Once I got over the smell that could not be snuffed out even through multiple water-soaked layers over my mouth and nose, my eyes stopped watering enough to see the carnage. Blood pooled on every path in the city providing nowhere to walk without getting blood on your soles. Bodies lie everywhere my eyes looked, skewered straight through, limbs cleanly cut off by something that was not a normal weapon. Clothes and skin alike, burnt, fear covering every face I dared to look at, even after death. The only things that moved in the city were us. No sounds, no scavengers, no breath."

"I searched the mountains and plains nearby for survivors and found far too few in order to rebuild a city ourselves, each mentally incomplete after going through such horrors, but there was a consensus from each one of them. Bloodborn - a crimson Bloodborn - and only one. But why? How? If I were there, would they have slaughtered me, too? The normally peaceful Bloodborn turning into such ravenous creatures. I couldn't believe it and so I will set off back to Purtghast to find even more answers."

Olibtine turned the page, the writing revealing no further information about the Bloodborn or the ritual or Natalie's trip back to Purtghast.

He closed the book, taking a drink of water to clear his parched throat, then sat in silence with Daria as the fire crackled beside them. *Does the ritual have something to do with these incidents? This text and the others back in Gbinti all say something like that happens after a passing, but can it be coincidence?*

"Well, that wasn't pretty," Daria broke the silence, her arm resting on the fireplace mantle after standing, staring into the ever-burning fire. She glanced over to Olibtine. "Does this mean that the ritual makes them do that?"

He locked eyes with her, a deep frown on both of their faces, then glanced at the cover of the book. "I'm... not sure, but from everything I've read, from the manuscripts and drawing in Gbinti to this first-person account, it seems more and more likely." He rubbed his eyes. "But why? What changes during the ritual?"

"Regardless, this is enough information for me to sway the Minds into action. Proof that the coming passing could spell destruction for Gbinti." He placed the book and canteen in his pack. "Should we return home?"

The fire crackled, reflected in Daria's dark eyes as she stared at nothing.

"Daira?" Olibtine asked, shaking her shoulder. She shook her head, looking over at him, then glanced towards the spot where they killed the sorcerer, only a black robe left behind.

"I want to see the top," she demanded, a boldness in her voice that didn't reflect on her face.

"What?" Olibtine asked, eyebrows narrowing as he removed his hand from her shoulder to take a step back. "Why? We have what we came for already."

"You think that's enough to convince the Minds? One written account? Why didn't the other ones work if that's all it took?" she protested with raised eyebrows, a harshness to her voice. "What if there was something else at the top of the tower that we could find? More answers to the questions we have even. We've come this far, what's one more floor?"

Olibtine shuffled his feet, feeling uneasy. This isn't the Daria he was used to - she needed this. *It was like her in the ujuntu rooms except this time it's a need, not a want. Is she right? Do I need more evidence than this?* He thought of the book. *Would this convince me if I were skeptical?* He looked up at the domed ceiling, picturing the top of the tower from the outside looking up. *Just one more floor,* he promised himself. "Okay," he agreed, nodding and turning back to Daria, mouth narrow, "but if we get any feeling like we did when that one came nearby, we get out of there."

Daira smiled, then nodded with a quick jerk of her head. "Deal."

Chapter 35: New Omens

Olibtine readied himself for the unknown above, palming the knife and shouldering his pack while Daria unslung her bow. The firelight illuminated the stairwell leading down to the previous level, but their goal was up where the darkness held. Olibtine spun the knife around in his hand, a nervous tick he realized, looking up towards the unknown, the left side of his face feeling the coolness in the stone stairwell, the right side wanting to stay in the warmth of the fireplace, basking in the glow of knowledge. He stepped from the warm light, Daria following, then began the silent climb up the steps.

These steps feel larger, Olibtine noticed, having to look down at his next step more than once on the climb. *Could it just be the oppressive air that has been lingering over us the last two floors?* He stumbled again, his injured hand catching himself on the stairs above causing him to grunt in pain, eyes watering. Daria gripped his shoulder and held him down, forcing him to stay seated. She pulled a vial out of her pack, opened it up, and beckoned for Olibtine's hand. *The medicine,* he saw, holding his hand out while she applied it into his bandages, the pain not nearly as bad as it was below. She put the vial away after applying a generous amount, then stood, eyes narrow and determined, holding out her hand for his. Olibtine grabbed it, allowing himself to be hoisted to his feet again, then started the rest of the climb.

Seeing the top of a closed wooden door a few steps above made them both pause and wipe their brows of the sweat that had accumulated even with the cool air of the staircase. A reddish glow escaped the cracks and crevices around the door, illuminating the stone landing and walls above, creating a gateway that gave Olibtine pause. He glanced at Daria who held her gaze towards the landing, eyes narrow, jaw clenched, and knuckles tight on her bow.

Olibtine steeled himself, nodding. *This could be it.* Daria glanced at him, nodded in return, then without waiting for his response, took the lead up to the door.

The reddish glow enveloped their heads, shoulders, chest, bodies, then feet as they reached the landing. They listened, but only silence returned. Daria gripped the handle, hesitating for a second, then upon an exhale, slowly opened the door inch by inch, an occasional creek in the doorframe causing breaths to be held before continuing. A solid red glow enveloped the room with a small slit open to the landscape beyond in the wall about head high. A small, wooden table sat flush against the wall near the entrance, a small ujuntu basin resting on top. She continued to open the door to reveal that the stone room was circling back on itself in the distance, its ceiling coming to a dramatic point. With the next crack of the door, she noticed the start of a circular, wooden platform about a foot tall, the red light more intense as her eyes continued towards the center of the room. Another push, and...

She froze, eyes wide in horror. *Is that.... A black robe?!* She fumbled the bow in her hand, a wood on wood *thunk* echoing in the room as she smacked it against the door. *Moss, moss, moss!* Daria held her breath, heart racing, trying to stand as still as possible, listening for a response from inside of the room. None came. She glanced back at Olibtine who was holding his breath as well from the looks of it, his eyes bulging as if they would pop out of his skull. *Okay,* she nodded, slowly releasing her breath and turning back towards the door, pushing it open slowly again while keeping her eyes locked on the black robe.

It's not just a black robe, Daria realized, opening the door enough to reveal the source of the red glow - a large ujuntu basin along with gray hands sticking out from the robe, fingertips resting motionless in the water within. *It's a sorcerer!* She panicked, eyes wide, both hands moving to the bow and arrow as she softly shouldered the door open another foot. She gulped upon noticing yet another lump - another sorcerer - in the same position as the first off to its right, robe hiding their entire bodies except for their hands. Bow knocked and ready, she crept inside, nodding Olibtine in while giving him a wide-eyed nod down towards the motionless bodies.

What? Olibtine's heart raced with anticipation. Responding to her motion he tried his hardest to creep silently through the doorway. He was enveloped by the soft red glow as he entered, looking right to where Daria had her sights transfixed upon, then froze, throat caught, unsure of what to make of it. The lumps under the robes didn't move - the glowing water inside of the basin didn't even ripple. *Moss,* he cursed to himself, relaxing slightly after realizing they weren't moving an inch, then catching Daria's eyes to mouth the word, "What?"

Daria shrugged, then slowly started making her way around the circular room to see if she could get in front of the sorcerers. Bow and arrow focused on the closest sorcerer, she crept, kneeling as she'd done when hunting, and could only see the hands in the basin - nothing underneath hoods or flayed out robes. She continued to finish the circle, ending behind the robes, careful not to step on them, then slowly lowered the bow once her eyes landed upon a book on the floor between them. She looked up at Olibtine who raised his eyebrows when he saw it too. He crept the opposite way Daria just had, ensuring he wasn't within reach of the sorcerer's robe, then got close enough to the book to see it open to a page with letters and words that resembled the ones in the book on the pedestal below - ones he couldn't read. Drawings accompanied the words on the opposite page. The first looked like a group of dead bodies with blood pooled around them, a red cloud above them. The second was a depiction of a human's face, eyes glowing with a deep blood red that sent a chill up his spine. He narrowed both eyebrows, glancing at the two sorcerers hunched over. *Is this a spell they are performing right now?!*

Olibtine could hear Daria's throat catch once she noticed what she was actually looking at. His head jerked up to her, her eyes wide in horror. He grabbed her arm and motioned his head towards the door, knowing that there wasn't anything else for them on this floor. She shook her head, jaw flexing visibly, not wanting to leave quite yet. Olibtine yanked, his eyes practically yelling at her now. She yanked her arm from his grip, still holding the bow and arrow in her right hand. Staring down at the sorcerer in front of her, she held her breath and cocked her bow while standing tall, pointing it straight at what should have been the head of the sorcerer.

Olibtine froze, body and mind fighting for his next move. *Moss! This is not how the Minds would handle this! All of the senseless contracts that these monsters have performed, they deserve this, but should we be the ones to do it?* He glanced from the lumps back to Daria, noticing that her hands were shaking. *She doesn't know either! To save whomever is on the other side of that magic and becoming an executioner or to let them continue their murdering?*

She loosed the arrow, the flight towards the black figure taking only a heartbeat.

A loud *CLANG* echoed through the room, arrow bouncing off of something unseen, the shaft crumbling into itself towards the arrowhead, then falling to the stone floor with a soft *clink*.

Daria lowered her bow, her jaw following suit by dropping open, and looked over to Olibtine who had the same dumbfounded expression on his face. *What was that?!*

Daria collected herself, gritting her teeth. She had an arrow recocked by the time Olibtine could blink, then leaned closer to the kneeling sorcerer, the arrow only a few inches from the black cloth. Taking careful aim at its spine now, hands steady, she loosed another.

CLANG rang the sound again, the arrow having no impact whatsoever.

Olibtine uncovered his eyes. *No good. They must have another spell active while performing theirs.*

Daria released the breath she had been holding, exhaling loudly, her hands falling to her sides as if defeated.

Olibtine glanced towards the book between the sorcerers again, deciding that if they weren't going to get more Bloodborn evidence, this should help their cause. He bent over and picked up the book, giving the pages one more quick glance before shutting it and throwing it in his pack with the other. Daria, frozen in place, didn't notice as Olibtine took the book and yanked her away again. This time, she didn't stop him from doing so.

I was ready, Daria internalized, feet unconsciously following Olibtine out the door and down the steps. *I was ready to take them with me. Ready to end everything these monsters are doing. I could live with Olibtine and Guane not understanding so long as they don't keep killing. Maybe this is the better way - we'll have the evidence of senseless killing that we can take to the Minds and they can figure this all out.*

Olibtine practically ran out of the room and down the stone staircase with Daria in tow. He wasn't about to wait around to see if the sorcerers would awaken from their trance, and so he ran - ignoring the pains all throughout his body from his throbbing hand to swollen leg. *At least this time she didn't fight me.* He stumbled down the darkened staircase towards the library.

They reached the landing for the library, firelight spilling out just as they left it, and paused, both taking quick breaths. Olibtine glanced up the stairwell, trying to see if anything was following them. Nothing. He noticed that Daria still had her bow in her hand and was staring off into nothing as if deep in thought.

"Daria," he called out. She didn't even so much as flinch at her name. "Daria!" Olibtine repeated as loud as he felt comfortable with while shaking her shoulder. She shook herself, blinking a few times, then met his eyes, his face alight from the fire spilling into the landing. "Are you going to be okay?" Olibtine asked.

She nodded, face still flat, and then threw the bow over her shoulder, string sitting against her chest.

"We need to get out of here. There is no way the sorcerers leave the way we came. Let's search this room first to see if there is anything but books in there and then try the room below that we passed over." He glanced up the stairs. "And we should be quick about it. Good?"

Daira nodded. *Good enough.* Olibtine entered the familiarly warm library with the pedestal in the middle. He couldn't help but to glance over the collection of books once again, completely in awe of the collection.

"Start on this side..." he pointed to his right, "...and I will start on this side," he finished, pointing to his left.

They made their way around the room, poking and prodding the walls, pulling on random books, moving stacks of books around to see what was behind them, and even checking the floors for trap doors until they met on the far side of the room, unsuccessful.

Moss! Olibtine cursed while rubbing the sweat from his forehead with the back of his hand. He glanced around once more before leaving, eyes landing on the pedestal in the middle of the room. He walked slowly over to it, the book still open on top and the basin water still as night, then glanced down, staring at the base. His head cocked sideways before kneeling. *What's that?* There were little circles on the floor that hinted at the pedestal being moved. Curious, he shook it, but it didn't budge due to its weight. He stood, wanting to get better leverage, then grabbed it on both sides and rocked it side to side as hard as he could. It rocked slightly and the more he did it, the more it rocked. A loud echo of metal on stone sounded throughout the room, but there was nothing to do about it. Straining with its weight and ignoring the pain shooting through his hand into his body, he twisted it while rocking it, making slow, but steady, progress. Eventually, he cleared the previous circle that the pedestal sat in revealing an odd, darker gray stone block. He looked up at Daria, eyebrows raised. She shrugged in return.

He knelt again, feeling around the block, sweat dripping from his eyebrows and nose to splash on the stone. His fingertips felt something rough on one side of the block, standing out in an overall smooth stone. He dug his fingernails in the crack by the rough spots trying to see if... *There!* The stone moved an inch, his fingernails finding room for his fingers to slide into the crack. He forced his fingers down more, the sweat helping them slide along the stone, which lifted slightly off of its resting place until the first bend in his finger hooked under the stone itself. He set his feet wide in a squat, breathed in, then strained with all the strength he could muster. The stone lifted an inch. A cool breeze slapped him in the face, cooling the sweat immediately, which sent a shiver down his skin. It moved another inch. His eyes squeezed shut and his legs quivered as he felt his hands slipping from the sweat and effort and just as he was about to drop it, he felt it lighten. He opened his eyes to see Daria beside him pulling on the stone block, her face strained with effort.

Once the stone was half way up, he shifted his hands to push, glancing down to see nothing but pitch black. They held it upright for a second to catch their breath, sweat dripping off of both of them even with the cool breeze from the opening greeting them.

Olibtine nodded to Daria, then they both worked their way around the side of it so they could set it down as soft as possible. Upon setting it down with a thunk that echoed through the room, they both collapsed to their knees, catching their breath and taking swigs from their canteens.

"You still have that mushroom vial for light?" Olibtine asked.

Daria pulled out the vial, a slight blue light emanating from it, then tossed it over to Olibtine.

After shaking the vial vigorously, Olibtine held it out as far as he could, illuminating the tunnel, noticing that there was a metal ladder on one of the walls leading into the cool darkness. He looked up at Daria, nodded, her eyebrows narrow above a flat mouth, then put one foot on the ladder, testing the strength until satisfied, then climbed on, wincing in pain. Pulling himself close to the ladder so his pack could fit in behind him, he took a few steps down until his head was inside of the hole. He wrapped his left arm around one rung, then released his right hand, which had the vial in it, and extended it below to try to see more of what was to come, but with little avail. Slowly, he made his way further into the darkness, step by slow step, until Daria appeared above him, taking her steps just as slow.

He stepped down again, then froze, feeling around with his foot. *No step,* he panicked.

"Wait!" he called out to Daria above, only two steps above his head.

He released his hand again, shining the light below him, only to find that the light only extended to his feet, useless, the darkness sucking in the light.

"There is no step here," he warned, looking up. "I'm going to drop the vial to see how far it goes. Look down here to see if you can see the same."

"Okay," he heard Daria say above, her clothes and pack rubbing against the walls as she looked down.

He scooted as far as he could to his left, squatting as low as he could, making room for the drop, held out his arm to his side, then dropped the vial with held breath. His throat dropped into his stomach with the same speed as the vial as he envisioned the fires the previous ones created. *Oh Moss*, he cursed. Just as he was about to yell up to Daria to retrace their climb, the vial hit a stone floor with a *CLANK* CLANK CLANK, bouncing around not even a few feet below him. He released his breath in a huff.

He looked up at Daria again, only seeing her outline above. "Looks like we just have to jump a little ways. Not far at all."

Steadying his breath, Olibtine bent his knees to move his hands down one more rung, spotted his landing spot below him in the light of the vial, then jumped the four or so feet to the bottom, an echo of boots and pack bouncing off of stone. "Uhmf," he landed in a squat. Relieved as he picked the vial up he briefly looked around with an extended arm around, then stood up, holding it above his head to illuminate his face and the ladder above.

"It's okay, I'm down," he relayed up to Daira, who was already making her way down the last few steps. While she was doing that, he squinted into the dark, glancing around again, this time noticing a dark tunnel leading off to his right that he'd have to bend over to get into, but only slightly.

He noticed Daria feeling the air below the final rung. "That's the final rung," he said, illuminating the space for her to see. Upon watching her land gracefully, albeit with the ujuntu clanking around in her pack, he turned, bending his neck forward, scooting into the tight tunnel.

"There's a tunnel right here - the only one I saw," Olibtine directed over his shoulder. Pack scraping against the walls, he extended his arm out in front to light the way ahead. It wasn't a dozen slow steps later when he noticed the tunnel curving off to the right, each step becoming easier like he was heading downhill. The right curve became more prominent with each step until he was having to lean back slightly, putting his feet further in front of himself for fear of falling forward. With the light extended in front of him, he saw the wall curving dramatically to the right, forcing his eyes the same way, and then he noticed something he never thought he'd be so happy to see if his life ever again.

"Stairs!" he exclaimed, hurrying forward the last few feet. Daria closed the gap, approaching his back to see a stone staircase not unlike the ones they had been climbing before, except for it spiraled the opposite way.

"This must be the way out," she practically pleaded, a smile appearing on her lips.

Olibtine nodded, taking in her smile, his pains evaporating as if they were but a passing nightmare, and then he smiled too.

"Let's get out of here." He wanted to rid himself of the dread that the tower forced upon him. Attacking the steps as quickly as their sore and injured legs would allow, their packs clanged and bounced around, their lungs burnt, and their footsteps echoed from wall to wall as if they didn't care who, or what, heard them, they descended.

They descended until hitting a flat area, then doubled over, hands on knees, panting loudly. Affording themselves a quick break to catch their breath, they took gulps from their canteens, then stored them away once more. Olibtine stepped forward into the unknown darkness, vial lighting his way to reveal a flat black stone wall.

What? Olibtine panicked, prodding at the cool stone wall in front of him. Squinting, he examined the wall, moving the vial up, down, and side to side, searching for a hint of something upon the single stone slab of a wall.

Daria noticed him frantically searching, the light illuminating a stone wall at the end of the landing, and made her way to his side. She placed her hand on his shoulder causing his head to snap to meet her calm eyes, a smile on her lips. His eyebrow rose before lowering his arms to his side. Her calm demeanor made him realize that he was the complete opposite. Closing his mouth to breathe from his nose, he took a few deep breaths to calm himself. *Why is she smiling?* He cocked an eyebrow. But even though he didn't know why, it calmed him. His cheeks went red and he had to divert his eyes away from hers.

After grabbing the vial from Olibtine, she stepped forward without saying a word while Olibtine scooted to the side. Moving from corner to corner, she searched, eyes focused, her fur not but a foot from the wall. She paused on a spot to the far right of the wall, placed her free hand flush against it, then with a little effort, pushed on the wall, a stone on stone grinding sound echoing loudly through the landing causing Olibtine to jump. The wall - or door it seemed - slid open with little effort, revealing a drop-off into yet another dark room. Daria illuminated what she could, unable to see the bottom.

"What do you think? I can't see the bottom or anything in the room," Daria asked, kneeling and shining the vial as low as she could into the room beyond.

Olibtine knelt beside her only noticing a flat stone wall below them like a cliff.

"Should we drop the vial again?" he asked, knowing they couldn't be far from the base of the tower.

Daria shrugged. "Sure. Ready?"

Breath held, they watched as the vial tumbled into the darkness until it exploded with a sudden blinding blue light that made them squint and shy away as it crashed open on solid stone, water and mushroom expelled from its holding ten feet below where they crouched.

They glanced at one another, then back below at the fading mushroom.

"That's not far," Olibtine noticed, imagining the ladder above and how easy it was to get down from there. "I'll go first."

He took his pack off first, placing it near Daria, then sat down, legs dangling over the wall, feet lit from below. *Moss, that's further than I thought.* He scooted further over the ledge, staring down at the mushroom on the ground that was losing its light every second. He held his breath, then pushed off the ledge, the ground rising to meet his feet. He landed with a THUNK, his whole body feeling the jolt. Exhaling, he stood, then looked up at Daria. *Moss, that looks high!*

"Toss the packs down first." Daria obliged, tossing his down first, then hers. By the time Daria sat on the ledge, the mushroom was on its last light, but she jumped without hesitation, landing in a crouch.

"Showoff," Olibtine teased, grabbing his pack and shouldering it. He quickly glanced around in what blue light there was left as she grabbed her pack and threw it on, but all he could see was the darkness closing in around them. They stood shoulder to shoulder, the dim light revealing nothing in front of them, only a wall to their left.

"Let's follow that wall," Olibtine suggested, pointing as the light blinked out. He felt a warm, soft hand on his that sent chills throughout his body. He was happy that the light was out or else Daria would see his face beat red. Without a word, he felt his arm go taught as Daria pulled him to the wall he indicated before. He reached out and found the wall as well. Step by step, they made their way along it, only the sound of their feet on the stone floor and the packs rustling on their backs to accompany them. He felt Daria stop in front of him.

"Daria?" he asked, "Daria, what is it?"

"Feel this." She pulled his hand to hers. Warm stone met his hand. He brushed over it, his eyes growing wide.

"The door!" he exclaimed, trying to see the scratch marks he had recognized from before. "It's the door we came in!" He blinked, and upon opening them again, he had to shield them from the intense light making his eyes water. The air was warm, the ground beneath his feet loose. *Am I?* He heard a *POP* next to him, then a moan.

"Daria?"

"Yeah. Did we... are we..."

Olibtine squinted, blinking over and over until he could see without looking through tears. His heart skipped a beat, proper tears forming in his eyes as he no longer saw stone beneath his feet, but instead, sand.

"Sand!" he exclaimed, looking over at Daria, whose eyes were blinking rapidly. "We made it! We made it, Daria!"

"We made it?" she asked softly, still skeptical until she was able to open her eyes herself and see the sand. "We made it!" she exclaimed, falling to her knees and grabbed two handfuls of sand. "I never thought I'd be happy to see sand," she laughed.

Olibtine straightened, throwing one arm over her shoulder. *How long have we been in there?* Daria turned, fists full of sand, and embraced him fully, his other arm hugging her with tears filling his eyes from both the light and sheer joy of being out of such a repressive place. He felt her shaking against him, then heard her sobbing, even happier than he was to get out of the tower.

He reluctantly leaned back from her. They weren't out of it yet. *We need to get as far away as possible.*

"Daria, can you walk?" he asked, meeting her teary eyes. She nodded. "Yes."

"We should get as far away as possible from this place, as quickly as possible." He stood while wiping the tears from his eyes, fresh ones taking their place, then held out his good hand for her. "Let's go."

She let the sand tumble from between her fingers before reaching up for his hand, willing herself to rise, then brushed her hands on her clothes before wiping her eyes.

With Daria in the lead, they set their backs to the ominous tower and its never ending, dark pressure, towards Gbinti, a renewed vigor to their step.

Chapter 36: Duties Inside the White's Tower

Kausha, cleaned and forced into a dress of white that covered her from neck to knees with a white cloak overtop that hung to her calves - the color of the first - followed an older slave woman with thick white hair, draped in a similar white cloak, through the candlelit hall. A drab gray and brown carpet muffled their footsteps as Selene walked her through the duties that were required of them.

"...and this," Selene pointed, her tone quick and demanding that said she had done this same routine countless times, "is where you will be sleeping." She opened one of the seven large, wooden doors on the floor, illuminating the inside with the wall's candlelight to show six beds lining the walls in a square with barely any room to walk in between. Selene closed the door nearly as quickly as she opened it, meeting Kausha's eyes. "Guards will be posted here at the end of the hall to ensure we aren't wandering off in the night. We have it easy compared to those outside, but don't get it wrong - if you upset one of the six, especially the first, you will be hauled off to the mines never to return. I've seen it happen before and wouldn't want your pretty little head to suffer the same fate." Her face softened as if remembering something. Selene snapped herself out of her trance, blinked, then hardened her face once again. "Now, follow me and we'll get some food for us and have you meet the other girls."

Without a word, Selene retraced her steps down the hall and up the wide stone staircase, each step requiring three steps to clear. They passed another slave draped in white in the process. They exited the stairs one floor later into a hivemind of activity. Women of all sizes, shapes, and types moved about in their white cloaks carrying bedding, herbs, pots and bowls, fruits, fresh vegetables, books, and more. Every one was focused on their duties with eyes forward, mouths drawn in a line, as they hurried towards their destination. This floor was one Selene had already shown Kausha with it being one of the most important in that it housed the kitchens and direct entry to the gardens, stretching the entire width of the first's tower. Each tower had the same layout, which made escape that much easier to Kausha. Selene barked a few orders to those passing by with empty hands, then turned to Kausha.

"We will have you," Selene weighed her options, looking Kausha up and down, then grabbing her hands feeling tough skin on both front and back, "pulling herbs from the garden and assisting the cooks," she decided with a satisfying nod to herself. "Go find Linil in the garden and tell her I sent you. You can't miss her. She will be half covered in dirt with a big hat on." Selene glanced over Kausha's shoulder, eyebrows turning down, then stomped away without a word. Kausha watched her go in admiration, thinking, *A strong woman that Yaula would have gotten along with. Yaula. You wouldn't have gotten yourself into something like this.*

Heading the opposite direction of the women carrying fruits and vegetables, Kausha found a broad exit that opened to the garden that was wide enough for multiple women to walk by one another with room to spare. The garden itself was an expansive area between the first and second tower where all types of plants grew directly out of the water, a type of hydroponic harvesting. She had seen this only a handful of times down in the swamps, so to see it in the north, between giant towers and sitting atop of an ujuntu base, made it feel unnatural and yet calming all at once. One of the slaves stepped out of the water onto a thick piece of cloth, drying her bare feet, then, confident she had dried completely, stepped into slippers and continued the direction the others were headed. Kausha turned to look out over the garden again, eyes focusing on the ujuntu floor beneath the water. She shook her head at the opulence, then searched through the plants and other slaves for the woman with the big hat.

There, she glimpsed, finding the wide-brimmed dark green hat poke up from behind a group of thick green and purple leaves. Kausha removed her slippers and made her way into the shallow water - body shivering and arm hair standing on end from the unexpected coolness of the water itself. After the initial shock, both feet in, the water only coming to her ankles, she made her way down one of the rows towards Linil, who was so focused on what she was tending to that she didn't realize Kausha was standing right beside her. The woman was a wrinkly-faced, unnaturally tan human from too many hours in the sun with unkempt gray hairs sticking out from all sides of her hat, and was shorter than Kausha, but with muscles taught from her time kneeling and lifting things. Kausha cleared her throat. The hat tilted upwards to see who it was, green eyes meeting hers. A smile appeared on Linil's lips, the wrinkles around her eyes becoming more prominent as she did so, then looked back down towards her ever-moving hands.

"I see there is another," she sighed in a slow, motherly tone like that of Kausha's grandmother. "When will enough be enough?" she asked, but to no one in particular as she continued to gently pull leaves from the plant, then scooting over to the one next to it. After finishing another, she held up the leaves to Kausha without looking. After hesitating for a moment, Kausha grabbed them, replying with, "Selene sent me."

Linil continued to toil away without an answer, handing two more handfuls to Kausha's arms.

"Do you know how all of this works?" Linil asked.

Growing plants? Kausha looked around at the different plants being tended by other slaves like her. "Rather than needing soil, the nutrients are put directly into..." she started, glancing back at Linil who was looking up at her with raised eyebrows.

"Oh, you didn't mean the plants." Linil smiled again, then returned to what she was doing.

Kausha glanced around to see if anyone else was close enough to hear. *Is this really the place?* She watched a slave slowly make her way back to the tower with a handful of orange and yellow vines, but answered anyway. "I know that the six rule over everyone in this city and it's clear now that they just take visitors and enslave them as soon as they enter." She imagined Shaum and Skirm breaking rocks in a dark mine. Her eyes shut, fists clenched into a tight ball, knuckles white, then she felt a warm hand cover hers, which jolted her eyes open. Linil was holding her hand, looking up at her again with a comforting smile.

"That has only started recently with more and more girls like yourself showing up draped in white. It seems that the old ways are through and the six are becoming desperate." Linil moved her hand away from Kausha's, continuing her toiling. "In the towers of the six, we don't live a lavish life, but it is one far better than in the mines where they break rock day in and day out until the moon rises over the walls. I've heard stories of late where men and women alike are dropping like leaves after being forced to increase their breakage. I've also seen women in the towers be sent off to those same caves after they upset one of the six. Keep your head down and do as you're told and that won't happen to you."

"Have any left the city?" Kausha asked, grabbing another bundle of leaves from Linil.

"In times past, yes, but I fear that these newer six do not catch and release."

Moss. No way we could have sat around and waited for that anyways, but this makes things slightly more difficult.

"Wait. Newer six?" Kausha asked with a frown as they moved to another plant with thin yellow leaves with purple veins throughout.

Linil glanced up at Kausha with an eyebrow raised, then returned to work. "The six are constantly shifting based on how much wealth they have. More slaves means more ujuntu to mine. The lower five have been shifting in and out for some time, but within the last moon, there have been newer sixes leading both within the same household and outside as well. The bottom four are new to the six while the top two have stayed the same with the first and second changing heads at the last counting. Change has put this city into a fervor and we should expect more to come."

"Why are you telling me all of this?"

Linil finished gathering the leaves, stood, then placed what she had in hand on top of Kausha's pile. She stretched her back, looking up towards the sun, then back down to meet Kausha's eyes, an intensity to them that wasn't shown earlier.

"Why, isn't it obvious? You need to know what you've gotten yourself into by coming to Nortmund. I am a slave, but this is all I have now and no matter what happens, I will always tell those that need to know. What you do with it is up to you. Now, run those plants inside and help with the cooking. Don't forget to dry your feet - women have been sent to the mines for less," she finished as she moved the opposite way down the row, gently stroking the leaves of the next plant in line.

Kausha did as she was told, thoroughly wiping her feet dry, then sliding the slippers on and making her way towards the kitchen. Falling in line with the others, she entered a kitchen full of smells of fresh bread and meats drying, sounds of pots and pans being struck with wooden spoons, and three larger-set women directing each slave on where the items they carried went. Kausha was told to add the leaves to an already existing pile on top of a counter that ran the length of the far wall, then was practically pushed out by the others behind her. *Go with the flow and find Nalia and Skip first,* she told herself as she continued out the kitchen into the main area where slaves milled about, heading every which way. *Wait, I was supposed to help with the cooking.* She paused and turned back to the ever-swinging door. Then, she saw her out of the corner of her eye heading up a stairwell. *Nalia!* Her feet knew what to do even before her brain, which carried her off quickly towards the stairwell. *Was it really her?*

Kausha ascended the stairwell, taking two steps at a time, stopping at the landing where two women were walking across a walkway above the floor with the kitchens. She ran over to the two, noticing furry ears before anything else, then grabbed her shoulder and spun her, orange eyes wide at the unexpected grip.

"Nalia!" Kausha exclaimed, grabbing her by the elbows.

"Kausha!" Nalia responded through a toothy smile, grabbing Kausha's elbows in return. The other woman draped in white had taken a few steps before noticing Nalia had stopped, but as soon as she noticed she was alone, she stopped herself, but didn't try to break up their embrace, only sighed and looked out over the hivemind below.

"Are you okay? Have you seen Skip?" Kausha whispered to ensure the other woman didn't hear.

Nalia nodded, "I'm okay - seems we're doing the same thing," she said, ruffling the white robe, "but I haven't seen Skip."

"I'm sure he's fine - he's a bard afterall. The old lady in the garden told me to not ruffle any feathers right now - tensions are high. Let's plan to meet at this stairwell entrance tonight after supper to talk more."

Nalia nodded, the brief moment of a smile gone, eyes as piercing as ever. Kausha returned the nod, wishing they could talk right now, but she knew the woman she was with couldn't be trusted. No one but their group could be. Reluctantly, she lowered her arms, then turned to escape back down the stairs as quickly as possible. Upon descending, she looked up towards the walkway where Daria stood a few seconds before, but she was gone. Kausha reentered the kitchen after a break in the flow of those leaving.

One of the larger women glared at her when she entered through the door everyone else was exiting from. "What are you doing?!" she yelled, face red and furious, while amazingly still directing the women carrying items into their proper places. "Well?!" she followed up with a gruff, booming voice.

"Um, Linil sent me to help with cooking," Kausha replied in her meekest tone, watching the next woman exit the kitchen next to her.

"What do you know about cooking?! Bah, Linil thinks she knows everything! Fine, get over here and stir - I'll make it easy on you at first," the large woman wheezed in a gruff voice that indicated she smoked too much. She pointed with her oversized finger while simultaneously padding her sweaty forehead with a cloth in her other hand. As Kausha made her way towards the pot the woman pointed at, she noticed that the woman wasn't as old as Selene or Linil. She had short, black hair with a few gray streaks that looked like she had just been rained on, but that was clearly just sweat, and dark eyes that darted back and forth from the piles of items around the kitchen to the incoming slaves, a seemingly ever moving flow. She barked orders and pointed over and over, never taking a break, never losing her drive.

Kausha, mesmerized by the large woman's endurance, stirred something in a large pot that smelled like cooked mushrooms and herbs, making her stomach groan. *Nalia and Skip.* She forced her mind back to the issue at hand. *First we need to find Skip, then escape into the city to find Shaum and Skirm, then find Nalia's sister, then find our way back out of the city. With the size of the city, I bet we could dodge the guards enough if we needed to. Find a home to hold up in if needed. Where are the exits into the city itself? The mines go directly into the mountains - we need to get an idea of where Shaum and Skirm are digging. Oddly enough, there aren't too many guards in this tower so it shouldn't be too hard getting out of here. I could see how hard it would be to leave the city the way we came with all those long sections between the walls, but maybe they don't envision anyone wanting to get into the city itself.*

Her mind reeled with the what ifs and hows until a large hand slammed on the table next to her, causing her to jump and smack the spoon against the pot.

"Girl! Don't go ruining my good spoon! I was calling you, did you not hear me?" the large woman asked, patting her forehead.

"I... I didn't. Sorry," Kausha replied, turning down her eyes.

A loud exhale released from the woman. "Guess I should have learned your name if I'm going to call on you. What is it?"

"Kausha."

"Kausha then? Alright, Kausha, call me Chef - everyone else around here does. Not sure if any of the lot even know my name if asked. If you're going to be between Linil and me, you'll need to be a quick learner. Ever cooked before?" Chef crossed her arms in front of her chest as well as she could. Kausha looked up at the woman, her arms looking like tree trunks - almost as big as Shaum's, the normally pure white cloak discolored throughout from the grease, sweat, and other mixtures clinging to her from the kitchen, her plump face hiding any semblance of bones beneath. *How long have you been here?* she wondered.

Kausha's eyes shot wide, forgetting to answer. She shook her head.

Chef said something under her breath that Kausha couldn't hear, but she sure smelt the onion on her breath that drifted over. "Fine, fine." She rolled her eyes and waved the hand with the cloth in it. "Ah hah, I've got it!" She measured Kausha up and down with her dark eyes. "Whatever you get from Linil you will chop for prepping. Do it on this counter right here," she pointed to the wooden counter next to where they were standing where she had dropped the leaves earlier, "and always chop into a fine substance, meaning chop the leaves, or whatever you bring in, as small as you can. Don't upset my kitchen balance and I won't have to report you. Understood?"

Kausha nodded. "One thing. What knife do you want me to use?"

Chef rolled her eyes again, reaching for one of the larger ones from the center counter and held it up to her eyes before placing it on the countertop where she would be cutting. "This one. Now, it's nearly time to eat. Hand me that spoon and go get yourself cleaned up with the others. You were told how to do that, weren't you?" she mocked with a raised eyebrow.

Kausha handed the spoon to her and nodded. "Yes, Selene showed me."

"Then run along," Chef finished with a shoo of her hand.

Kausha set off for the exit, glancing at the knife from the corner of her eye. *They really just allow slaves to walk around in the kitchen with knives lying around?* She exited the kitchen through the correct door, which she noticed no one was filing out of anymore. She made her way down to the sleeping quarters where the bathing room was located, which was bustling with women running this way or that. Some were draped in just a towel, others putting their hair up, with the majority walking into the bath towards the far end of the hall. Kausha could see steam constantly escaping the room whenever someone opened the door. Not wanting to be left behind, Kausha hurried to the room Selene indicated was hers where three other women were gathering their things from under their beds before heading into the bath. Kausha did the same, grabbing the pile of things beneath her bed - a towel, a bar of soap, and a small bucket - then followed the others from her room. She entered the bath, heat smacking her in the face as she did, a haze of steam enveloping the room so she could barely see her fingertips when she outstretched her hand. *Is Nalia in here?* She tried to force her gaze through the steam. *I can't see anything in here. Best to not waste time and think about how to get out of here.*

Kausha disrobed near the edge of the large pool of water that practically engulfed the entire room in an attempt to keep her distance from everyone else. As soon as she lowered herself into the hot water, a hushed murmur from all directions popped up out of nowhere that mixed with the bubbling water. *Interesting. Couldn't hear this from up above.* Kausha closed her eyes, attempting to focus on the one closest with no luck. *Should I scoot closer?* She imagined a wave of water being sent to those she was trying to sneak up on, which gave her pause. *I have to try.* Using her feet and hands with baited breath, ears focused, she inched her way around the edge of the pool.

"...shouldn't have done that or else she'd still be here," came a hushed voice from her right side.

"Don't say that! The six have become short tempered these days!" replied a separate voice.

"Hey! Keep it down, you don't want anyone else to hear us," answered another voice as a ripple of water reached Kausha.

The group quieted down to a whisper, which left Kausha out of ear shot. She backed away slowly to the spot she entered, quickly cleaned herself, then left back to her room to clothe herself and then follow the rest of the slaves to serve the supper.

The women, all dressed in the same white robe, began lining up right outside the kitchen, so Kausha thought she'd fall in line as well, looking up and down the line searching for Nalia, who wasn't there. *I wonder what she's been doing.* The kitchen door swung open, drawing her attention. One by one, the women in line disappeared through the door. Kausha was next, and as soon as she entered, was handed a basket by Chef, then pushed off out through the opposite door. Looking ahead, Kausha could see a line moving like a giant snake, each woman carrying something in her hands. A straight line of women led her across the main corridor and up a long flight of shadowed stone stairs until they exited into a square, brightly lit room from the numerous wall-mounted candlelight sconces. A fluffy white rug underfoot took up the entire room and continued through a large set of double wooden doors, wide open to expose the dining hall beyond.

Peeking around those in front, Kausha could see one of the larger women that was in the kitchen earlier dividing the slaves into two groups and sending them off down each side of the long, wooden table that could have fit the entirety of the slaves she'd seen on just one side. Kausha had never seen such a large table before, not even at home in Purtghast. *This must be from one of the largest trees from The Forest,* she awed, mouth agape. On either side were countless, finely carved wooden chairs, all outfitted with plush seating and high backs for any guests to sit in comfort, with two in particular catching her eyes towards the middle that were larger and much more ornate with streaks of ujuntu lining the top and sides. There were three large stone fireplaces in the hall, two on either side of the table as well as one at the far end, being tended to by slaves. A painting hung above each, depicting a group of dwarves holding a large ujuntu shard above their heads. Kausha was herded towards the far side of the table with her basket in hand, then was directed to place it towards the back half near two ujuntu spheres wrapped in a yellow shell that gave off the same color light as the fireplaces on each wall. Another group of women, half as many as before, were entering while the first group was dismissed back out into the long hall. Wanting to see the entire process, Kausha stayed behind in the corner closest to the exit. Even though her robe was the same color as the rug, she wasn't hidden while standing in the shadows, but no one challenged her on it at the moment. The women scurried about, removing food from baskets and placing them on fine plates, filling glasses with wine, and organizing silverware.

Nothing out of the norm. Before she took a step towards the exit, a door on the far end of the dining room slammed open. She heard it before she saw it, her blood instinctively moving to the opposite side of her body, fingers feeling bloated with blood. Her head snapped towards the noise where she saw a dwarve with a brown beard and a colorful cloak backlit by natural light from outside. She squinted, *Is that the dwarve from earlier?* Oddly enough, the other women slaves refused eye contact, hiding their eyes from him as he barked orders on silverware placement, food order, and how much wine was poured into one of the glasses. He did that up and down the long table, not once happy with what he saw.

"This is a very important supper! The first will not be happy if this doesn't go just as planned!" he yelled at no one in particular, his voice booming up and down the room. Once he finished his tour of the table, he left the room through the same door as he had come, slamming it hard behind him. The tense feeling shared by everyone lifted from the air nearly as soon as it came. *An important supper?* Before she could think more on it, one of the larger women from the far side of the room started making her way towards her, herding the other women that were finalizing the table. Kausha simply stood there as the woman approached - a woman nearly as large as Chef with fading blond hair, permanent wrinkles on her face from smiling too much, and hands behind her back. She didn't speak a word to Kausha, only stared with a creepy smile on her lips, eyes drowned out by the white in her cloak, but Kausha understood and quickly made her way to the door, letting the others file out before her.

Nearly to the exit, she heard a door open from the other side again and a mumble of voices echo throughout. Kausha looked back just in time to see the dwarve from earlier holding the door open, head bowed, and a much smaller dwarve in a pure white robe entering. It was impossible to make out what they were saying, but the glimpse was gone nearly as soon as it started, the large woman closing the doors behind her and Kausha. She looked down at Kausha over a pointed nose, brown eyes visible now that they were in some candlelight, and without a word, got Kausha to retreat from the door and back down the stairs to the kitchen for supper.

***

Kausha's stomach growled while ladling out a thick, reddish-brown stew from the pot she was stirring earlier, slopping it down next to the colorful vegetables and fluffy bread. She made her way out of the kitchen into the large common area that opened up to the garden, then decided to keep her space and found herself a quiet area off to the left of the door where she could think about her meeting with Nalia. Sitting, she began replaying the technicalities of the escape in her head, but her mind wandered to earlier. *Was the dwarve a child? Is one of the six a child? Can a child be blamed for the recent changes that Linil was referring to? It doesn't change anything that needs to be done, but if one of the six is indeed just a child, there is much more to this than meets the eye. The attempts at my life, the six shifting so much recently, enslaving all visitors that enter the city.*

Her mind raced and she found herself moving her food around instead of eating it. She sighed, closing her eyes and resting her head against the stone wall behind her. *What is going on?* Frustration boiled inside of her. *I need to get home!*

"Hello," came a soft, high-pitched voice to her right.

Kausha's eyes shot open to stare at the woman next to her. *I should have heard her.* She was a Lodarian with scaly green skin that seemed to reflect light like a mirror and yellow eyes that never blinked.

"You going to eat that?" the woman asked, nodding to something on Kausha's plate. Kausha shook her head handing the plate over. The Lodarian smiled with flat, straight teeth showing her gratitude, then accepted the plate and pushed the vegetables from Kausha's plate to hers and then handed the plate back. Kausha accepted it, placing it on the floor and watched the Lodarian cut everything into tiny pieces, forking one bite at a time, then licking it off the fork with a long, red tongue that looked slit right down the middle.

The Lodarian ate without saying a word, not even one to tell Kausha to stop staring. Once the last piece of food was cleaned from her plate, she looked over to Kausha, nodded her head, then said, "Thanks." She began standing, ready to walk off until Kausha stopped her. "Wait."

The Lodarian looked back and down at her.

"So... is this how it always goes?" Kausha asked, nodding towards the tables the other slaves sat at - most in small groups of hushed conversations.

Lodarian followed Kausha's eyes, nodded her head, then looked back. "It is. Different food when we aren't serving something important."

"I see. And the freedom to do this?" Kausha asked.

Lodarian's eyes squinted for a moment before returning to their normal state. "Freedom. Yes."

Kausha heard hints in her tone that the Lodarian had much more to say, but feared doing so. *It's because I'm new.*

"How long have you been here?"

The Lodarian's yellow eyes wandered off over Kausha's head as if staring at something and nothing all at once. She shook her head. "Too long."

Kausha didn't want to push too hard, but seeing as this woman was holding back, it was a gamble she was willing to take.

"Has anyone tried to leave?" Kausha spit out in a jumble.

The Lodarian shot her gaze at Kausha, eyes squinting again, unsure of what to make of her. She looked around, then back to Kausha.

"Tried? Yes. Succeeded? No. This city used to be one with beauty and prestige where all walks of life dreamed to visit. Now, those same dreams are the ones halting others before they come to life."

She sounds sincere. Kausha noticed the Lodarian close her eyes and clench her left hand.

"And the six are doing this?"

"Yes," the Lodarian replied, fidgeting with her plate and utensils. "They are, afterall, the ones making the laws."

"Kausha."

The Lodarian pried her eyes up from her plate to meet Kausha's eyes, then nodded. "Puid," she responded, before heading towards the kitchen door before Kausha could ask anything else. *Puid,* Kausha repeated, picking her plate up while standing, then circling back around to the entrance to the kitchen to drop it off like the others had. Her stomach fluttered in anticipation for the meeting with Nalia. *I hope she has more information than I do.*

She exited the kitchen, veered off to the left while others went right, then casually searched the area to make sure no one was around. Rousing suspicion, even if only other slaves were nearby, would hinder any chance of escape. Satisfied with her search, she gathered her thoughts one last time while leaning against the white-washed wall near the exit to the staircase.

Kausha audibly relaxed at the sight of Nalia coming down the stairs, only knowing it was the tail end of supper due to most of the women already retreating down the steps towards the sleeping quarters. She closed the gap between them in a flash, hugging Nalia, who stiffened from the intimate interaction.

"I'm glad you're here," Kausha pulled away to meet Nalia's wide eyes, which made Kausha chuckle.

"What?" Nalia asked.

"Oh, nothing. Where are they keeping you? Did you eat?"

Nalia shrugged. "Upstairs in a small room with three others. A little."

Kausha nodded. "They have me downstairs with dozens of others, but same. Something isn't right here lately from what I hear. As if slavery wasn't enough to be 'not right', there have been a lot of changes in the last few moons, including what happened to us where they just took us. Have you found out anything about your sister."

Nalia's eyes softened, then turned down as she shook her head.

I see. Kausha had to ask. "Skip? Shaum? Skirm?"

Nalia shook her head again.

Moss. "I'm sure we'll find something. Keep asking around. I think I have a plan." Kausha laid out the plan, which was used in the loosest meaning possible. After hearing the entirety of it, Nalia nodded, eyebrows scrunched in thought. "As long as we find my sister."

"We will," Kausha promised, nodding.

The two stood there leaning against the wall, watching silently as the final few women disappeared behind the kitchen, undoubtedly down the steps to sleep.

"Do you think we'll really find them? Shaum and Skirm, I mean," Nalia asked in a soft tone.

Kausha felt Nalia shrink against the wall, head leaned back, ears drooping. *Can we?* Kausha imagined the vast, endless caves beneath the Uhlbrar Mountains. Her fists clenched, the blood churning inside of her itching to be released.

"We will," Kasha answered forcefully, realizing that she actually meant it, even against the seemingly insurmountable vastness of the city.

Chapter 37: New Information

Time is slipping by. Kausha squeezed her jaw tight while squatting with Linil in the garden the following morning, completely missing what she was explaining. After a breakfast of bread and what was left over from last night's supper, she had been with Linil all morning working their way through the vegetables they were picking for today's supper. Even with the sun nearing its peak, Linil had only talked her through two separate plants, explaining everything from the planting process to grow time to gauging when they are ripe for plucking - a testament to how much she knew regarding the plants.

"And that is why animals grow from the ground, correct?" Linil asked, looking at Kausha, hands still caressing the leaves of the knee-high bluish-purple plant they knelt by.

Kausha nodded, not listening to what was said, she was simply repeating what she had done when her mother went on her educational rants.

Linil sighed that perfect motherly sigh, but didn't chastise, only replied with, "You weren't listening." It wasn't a question, but a statement of fact.

Kausha shook herself, eyes landing on Linil's. "I'm sorry," Kausha replied, her eyes falling to the water they were standing in - a better alternative to telling her what she was thinking.

Linil's eyes fixed on the plant again, turning a leaf over to check something on the bottom. "When I was first enslaved, you could earn your freedom by serving for some time. The exact time varied, but if you did as you were told, it was there within your grasp. I've seen women come and go for decades. Some were unable to earn a living and unwilling to submit themselves to the darker side of Nortmund, while others simply upset a guard by denying their advancements. Life has changed for everyone here, and along with

255

change comes ideas." She paused, looking up from under her large hat, sharp, strangely youthful eyes piercing Kausha's. "Whispers are everywhere now, you simply have to know where to listen."

Kausha stared back, unsure of what to make of the sheer open discourse that Linil displayed for the second time in two days. *Why is this woman telling me all of this? Does she know what I am? Does she do this with everyone?* The conversations only created more questions than answers. After Linil had plucked a few leaves from the plant, taking care to snap it cleanly from its stem between fingernails, the two moved down the row a ways to a cluster of small, green and yellow plants with leaves only a thumbnail in size. Kausha could smell them before even squatting, causing her nose to wrinkle as she breathed in and out quickly as if trying to rid herself of it.

"These," Linil started, setting her feet and squatting, "are called Dungung. Indigenous to the marshes to the far south. Pretty easy to understand the name." A smile appeared on her lips. "It is only used in dishes that have their own unique smell that can overshadow this. Surprisingly, the taste is rather enjoyable with a slight twinge of sour," she finished, removing one of the tiny leaves, placing it on her tongue, her face puckering almost as soon as it touched.

Kausha laughed aloud looking at the normally wrinkly faced woman's face pucker, causing even more wrinkles than she thought possible. Linil smiled, the sour taste fading from her tongue. She reached down again and pulled another leaf off of the plant, then handed it to Kausha, who accepted it in her palm. She shrugged, briefly glancing at the smiling Linil, then placed it on her tongue. Her eyes squeezed shut as a shock of sour exploded into her tongue and through her jaw, causing it to convulse while her fingers gripped her knees in front of her. It was gone almost as soon as it started, ending with a pleasantly soothing tingle, her mouth feeling like she had just drank the coldest water from a mountaintop.

Kausha opened her eyes to see that Linil was laughing joyously at the sight, her hand slapping her leg over and over with her head tilted towards the sun, hat nearly falling off her head. Kausha smiled at the woman, feeling a slight pang in her chest for ever thinking poorly of her intentions. *Surely there is no way that this woman is out to cause me harm.*

Linil wiped her teary eyes, forcing herself to calm down. "Oh, thank you child," she thanked with a final chuckle. "I haven't laughed that hard in ages. But tasty, right?" Kausha nodded.

"Okay, now that we have that done, go ahead and pluck a handful of the three plants we discussed today and take them to the kitchen for supper," Linil directed as she stood, knuckling her lower back with both hands, face to the sky.

Kausha did as she was told, starting with the smelly plant, working her way back to the others, and then carrying it all into the kitchen, dropping them on the counter where Chef asked. Remembering the conversation from yesterday, she grabbed the big knife from the center island, feeling Chef's eyes on her back, and began to chop - or at least attempt to. Kausha had handled all sorts of blades in her day from the rigorous training growing up, always hearing from her mother that there would be a time where she wouldn't be able to resort to her powers to get out of situations. She had a feeling that this wasn't what her mother meant.

Upon completion, Chef was standing next to her in an instant, her body moving quicker than Kausha thought possible for a woman her size, even if she was breathing heavier. Kausha looked up at her, her extra chins moving side to side in a ripple as her head vigorously shook.

"Tsk tsk. These are far too big of cuts to use in food, especially with the Dungung, which would send anyone's face into a convulsion. Here," Chef held her hand out asking for the knife, which Kausha handed over hilt first. Chef twirled it casually. "This is how you chop fine pieces. First, fingers positioned down, the front of the blade should never leave the surface. Pull, then push. Don't force it. The knife should do most of the work for you." Her chubby fingers handled both the vegetables and knife with a precision only learned through countless hours of work. Kausha nodded. '*Keep your blade sharp,*' echoed in her mind, something her mother always said. She accepted the knife from Chef and after repeating what she was taught, Chef nodded, dried her sweaty brow, then turned to continue working through the other parts of the meal.

Satisfied with her piles of finely chopped vegetables, Kausha spun the knife in her hand like Chef had, then set it down next to the piles. She turned to face Chef, who was throwing something fine and white into the mixture she was tasting with a wooden spoon. She must have felt Kausha staring, for she smacked her lips and without turning, dismissed her, "That is all. Run along." Kausha set off towards the exit, glancing, once again, at the knife lying on the counter.

The common area was a hivemind of activity - women speeding this way or that, white cloaks fluttering behind each as they set off to finish their duties. Some carried baskets while others carried spindles of cloth or half-finished clothing, but each held their mouths in a line with eyelids soft. She leaned her back against the wall thinking of the others until she noticed Selene walking away from her with two women in tow, both darting their heads left and right like they were watching for something. They disappeared through a door on the far side of the room, further than the gardens. Kausha frowned after them, unsure of what to make of it. Nearing supper, Kausha fell in line with the others awaiting their items to be carried to the first's table. This time around, she was handed a heavy tray of polished silverware. Following the line of white cloaks, she realized that the awe she first felt when seeing the large dining room turned into a sour taste in her mouth upon seeing it this time. *All on the backs of slaves.* She clenched her jaw while slowly working her way from one end of the table to the other placing a spoon, knife, and fork, as instructed, to the right of each plate. Nearing the far end of the table near the fireplace, she looked up from the monotonous task to see that the only two left were her and the same larger woman that stood at the door the last time. She jumped as the door opening nearby caught her by surprise, light from what she now noticed was a sun-lit hallway forcing her to squint as it covered her from head to toe.

A silhouette paused in the doorframe, cloak flapping as a cool breeze reached her cheeks along with the word, "Kausha?"

Kausha dropped the fork she had in her hand to shade her eyes as the silhouette started towards the edge of the table.

"Kausha, it IS you!" came the voice again.

She remembered the voice before she saw who was behind it. "Skip?" she asked as he rounded the corner of the table, the light shining on his red hair, backlit by the fire making it look like flames coming out of his head. "Skip!" she exclaimed, placing the tray down on top of the next two plates in line as he closed the gap while opening his arms. She returned the gesture, embracing him equally, feeling his instrument strapped across his back. They let go of one another, a smile on both faces.

"Where have you been?" Kausha asked, shifting her weight so the fire was directly behind him.

"Well, here as well as the other towers. I guess I made too good of an impression the first time playing and the first wanted to show me off to the other five. Have you seen Nalia?" he asked, glancing at the tray then back to her.

Kausha nodded, remembering her job, picking up the tray, then placing a spoon down and glancing over the room to make sure no one else was near. "I'm not sure what she is doing, but I've seen her twice and I have a plan."

"A plan?!" Skip responded a little too loudly. Kausha shot a look from the corner of her eyes.

He cringed, repeating it again in a whisper. "A plan?"

Kausha shook her head in exasperation, placing a knife on the table next to the spoon. Without looking up, she responded. "Yes, it seems that the water is near a boil and the six are the cause of it. How are they? The six, that is?"

"Hmm. Well, the first is just a kid, thrown into something he doesn't understand from the looks of it. He's rather new from what I've heard. The second is a graying dwarve that just sits around, not a hint of pleasure in my songs, even when I..." he stopped himself abruptly, "... I, um, play newer songs. The other four are seemingly normal from what I witnessed. Then again, the only time someone brings a bard in to play is when they're eating, drinking, or mourning, and they're not doing the latter. How are they causing it?" he asked, shifting his instrument to his front to pluck a few notes, pretending to tune it after realizing he was just standing there.

Kausha moved down the table to the next plate, gently placing a fork to the right side of it. "I see. Well, they are enslaving everyone and everything that comes through the walls and nearly all of the six are new in the last few moons. Even the older slave women that voluntarily went into it, who were once able to leave, are no longer allowed to. Their greed for ujuntu has not gone unnoticed with the women, both young and old. I have a plan though, but first we need to find Nalia's sister, who I think is in one of the towers. Have you seen another Catsnif slave anywhere in the other towers?"

He plucked a few cords while his eyes drifted, thinking. "I don't think so. Would have remembered seeing someone like Nalia. I'll see if I can somehow get over to the other towers, but they barely give me time to think. I've been playing almost nonstop since we got here."

Kausha glanced up after placing a spoon, only now noticing that four of his fingers had wrappings on them.

Skip noticed her eyes on his fingers and clenched his hand into a ball. "I'll be fine though. It's Shaum and Skirm that I'm worried about. I wouldn't want to spend a single day in those things."

Kausha nodded in agreement, nearing the middle of the table where the fireplaces warmed her, threatening to force her into sweating. "Okay, so you'll keep on the lookout for her while we do the same."

Skip nodded. "Right. Might want to speed that up though, the woman over there is staring daggers into you."

Kausha could feel those eyes now that he said that, practically boring a hole into the side of her head. "Okay, can we meet here tomorrow?"

"I'll try."

"Great. See you then."

With that, Skip nodded, then retreated back towards the end of the table still strumming his instrument while Kausha placed the last few utensils and retreated to the opposite side of the room, eyes down to not make contact with the large woman at the door.

"He's an exotic one, that one," the large woman growled, shutting the doors behind Kausha. "As much as I'd want to jump his bones too, don't go letting the dwarves see you pull that stunt. Leave me out of whatever you were talking about and don't let the dwarves catch you doing it either."

Kausha looked back at the woman, cheeks red. "I wasn..." Kausha began, but was interrupted by the woman putting a single finger over her lips. "I told you, I don't want anything to do with it. Now, get on downstairs."

So the first is indeed a kid. Kausha headed down the steps towards the kitchen with the large woman keeping pace behind. *He's more than likely a puppet, but who is pulling the strings? Does it really matter? We need to find Nalia's sister and get out of here.*

The other women were eating in the common area, a low buzz reaching her ears from the close talking whispers throughout the room. She entered the kitchen, placed the tray down on the stone countertop, then grabbed a portion of the meat, bread, veggies, and cheese that was there. She exited out the opposite door, aiming for the spot she had eaten before, just left of the door, and was met with yellow, unblinking eyes.

"Puid?" Kausha asked, meeting her eyes.

"Hello," she replied with her toothy smile again, faint wrinkles appearing on the outsides of her eyes on her green skin.

Kausha proceeded to sit next to her, crossing her legs to create a place to put her plate. Without saying a word, they both ate - Puid with her methodical cutting, Kausha scooping everything within reach, uncaring what touched. Once Kausha had her fill, which never took very much, she held her plate out towards Puid, who looked at it, then at Kausha, her toothy smile returning.

"Thank you," she said before sliding the vegetables onto her plate.

Kausha set the plate down between them, then leaned her head back against the wall, closing her eyes attempting to hear one of the conversations nearby.

"What were you talking to the Catsnif about last night?" Puid asked, forcing Kausha's breath to catch, her eyes shooting open to look at the woman who was still cutting her food into small pieces. *Why would she ask that?*

"Nothing important," Kausha replied.

Puid put the fork to her mouth taking a small bite, swallowing, then responding without looking at her. "I'm sorry, I was just curious."

Is she being sincere? Kausha's eyebrows narrowed. *Maybe I can use this to my advantage.*

"It's okay. We were talking about getting out of here."

Puid paused, holding the fork with a single square green embedded between tines, half-way to her mouth, her eyes widening, then shrinking back to normal almost as soon as it happened. Kausha even caught herself off guard with that, her legs twitching, preparing her to fight. *Moss! Why did I just come out and say that?!* she cursed to herself.

Puid nodded, finishing the bite on her fork, then placed the plate between them on top of Kausha's. Kausha noticed that, unlike yesterday, she didn't clean it.

"I see. And what I said meant nothing to you?" she asked.

Kausha thought back. "That some have tried while none have succeeded?"

Puid nodded, her fingers rubbing between her knuckles while her hands sat on her lap.

"Have you seen any other Catsnif around, Puid? She would only have arrived a few moons back by herself."

Puid's eyes squinted as she thought, and then to Kausha's delight, she nodded.

"You have?! Where? When?" Kausha asked, nearly jumping to her knees.

Puid turned towards Kausha, the skin on her face and neck reflecting the white of her robe. "I saw one that looked similar to the one you were talking to. It was four moons back, I believe, and she was clearly frightened."

"So she WAS here. Do you know where they took her?" Kausha's heart drummed quicker.

Puid gave a small nod. "To the third's tower."

This time, Kausha did jump to her knees, fully facing Puid, who gave a start at the sudden movement and shied back an inch, but made no effort to move. "Do you know if she is still there?"

"I don't," Puid replied, her eyes moving down and away from Kausha's, clearly uncomfortable.

Kausha fell back on her heels, her hands resting on her legs, then nodded. "Thank you for this, Puid. Really, it means a lot."

Puid nodded, but continued to stare down at the floor between them.

"What is it?" Kausha asked.

The question hung in the air, Puid's fingers turning a lighter shade of green as she struggled to answer, opening her mouth a few times to speak, but holding back until looking up and meeting Kausha's eyes with a determination that made her swallow. "Take me with you. I don't care if I get caught and thrown into the caves. I need to get out."

Kausha could have sworn that she saw her cheeks turn slightly yellow after she finished the statement, but her yellow, unblinking eyes, meant she was serious. *Can I?* Kausha wondered how she was going to get herself, Nalia, Skip, Shaum, Skirm, and now Puid, out. She found herself nodding, nonetheless.

"Okay," Kausha finally answered. Puid's eyes returned to their normal, softer self. "For now, don't say anything to anyone and act like nothing is happening. I have a plan and now that I know where Nalia's sister is, we can begin preparations."

Puid nodded a quick jerk of her head. "I'll be ready whenever you are."

Kausha only then noticed that the buzz in the room disappeared, leaving only a few women remaining at a table far off at the opposite end of the room.

"I think we should get moving," she decided, picking up the plates, handing one to Puid and keeping the other for herself before standing. Puid nodded, then the two headed into the kitchen to drop their plates off before heading downstairs in silence, only the sound of her footsteps accompanying them. Kausha glanced down to Puid's feet, attempting to hear her footsteps, but nothing reached her ears. *Interesting.* They reached the bottom floor where women shuffled back and forth from bedrooms to the bath, its steam warming the entire floor. After a quick nod, Puid cut right into her room, Kausha left to hers, gathering her towel, bathing, and then heading back to her room where all of the beds were filled except hers. Lying in her bed with renewed vigor, she went over the plan in her head again, adding Puid into them and filling in holes previously unfilled, until sleep overcame her.

Chapter 38: Reanimation

Death in the caves was commonplace in Nortmund and the sorcerers knew that. Countless dead slaves piled deep in the long-abandoned caves where ujuntu was mined dry, lost in time. Until now.

The sorcerer's minds, invisible and formless, hovered over dozens of fresh bodies that had been discarded recently, skin taught to their bones, faces hollow with eye sockets seemingly deeper than the caves they rested in - worked until their hearts gave out. What little blood that remained in the husks began to seep from every orifice from hundreds of names long forgotten, pooling into little droplets, hovering in mid air until the entire cave was filled from walls to ceiling. The droplets split again and again until each was the size of a fingernail. The sorcerer's combined minds enveloped the droplets, forcing their bidding as well as images of Kausha and the others into each with an absolute goal: Take over a host and kill the Bloodborn and her companions.

The droplets reverberated before becoming perfect spheres, then shot out of the cave, hunting for a host.

***

With a quarter moon overhead, a group of dwarven guards relaxed on large, jagged stones, smoking through long wooden pipes under a tent near the base of a ramp leading towards the caves. After a long day of guarding slaves, helmets were off and halberts were discarded, leaning neatly on a metal stand nearby. Deep, bellowing laughs shot out into the open air, uncaring of who would hear.

A droplet of blood splashed into one of the dwarve's eyes causing him to curse and blink hard in an attempt to expel whatever it was that hit it. The other guards looked on curiously,

266

then were hit by seemingly the same thing, each dropping their pipes and rubbing their eyes hard, finding red on their hand upon removing it from their faces. A blood curdling cry sounded off somewhere in the dark causing each dwarve to shoot up out of their seat and squint towards the sound in an attempt to see what it was. They were met with only silence until the first dwarve let out a similar cry into the air above, arching his back unnaturally as if he were going to fold in half. The others shied back, cringing, quickly covering their ears. The cry ceased, and yet the dwarve's chest heaved up and down, back still arched with his head facing the dark sky above. A stillness hung in the air as they watched in horror as the dwarve lifted its head towards them, deep, blood-red, glowing eyes staring daggers into them. Wide eyed and paralyzed with fear, the dwarves lowered their hands from their ears, not knowing what to do next. Then, a dwarve off to their right cried, then the left, and soon the entire squad was overtaken, blood curdling cries echoing into the night.

Cries rang out everywhere, a wave of pain rolling through the tents, shacks, and run-down homes that were unlucky enough to be chosen by the blood droplets. Those that were not chosen scrambled into the dusty streets and were met with similar cries for help from everywhere they turned. The quiet night became a mix of fear and panic as the red, glowing eyes cut through the night, focused on one thing and one thing only - death.

Chapter 39: Rescue Attempts

Kausha's eyes shot open as a loud bang sounded on the other side of the door, her body moving before her mind could process anything, forcing her to her feet before her eyes could even see through the darkness. She could hear rustling throughout the room as the other women began moving. Another loud bang had the women in a frenzy, each jumping to their feet and throwing their robes on, just as Kausha had. One of them slowly opened the door, candlelight from the hall, as dim as it was, blinded Kausha forcing her to blink until her eyes were used to the light. Slaves were flowing from the doorway opposite hers, the women haphazardly dressed, some without robes on at all, but all with fear in their eyes.

What the, Kausha wondered as she watched a few of the women in her room file out, look left down the hall towards the other rooms, then turn heel and run the opposite direction. Mayhem ensued. Screams echoed throughout the hall, white robes flying by the doorway in a blur followed by another bang nearby, this one closer than the ones before. She stood by her bed, blood coursing into her arms and hands as the final woman fled the room, disappearing into the wave of white robes.

A short silhouette appeared in the doorway, helm and shoulder armor glistening in the candlelight from behind. Glowing red eyes pierced through the room directly at her. *Is that a guard?* She squinted, trying to make its face out as it stood unmoving with halbert in one hand with the butt resting on the floor.

The hall was empty of slaves, the candlelight returning back to its steady, unwavering self, but Kausha could hear muted commotion coming from up the stairs signaling something more was happening. She bent her fingers to face backwards so as to not raise suspicion, then began pushing blood from beneath her fingernails, her trusted blood knives appearing from her index fingers. Before she could move, a flash of green appeared behind the dwarve followed by a loud metal on stone crunch echoing through the room as the dwarve fell face first onto the stone floor besides its halbert.

Candlelight reflected off of Puid's green body as she appeared in the doorway with a stone pan in hand, motioning for Kausha to follow. Kausha sucked her blood back into her fingertips then strode to the doorway.

"Puid!" Kausha exclaimed while stepping over the dwarve. "What is going on?"

Puid shook her head as she gripped the pan with both hands, knuckles a shade of light green. "I don't know, but they're searching for someone. None of the women from my room were bothered and I didn't see you upstairs so I came back down. They have glowing red eyes, Kausha, all of them."

Kausha nodded, glancing back at the fallen dwarve. *What do those eyes mean?* "So there are more upstairs?"

Puid nodded, a frown appearing on her face. "Lots."

"Moss," Kausha cursed, "Okay, we need to get to the kitchen. Let's hurry." Before Puid could answer, Kausha was already off towards the stairway, taking them two at a time on her toes.

They approached the top of the stairway where the commotion was at a fever pitch - women everywhere huddled in small groups either chatting or deathly afraid and completely silent as they watched dwarven guards, all suited with armor and halberts in hand, pace throughout. She noticed Chef standing a ways off, arms crossed in front of her chest, a deep scowl on her face, doing her best to look intimidating as the oldest of women, including Linil and Seline, stood behind her.

Kausha shook herself, forcing her sights back to the kitchen. *No one around,* she noticed, glancing from dwarve to dwarve. Without a second thought, she darted from her hiding spot directly towards the kitchen door. Reaching it, she quickly glanced behind to see Puid directly on her heels, then pushed it open as quickly and quietly as possible with her left hand while her right hand prepared a blood knife. No one was in the kitchen and so she retrieved her blood and shut the door behind her in a flash, nearly clipping Puid in her heel.

The guards could be right behind us. She hurried towards the knives on the center island, grabbed the two that were roughly the size of her hand, weighing each by flipping them head over handle.

"What are we going to do?" Puid whispered from behind her.

Kausha turned to look into her yellow eyes, then down at the pan she still held clutched in her hand. "Do you want to use that?" she asked, nodding towards it. Puid held the pan up, a dent showing in the middle from striking the dwarve's helm. She looked up, then nodded. "If I have to, yes."

Kausha nodded. "Okay, well, the plan I had before this is useless now, and whatever those things are, they aren't the normal dwarves from before. First, we need to find Nalia and Skip on the next floor, then Nalia's sister, then we're heading to the mines to find Shaum and Skirm." *Sure sounds like a lot more than I thought.*

Kausha noticed a brief moment of fear crossed Puid's face upon mention of the mines, one that she'd seen too many times before, so she placed a hand on her shoulder. "We'll get out of here," she promised. Puid's eyes narrowed, determination returning, and answered with a nod.

"Right, let's head out the opposite door and up the back stairwell first. Ready?" Kausha asked.

"Ready," Puid responded close behind, clutching the pan tightly.

Kausha reached the door, pushing it open just enough to peek out as the conversations beyond continued, albeit subdued from before. The dwarves from before were still pacing throughout the room, occasionally staring at one of the women as if measuring them.

Right. Kausha quickly glanced back at Puid, then snuck out crouched, cutting directly left towards the back stairs, reaching it in a dozen quick strides. She placed her back against the inner wall of the stairs. Puid slid in beside her. She listened for commotion, knives at the ready, but none came and so she took to the stone steps, silently ascending them towards the walkway above. She stopped, throwing herself towards the inner wall again upon noticing an armored foot at the top. She looked at Puid, bringing her finger to her lips telling her to be silent, then took a deep breath. Driving blood into her legs, she charged up the stairs two by two, reaching the dwarven guard before it could move its halbert from its resting place, then slammed both knives up into the dwarve's chin, silencing it before it could set off any alarm. She let go of both knives, catching the halbert before it could fall with her left arm as the dwarve slunk into her blood-strengthened right arm. She let both down softly on to the stone floor, no one the wiser to what just occurred. Retrieving the knives from the dwarve, she glanced down to Puid and nodded, the woman showing no signs of awe or fright on her face.

Kausha looked forward across the walkway - a wide enough stone path for two to walk side by side with stone railings on either side exposing it to the room below. She slid the knives into her waistband beneath her robe, then got on all fours and began crawling across. While crawling, she glanced down into the room noticing that some of the women were sitting down now, their initial shock replaced with anger as they glared at the dwarves searching faces for something or someone.

They stood again upon reaching the end of the walkway, full walls replacing railings as they turned left to enter a candlelit hallway void of anything but light. Even the sounds of the women slaves in the previous room going mute. She retrieved the knives from her waistband and proceeded down the hall with Puid in tow until she approached the end, the familiar sound of women chatting reaching her ears once again. *Here too, then.* She glanced around the corner to reveal a common room not too different from the one below, except smaller with only one wooden table with wooden benches on either side. A handful of women were seated in the white slave robes of the first - impossible for Kausha to tell if Nalia was one of them.

The room itself was illuminated by one large fireplace that could fit three of her inside with room to spare, a painting of what would have probably been the first's family above the mantle. The rest of the room's walls were bare, the white-washed stone similar to the rest of the interior of the tower and the only other exit Kausha could see was on the opposite corner next to the fireplace.

Two dwarven guards paced back and forth on opposite sides of the table behind the women, occasionally casting a shadow on their faces as they passed in front of the fireplace. She leaned back into the hall, the absence of the firelight on her face noticeably cooler, and explained the situation to Puid, who nodded along.

"Stay here and I'll handle these," Kausha whispered, turning towards the room again. She glanced in and waited for both dwarves to turn away from her once more, then took two quick steps inside while rearing back the knife in her right hand, robe rustling at her movement, aiming for the dwarve on the far side of the table. A gasp came from one of the women as she noticed Kausha enter with a gleaming knife at the ready causing the dwarve's glowing eyes to search for the commotion, but Kausha was ready. She let loose the knife directly at the dwarve's throat, confident that it was going to hit its mark, then immediately bolted towards the closer dwarve, closing the short gap between them in three strides. It raised the halbert, spinning it backwards, head over shaft, in an attempt to catch Kausha from underneath. She sidestepped to her right, clearing the glistening metal of the halbert as the corner of her robe was sliced through. Planting her feed, she spun with her left arm outstretched, knife slicing through the air along with the dwarve's throat and braided beard alike causing blood to gush down its chest over armor and white cloak. The dwarve went limp as its eyes went dull and toppled back with a crash. She glanced at the women at the table, all of them huddled together, horror on their faces as blood dripped from Kausha's knife. *No Nalia,* she noticed.

"You're free! Go!" Kausha yelled, possibly a little too harsh. The women only stared wide-eyed at her in the firelight, either not wanting to move in fear, or unable to.

Kausha shrugged, looking back at Puid who was staring down at the dead dwarve at her feet. Wiping the blade off, she made her way to the other side of the table, pulling the knife from the dwarve's neck, a puddle of blood reflecting the firelight underneath its head. She stood, all eyes still fixated on in horror, then she made her way to the doorway, her eyes unable to pierce into the darkness beyond.

Knives at the ready, she stepped into the darkness with eyes wide trying to force them to adjust. As she crept forward into nothing, the crackling of the fire faded behind her leaving her heart thumping in her ears. Out of the corner of her eye, she noticed a few slivers of light close by to her right and crept up to them with an outstretched hand feeling wood on her fingertips. *A door.* She searched for a handle, finding metal, pressing the knob down and then cracking it open. Dim candlelight cut across her eye as she peeked out.

She pulled the door open slowly until enough space was left for her to stick her head out to see a stone hall with a few candles along the wall with only half of them lit, creating a patched looking hall where light and dark fought for supremacy. She looked both ways but didn't see or hear anyone there, so she silently crept the door open the rest of the way, knives at the ready again just in case, and entered the hall. *Which way?* A tap on her shoulder sent her heart racing, insides responding immediately by shifting away from her center. She looked back to meet Puid's eyes who nodded to the left. *Okay, left it is,* Kausha nodded, wanting to ask how she knew, but now wasn't the time.

She turned left down the short hallway, entering light and then darkness, then light again until approaching a corner with two open doors on the opposite wall, both pitch blank on the inside. She peeked around the corner to see an empty hall similar to the one she stood in.

"Kausha?!" she heard, making her jump, knives ready as she turned, staring into the dark room opposite of where she stood.

A pale face with red hair emerged into the light as if detached from the body.

"Skip!" she exclaimed in a whisper. "What are you doing here?!"

He left the room, crossing the hall in a hurry, supporting an instrument on his back with his left hand.

"I could be asking you the same thing," he answered looking back at Puid.

"Skip, Puid," Kausha introduced, both nodding as a hello.

Skip looked back at Kausha again. "So what's the plan?" he asked.

"No plan, we just need to find Nalia and her sister, then get into the city to find Shaum and Skirm," Kausha answered.

"Sounds like a plan to me. I found Nalia's sister earlier today and while everyone was running around, ran into her and told her. She told me to stay here to watch out for you as if she knew you were going to come, then ran off." Skip scratched his chin.

Moss! Kausha cursed. "Where was she?"

"In the second's tower."

"Can you lead the way?" Kausha asked.

"Sure, but I'm no fighter, you know that."

"That's fine, I can take care of most. And Puid here can handle her own too," *I think*.

"Follow me, then. The connection isn't too far away," Skip ended, taking the lead turning the corner down the hall.

Compared to Kausha and Puid, Skip sounded like he was actively trying to make noise even though he was clearly trying his hardest to tiptoe around. It didn't help that the strings on his instrument kept snagging cloth on his back, letting off a twang every so often. He led them down the hall through periodic candlelight, passing closed wooden doors on the left-hand wall until they reached another corner. Peeking around it, seeing no one, they proceeded towards a bright intersection shaped like a t where they could go straight or turn left down a hall where bright candlelight was spilling from.

Without entering the light, Skip turned towards Kausha, then whispered, "The connection is right here."

She looked at the intersection, nodded, then took the lead, hugging the wall while approaching the corner, then crouched. Out of the bottom corner of her eye, something reflected the light. *Blood.* She gripped the knives and moved her head into the light to see where the blood was coming from, first seeing the tip of a helmet, then the unmistakable beard covered face of a dwarven guard, eyes dull. Before she could inspect further, a shuffling sound of feet down the connection hall made her retreat into the dark around the corner. The shuffling grew more numerous and louder as if multiple feet were moving towards her. She glanced back at Skip and Puid, motioning them to scoot back away from her a little, then stood with her back flush against the wall, knives at her side pointed out, ready to pounce. The shuffling was nearly upon her. As soon as she heard the sound of a foot stepping in the puddle of blood next to her, she acted, swinging her right arm in a long arc at what she assumed was face level with a dwarve.

Her face and muscles strained upon recognizing Nalia's furry face, eyes wide in horror at the knife approaching her chest. Kausha forced blood into her arm, pulling her elbow in, forcing the knife off course and slamming it into the stone wall. A loud clank echoed through the halls as metal hit stone causing a painful shock to shoot up her arm, forcing her to drop the knife and close her eyes with a clenched jaw.

"Kausha?!" Nalia quivered. "Skip?"

Kausha opened her watered eyes, blinking and forcing the blood in and out of her hand to get feeling back.

"Moss, that was close," Nalia cursed, looking at the gash in the stone wall. "You okay, Kausha?"

Kausha nodded through watery eyes, shaking her hand. "I'll be fine." She looked past Nalia to the smaller Catsnif beside her.

Nalia followed her gaze. "Oh, right, Roana, this is Kausha and Skip, friends of mine." Nalia's soft eyes looked back at a smaller Catsnif behind her. "And this is my sister, Roana," she finished, turning back towards Kausha and Skip.

"Nalia, you're safe." Kausha squeezed her hand once more, the tingling feeling nearly gone. "Skip said you'd ran off to the second's tower to get your sister. Seems you found her." She glanced at Roana again, noticing the same striped brown and tan fur covering her face and hands that Nalia had, her pointed ears turning towards sound Kausha couldn't hear. The only difference was that Roana was smaller in height and in mass and had light brown eyes instead of orange.

"I was coming back for Skip and you," Nalia replied, only then noticing Puid.

It was Kausha's turn to follow her gaze. "That's Puid, she's helped me find you and Skip."

"Hello," Puid responded, light reflecting off of her green skin, pan still grasped in her hand.

Nalia nodded, then returned her eyes back towards Kausha, eyebrows narrowing. "They're everywhere. We need to get out of here."

"Right," Kausha nodded, "but first, we need to get into the city to find Shaum and Skirm. How do we do that?"

"I think I can help with that," Puid broke in from behind Skip, causing everyone to turn their heads towards her. "I've been here too long and know the way from this tower to the gate."

Kausha nodded. "Lead the way."

***

Shaum sat upright, eyes wide, but still seeing just as much as he was with eyes shut. Was it his imagination or was something happening outside of the tented cage? His hands and feet were raw, his muscles and bones were sore, but was his mind gone already? Dozens of other slaves slept nearby, none churning awake like him. He focused past the snores and heard it again, this time nudging Skirm awake.

"Oy. Di ya ear tha?" he whispered, eyes shifting to where he recalled him falling asleep next to him in the dirt. Skirm groaned, sitting up.

"Hear what?" he asked, stretching his sore arm across his body.

A cry reached their ears, then another and another until rustling from the other slaves proved that they weren't just hearing things. Murmuring began to rise throughout as the slaves began standing and shuffling towards the metal bars.

Shaum and Skirm were the first to reach the edge of the cage. They reached through the thick metal bars to grab the tent flap, shifting it from one hand to the other in an attempt to create an opening. Slaves gathered behind, pushing and shoving for the best view between the burly Spearheads. The flap opened enough for a faint light to cut through the pitch black accompanied by clear, blood curdling cries coming from everywhere outside. Talk from behind them grew louder as the ones in the front relayed what they saw to those behind.

"It's Doinun, he's screaming up into the air!" came a voice right behind the two, referring to a dwarven guard that regularly watched the cage. Shaum and Skirm stared at the guard until the cry stopped, his chest heaving in and out, followed by his head rightening back to normal.

Those that could see gasped, some tumbling backwards into others as the guard's head jerked towards them, blood red eyes glowing while staring directly at the opening. With the blood curdling cries growing louder in the distance, the dwarve began walking towards them, not an ounce of urgency to his movement.

Shaum dropped the flap, throwing the entire cage into darkness once again. He grabbed Skirm. "Wha was dat?" he asked, keeping hold of Skirm and shoving their way through the crowd towards the middle.

"I'm not sure, but it didn't look good," Skirm replied, a slight tremble in his voice.

"Well, we can't jus sit ere!" Shaum yelled over the growing commotion. Some nearby agreed as if he were talking to all of them.

"We're in a cage! What *should* we do, then?!" Skirm replied, catching himself on Shaum as someone ran into him.

Before they could decide, the tent flap at the door of the cage parted, revealing glowing red eyes staring directly at them. Skirm felt Shaum's hand tighten around his arm as his breath caught, heart pounding in his chest. All around them, slaves turned on their heels to stare at the dwarve, the cries from outside the tent drowning out those on the inside. The two took a measured step back. The dwarve pulled something from his waist and reached for the door.

"He's coming in!" Skirm exclaimed, which seemed to shake the other slaves from their stupor, each retreating towards the back of the cage leaving Shaum and Skirm alone in the middle, the triangle of light from outside illuminating their faces and bodies.

"Moss, moss, moss! Es e afta us?" Shaum panicked, eyes darting around seeing no one close. The dwarve's eyes were still fixated on them as he reached for the lock. "Es afta us int e." It was more of an answer than a question this time.

Skirm nodded, prying off Shaum's hand to wipe his brow with the back of his hand, sweat building, even in the cool air close to the mountains.

The dwarve unlocked the doors, shoving them open, then stepped forward. The tent cloth slid closed behind him except for a small sliver that back-lit the halbert in his right hand and metal armor donned throughout. Unblinking, glowing red eyes fixated on them as if they were the only ones in the cage. The slaves behind Shaum and Skirm gasped as the dwarve stepped forward again, tension and hot breath filling the air.

"We have to move!" Skirm whispered out of the corner of his mouth. "You go right, I'll go left. His reach isn't long so if we stick by the bars we should be able to get away. Whoever he comes after, the other will sneak behind him and ram him in the back. Deal, brother?"

"Deal, brotha," Shaum replied, then started shuffling towards one side, Skirm shuffling towards the other.

The dwarve stopped, feet shoulder-width apart, the butt of the halbert slamming into the floor driving up dust into the sliver of light as his eyes slowly moved from one to the other, landing on

Skirm. He turned to face him, pointing the halbert, now held in both hands, directly at Skirm's chest. He began his slow walk again, eyes fixated on his target, only a few feet out of range. Skirm tried to force himself to move, but the eyes froze him in place.

Move, Moss! Move, he cursed, trying to will his legs without success.

The tip of the halbert was within arms reach. A thrust could have skewered him. He sucked in a breath. But before the dwarve could rear back, a blob of bodies slammed into the dwarve from the side, the red glow disappearing as its head snapped away, halbert flying from its hands and slamming into the dirt. Skirm blinked, finding he was able to move his body again as Shaum appeared in front of him, mouth agape beneath a glistening face and forehead.

"Go!" a gruff voice grunted off to his left where the blob of bodies lay on top of the dwarve. "Go, Moss you!" the gruff voice yelled louder again between cries of pain and growls of anger. The slaves wouldn't let this moment of revenge pass them by.

Shaum pulled Skirm around the writhing blob of bodies of slaves and out the open door into a mass of confusion and noise with citizens running and yelling everywhere off in the distance closer to the inner walls. Embers danced into the sky from unseen fires below that made the shacks and lean-tos glow.

"Did they just..." Skirm asked, glancing back to the large tent.

Shaum nodded looking around. "Tha way." He pointed towards the barracks that normally held the guards, its door swung wide. "We need weapons," Shaum explained, starting the run with Skirm right on his heels.

They slowed to a silent walk, wiping their sweaty hands on their dirt-stained skirts as they approached the wooden barracks, one of the larger structures on this side of the wall with its polished stone walls that nearly glistened in the faint firelight. They listened for the sounds of guards inside, but the only thing they could hear was what was around them outside. After nodding to one another, they crept, fists clenched into balls, through the door into a bright, candlelit room that ran the width of the building. Littered throughout were circular tables and wooden chairs, some looking as if pushed back, others simply toppled over as if shoved away for a quick getaway. It seemed that all of the guards heard the commotion and ran off to help. The two continued, entering the main sleeping quarters, filled with beds stacked in twos, which wasn't very much more impressive than the slaves sleeping arrangements, but at least they had beds. Off to the right were racks of halberts and swords neatly situated by armor in case a quick getaway was needed. The two looked at the armor then at each other, shrugging.

"Seems like it'll only be a weapon for us." Skirm lifted one of the helmets next to his head, which clearly wasn't going to fit. He set the helmet down, then grabbed the longest halbert he could find, testing it with a thrust in front of him. Shaum, as different from his brother that he was, grabbed a smaller one, snapping the wooden shaft in one quick motion, then repeated with another to hold two short halberts that mimicked long axes.

Skirm huffed. "You just can't be normal, can you?"

Shaum shrugged. "I gotta look cool," he smiled, twirling the handheld halberts, then nodding to himself, satisfied.

"Okay, so I don't know why those things are after us, but it seems like they are and they are everywhere from the sounds of it. This is our chance to get out of here to find Kausha and the others. Let's sneak around the outside towards the towers, find a door, then search for them inside," Skirm explained awaiting confirmation from Shaum.

Shaum's eyebrows scrunched, shoulders slouching. "Wha if we can find em an we get caught again?"

Skirm exhaled audibly, putting his hand on Shaum's shoulder, willing him to meet his eyes. "We will get out of this. If I know us, we can do this. We're Spearhead, afterall. Once we find Kausha, she'll handle everything else, I promise. She's Bloodborn, afterall. We all make one impressive team."

Shaum straightened him back, forcing a smile to his lips, revealing the sharp teeth beneath. "Yer right."

Skirm slapped his shoulder once before removing it completely. "Oh, and don't stare those things in their eyes. I'm not sure what happened back there, but I couldn't move when we held eye contact."

Shaum nodded in confirmation.

"Let's go." Skirm led the two towards the exit, pausing to glance around before rounding the backside of the barracks. They crept in the dark from building to tent to outhouse, the constant screams and noise from the citizens coming in handy, overshadowing any noise they made. They only ran across two of the glowing eyed dwarves while they crept, neither catching a glimpse of the two in the dark. They were as close as they could get to the innermost wall without leaving the cover of darkness and their hiding spots. Glancing along the wall, they could see the towers looming not too far off in the distance, white points lit by the faint moonlight overhead on one side and firelight from the other. Below the towers, the gigantic wall curved off into the distance, now glowing from fresh fires dancing nearby. They could see one of the steel gates not too far off, drawn down like normal.

"The guards, if there are any, are probably inside of the gate." Skirm moved his head to change his line of sight. "Do you see any?"

"No," Shaum replied, shaking his head. "Only a gate. Where's tha door?"

"There," Skirm pointed, "just beyond the gate. It's a wooden door for the guards to pass through without going through the gate itself. We'll have to try to break it down if it's locked."

The two crept forward to the next tent, the cries for help growing louder alongside fires crackling, wood breaking, and curses being tossed towards the dwarves.

"Moss! Say something! You can't just enter without saying why!" a high-pitched voice shouted from off to their left. Before jumping between tents, Skirm paused, peeking around a small tent to find the voice. It was an older human standing in his doorway facing the dwarve head-on. The dwarve didn't say a word, didn't even look at the man as he shoved the man to the side as if he were a pebble. Skirm slinked back into the darkness, focusing again on Shaum ahead of him.

What is happening?! Skirm crept forward to squat behind Shaum. *Why did they try to kill us but not him? And those eyes. Those unnatural eyes were not right. The guards never had eyes like that before.*

Shaum paused ahead of him, quickly glancing around the corner, then looked back. "Es a dead end. No otha dark to hide in."

Skirm huddled around Shaum seeing that the wooden structure they were at was the last one before a wide, dirt road that led from the gate, which ran alongside the wall a short span, then curved into the shacks, hobbles, and lean-tos the slaves with more freedoms called home. Whatever had a roof and at least three walls could be called a home here. Opulence on one side of the wall, poverty, hardship, and death on the other. And all for pieces of rock.

Mayhem spilled into the street where slaves ran every which way pleading the dwarven guards for help. Fires burned sporadically in the distance while others took advantage of nightfall and confusion to rob or steal. It all fell on deaf ears, the dwarves shoving aside anyone that got in their way of the search for...

"Us," Skirm blurted out, a chill running through his spine. "They're searching for us."

Shaum's eyes peeled away from the road and mayhem, placing his back against the wooden structure they were hiding behind, then sighed, eyes connecting with Skirms, a cold calm to them.

He knew. Skirm narrowed his eyebrows. *But how?*

Before he could ask, Shaum spoke with a new resolve that he hadn't had earlier. "Les make et through tha door ta Kaush and tha others. If they're after us, they're probly after them."

Skirm didn't want to say it, but he knew that was right. *We're all connected now.* He gripped his halbert tighter in one hand.

The structure was large enough for them to stand next to and not be seen from the other side, but it still made their skin crawl.

How I wish I were sometimes smaller. Skirm ignored the sweat dripping down the sides of his face, setting his sights on the door next to the gate.

"On three." Skirm readied his legs for the run.

"One. Two. Thr..."

Before he could finish the word, the thick, wooden door flew off its hinges as if a giant had kicked it away. It should have made a booming sound, but the fires and shouts nearby muffled it down to a small part of the overall noise. Shaum and Skirm's mouths fell open as Kausha appeared where the door previously stood, draped in a white cloak that was dirty and tattered with blood splotches in various places. She looked back into the dark doorway, motioning and saying something out of earshot. To their shock, Nalia, Skip, and two more accompanied them that neither of the Spearheads recognized.

"Kaush!" Shaum yelled, causing Skirm to jump unexpectedly. He looked left down the dirt road towards the dwarves and commotion happening nearby. None of them seemed to hear Shaum yell, but Kausha did. She froze at first, arms splayed, ready for a fight, but then looked directly at the two, a smile reaching her lips. Before she could respond, Shaum was already running towards her and the others, long legs covering the width of the road in a few thumping strides, while Skirm, initially taken aback by Shaum's immediacy, followed close behind.

"Kaush! Whatre ya doin ere?!" Shaum asked, pausing short, blocking the light from the flames from the group's faces with his large body. "An Skip n Nalia n... these two!"

"We're here to rescue you, but it seems like that wasn't needed," she replied, glancing down at the weapons in his hands and raising an eyebrow. "Now, let's get out of this city! Puid..." she turned and nodded towards the shiny green woman in white, "...knows the way the six get out of the city so they don't have to go through the main paths that we took getting in here. Puid."

Puid nodded, her yellow eyes soaking up the firelight as it danced into the night behind Shaum and Skirm. "Follow me," she led, turning back towards the doorway they had just left.

Kausha took the place behind her, followed by Nalia and her sister, Roana, then Skip, Skirm, and Shaum bringing up the rear.

Chapter 39: Fight For Your Life

They entered the doorway, the flickering of candlelight greeting them by lighting the hall and area ahead, leaving the cries for help and firelight behind only to enter the lavish tower of the first with slaves in white running every which way after seeing skewered dwarven guards lying on the ground motionless, blood pooling beneath their bodies.

Puid paid no mind to anything going on around her, turning the group down a wide, plain hallway with gray stone on all sides lit by candlelight along the walls every few feet to provide ample light throughout. They hurried forward, slave women gawking at the two Spearheads in their skirts, chests bare, as they scampered in opposite directions. Descending a curved staircase at the end of the hall, they heard a scream above causing Puid and the others to pause before reaching the bottom of the stairs, glancing back up the way they came. Turning back towards the exit of the staircase, red eyes that weren't there a moment ago fixed on them from below, face hidden by the candle just above and behind the dwarve in the hall beyond. The dwarve gathered its halbert in both hands before taking a step up the curved stairs towards Puid.

Moss. How many are there?! Kausha wondered as she pushed blood from under her fingernails to produce the knives she'd become accustomed to. Before anyone could say anything, she was in the air falling towards the dwarve, knees tucked into her chest, blood knives glistening in candlelight. Before the dwarve could lift its halbert, she came crashing down on its chest, knives finding flesh between the neck and top of the chestpiece. A loud crash echoed up the stairs and down the hall as metal met stone. Without even so much as a grunt, its red eyes sputtered out, leaving only deep brown in their stead.

Kausha retracted her blood and stood, the dead dwarven body motionless beneath her, then looked up at the others, their eyes wide and mouths open.

"Well?"

They shook themselves, a big smile appearing on Shaum's lips.

Puid took the lead again, stepping over the dwarve at the bottom of the stairs, Kausha falling in line behind her, more alert than before as they headed down another hallway similar to the last.

Puid stopped the group towards the end, then glanced around a corner. Kausha followed suit pulling up beside her. Three dwarven guards stood before a doorway on the opposite corner of a dimly lit room, glowing red eyes piercing through the darkness brighter than the four candles on the walls, the butts of their halberts resting against the stone floor. The two moved back, Puid looking towards Kausha for a plan. Kausha turned towards Shaum and Skirm and held three fingers up, then pointed around the corner. The two nodded, faces taught, understanding what she meant, then crept up to her side preparing their weapons. Kausha felt the two looking at her for the next step, then she nodded, knives appearing once again under her fingernails. The three stood upright, entering the large room that was bare except for the four candles, one placed in the center of each wall to illuminate small pockets of the room, along with a few wooden crates stacked haphazardly in each corner, lids ajar.

The three dwarves fidgeted, halberts moving into both hands, their stances shifting to one of practiced precision upon seeing the three approach. Kausha began stepping leg over leg, making her way left in an arch with Skirm doing the same on the opposite side, except to his right, while Shaum moved straight ahead, sharp teeth bared for the dwarves to see.

The dwarves emulated the three, quiet clanking scattering throughout the room, bouncing off of the stone walls with every step, their eyes transfixed on their goal.

The dwarve approaching Kausha wore a white cloak, highlighted on his right side from candlelight. He reared back his weapon as he walked, armor clinking with each step, brown beard swinging softly from one side to the other underneath a metal helm that covered everything but the center of his face. He lifted his foot to take another step. Kausha sprang, running towards the side opposite the weapon as her insides shifted to ensure even if she were hit, it wouldn't be life threatening. The dwarve swung the halbert level with the floor in an attempt to slice her in half. She stopped her forward movement and jumped back just out of reach, her robe nicked by the blade as wind buffeted her cheeks. The top-heavy weapon made the dwarve follow through past Kausha, thick hand and arm muscles failing to halt its movement giving Kausha just the right amount of time to dart inside the dwarve's reach, stabbing both of her blood knives up under the dwarve's chin through the top of its head, lifting the helm it wore until the chin strap went taught. Its bright red, hollow eyes, once fierce, sagged as Kausha stared directly into them. She retracted her blood in one smooth motion and it toppled over, the lifeless body falling into a heap that caused a loud clang to echo throughout the room.

Kausha lifted her eyes from the body, looking over towards Shaum. He deflected the dwarve's halbert towards the ground with his own makeshift weapon, sparks ignored by both as metal met metal. He swung the one in his other hand in a quick downwards motion, the tip connecting with the dwarve's chest piece, sparks flying into the air once again, accompanied by a bone chilling scraping sound as the weapon sliced through the chestpiece. It would have sliced the dwarve in two if Shaum had been even a step closer. Unperturbed, the dwarve reared back again, unaware or uncaring of the sheer size difference, and swung again, this time in an upward motion, metal tip flashing through the air, forcing Shaum to dodge to his right. He bared his sharp teeth again, this time for the pain, not intimidation, shaking his right arm as it hung to his side, numb from the last hit.

Recovered, the dwarve slammed the halbert straight down from over its head, barely missing Shaum's left arm. A loud crash filled the air as metal met stone causing stone chips to fly into the air nearby. Eyes wide, staring down the shaft at the dwarve, Shaum stumbled back a few steps as the dwarve struggled with the weapon, now lodged into the stone floor. Shaum saw this and pushed himself forward with a clenched jaw and narrowed eyes, his right arm moving again. Then with two huge strides, he was at the side of the dwarve who was still yanking on the halbert's wooden shaft, only the muscles on its hands and arms giving any indication of strain. Shaum lifted both of his handheld halberts over his head as the dwarve gazed up at him with its glowing red eyes. Letting out a roar like that of a wild beast, he slammed them both down into the dwarve's helm, a nasty crunch following as the metal helm caved in, crushing the dwarve's skull. Shaum let go of the weapons, letting his arms fall to his sides while his chest heaved in and out. The dwarve collapsed in front of him, halberts still lodged deep into its helm and skull.

She looked past Shaum to Skirm, who was breathing heavily and glistening in the faint candlelight from his sweat. He held the long halbert in front of him, the tip of the weapon resting on the ground as the dwarve opposite him held its in front, solid and unmoving. With some struggle, Skirm lifted the halbert to his shoulder, letting one hand drop to his side. He flexed it over and over, muscles not used to the strain of a life or death fight. The dwarve took its opportunity and stepped forward, thrusting. The distance was too great for the weapon to reach, but Skirm took a small step back reflexively, seemingly unphased. He turned his body, positioning the shoulder his halbert sat on behind him, his left arm facing the dwarve. He took a deep breath to steady himself, then crouched, placing his left hand at the very bottom of the shaft while sliding his right hand down to meet it causing the halbert to hang behind him, metal tip nearly hitting the floor. The dwarve pulled his weapon back, took one step forward, but before he could plant his foot, was split directly in half from head to toe as Skirm slammed down his halbert through the top of the dwarve's skull using all of the force his large body could muster. A loud clang echoed throughout the room as metal met metal, bone, and then stone in one, jarring moment. The dwarve's body crumpled into itself, a pool of blood and guts spilling onto the stone beneath. With hands still tight on the halber's shaft, Skirm froze bent over, chest heaving his back up and down as he stared at the floor, the faint candlelight shining off his glistening body.

Shaum ran over to his brother, lifting his chest to help him stand, then threw one arm around him while the other punched him in the shoulder. "Oy, I dint know ya could do tha!" he exclaimed with a wide grin on his face.

"Now that is something you don't see everyday," Skip commended as he and the others left the hallway. "Cutting through armor and bone in one swing," he whistled as he glanced at the other two dead dwarves across the room. "This will make a fine song."

Puid and Roana made an effort to not look at any of the bodies as they walked with Nalia towards Kausha who was looking her up and down for wounds.

"I'm fine," Kausha assured, noticing their eyes. She shifted her gaze, watching Shaum and Skip slap Skirm on his back, the two talking over each other as they made their way towards Kausha.

"How much further?" Kausha asked, looking back at Puid whose mouth was tight in a straight line.

"Not far. Just through this room, down the stairs back there, then into the underground tunnel," she explained, nodding towards the back part of the room where the dwarves were standing when they entered.

"I'll lead, then. Everyone good?" Kausha asked to the group, but focusing on Skirm who seemed to be out of it, staring at nothing, not even responding to Shaum and Skip when they applauded his fight.

Everyone nodded though, even Skirm, even if lazily, and so Kausha turned heel and led the group towards the back doorway. They exited the room, entering a pitch-black stairwell without so much as a single hesitation. The climb down was slow and methodical, Kausha wanting to ensure everyone made it down safely, and with only walls on either side to support them if they needed them, she went much slower than she wanted. The sound of footsteps sliding along stones echoed through the staircase as they descended.

If there is someone at the bottom, they will certainly hear us, but we won't see them. Kausha clenched her jaw at the noise coming from behind. She instinctively split her insides to leave the middle of her torso void of blood and organs in case there was in fact anyone down below listening, waiting. To further protect herself, she rolled up her sleeves and then pushed her forearms together in front of her chest, one on top of the other. Forcing blood through the pores in her forearms, she connected the blood from both, separating each, moving one up and one down, creating a blood shield that was just as strong as any other in Uradaria, if not stronger, that was the width of her body and covered her from hip to neck. Head swimming, she realized she couldn't afford to snap it off this time after losing blood from the escape earlier, so she held it awkwardly like a scholar might hold a scroll.

Step by slow step, they continued down until Kausha heard, "Light," whispered from behind. It was Nalia with her sensitive Catsnif eyes. Kausha didn't notice anything until a number of steps later, and only then was it just barely visible.

That means there is no one else here, then. Good. Kausha let out a sigh that she hadn't realized she was holding in. *An underground tunnel next.*

Kausha reached the landing to see a glowing stone wall directly in front that had a sharp left turn to it, hiding the tunnel from immediate view. She pushed her forearms together, decided it was safe to retrieve her blood from the shield, then peeked around the corner into the tunnel in the direction of the light while the others made their way down the final few steps. Her eyes shot open at the sight, her body reacting unconsciously by shoving her organs to the right side of her body. She pulled her head back, cursing softly.

"Moss!" she whispered, looking down at her feet thinking.

"Wha es et?" Shaum asked in a hushed tone. No one moved a muscle as they watched Kausha glance over each one of them with clenched fists and furrowed eyebrows.

No. Kausha forced herself to calm down by slowing blood flow momentarily. She narrowed her eyebrows, forcing her mouth in a straight line. *Remember your training.* She inched silently back towards the stairs where the others were standing, measuring at each in turn, only Nalia's face calm and collected.

"Okay," Kausha whispered, "there are red eyed dwarves blocking the tunnel exit. It's skinny, so there is only room for one at a time, which gives us an equal playing field." She glanced at each again to gauge their faces, Skirm back to his normal self with downturned eyebrows and intense eyes. Shaum and Nalia had the same intensity as Skirm, while Skip stood with arms crossed in front of his chest as if he were taking notes in his head trying to come up with a new song. Puid and Roana glanced at the entrance to the tunnel, then back to Kausha, foreheads scrunched, worry clear on their faces.

"I'll lead with Shaum behind me, Skirm taking the rear." Out of the bottom of her vision, she noticed the two Spearhead's hands clenched into fists as if they were thinking of protesting. Kausha cut them off before they could. "Don't worry, I AM a Bloodborn after all. My grandmother could beat these things."

Their hands didn't unclench, but their eyes shifted to her hands, then back to meet her eyes, faces no longer seeming to want to protest the order. Kausha nodded, then looked to Shaum. "Don't get too close to me, but follow through and make sure the ones I pass don't get up again."

Kausha turned towards the tunnel, pushing blood from four of her fingertips creating small throwing daggers, snapping them off and placing them between her fingers, two on each hand. She breathed deep, envisioning the training her mother put her through so long ago and moving her insides down and back, just as she'd done thousands of times before.

Steadying her breath, she stepped into the tunnel.

Light from the candles placed high up on the walls on either side of the tight tunnel illuminated her tattered white cloak scattered with red blood streaks. Her crimson hair, which was tied into a tight knot in the back of her head, seemed to ignite under the candlelight. The blood daggers glistened as the shuffling of boots and armor cascaded off the walls towards her as the dwarves prepared their halberts. She stared straight ahead, meeting the first dwarve's glowing red eyes beneath a metal helm that expanded to engulf the pale skin surrounding them - mouth, nose and all. Its neatly braided light brown beard hung to its chest as it squatted, feet spread, halbert threatening. How many there were, Kausha did not know, for the first hid the heads of those behind.

Good, they have those clumsy weapons still, she noticed with a smirk. The air was cool and still, candlelight steady throughout. Sweat slid down the side of her jaw, her body warm from blood coursing throughout her body. She waited. Until...

Blood strengthened her legs, then she shot forward, muscles tightening instinctively as memories of her training blinked into her head. 'The floor isn't your only platform,' she could hear her mother say before the dwarve reared back, shoving his halbert straight ahead at her chest. Sprinting forward, she jumped over the weapon clearing it easily, and reared back the two daggers in her right hand as the dwarve looked up at her, unblinking glowing red eyes unfazed. She loosed the daggers in a flash, both hitting home, one in each eye, snuffing out the red light. Landing on its broad shoulder, its body collapsed beneath her weight, the grinding sound of metal on stone echoing down the tunnel. Eyes up, she leapt off the body, white cloak flapping as she spun in mid-air. The second dwarve stabbed his halbert into the spot she had been not one second earlier, skewering the dead dwarve. Using her spinning momentum, she let loose the final two daggers she held, hitting the dwarve in the throat before it dropped its weapon to clutch the blood spilling from its body. It fell to its knees, metal armor thudding into the floor. Its eyes dimmed into nothing, then fell towards her, lifeless.

Without hesitating, she strode forward, then jumped off of the dwarve's corpse, angling toward the right wall while pushing blood from underneath her right fingertip again to produce a blood knife, leaving her other hand free. Upon landing, the wall quaked as a halbert slammed into the ground near the corner of the wall, creating a loud ringing in her ears. Before the dwarve could recover, Kausha kicked off the wall, snuffing out a candle nearby in the process, and while coming down just behind the dwarve, she pushed blood into her arm to strengthen it, then grabbed its helmet with her left hand, snapping its head back towards her landing spot, its body snapping backwards with it. With feet solid beneath her, she reached back with her right hand and slammed her blood knife straight down into the dwarve's right eye. Without waiting to see if it was dead, she ripped her knife out, sidestepping to flatten herself against the wall in anticipation of the next dwarve's strike. Wind buffeted her face as the shiny face of a halbert glimpsed upwards in front of her, narrowly missing his nose. She ducked underneath the weapon, spinning on her knees towards the center of the tunnel before the dwarve could stop its momentum, then thrust her dagger under the dwarve's chin, a crunch reaching her ears as the knife slid through bone meeting the metal helm, glowing red eyes emotionless not inches from her face. Blood shot out like a geyser as she yanked her hand down removing the knife. The halbert crashed down behind the dwarve, bouncing off of the stone floor, its owner's body collapsing in front of her to reveal the next set of glowing eyes.

Four down. She took a step back, counting as blood pooled at her bare feet. *Four to go.* She could hear Shaum and the others making their way through the death she left behind. She stared into the next dwarve's emotionless eyes, except this time noticing a slight unease in its grip as it adjusted the weapon in both hands. She smiled, her mother's voice sounding in her head once again. *'When your enemy falters, you must strike - there is no honor in waiting for them to recover. If they had honor, they would not falter in the first place.'*

Kausha pushed more blood from two of her fingertips on her left hand, producing two daggers, then snapped them off placing them between her fingers.

She kicked the shaft of the slain dwarve to pendulum towards the next, following it as it fell. Kausha jumped, aiming for the wooden shaft's center. The dwarve released a hand from its own halbert, throwing it above its head to block the incoming shaft just as Kausha landed on it, forcing it down with all her weight. The dwarve's arm was not enough to block the full brunt of the attack. The shaft slammed into the top of its helm, a loud ring echoing through the tunnel as wood met metal followed by the wooden shaft snapping where Kausha landed. The dwarve fell to a knee, looking down, dazed. Kausha took two steps forward to reach the dwarve, and with an uppercut, slammed her blood knife into its face before it could look up. She jerked her hand away, focused on the next dwarve. It shot forward, stabbing wildly in quick succession causing Kausha to step back towards the previous dwarve so as not to be hit. The dwarve snarled, glowing eyes narrowed as it crept forward, stabbing at different parts of her body, slicing her robe a few times.

"Kaush duck!" she heard from behind. She looked back just in time to see Shaum rearing back over his head with half of a halbert in his hands. She threw herself to the ground right before he let go, the shiny head of the weapon toppling end over end in the candlelight as it raced towards the dwarve before a loud crunch met her ears when the halbert slammed into the dwarves face, throwing it backwards at the force of the blow. She glanced at Shaum, nodding. He only shrugged in return with a smirk on his face. *Mossing Spearhead.* A smirk crossed her lips.

Two left.

She stood again and faced the remaining two that blocked their exit to freedom. She took one step forward, a squishing sound beneath her from the blood that filled the floor. Then another. Then, she ran, leaping over two corpses, landing lightly on one foot as the next dwarve stabbed forward like the previous one, but

Kausha was ready. She reared back and threw the two daggers in her left hand at the dwarve causing it to halt its attack while it blocked the daggers with its forearm before they could hit its face. With her left hand free, she forced blood into her legs, gripping the shaft of the halbert, then yanking it towards her in an attempt to pull the dwarve off balance. With its stocky limbs, it held on with one hand, and instead of losing its balance, it yanked the weapon and Kausha along with it, her feet sliding along the stone. *Moss!* she cursed, face taught while holding on to the shaft being yanked towards the dwarve.

With the dwarve's next yank, she jumped straight up, giving in to the momentum, and flew towards the dwarve as it pulled with all its might. She lifted her knees, then threw her feet out ahead of her, a painful vibration shooting through her body from her toes into her head as she slammed into the dwarve's breastplate. She fell to the stone floor, another bout of pain shooting through her right side. The dwarve stood over her, seemingly shrugging off Kausha's weight. It lifted its halbert, pointing the tip directly at Kausha's chest, then slammed it down with a force only a dwarve could muster. Kausha rolled to her side, but not quite quick enough as the point of the halbert sliced into her left side, ripping cloth and skin alike, the familiar sound of metal on stone bursting in her ears. A wave of pain shot through Kausha's body as she glanced down at her side through tears. *No blood,* she noticed through clenched teeth. She stared up at the dwarve hunched over her, glowing red eyes only a foot away, jaw tight as it struggled with removing the tip of the halbert lodged into the stone floor.

Before she could think, her body was sitting up, twisting, while her right arm shot out from beside her, knife slicing through the air in an arc as she slammed it down into the dwarve's left foot through metal and bone alike. She removed it almost immediately, blood spurting upwards from the wound. It let go of the halbert, falling backwards off balance as it grabbed its injured foot with both hands. Kausha sprang to her feet in a kneel, then lunged forward, driving the blood knife up into its left eye in a crunch, its arms going limp in front of her as she yanked the knife from its home. She heard it before she saw it. The final dwarve stepped forward, slicing its halbert through the air overhead causing the candles on both sides of the tunnel to wink out. Kausha rolled forward over the fallen dwarve's body right before the halbert slammed into the stone floor behind her with a loud clang. With feet steady on the ground beneath herself, she rose, slicing upwards with her right arm, blood knife severing the wood shaft as if it were just the wind, causing the dwarve to fall backwards from the force it exerted trying to regain the weapon, now only a small piece of wood in its hands. Standing over the dwarve in the dim light, Kausha watched as it pulled the broken piece of wood close to its eyes, fear showing in the glowing red for the first time. It lowered its arm, met Kausha's eyes, then spoke in a voice that seemed like it was two instead of just one.

"Join us or else you WILL kill those you try so hard to protect. Join us or else all are doomed."

Kausha shivered, the voices chilling her to her bones. *The Bloodborn Sorcerers!* Eyebrows narrow, she opened her mouth to respond, but before she could, the dwarve turned the fractured end of the shaft towards itself, lifted its chin, then drove the jagged splinters into its throat. Blood gushed from the wound and mouth alike as it gasped for air. Its eyes dimmed slowly while Kausha looked on, her chest heaving in and out, sweat dripping from her brow. *'Join us or else you will kill those you try so hard to protect. Join us or else all are doomed,'* she repeated to herself as the dwarve's eyes completely winked out leaving a bloody shell.

She tensed as a burly hand gripped her shoulder. "Kaush," came Shaum's voice from behind her, soft and low.

She let herself relax and drew her blood knife back into her fingertip, then turned to face him, his large body blocking everything behind from view. She looked up at his face, barely visible in the candlelight from behind her, not knowing what to say or think.

"We should go. Tha exit int far," he nearly whispered, glancing over her head down the tunnel.

She nodded, lowering her chin to look down at her robe, smeared with streaks and gobs of blood, only a few small pieces of white showing between the red. With an exhale, she turned back around, Shaum's hand falling from her shoulder as she set her sights on the tunnel ahead. Without a word, she stepped over the dwarve and continued down the tunnel, the only sign of the other following behind was that of footsteps squishing through pools of blood.

They followed the tunnel a ways until Kausha noticed the walls becoming less finished than the ones near the stairway, the stones producing more and more shadows from the candlelight from their jagged faces. It wasn't long after that she felt the air growing warmer accompanied by a breeze that played with the flames above, cooling the sweat on her forehead and arms. She placed her hand on the cold, jagged stone wall once the final candle passed overhead, plunging her into darkness, signaling they were nearing the end of the escape tunnel. Something cool met her fingertips along the wall, her breath catching before tracing the cool spot and realizing that it was a leaf attached to a vine with numerous other leaves running along the length of it. The sound of dirt rubbing on stone underfoot followed until she saw a faint sliver of light ahead - the distance unknown in the confines of the pitch-black tunnel. The light grew larger and brighter with each passing step until she felt the need to put her free hand in front of her body, not wanting to run into anything at the end. The sound of rushing water reached her ears as the light felt right in front of her eyes until she hit something moist and soft in front of her, the light shifting as something moved at her touch. She stepped to it, and using both of her hands, parted, what she noticed were vines covering the exit, to reveal a large, open mouthed cave with a waterfall gushing over its mouth. Moonlight illuminated the water, which refracted into the cave as if it were daylight. She stepped into the mouth of the cave, waiting for the others to exit the tunnel, eyes growing wide in awe of the beauty. The rushing water, roaring past the mouth, made it impossible to talk and so she glanced around for a path, hopeful that this wasn't just some spot that the six come to relax, then noticed a ledge a few feet across to the left of the waterfall. She made her way to it, relieved to see that it hugged the wall out of sight. Glancing back at the others, she motioned them to follow, stepping carefully out onto the wet ledge.

Standing sideways with her back to the jagged stone, she slid slowly across until she cleared the waterfall, unbroken moonlight in a cloudless sky illuminating the land around her. Noticing a wall on the other side of the waterfall, sheer and tall, Kausa thought they seemed to have come out on the opposite side of the massive moat they saw upon entering the city, the waterfall filling the moat from the runoff high up the mountains. She followed the gentle slope of the path, a light mist wetting her hair and face from below, the roar of the waterfall quieting as she reached a flat landing a foot below the grass that marked safety. She stepped up out of the path, feet crunching grass and rock alike, then turned to watch the others, assisting them up and out of the path.

Everyone stood near the edge of the moat looking towards the city with its white towers glowing from the moonlight, the everlooming mountains as a background, and its giant, layered walls providing not so much as a hint of what was occurring inside.

We made it? Kausha questioned, looking to her right at Puid, Nalia, Roana, and Shaum, then to her left at Skip and Skirm, a smile rising on her lips. *We made it.*

"Well, I ope tha I neva ave to come back ere again." Shaum wiped the water from his spear-shaped head.

Everyone nodded in agreement.

"We better get moving," Skirm suggested, turning towards Kausha. "Where to?"

All eyes focused on her. *Moss,* she cursed to herself, glancing at each in turn.

"I..." she started, not sure what to say. *We've gone this far together and they know who I am now, so I should tell them.* "I lied to you all earlier when I said I needed to go to Nortmund," she blurted out in a jumble, pausing to see their reactions, but when none showed shock upon their faces, she went on. "I was heading through The Forest to my home in Purtghast to the west. I didn't need to go to Nortmund, but I went anyway for the safety in numbers. Now, though, I must head there alone," *in order to see my great great grandmother's passing,* she finished in her head, deciding they didn't need to know that part.

They all glanced at one another silently, waiting for the other to speak.

Suddenly, Nalia leapt forward taking Kausha by surprise, and threw her arms around her.

"Thank you," Nalia whispered in her ear, her fur tickling Kausha's cheek.

Kausha returned the hug, closing her eyes, then whispered back, "Thank you, too." She felt more hands on her shoulder and back as Shaum, Skirm, and Skip wrapped them both in their arms.

"Come find us when you're done. We'll be in Gbinti for a while before heading home," Skirm sniffled.

"An I'll buy tha firs round," Shaum replied.

"And I'll have songs that will fill any tavern from coast to coast," Skip promised through a smile.

They let go one by one, Nalia the final one to pull away, met her eyes, teardrops threatening to fall, then she let go, turning to move back to her sister's side.

Kausha looked to Puid, exchanging nods, then glanced over each face in turn, and with a final smile and nod, turned southwest towards Purtghast, then began walking.

Chapter 40: Failure

The sorcerers ended their spell, returning their minds back to their bodies at the top of the tower.

"Ahhhhh!" the monotoned sorcerer yelled in frustration while sitting up from the knelt-over position while the other did the same, although not saying a word.

She pounced up with clenched fists beneath dark sleeves, her body aching, but the only thing on her mind was continued failure.

"How could they have gotten away again?!" she yelled while striding towards the slit in the wall, looking towards Nortmund over the top of moon-lit trees that were The Forest.

"She was trained well," the sorcerer with the rumbling voice replied, standing slowly, staring at her sister's back. Peeling her eyes away while twisting her back, she froze. "The spellbook! It's gone," she grimaced, glancing left and right around the room.

"What? How can that be? Did our sister take it?" the monotoned sorcerer asked, turning quickly with eyes wide hidden inside of darkness, then glancing towards the cracked door. She returned her eyes back to the other sorcerer in the room to see her kneeling to pick something up.

"What is it?" she asked.

"An arrow," the rumbling voice replied, holding the broken arrow up for her to see.

The darkness emanating from the sorcerers grew denser, spreading throughout the room, overflowing and spilling from the small slit in the wall.

"The Mind," the monotone voice said through gritted teeth. "And I do not feel our sister either."

The other sorcerer enclosed the arrow in her hand, squeezed, then turned her hand over, dropping ash.

"We have failed on two fronts this moon, sister," the monotone sorcerer admitted in a quiet tone, the darkness retreating inside of her as she closed her eyes and bowed her head, hood hiding her expression.

"What should we do? Go after the Bloodborn or the Mind?" the rumbling voice quickly asked as if trying to counteract her sister's change in tone. She wiped her hand on her pitch-black robe while making her way around the basin to stand at her sister's side.

The monotone sorcerer lifted her head, turned, then stared out over the trees again, the first touch of the rising sun brightening the sky, and for the first time in as long as she could remember, she didn't know what to do.

Chapter 41: News and a Vote

"This is a dangerous precedent. Olibtine is putting his life on the line as we speak in search of answers and he proposes this?" a tall, dark skinned man with light blond, short cut hair named Fexule, protested to the Chamber. "This is completely unbecoming from a Mind when we are here to help make the lives of our citizens better."

A light murmur wafted through the chamber as the Minds throughout shared their thoughts with the ones next to them.

A tap of wood on granite echoed over the murmur, each Mind going silent in an attempt to find the one that produced it.

Bjorgene, seated in the Leader of the Mind's chair at the bottom of the Chamber, cleared his throat, unfolded a piece of parchment and read it once over as if he hadn't read it numerous times already.

"Are you aware, Fexule, that Nortmund was attacked?" Bjorgene asked.

A collective gasp shot through the Chamber as if a stiff, cold wind had blown through. Clothes ruffled throughout as numerous Minds stood, bellowing out questions one after another, not waiting for an answer before voicing another.

Bjorgene tapped wood against granite, silencing the room while tension hung in the air.

"Who did this?!" a quick voice shot through the air, unwilling to wait on decorum.

Bjorgene tapped again, cutting off any further interruption, waiting a few seconds to make sure before continuing. "We have only reccccieved word thisss morning, but the woundssss are irrefutable. It wasss the Bloodborn," he explained, emphasizing the final word.

Pitched conversations echoed through the Chamber. Anger from some, curiosity from others, and a silent contemplation from a few of the elders on the second level. Bjorgene stood next to the high-backed wooden chair, allowing the conversations to continue as he glanced around the room to further measure the different feelings towards the news.

A tap echoed behind him, the Mind's conversations cutting off once again to find the source. Bjorgene turned to lock eyes with Wilbur, a tan man with deep, brown eyes and a thick, braided beard to match. His hair was the same color as his beard, except for a few white streaks forming on his temples above ears. He stood, a head taller than those nearby, and as broad as two side by side.

"Do we have proof of this?" he asked in a deep, rumbling voice that seemed to shake the very granite they stood on.

Bjorgene nodded. "We do," he started, holding the parchment up for all to see, "Two of the sssix themssselvesssss, the firsssssst and the third, provided their housssse sssssealssss to confirm the letter."

"And did the dwarves provoke the Bloodborn in any way?" Wilbur replied.

"The letter doessss not ssssay," Bjorgene responded.

The thick Mind tugged on his beard, eyebrow rising. "And what of the destruction? Does the letter say that?"

Bjorgene nodded. "Yessss. There were no less than 20 guardssss killed, ssssome sssssplit in two asss if they were firewood to be hacked, as well as a dozen citizenssss ssssslaughtered and numerousss homessss and worksssshopsss burned to the ground."

A silence hung in the air as the Minds mulled it over, contemplating the turn of events.

The thick Mind nodded, a deep frown forming on his lips as he continued to tug on his beard while retaking his seat.

A subdued rustling swept through the Chamber as the rest of the Minds, just moments ago yelling and questioning one another, took their seats as well.

Bjorgene smiled in his head as he folded the parchment onto itself, placing it in the chair beside him.

"Thissss isss but a tassste of what the Bloodborn are capable of. Hisssstory hassss sssshown usss that when a passssing occurssss, dessstruction followsss, and I fear, my fellow Mindssss, that thissss issss but the beginning, and we may be next," Bjorgene warned in a rough tone, turning slowly as he spoke in order to communicate with the entire Council and not just those immediately in front of the chair.

The sound of wood on marble echoed through the chamber as a middle-aged Mind named Manu, with a clean shaven head and a smirk that never left his mouth, stood. "And what of our force? Can we attack with the expectation of winning?" he asked in a high pitched, yet sultry voice.

Bjorgene nodded to the man, his eyebrows dipping, spoiling his answer before he even spoke. "Alone, I fear that we are not enough."

A murmur began, but before it could spark conversations, Bjorgene interrupted. "But... If we combine forcessss with Nortmund, attacking in tandem, we sssstand a chance," he finished, nodding to the Mind that asked the question.

"Are you proposing we go to war?!" exclaimed a middle-aged, bald Mind on the top row named Peitrin. Bjorgene's eyes narrowed, his mouth twitching in a line as he watched the man stand with both hands placed solidly on the granite in front of him, leaning forward. "Gbinti does not go to war. We are not killers - we are here to use diplomacy in all of its facets to protect those around us with our Minds. Do you honestly think that we are capable of fighting the Bloodborn? Those that have demolished cities and everything inside with their bare hands? That would be a death wish and bring nothing but ruin to Gbinti."

Silence returned to the Chamber as the Minds contemplated both sides.

The sound of wood on marble echoed again, Fexule speaking up immediately. "I propose a vote. Seeing as the circumstances are imminent, we cannot afford to wait another day to decide."

Feet shuffled and clothing rustled throughout the Chamber as a sudden weight pressed down on them, but no one objected to the notion. With a sigh, Peitrin returned to his seat.

"Very well," Bjorgene started, "we will vote on going to battle. Right hand in favor, left againssst."

Right hands shot up immediately from a number of Minds while others glanced around, gauging the sentiment. A few left hands rose on the second level - some of the older Minds - while more right hands rose slowly on the top level.

Bjorgene's lip quivered as he forced a smile down while counting hands. "The rightssss have it. We will begin preparationsss by contacting the ssssix and gathering sssssupliesss for the battle."

"The meeting issss adjourned," he announced with a wave of a hand, ending the meeting. While the Minds were shuffling out in murmured conversations at the news, he bent down, picked the parchment up, and then sat down again, reading it once more with a smirk on his lips.

Chapter 42: A Feeling

Olibtine felt something in the back of his mind and afforded himself a glance behind for the first time since leaving the tower. They had walked the rest of the day and unknowing hours into the night, only stopping momentarily to grab food or water from their packs. A rolling, silent landscape lit by a full moon met his gaze almost as if it were daylight out. He no longer felt the overwhelming darkness that the tower put off, but he knew that it was in the direction he looked. Daria stopped when she noticed he wasn't walking at her rear, looking back as well.

"We're still in the desert," she warned, eyes drifting above his head towards the tower.

He nodded, not sure if she could see him, so he put words to it as well. "I know. I just..." *felt something,* he finished in his mind and then shook his head trying to shake the feeling as well. "Nothing," he ended.

She narrowed her eyebrows at his hesitation to speak up.

"But it isn't long until we're out of the sands and then we can rest." She led them down another dune, feeling something in the back of her mind, but refusing to give voice to it.

Chapter 43: A New Task

"Your services are no longer required with the Bloodborn," the disjointed face in the ujuntu basin calmly broke the news. The sorcerers provided their account of Nortmund to little care from the other side. "We expect to be reimbursed in full for your failure."

The sorcerers knelt next to each other over the basin, hoods hanging straight down not even a hand's width from touching the water. The darkness inside of the hood fought the red glow of the face inside of the basin, an ominous outline of their faces only visible when they allowed it to be.

"Understood," the monotone voice replied flatly even though she clenched her robes tightly at her knees. "And of the Mind?"

The face in the water turned to look left, nodded, then faced the ujuntu basin on his side.

"This is your new focus. Do as you see fit, but the Mind shall not reach Gbinti. Understood?"

"Understood," the monotone voice replied as the face in the basin disappeared.

The two sorcerers stayed kneeling in contemplation while the red glow dimmed giving way to the sun's rays piecing the tower.

Chapter 44: Soup and Smoke

Kausha did what she could about the blood stains and bright white cloak, neither of which allowed her to stay hidden on the journey to Purtghast. First, she washed herself in the bitterly cold Veda River, which most simply call Green River, that flows from the Uhlbrar Mountains through The Forest all the way down to the Bloody Waters, named after the Bloodborn living in Purtghast. After the first attempt of cleaning the cloak proved unsuccessful, she found a mud pit and lathered a layer on top of the cloak, which seemed to work for a time until the dried bits started to flake off from the sun's heat the further she got from the mountains. Finally, she decided that visiting one town was safer than continuing along the flat plains where anyone could see her from miles away.

One such town, huddled against The Forest southwest of the main peaks of Uhlbrar Mountains, looked as inconspicuous as she would hope for at this juncture in her journey. First light had just occurred when she arrived, but the countryside beyond the town's fence was bustling with activity. Every plot of land was being worked on, the familiar sound of chopping wood echoing off of the trees nearby. Children ran over and through the gaps left in the faded white-stained fence long forgotten, and not a single resident gawked as she walked through the main gate that sat ajar, only noticeable due to the trampled dirt road.

The inn, she searched, kicking up dirt under bare feet, breaching the fence into the town, glancing back and forth for anything but a simple home. One of the kids cut her off, glancing over his shoulder at his pursuers, sticking his tongue out in defiance. "We're gonna get you now, Fin!" yelled one of the girls giving chase as they passed in front of Kausha, who was just another obstacle in their game. Kausha watched them disappear behind one of the many immaculate wooden homes on the only road through the town. Homes, she noticed, that were set in a perfect line along the road, each with perfect, circular shutters, whether opened or closed, small front porches perfectly swept clean of dirt and leaves, the little garden patches containing plants Kausha recognized from Nortmund, perfect without a weed anywhere to be seen. Practically everything she looked at was perfect from home to home. Her mouth moved into a frown. *It's a little too perfect.* She turned back to continue along the dirt road, meeting eyes with an auburn-haired woman carrying a wicker basket, wearing a patch-worked brown and dark green dress that exposed her tan legs at the knees. The woman smiled at Kausha and Kausha forced one in return.

"Hello. I don't see an inn. Is there one in town?" Kausha asked.

"We don't get too many visitors around these parts, but we do, if you can call it that - it's old Yauna's place right over there. It's the bigger one," the woman replied with a smile, pointing towards the widest of the homes near the end of the dirt road - the only one that wasn't identical to the rest.

Kausha looked at the home, but all she could think about was the name the woman said, causing her throat to catch. "Did you say Yaula?" Kausha asked.

The woman shook her head with a smile. "No, Yauna. She's the innkeeper."

I must be more tired than I thought... she trailed off, glancing around while continuing down the dirt road. Approaching the home that was two times the size of the rest, but still small compared to any other city, she felt oddly at ease. No sign greeted her on the short, dirt path that lay between green, yellow, purple, and red vegetables on both sides, some of which she had to step over to not step on, and others she recognized. Linil flashed into her head, squatting with her large, green hat rubbing a leaf. Her fists clenched as she shook her head. *This first.* Stepping on to the porch she reached the wooden door and knocked.

"What is it?!" shouted a woman's high-pitched voice somewhere behind the door. Before even answering, Kausha heard the wood groan beneath the woman's weight as she stood to make her way to the door.

"I am in need of clothing, food, and shelter," Kausha replied, taking a step back from the door as a groan reached her ears. The door flung open as a small, brown with white tipped quill covered Marpet with light brown eyes stood in the doorway. Kausha's heart raced, her eyes growing wide, as she stared at the Marpet envisioning Yaula's last moments.

"Well? What're you waiting for then?" the Marpet asked, sounding annoyed.

Kausha visibly shook herself, blinking a few times before replying. "Sorry, you just remind me of someone."

The Marpet named Yauna grunted. "Us Marpets are everywhere, hun. Don't make nothing of it. I've got a bed, food, and leave-behinds of old travelers on these parts if you've got the ujuntu," she finished, closing the door behind Kausha, leaving her in a comfortable living space with a wooden floor and multiple unmatching chairs spaced out in a half-circle with wooden side tables, also unmatching, placed between each. The walls were filled with hooks for cloaks, multiple shelves packed with nick-nacks, and paintings of various landscapes, trees, waterfalls, and one she noticed was of the town itself from the vantage of the end of the road just outside. The other side of the living space was a little kitchen with a tall, solid wooden table placed nearby and stools placed before it.

"About that," Kausha started, another grunt coming from Yauna as she sat down in what looked like the most comfortable chair of the bunch. "I just escaped from Nortmund and I don't have anything but the clothes on my back. You can have all of this in exchange." She motioned to her clothes.

Yauna looked Kausha up and down, another grunt, this one lower pitched, coming from her throat. "Fine. Take the bed back there to the right. You'll find clothing in the wardrobe, just take what you want and leave those on the floor in the bath. You missed first meal, so dinner won't be ready for a while now."

Kausha nodded in thanks, then retreated into the hallway behind the kitchen that led to all of the rooms outside of the main living space and kitchen, similarly covered with colorful paintings. She took the first door to the right that opened into a small room with one window on the back wall opposite one plain looking bed, one chair, and a large wardrobe. Kausha shrugged as she returned to the hall, closing the door behind. Three closed doors met her on the right wall, the final one opposite hers sat open revealing a tub. Making her way towards it, candles placed on the wall opposite the doors flickered while she passed. She closed the door behind her, then stripped down and tossed the clothing she was wearing into a pile near the door. A fire was already lit beneath the metal tub, water steaming, sending a pleasant floral smell through the air. Kausha stepped in, soaking her body until she began to sweat before getting out. She grabbed the towel from a table nearby, dried off, then scampered back into her room, closing the door, then opened the wardrobe. Robes and cloaks of all colors and types hung before her. From a patched brown and green cloak like the woman before wore to a blue and white cloak signifying the city of Gbinti to...

Her eyes grew wide and her hands shook as she shifted the cloaks away from the one her eyes were set upon. She turned the front towards her, holding her breath, then exhaled with an audible sigh. On the front of the red and purple cloak wasn't a teardrop as she expected, it was a candle with wax sliding down the side as if it were burning. She cocked her head. *What symbol is this?* She lifted it to see if there were any other symbols. Finding none, she threw it on the bed, crouched, then grabbed the rest of the hodgepodge outfit from the stacks of shirts, pants, and shoes at the bottom of the wardrobe, then dressed. She studied the cloak once more.

It's too close to Bloodborn to be a coincidence, but what of the candle symbol? She flipped the cloak over one more time for good measure, seeing nothing. She threw the familiar colors on, the cuffs fitting near-perfectly to her wrists and ankles, producing a smirk on her face. *This will do.* Tying her hair, she opened her door to see Yauna in the bath down the hall scrubbing the clothes she had placed on the floor, the pleasant sound of water splashing around reaching her ears as she took the few steps into the main living area to find a chair.

For the first time in a long, long time, Kausha melted into the chair and relaxed enough to close her eyes to the world around, the rhythm of scrubbing clothes calming her to sleep.

The world outside was already dark by the time Kausha startled awake at the sound of wood on metal nearby, blinking and sitting up straight in an attempt to regain her bearings.

Yauna grunted as she poured some water into a metal pot. "Ah, you're awake. Come, come, it's the least you could do after trading those ruined clothes for food and shelter. They were skewered through and through and will be used for excess. Can't be having the six's men stomping around and finding it and don't you go telling me anything, either. I don't want anything to do with what you've done."

Kausha stumbled over to the kitchen, still groggy, and noticed Yauna was standing on a stool while working, two pots, a pan, and green vegetables set out on the counter within arm's reach.

"Chop." Yauna nodded towards the vegetables as she pinched something next to her between three long fingers and threw it into the water.

Kausha did as told, chipping the vegetables in silence until her brain started working properly again. *So she knows then. Should I be worried?* Kausha glanced over at the woman. *This close to Nortmund, either they are followers or they hate them.* Once the vegetables were chopped, Kausha took a seat on one of the stools and watched Yauna as she pinched, poured, stirred, and tasted what was steaming in the pot.

"Stop staring and get us something to smoke. Grass is on the shelf in a wooden container next to the pipes," Yauna nodded off to the right without breaking her stirring movement.

Kausha grabbed the container and two pipes, then packed both in silence, handing one to Yauna and keeping one herself. Yauna lit hers using a dried string lit by using the wood fire beneath the pot and then did the same for Kausha's. Kausha took a puff and immediately coughed, her mouth sweating as her eyes filled with tears.

Yauna slammed her right hand down on the counter while bellowing out in laughter, placing the pipe down in order to wipe her eyes with her sleeve.

"This stuff comes from The Forest nearby. Old Harman was lost for nearly a moon in there and came out saying he found something growing as if nothing had happened. We ask him where he's been for the last moon and he just looks at us and says 'Smoking,' with a shrug." Yauna threw up her hands. "Smoking! Just like that as if it were the answer to everything. Anyways, this stuff is that stuff - it'll make ya forget what day it is."

Thinking twice about another puff, Kausha placed the pipe down nearby and took a gulp of water Yauna had slid towards her.

"I see you've chosen that one," Yauna noted in a more serious tone, taking another puff from her pipe.

Kausha looked down, seeing the melting candle on the front, then glanced back up to meet Yauna's eyes. "Do you know the symbol? It's not one that I've come across recently."

Yauna paused her stirring, puffing out a few circles into the air as she thought. Returning to the stirring, she placed the pipe down, puffing out the last of smoke before responding.

"I do," she started, eyes narrowed, focusing on the stirring. "Just like I do with all of the other robes of those that have passed through my door. To understand that, you have to understand something about this place we call Uradaria. It has had many names, but Uradaria for our sake. It has had just as many that have claimed the title of King as well, but none have lasted longer than a hair's breadth in the grand scheme of it all. I am old and have memory of the last that crowned himself King."

King Gadimar. Kasha remembered the name her mother taught her when she was little.

"He did not take the title willingly though. He was a man of trade and commerce, not bloodshed and death. But what's the difference to anyone when a title gets forced over the top of you unwillingly? Country men and women doing nothing but getting by in their small towns, enjoying their communities, and growing just enough food to feel comfortable, were all of a sudden under the rule of some King across The Forest. Enforcers came to impose taxes throughout the land that weren't there prior to the King, and if they were, this threw more burden on top of citizens. Word always spreads quicker with bad news than good, and so word got around of these enforcers taking certain... liberties with their duties."

Yauna shook her head when she said the last part until she puffed her pipe again, returning to her story.

"Well, as quickly as they were taken care of, it was too late to matter. His light was going to be snuffed out no matter what he did - it had been decided. Not a moon later, he, and along with an entire city, were killed at the hands of the one wearing a robe just like that with a burning candle surrounded by blood and darkness. The only thing that travels faster than even bad news is fear, and the news of a Bloodborn assassin spread like the wind. There hasn't been a King since, only ruling classes in different cities. "

Kausha looked down again, running her hand over the symbol as if seeing it together for the first time, sweat forming above her lip.

"Bloodborn... assassin? I thought the Bloodborn were kind and calm people," Kausha asked, turning her eyes up to look at Yauna once again, lowering her hands and gripping the cloak at her waist for fear she'd continue outlining the symbol in contemplation.

Yauna nodded. "They are, for the most part. Rumors said that they were trying to help the farmers and citizens throughout. Other rumors said that they see everyone and everything but themselves as something to be culled and killed when they see fit."

"And you?" Kausha asked.

Yauna stopped stirring and placed both of her hands on the counter before letting out a long exhale, then looking up to meet Kausha's eyes.

"I hope you're here to help and not harm."

Kausha's hair stood on end, her breath catching, nearly causing her to choke. Blood shifted into her hands. *How?*

Yauna peeled her eyes away, re-lit her pipe, then took a large inhale, holding, then releasing slowly, placing it down where she had picked it up and going back to stirring.

A long silence hung in the air as Yauna stirred. She tapped the wooden spoon on the edge of the pot, then removed it from the fire, smothering it with a cover.

"But how?" Kausha finally asked, letting her blood move freely throughout, deciding that Yauna meant her no harm. "How did you know that I...."

"Was Bloodborn?" Yauna interrupted, meeting Kausha's eyes once again, then shrugged. "A hunch. You know one of my kind as well and my kind always seem to be in the path of something important, even if we don't want it."

Kusha pictured Yaula looking down at her again in her home in Lumber after having saved her life.

The aroma of vegetable soup and the sound of a metal spoon being slid in front of her caused her mouth to start watering, shaking her from the daydream.

"Eat," Yauna instructed through a smile, "you look famished."

Chapter 45: Connections

After a night of restful sleep, Kausha awoke before the moon had fully fallen to give way to the day, but she wasn't the only one awake. Yauna was already in the kitchen stirring something in one of her pots that sent hints of spice and bitterness into the air. Lit by a single candle that illuminated most of the kitchen, she caught Kausha's movement out of the corner of her eye and turned with a smile on her face.

"Well good morning." Yauna banged the wooden spoon against the pot while stirred slowly.

"Good morning. I wasn't expecting you up," Kausha replied, taking a seat in one of the stools across from her.

"I could say the same for you. Figured you'd be sleeping until the children started playing."

Kausha shook her head. "I have a long ways to go still, but even this short of a break helps tremendously."

Yauna closed her eyes while placing her face over the steam coming from the pot, then took a deep breath, another smile crossing her face. She nodded to herself pleasingly, grabbed two mugs, ladled out the liquid, tossing one to Kausha, then held hers in both hands and took a sip.

"Mmm. Nothing like a cup of spiced coffee in the morning," she exhaled with steam enveloping the quills on her head.

Kausha looked down at the dark liquid, then grabbed the mug in front of her and did the same as Yauna. The bitterness made her face visibly scrunch, but the spices made it all worth it.

"So, where ya off to then?" Yauna asked over her mug.

"Home," Kausha replied.

"Ah, to Purtghast. I sure wish I could see it someday. The stories paint a pretty picture and you can see I like my pictures."

Kausha glanced over to the far wall at her paintings, eyes falling on one she had missed before. She put the mug down and crossed the space as Yauna watched on with a raised eyebrow. Kausha stood in front of a painting much smaller than the rest and if one didn't move back from it, it would just look like a random brown and green forest, but it was more. Her hands grew sweaty as she remembered playing cards in The Forest clearing, dodging acid rain, and the pain of acid hitting her shoulder. She involuntarily grabbed the spot the acid hit, long healed without a blemish on it.

"I know this place," Kausha pointed, voice trembling without meaning to. Yauna took another sip from her mug letting out a grunt.

"So you know Yaula?"

Yauna put her mug down, then looked towards Kausha, a hint of sadness in them as she seemed to look right through her.

"She's... my sister. We haven't spoken in many moons - too many to count. The Forest makes it hard for me to go to her or her to me," Yauna finished, picking up her mug again and taking a sip.

Kausha frowned and let her arm down as she glanced back at the painting. *Do I tell her? Nalia would want to know if it happened to her sister.*

"It looks just like it," Kausha replied, walking back to the stool and taking a seat. She picked up the mug with both hands and took a sip, the bitterness not as bad as the first try. She looked up at Yauna and opened her mouth to speak, but she couldn't find the words. Her eyebrows narrowed as she looked down at her mug, then she tried again, but nothing came out. *Why can't I say it?* She gripped the mug tighter.

"What is it?" Yauna asked as the sun made its first appearance on the day, sending faint yellow light into the windows. Kausha looked up again to see Yauna staring right at her.

"It's just. Well," Kausha started, sliding her hands off of the table and balling them into fists on top of her thighs. "Yaula is dead," Kausha blurted out, the pain of loss filling her eyes with tears causing her to look down.

A grunt sounded from Yauna. "She probably went out telling those around her what to do. Was it quick?"

Kausha shifted in her seat, positive she could hold back the tears, glancing back up, then nodded. "It was. A Trender got her saving mine and a few of my companion's lives."

Another grunt from Yauna, this one sounding higher pitched than the others as she took a sip from her mug. "I can see why you looked like you'd seen a ghost when you saw me for the first time. Why she would ever leave Lumber is beyond me. She loved that place more than anything."

"It was ruined by the acid rain."

Yauna grunted something deep and visceral. "Mossing sorcerers," she mumbled beneath her breath, then looked up to Kausha with narrowed, intense brown eyes. "I knew that nothing could tear her away from that place, barring a disaster. Where is her body?"

"In the thickest of trees north of Silpada on a dirt path. We buried her in a clearing along a path. The Trender was lying dead a few feet from her, so there might be some remnants of it nearby. I'm sorry, Yauna. If I was..."

A deep, rumbling grunt from Yauna interrupted Kausha. "Don't go blaming yourself for things like wild creatures, ya hear? There's no time for sulking over the past. Can't change it, so think about it after the moment, grieve, joy, whatever the feeling may be, then move on and take the next step. That one is always the hardest. I'm sure she had a reason to go with you, even if it was initially the sorcerer's doings, and knowing her, she would have stubbornly stayed behind and fixed the place up even if it were completely leveled."

She took a gulp from her mug as Kausha's began to cool, no longer warming her fingers like it had, but what was missing from the mug's warmth was replaced by the first rays of sunshine breaching the tops of The Forest trees and shining through the windows behind the chairs in the main sitting room. A weight had been lifted from Kausha's shoulders, at least for the moment, causing her to stand, brush her cloak flat with both hands, then decide what to do next.

"I must be going now. I hope you find Yaula's resting place, but if you do not leave by the next time I pass through, I will go with you to find it."

A smile appeared on Yauna's face, the same one Yaula had. Kausha felt warmth, sadness, determination, and comfort in that smile and returned one herself. "Thank you. Oh, before you go." Yauna grabbed something, then hopped off her stool and handed Kausha a small, brown bag. " Take this. It's a few meals to tie you over until you reach Purtghast. It's all I can afford to give when strangers come through with no ujuntu." A smirk reached her lips.

"Thank you!" Kausha replied, tucking it under her arm, then bending down to carefully hug Yauna, dodging the sharp quills on her back. Yauna simply grunted in return.

Kausha pulled back and Yauna nodded. "Good luck, and I hope that cloak doesn't mean a repeat of what happened long ago."

Kausha looked down, completely forgetting what she had on. "Right," she replied with a nod. Yauna walked to the door and pulled it open, the sound of birds and children playing rushing in to greet her. Kausha stepped through the doorway, sunlight warming her face, then nodded, taking the next steps towards Purtghast.

Chapter 46: A Forgotten Spell

The sorcerers tossed books haphazardly over their shoulders as they scoured for the one they needed. A thunk sounded through the library as another hit the floor behind the taller of the two.

It's here somewhere, the monotone sorcerer thought, snapping another book shut, throwing it over her shoulder into the pile with dozens of others. She glanced over once again to the open trap door in the middle of the room and then to the remnants of her sister who she'd stood by since she was born. Anger replaced sorrow as revenge was the dominant emotion in her mind - getting paid for it would only be a perk.

She turned back to searching, scouring shelf after shelf, books of all shapes and sizes piling behind her each step of the way creating an inner circle behind her and her sister. Reaching for another book on the shelf, her hand paused in mid-air. She studied the black and red spotted spine, a recollection jolting through her. She removed it from the shelf carefully, turning it to view the cover showing the red dots growing larger and more numerous the closer they got to the pages themselves until the entire edge was a deep red. She slid her hand over it feeling the smooth red dots over a rough, black background, then opened it to the first page. *Spoils of Blood,* she read. A smile appeared on her lips.

"I found it," she announced in a monotone voice without glancing away from the book. She heard her sister drop a book and stride towards her, her cloak flapping as she hurried over.

"Are you sure?" the rumbling voice asked as she reached her sister's shoulder. The sorcerer looked at the book her sister held and a slight exhale escaped her hood, a sign she knew it was the right one.

Turning page over page, they passed by Bloodborn spells that could both harm and help. From using blood to transfuse it into another to diminish the effects of poison to creating a slick blood surface with little blood tentacles on the soles of one's foot in order to glide across any surface to torture methods that involve shoving blood into the organs of their victim, squeezing, cutting, and moving things around that shouldn't in a normal body. The Spoils of Blood displayed everything a Bloodborn could hope to learn, including...

There! The sorcerer paused with trembling fingers, unseen from inside of her sleeves. She creased the left page to get a proper view of the drawing and spell they were searching for, a toothy smile appearing under her hood once again as the revenge inside of her began to overflow. She glanced to her sister standing next to her, the darkness under her hood hiding all emotions on her face, but she knew that her sister felt the same way. *Revenge*

"Let us prepare."

The two knelt once again in the room atop the tower, the final hours of the full moon closing in as dark gray clouds were split by the sharp point. Candles placed between them to brighten the pages of Spoils of Blood fought through the darkness emanating from the sorcerers to cast flickering shadows against the far wall that looked like creatures fighting to escape their bondage. They placed their hands into the water and began the chant in unison. Darkness spilled from their bodies dimming the candlelight. The water began to glow an intense red, bubbling and churning, fighting for supremacy against the deep black that pulsed from the sorcerers. The chanting grew louder, every passing word bearing the weight of something sinister and forgotten to time. Then, all of a sudden, blood gushed from each fingertip turning the water into a bubbling mass of deep red causing the sorcerers to grow weak, their voices slurring from exhaustion until they both collapsed in their hunched over positions. The blood water filling the ujuntu basin grew still as the candlelight flickered back to life.

Slowly, the blood water began to churn, spiraling into a whirlpool. The blood began to separate itself from the water, pulling itself towards the center. A wind began to spiral inside of the tower, snuffing out the candlelight and leaving the room in a glow of blood red. The unconscious sorcerers' robes fluttered uncontrollably in the wind. A whistling could be heard as the wind swept through the horizontal slit in the wall as if wanting to be free of the tower. The blood in the center of the whirlpool began to bubble, growing thicker with every pop until it seemed to barely move while the whirlpool continued to churn around it.

The thick blood in the middle expanded outwards, pulling in the blood whirling and bubbling around it. Two sharp points began rising out of the blood, growing wider as they rose, excess blood rolling down the sharp points until the start of a jagged, hollow circle formed to connect them. The shapes continued to rise out of the blood, the circle extending down into an oval revealing eyelids and a closed mouth above a sharp chin. The oval ended, revealing a bloody, calm face with sharp, unnatural features. Still rising out of the blood, a neck appeared, and below that, skinny shoulders that connected to a torso that was hollow on the inside except for three thick blood cords, one going from its left shoulder to right hip, one going the opposite way, and the final one extending from its neck to its newly revealed pelvis. Its skinny arms, resembling the inner muscles of a normal arm without skin, extended far past what normal arm lengths should have gone as the full length was not revealed even with the body rising still, forming thin legs that weren't meant for walking. Its hands, at the ends of arms that reached down below its knees, each had five long fingers that nearly reached its feet, which finally rose from the blood. Hovering just above the basin, the excess blood rose into the figure, filling gaps throughout, hardening as soon as it found a spot.

The room became still and dark, all of the light from the basin's water disappearing as the whirlpool slowed to a crawl, then ceased.

It opened its eyelids revealing an endless whirlpool of bright red, the center a black deeper than what even the sorcerers could muster with their combined powers. It did not breathe, it did not eat, it only did as its creators embedded into it with their emotions - a single duty. *Kill the Mind and his companion before they reach Gbinti.*

Chapter 47: To Protect a Mind

Olibtine and Daria watched the full moon race towards the horizon, the first light of a new day brightening the sky, illuminating the landscape surrounding their camp. They had escaped Baugroun and the ominous cloud near the tower for the most part, a tiny sliver of darkness hanging on in the back of their minds. With The Forest's massive trees off a ways to one side and grassland on the other, they sat just off of the main road that started to form. Even though they still had a ways to go to get back to Gbinti, they afforded themselves a rest in order to refill canteens, eat, and tend to Olibtine's wounds.

Olibtine, leaning against his pack sitting across from a small fire from Daria, was reading through *A Recreation of the Bloodborn Ritual* while puffing on his pipe - a welcome reprieve after such a long time sober. It was a small book, but he thought that the more information he retained, the better he would be at persuading the other Minds to begin preparations to protect the city.

Daria sat with legs laid flat, one crossed over the other at the ankles, leaning against her own pack, chewing on a piece of grass, and watching the clouds shift between orange, red, and yellow in the morning light. This was her favorite part of every day. The first few minutes of the morning where everything was still as if the collective continent were taking a moment to themselves to sit and reflect. Before Guane, the morning was a continuation of a growling stomach and aching muscles. Back then, the night was her favorite, especially the new moon nights when she could easily slink between the shadows.

She shifted, feeling the ujuntu in her pack stab her, then smiled. *Almost forgot.* "You thought about what you're doing with your ujuntu?" she asked absently across the fire that had turned into coals, still giving off warmth, but light not needed anymore.

"Huh?" Olibtine responded, a puff of smoke escaping his mouth as he peeked over the book.

"The ujuntu. What are you doing with it?"

"Oh, I told you, I am going to give it to those that need it."

"Admirable," she started, looking up as she rubbed her chin while working the grass beneath her tongue. "I think I'm going to buy Guane a new chair. There isn't a moon that passes where he doesn't complain at least a dozen times about it. He's old and needs something more... plush if he's going to try to keep up with the younger Minds. And then, the rest goes to me. Maybe I'll just buy a tavern or smoke house and never have to pay for liquor or grass ever again."

Olibtine frowned. "I'm sure Guane would appreciate it."

Daria sat up and took the grass from her mouth, eyebrows narrowing. "What gives? Why are you so..."

"Short?" Olibtine finished.

"Short, yeah," Daria replied, nodding.

Olibtine put the book down next to him, took a puff from his pipe, then gazed up at the clouds above, now a bright orange. "I'm worried that this still isn't enough to sway the Minds. Most of them are old and stuck in their ways after forgetting what it is like to have any sort of hurdle to overcome." He closed his eyes trying to envision what Guane might do.

"Old, wrinkly skinned, verge of their death beds, progress halters," Daria cursed, causing Olibtine's head to jerk down, wide eyes catching hers, but she went on as if not noticing. "Guane never did like the others, he told me so. He deals with them for the sake of the citizens, but he has become more and more agitated these last few years. Until you arrived. He talks about you when we're gardening all the time, you know? He thinks that you can be the young Leader to impose new changes and fight the old guard." She smiled and let out a little laugh before continuing. "He told me about a time when he was younger where he and Bjorgene were practically touching noses to one another as they argued in the Council's chamber. I just can't stop picturing them as they are now, white hair sticking out of their noses and touching each other's." She leaned back and let out a bellowing laugh and Olibtine couldn't help but do the same, their eyes watering by the time they gathered themselves.

"I didn't know Guane was like that with Bjorgene. Seems like they are joined at the hip these days." Olibtine wiped his eyes.

"Oh, no," Daria replied, shaking her head as she wiped her eyes as well. "They haaaaate each other. Guane sees Bjorgene as a mental game, eventually using him as a pawn in the Council."

"Wait, what? A pawn? How?"

Daria shrugged, putting the grass back into her mouth. "I'm not smart enough to sit on those meetings. Plus, isn't that thing fun to you all? Mental games, I mean. You have what you need right there." She nodded to the book. "You just need to find a way for them to argue with themselves."

Olibtine raised one of his eyebrows at her. Moss, *she could probably be on the Council.* He glanced down at the book by his side. *I must persuade them!* "Thank you, Daria. For everything." He met her eyes.

She grunted, a sly smile appearing in response. "If you want to thank me, toss me your ujuntu."

Olibtine frowned and shook his head as Daria chuckled at him. "Only kidding. Unless you...Nope, okay."

Olibtine couldn't help but smile at her after remembering how she changed in the tower. *That place could change even the bravest of us.* He blinked and before he had his eyes back open, Daria was stiff backed, her body motionless while her head and ears turned slightly as if listening for something. She jumped up in an instant, spitting the grass from her mouth and kicking dirt into the coals of the fire.

"Get up and help me clean this up. Grab your things and head into the tall grass over there. Now!" she growled frantically, pointing off towards the grass away from the road.

"What is it?!" Olibtine asked in a whispered voice, which felt right in the moment before standing and kicking dirt into the pile. Then, he bent over to pick the book up and shove it in his pack. He noticed his hands were shaking and sweat was beginning to wet his forehead, the ominous, dark feeling growing in the back of his head. He picked his pack up, threw it over his shoulder, and darted to where Daria pointed, who was quickly on his heels. He slid to a stop enough into the grass he was sure to not be seen, but also enough for him to see what was going on, which he still didn't know. Daria slid in beside him, her bow out before he could see her retrieve it.

"What is it?!" he whispered between breaths, his eyes darting up the road, then to The Forest's treeline, then the direction of the desert trying to find why Daria made them rush into the grass. He glanced over at her and followed her eyes, noticing she was staring up the road, her bow and arrow held down, ready to lift at a moment's notice. He stared just as she was, his heart pounding in his ears as he tried to calm his breathing.

"There!" Daria made Olibtine jump, his eyes darting along the road.

A dust cloud? He narrowed his eyebrows. A few moments later, a few figures crested a small hill in the distance. Without being able to make out their physical features, he could see that they were wearing the Gbinti colors of blue and white, undoubtedly with a scale over a book in the middle of their chests. He almost jumped out to greet them until he saw a twinkling of faint sunlight on them. Each was wearing chainmail armor from neck to toe under their cloaks, holding a helm under one arm, and wielding a long pike of varying type in the other. *Soldiers?* Olibtine frowned as more and more Gbinti men crested the hill, heading the way he and Daria had just come from.

"What are they doing?" Olibtine whispered, glancing over to Daria, who no longer had her eyes down the road, rather, she had them glued to something off to their left towards the desert.

He turned to see a large, circular, swirling cloud of deep gray, reds, and blacks surrounded by a clear, blue sky. He stared, squinting for a few seconds, then noticed that it was headed right towards them at a speed no normal cloud could move. The ominous feeling grew more and more oppressive by the second as the cloud swirled off in the distance.

"Moss, what is that?!" Olibtine exclaimed, eyes wide, not fully expecting an answer.

"Not sure, but it doesn't look good," Daria responded, a slight quiver appearing in her voice.

Olibtine glanced back towards the soldiers marching down the road three by three, noticing a few of them point up at the cloud as they began to chat to one another. He glanced back at the cloud, forehead scrunching as it swirled closer and closer. *Whatever it is, they're going to meet at the desert's edge.*

Without a second thought, he darted from his hiding spot, sprinting into the road directly in front of the first line of soldiers. Daria attempted to reach for his arm, cursing, but her reaction was too slow this time and so she followed after him, putting away her bow across her back. As soon as they saw him leave the grass, shouts rang down the lines, a domino effect of rows stopping in their tracks, each throwing their helms on and readying themselves for a fight.

Olibtine waved his arms above his head, open palms to the soldiers to show he wasn't hiding anything, then yelled, "Stop, stop! Something is coming from the tower!"

He wasn't positive that it was coming from the tower, but the ominous feeling that he had almost escaped now felt like a physical weight on his head.

"Who are you?" someone asked from the rows of soldiers.

"Olibtine, the Leader of the Minds!"

A gasp shot through the soldiers as a few called out, "He is who he says he is!" Clearly at least a few had been guards near the Minds before.

Olibtine let his arms drop and glanced over his shoulder into the sky - the rolling, circling cloud covering vast amounts of distance in just these few seconds. *Moss! We can't get away.* He halted in place, turning back to the soldiers who had lowered their pikes.

"It's too late to run, so we'll have to face whatever that is head-on." He lowered his voice to sound more regal. "Soldier..." he pointed at the one to the front left, "who is the Captain here?"

"I am," came a deep, booming voice that projected from somewhere unseen. Olibtine stood tall to try and see where the voice came from, then he noticed soldiers were parting from the middle a few rows back, continuing like a wave until the three in the front split to reveal a man a head shorter than the rest, his helm still under his arm, wearing the same chainmail armor as the rest. The only real difference was the way this man carried himself. His square, hairless face with a wide nose, bushy brown eyebrows the same color as his short hair, and brown eyes to match, projected an air of command. He scowled at Olibtine and Daria for only a moment and then his eyes shot up into the air behind the two, face growing even harder, jaw flexing as his mind worked.

"In formation!" he yelled, throwing on his helmet. A wave of chainmail rustling shot through the ranks along with boots stomping and men shouting to those in back that had not heard the order directly. The lines shifted, kicking up dirt to form ten rows of ten soldiers across

"Olibtine, was it? Come with me," he demanded, turning into the soldiers who parted ways for him to get through even before he got to them. Olibtine and Daria jogged to catch up with his surprisingly quick stride, passing soldiers as they advanced forward, spreading themselves out wide in separate layers.

The Captain turned heel once he was behind the lines and stood, feet planted into the dirt looking as immovable as a tree deep in The Forest. Olibtine and Daria didn't have to be told what to do as they passed the Captain and stood behind him.

"Stay here," he grumbled, glancing over his shoulder to meet their eyes, then began walking the same way he had just come.

"Wait!" Olibtine shouted. The Captain stopped mid-stride, glancing over his shoulder again, brown eyes intense.

Olibtine stumbled beneath the gaze. "Who sent you?" he fumbled, although he felt he already knew the answer.

"Why, the new Leader of the Minds: Bjorgene." He stalked back towards the front of the soldiers, the ranks closing in behind him.

Bjorgene.... Leader, Olibtine struggled, mind churning.

"Lads," he bellowed even louder than before while making his way to the front, "I know this isn't what we came to do this day, but it seems that we're backed into a corner. Lucky for us, being backed into a corner is what pikemen want! We won't hide, we won't shy away, we won't give in, but we will protect our home from anything, right lads?!"

"Ay! For Gbinti!" they yelled in practiced unison as they slammed the butt of their pikes into the ground, leaving Olibtine with visible chills up his arms.

The Captain made it to the front, right in the middle, and stood, straight back and confident, seemingly towering over the others even though he was a head shorter. "On my mark!" he bellowed.

"Huah!" he instructed, moving the pike into both hands, the point straight ahead, while at the same time turning his body at an angle, spreading his feet roughly shoulder-width apart.

A long silence hung in the air as the soldiers stood planted into the dirt road, ready for what was to come. Sunlight sparkled off chainmail throughout the lines, steady and unwavering. Birds scattered above, moving in the opposite direction the lines faced as if feeling the darkness expanding.

The cloud was close enough for Olibtine to see something odd about it, as if it wasn't odd enough with its gray, red, and black coloring.

"Is that... a human?" he asked out of the corner of his mouth so only Daria could hear.

"It looks like it," she replied, squinting.

It grew closer yet, nearly at the edge of the desert, close enough for Olibtine, and from the sounds of it, the soldiers, to see that it clearly wasn't natural as it hung beneath the cloud. Its deep red color sent chills up and down Olibtine's spine while the colors above churned as if blown by strong winds, but there wasn't so much as a piece of grass moving on the ground. The soldiers shuffled their feet as they watched the cloud blot out the sun, creating a large, shaded area around them as if a bird cage were being placed over the top of them.

The ominous feeling continued to grow in the back of Olibtine's mind as he gawked at the thing, now close enough to make out all of its features even through the cloud-covered shade. The entire figure was a deep red color, nearly black, with two unnaturally long and skinny arms and legs that reminded him of medical cadavers if they didn't have skin. In fact, the entire thing looked like it didn't have skin and was mostly bone with some muscle on top. The chest wasn't even a chest at all. Its mid-section was entirely hollow except for a few rope-looking connections running throughout. If that wasn't bad enough, the head, Olibtine decided, was the most terrifying of all. It ended at two points resembling horns that poked straight up from the sides of its jagged, hollowed out skull. The face was calm, leaving no hint of its goal in its mouth or its bright red eyes surrounding a deep, endless black that threatened to pull him in.

It's staring at me. Olibtine felt overwhelming foreboding. He knew it was even though it was still just far enough away to make it seem like it was staring at all of them at once.

He glanced over to Daria at his side. Sweat matted the fur on her forehead as she held her knocked bow down, but ready. Realizing he was empty handed, he reached into his robe and pulled out his knife, turning it so the tip pointed down.

He glanced back to the thing overhead, just in time to see it come to a halt with the cloud's churning slowing to a crawl. It continued to stare at him. Then, it pointed directly at him with its long, unnatural finger, causing his throat to catch and body to stiffen.

It opened its mouth revealing the same, seemingly endless swirl of darkness its eyes held and spoke with what sounded like two voices in one, combining into a calm, monotone voice that seemed to carry the distance between them in an instant as if it were directly in front of them.

"Give me the Mind and his companion and the rest will be spared."

A shuffling of feet and chainmail sounded through the ranks of soldiers as some looked to see where the thing was pointing, but most already knew, shuffling to reaffirm their stances knowing that a fight was inevitable.

"Bah!" came the deep, projecting voice of the Captain. "You can fly back off to wherever it is you mossing came from! You won't be getting any Mind from us!"

Daria quickly exhaled next to him as if agreeing with the Captain, an audible tightening of the grip on her bow heard immediately after.

"So be it," the thing replied as it lowered its arm and then began to slowly drop until it hovered just above the ground in front of the Captain and his soldiers, half of its body still visible to Olibtine and Daria in the back.

It held up its right hand next to its head, splaying its fingers. The fingers separated from the main part of its hand in an instant, hovering just above the positions they were in just a moment ago. The fingers turned in unison, the tips pointing towards the soldiers, and then they disappeared. Olibtine's eyes went wide, his head swiveling to try to locate the fingers with no luck. He glanced back to the creature, fingers back and hovering there as if they had never disappeared in the first place. Olibtine gulped. *Did I imagine that?*

The sound of chainmail crashing to the ground sounded in front of him and to the left where the soldiers stood, forcing his head to shift that way as he clenched his dagger, seeing five soldiers in the back-line fall backwards as if being hit by something from the front. *Moss!* Olibtine cursed, noticing the same thing happening to each of the lines ahead of those five. Soldiers all around the ones that fell scrambled to see what was going on, kneeling over the fallen as numerous voices scrambled together, unintelligible, until one in the back, a short, young man from the looks of it, yelled out, "They're dead!"

Soldiers everywhere began to talk to one another, shifting their pikes and feet as they waited for an order. They didn't have to wait long though, for not a second later, the Captain held up his pike and yelled, "Charge!" at the top of his lungs, drowning out the chatter.

Some of the soldiers were waiting for the order and immediately bolted towards the thing, pikes pointing up at the thing's chest, while others were frozen in place as if still digesting the message, but joined in on the charge as well once their training took over. They circled the thing from all sides, but it held its focus on Olibtine and Daria as if nothing else mattered.

Olibtine watched an arrow fly over the heads of the soldiers as they ran, headed right at its face. He held his breath as it closed the distance in a flash, but it never made it all the way, somehow being thrown off course right as it was about to hit. His jaw clenched. *Moss.*

"Moss," he heard Daria curse beside him as if reading his mind. He glanced over and she already had another arrow knocked and ready to loose. She let it fly and he watched, hoping this time would be different, but it wasn't as the arrow ended up flipping head over tail off to the right of the creature before it could hit its mark.

She lowered the bow. "Well that's not going to work."

What can we do? Olibtine watched as the soldiers poked at it from all sides, never quite reaching it for some reason.

The creature lifted its other hand near its head and separated those fingers as well, causing the soldiers to pause, frustration mixing with fear as all ten fingers hovered above the main part of its hand. The fingers rotated just like before and then disappeared. A second later, the fingers returned to their position above the hands, then reconnected, a stillness filling their air. Olibtine watched on in horror as every soldier, no matter where he stood, crumpled to the ground, the stillness evaporating in an instant as the sound of armor and pike heads alike came crashing down, leaving a circular, motionless mass of blue and red.

Chapter 48: Purtghast

Kausha stared at her home of Purtghast in the pre-morning light. A warm breeze swept up from the ocean along the cliffside, over the city and its walls, down the rolling hill, batting at the front of her cloak. Except for short sleeps, she had trekked there nearly non-stop for fear of missing her great great grandmother's passing. A wave of emotions flooded through her as she stared upon the place she spent so many years of her life.

The city, while having similarities with others, namely Nortmund, had a calm air that no other city could match. The squat white towers and buildings throughout were highlighted and tipped by red outlines, ensuring that even if a stranger stumbled upon the city, there would be no mistaking who resided within. It was situated on a sheer cliff face overlooking the Bloody Waters, aptly named after the Bloodborn lineage, that protected the city on one side while the opposite side, the one Kausha stood at, had a relatively short wall to keep any would-be intruders thinking. Rolling hills crested for leagues around. In the history of the Bloodborn lineage, only once had it been attacked in all that time, which resulted in death to all those that attacked. The Bloodborn have been feared or respected by all for thousands of years, so walls resembling the hulking ones of Nortmund are unnecessary.

The white stone wall itself spanned from a set of sheer rocks, not dissimilar to the ones on the back side of the city that ran straight up into the sky and were sharp enough throughout to cut even the thickest of animal hides, to an inlet that had cut away the land to create a natural downslope that led to the ocean. Spaced out upon the wall walked a handful of guards wearing the Bloodborn cloak of red and purple with the bloody teardrop symbol on the front. A stark contrast against the mostly-white backdrop of the city.

Walking up the slope outside of the wall, the gate began to open as Kausha approached. Two of the middle stones lifted first, then the set outside of those as they continued down the line until the sequence left a half-moon shaped opening that could only fit a few people in abreast at a time.

As soon as she crossed the threshold into the city, she was met with morning bird calls from the numerous trees that lined the white painted cobblestone streets that wound throughout the city. Continuing along the cobblestone, she gazed right and left at the small, square, two story-homes placed side-by-side just behind the trees that housed the smaller Bloodborn houses - those that were either dying out or, in rare cases, starting anew. Men smiled and nodded to her when she passed as they carried out their morning duties, tending to cleaning or the gardens, gathering produce for meals for the day, or anything else that was needed of a man.

Following the winding of the street, she entered the main circle of the city where the citizens congregated. A giant white water fountain in the shape of an upside-down teardrop sat directly in the middle that commemorated the first 1000 years of the city that looked like it was just built yesterday. Even now, men and women sat at the base of the fountain chatting and drinking their morning coffee or tea. There were no carts or booths to be seen like there were in other cities. The Bloodorn were a society of post-capitalism, which is to say that with the abundance of food, shelter, and comfort, everything of need was given freely. Six separate roads branched off from the city center, the one Kausha just walked down, along with five others that wandered through the city bypassing homes, workspaces, fields, and towers along the way.

Kausha started up the left path towards her family's home - the largest and oldest one in the city. Following the path, she couldn't help but to look up at the plump trees lining the street which sat upon square carpets of picturesque green and yellow grass. When she was a child, she was told that the seeds for all of the trees in Purtghast were picked from deep within The Forest ages ago, but they weren't as large as those due to the proximity to the ocean and its salty air. She closed her eyes and breathed in, the familiar salty smell bringing back memories of running through the streets as a child, chasing birds that were unlucky enough to land on the cobblestone, or eating under the warm sun. Letting out a long exhale, she continued up the slope of the street until she could see the top of her home, a sheer white, sloped roof with a red outline - a striking sight against the clear blue sky behind.

Continuing up the slope, the full home came into view. A three story, rectangular building that was wider than it was tall. Each floor contained a number of thick pillars that allowed each floor to be open to the elements. Even now as Kausha looked on, all of the doors were open, white cloth with red fringes draping each, flapping in the breeze coming from the opposite side of the home. Sea birds flew overhead calling out as she approached one of the doors and slid the cloth to the side, the breeze threatening to pull the cloak from her body as she entered.

The ground floor was similar to the ones above consisting of a pair of large, open common areas that contained finely carved tables and chairs throughout. A central firepit was situated in a divot dug out of the natural stone circled by three wide steps for seating. The floor itself was the natural rock of the cliff, polished to almost glisten in the sunlight.

Kausha proceeded forward towards the opposite side of the room, passing the firepit and weaving her way through chairs and a large dining table to pull back the flapping cloth to reveal a skinny landing and a view of brilliant, endless blue as far as her eyes could see. She took another deep breath, memories from her childhood racing through her mind again. *I almost forgot how blue it all is.* She stared, transfixed, the crashing of waves against rock making it to her ears from below.

"Kausha?" she heard from behind her off to the left. She turned, hand still holding the cloth out of the way.

"Kausha, it is you," her mother smiled.

"Hello mother," Kausha replied, turning while dropping the cloth, then walking over to give her a hug.

Her mother, still young for a Bloodborn, looked exactly like Kausha - crimson hair and dark skin with a short, slender build.

She pulled back from Kausha looking down, then gave her a raised eyebrow once catching her eye again.

Kausha looked down at her cloak, understanding. "Oh, right, this. It's nothing, just something I traded for in a town I passed through."

"I see," her mother replied in a questioning tone, her eyes going distant for a second, then returning to normal. "Come, we are having our morning coffee." She grabbed Kausha's hand and led her outside through one of the cloth covered doors, up a short, wide staircase to the airy outdoor seating area. It was covered with a cloth canopy draped cross-ways from corner to corner from the four thick wooden pillars - the same exact one from her dreams.

"Look who is here," her mother announced as she reached the top of the steps.

Kausha glanced around the circle, meeting the eyes of her grandmother, great grandmother, and great great grandmother, each wearing the customary Bloodborn attire along with a smile on their faces as they met her eyes.

"Ah, Kausha, right on time. Come, sit." Her grandmother rimmed her mug while patting the seat next to her.

Kausha crossed the space, finding a seat between her mother and grandmother.

"How was the rest of your journey?" her grandmother asked before she took a sip from her steaming mug.

"It was... eventful, but I made it in time," Kausha replied as she looked at her great great grandmother who was leaning forward, both hands resting on her cane, her chin resting on her hands.

"That you have. How was Nortmund?" her grandmother asked in the same tone she would ask someone about how their meal tasted.

Kausha darted her head to her left to look at her grandmother. *How did she know?*

"It was eye-opening to say the least. How come you didn't tell me how brutal it was there?"

Her grandmother took a sip from her mug before lifting her eyes again and answering in a soft tone. "Books and stories can only do so much to impact your perception. It is better to see these things on your own and judge for yourself."

"I could have been sent to the mines or been killed!" Kausha exclaimed, looking at each in turn, landing on her mother, who scoffed.

"You are fully capable of escaping any situation alone, we made sure of that in your training," her mother stated matter-of-factly while staring into her mug.

Kausha glanced around again to see each nodding at that, her heart beginning to race at the candid nature of their emotions. She returned her eyes to her mother.

"And what about the sorcerers? Did you train me for that as well?!"

Her mother's eyes went wide for a brief moment before she blinked, opening them to stare across the space. Kausha followed her eyes to see her great great grandmother staring not at her mother, but at her with those intense purple eyes. Her arm hair stood on end under the gaze.

"What happened in Nortmund? Only in regards to the sorcerers, nothing else," her great great grandmother asked while lifting her head to sit up straight, the haggard look from only a moment ago forgotten.

Kausha cleared her throat, gathering her thoughts, then responded. "I'm not entirely sure how it happened, but every single one of the guards seemed to be in a trance, or something worse. They each had glowing red eyes and only attacked me or those I was with. We all escaped, but the last one I killed said something I am still working out. With its final breath, it said 'Join us or else you WILL kill those you try so hard to protect. Join us or else all are doomed.'"

Upon finishing, she heard rustling of clothes to her left and right, while at the same time, great great grandmother clutched her cane tighter, white knuckles appearing through boney hands.

Silence hung between them, only the wind refusing to quiet itself.

"What does it mean?" Kausha asked, breaking the silence, never taking her eyes away from her great great grandmother, who slowly turned her eyes down to her hands resting on her cane.

"And you are sure this happened inside of the walls of Nortmund?"

Kausha nodded. "Inside of the first's tower."

She shook her head, visibly blinking, then turned her eyes up to meet Kausha's again, the intensity vanishing, replaced with that of understanding. "As for what was said, I do not know. It may as well be something they are trying to plant inside your head to make you turn to their side. I would not put it past the sisters. As for the first part," she blinked slowly and let out an exhale, "that is a blood magic that I thought was lost in time. One that was found even before my time and locked away deep in the forbidden parts of the library. Neither your mother, nor your mother's mother, knows of this. It is very troubling that they would go to these lengths inside of a city, but at least now we know that the contract did not come from Nortmund. Would you agree?"

Kausha glanced left and right at the stunned faces of her grandmother and mother, their jaws flexing as they stared, breath bated, awaiting more information. She then returned her eyes to her great great grandmother, nodding.

"It involves a spell that requires dead bodies that still have traces of blood flowing through the veins. The blood is extracted from each, a demand is implanted into the droplets, then it is pushed to find hosts, overriding even their most basic of needs and wants. That, child, is what you ran across in Nortmund." She finished with a cough, her mother darting over to offer her water that she took in both hands as her mother grabbed the cane. She took a sip with her eyes closed, then handed the water back, placing her hands on the cane again and hunching over to place her chin on her hands. She opened her eyes upon settling herself, a pain replacing the understanding from before beneath narrowed eyebrows.

"So those were... puppets?" Kausha asked.

Her great great grandmother nodded.

Moss, Kausha cursed to herself, replaying the battle she fought in the tunnel. Her head drooped, staring at the stone ground. *Does that mean I killed innocents that day? Could we have escaped without killing?* A stiff gust played with the cloak dangling between her legs.

"You did what you had to," her great grandmother spoke up for the first time as if reading her mind. Kausha's head shot up, stomach churning. "Even if you would have known, you may have been able to escape alone without killing, but you would not have been able to escape with your companions in tow. Preparedness can be both a blessing and a curse at the same time, but actions taken to save your life and your companion's lives should not be second guessed."

She caught her grandmother nodding out of the corner of her eye to her left, but the churning in her stomach didn't stop, it only grew.

"Why has so much been held back from my teachings?" she asked, turning to her mother, who shook her head.

"I didn't even know of this," she responded without looking at Kausha.

"It isn't just that, though. It's the sorcerers being Bloodborn. It's the Nortmunder's slavery and oppression. It's the Bloodborn assassin that killed Gadimar. What else is there?!" she demanded, her volume increasing with each question.

Her mother's hands tightened around her mug, her mouth tightening and eyes squinting along with it. She then turned to Kausha to meet her eyes, face returning immediately to her calm and collected self.

"Every Bloodborn has her own hurdles to overcome. Yours may be unique this time around, but they are still yours to have. I had questions, your grandmother had questions, your great grandmother had questions, and your great great grandmother had questions. There is more Bloodborn history than can be taught in a lifetime. You will receive more answers than you can possibly fathom during the passing, but you must wait," she ended, nodding with a finality that she'd used hundreds of times before with Kausha.

Kausha sat staring at her mother taking a sip of her tea, numb. *Still they won't answer?* She fixed her eyes on her great great grandmother. *What does the passing have to do with this? Moss!*

"I think that is enough for this morning." Her grandmother stood, placing her empty mug on the table nearby. "Kausha will need to clean up before the passing and great grandmother must finish her final duties." She crossed the space to Kausha's great great grandmother, standing on one side to help her up while Kausha's mother took the other side doing the same. Each departed down the steps leaving Kausha alone with her thoughts.

Chapter 49: Destiny's Demand

The following evening was the passing. Kausha, in a formal Bloodborn robe of red and purple with black embroidery down the seams that also outlined the symbol embossed on the back with a high collar, stared west watching the sunset that was giving way to the full moon of the night. The anticipation was palpable throughout her home and the city - a passing did not happen often, let alone to such a prominent family as Kausha's. Men ran this way and that way, double checking to make sure everything was prepared for what was to come while the women partaking in the passing dressed themselves in a similar robe as Kausha's.

She felt a warm hand grasp hers as she watched the last slivers of the sun retreat beyond the sea, the brilliant purple and orange wispy clouds evaporating.

"Are you ready?" her grandmother asked from behind.

Kausha nodded, tearing her eyes away from the sea to make eye contact with her. "I am," she promised herself.

Her grandmother nodded in return. "Let us be off."

Hand in hand, Kausha walked with her grandmother out of the front of the house, took an immediate left towards the ritual tower - a large, half-oval structure that resembled a half moon. It was the highest point in the city, and the most important. Walking up the cobblestone path with her home to her left, she couldn't help but to stare up in awe. She had only been inside of the ritual tower a few times in her life, each time sneaking in with her childhood friends under darkness. Her stomach fluttered and her heart raced the closer she got. She gripped her grandmother's hand tightly. It wasn't that she was afraid, afterall, her entire lineage had gone through a passing themselves, but something seemed to weigh down on her mind.

She shook her head in an attempt to rid herself of the weight, but it still held. She watched as the final Bloodborn woman filtered through the broad, wooden doors as the sun had fully given way to the night, a bright, full moon rising slowly on the horizon.

Kausha paused at the steps leading up to the doors, staring into the darkness on the other side. Her grandmother took an extra step as her arm extended, only then realizing Kausha had stopped. She looked back at Kausha, face level.

This is something all Bloodborn women go through, she reassured herself. *You will be alright.*

She met eyes with her grandmother, a quick smile touching her lips in encouragement. A slight squeeze at her fingertips provided comfort in what lay ahead. Her feet began to move without thought, up the steps, into the darkness beyond.

It was just as Kausha remembered from her childhood; a large, open room with a glass dome above, the moon shining inside making it light up as if the sun were out. In the middle of the room were two beds, her great great grandmother already lying down in one. The beds were set on top of a large ujuntu basin surrounded by smaller basins placed at the feet of a dozen women, each wearing a red and purple Bloodborn robe with their hoods pulled up, faces completely hidden from view.

Kausha's eyes drifted away from the middle of the room to her hand that she felt her grandmother let go of. She smiled, then pulled her hood up, finally turning to pace across the room to stand behind the final empty bowl on the ground.

Kausha took a deep breath, then started towards her destiny. The heads beneath the hoods surrounding the beds turned to watch her approach causing her hands to sweat under their faceless gaze. A heavy silence filled the air, not even her robe rustling making it to her ears. She closed the gap to the bed, meeting the purple eyes of her great great grandmother, glowing in the moonlight. A smile appeared on her lips as she held out her hand. Kausha smiled back, taking her hand in kind as she sat down, then pulled her legs up to lay down, holding eye contact the entire time.

As the full moon continued to rise, revealing more of itself every minute, Kausha noticed age lines upon her great great grandmother that she hadn't noticed even the day before. A lifetime and more of experience. Kausha gripped her hand tighter as she watched a tear slide down the side of her face to the bed. Her great great grandmother returned the squeeze with a small nod, barely discernible, then smiled in that comforting way Kausha remembered from her childhood.

With the room alight from the full moon nearly directly overhead, the ritual began.

Out of the corner of her eyes, Kausha caught the women surrounding them drop to their knees, faces completely hidden beneath their hoods. All at once, they placed their hands into the basins in front of them. As if connected by an unseen conductor, they began to chant in a slow, quiet harmony that Kausha did not recognize. Her heart began to race as she listened to the familiar, but unknown chant. A soft, red glow rose from the smaller basins, surrounding her in a complete ring on all sides. As the chanting's tempo picked up, the red glow expanded from the small basins, first connecting in a complete circle between women, then fully enveloping her and her great great grandmother. Kausha's heart continued to race, beads of sweat covering her forehead as she forced herself to hold eye contact.

Suddenly, the harmony in the chanting changed - replaced with a fervent, mismatched chant that sounded as if each were fighting for supremacy. The air grew heavy as the moon reached its peak directly above them.

Kausha gasped as her great great grandmother's eyes squeezed shut, her back arching, then blood began to seep from every pore and float above her as her skin grew white, glowing in the moonlight. She stared at the glistening blood - her great great grandmother's blood - floating above in the shape of her body. The chanting grew louder and more confusing, harmony lost. The chanting reverberated throughout her body, shoving her blood wherever they wanted without her consent. First slamming into her legs, then thrust up into her head, then forced down into the pit of her stomach. She closed her eyes, giving in to the ritual as blood coursed through her hand, tightening her grip on her great great grandmother. With a shock, she felt new blood rush into her through her fingertips, cooler than her own. Then something unexpected hit her - memories.

Flashes of faces, figures, landscapes, death, blood, pain, love, hatred, comfort, and revenge filled her mind. Her body convulsed as it was enveloped in new blood and thousands of years of memories.

A breeze flowing through her hair as she ran along the beach hand in hand with three other girls.

A calm serenity of staring into an orange and pink sunrise.

Chipping away at stone atop a hill overlooking the sea. Swiping her brow before glancing behind her to watch as a square stone was hoisted on top of another.

Hearing her daughter's first scream.

Blood splattering her face as she killed a man with fear set upon his face. Watching a woman with a child in her arms look back while running away, a blood dagger finding her back a second later.

Pain shooting throughout her body as dozens of knives drew blood, a manic human face laughing as he caught the blood in a jar.

Revenge.

Kausha's body continued to convulse as memories and blood alike filled her body to the point of bursting. She opened her mouth to scream, but no sound escaped.

A Catsnif deflecting a blood blade with her sword, only to be struck in the eye with a blood dagger, toppling backwards.

Kicking in a wooden door, a group of men turning, eyes and mouths wide in horror plastered on severed heads toppling to the ground leaving a woman lying naked on a bed.

Revenge.

Watching on from a distance as smoke and fire engulf a small village.

Looking up at her arms, wrists bound and chained to a wall behind her head. A man hidden beneath a dark hood grabbing her face, forcing her to look forward, a smell of garlic on his breath. "So you're healed," he spat, turning her head back and forth. "Good. They will be pleased." Four others with hoods hiding their faces closed in on her as she watched them place jars on the stone floor beneath her, sharp pain shooting through her body as they stabbed her repeatedly along her arms and sides. Overwhelmed by the number of stabbings, she couldn't move her blood away quick enough to dodge them all. Eyes wide, manic with lust, they caught blood in jars as it dripped from her wounds. Through watery eyes, she glanced around to search for something, anything, but all there was was dark, dirty stone and a metal gate on the opposite wall. She groaned, blinking tears away, vision swimming, then black.

Hobbling up a dirt hill, The Forest ahead, bells sounding behind. Glancing back to see a walled city with a blue and white banner flapping in the wind.

Revenge.

Kausha stilled, memories ceasing for a moment, but the emotions lasted. *Revenge.*

She jolted up, rubbing both hands to her forehead. She realized the chanting had stopped, the moon still illuminating the room. *Great great grandmother.* She looked over to see a motionless husk of pale white skin, robe sunken in as if only bones remained, arm still extended to her side.

Kausha watched as the women previously surrounding them, hoods now fallen behind their heads, walked slowly to her great great grandmother, placed their hands upon her skin wherever they were, then recited something beneath their breath. Once finished, they walked to her, repeating the same touch and under-breath saying. Afterwards, they filed out, the moon casting long shadows on them as they departed, leaving only her family standing beside the beds. Sweat glistened on their foreheads above weathered faces.

"You did well," her grandmother comforted before removing her hand. Kausha's mother and great grandmother nodded in agreement.

Her body tensed, back arching as pain shot through her mind. Not physical pain, no, the pain of an unfulfilled revenge and anger. Flashes of blood pooled on dirt reflecting firelight, men and women screaming in the background as a blue and white banner wrapped in flames slowly turned to ash.

She hunched over, taking quick, shallow breaths.

"What... what is happening to me?" she whispered with a dry mouth.

Nothing but silence came from her mother, grandmother, and great grandmother.

"What did you do?!" she yelled, lifting her head to stare into each of their eyes in turn.

"It is the passing," her mother replied after a long silence. "Memories and talents are passed down through generations. No two are ever the same."

"These aren't just memories!" Kausha fumed, gripping her robe tight at her knees. Even now, she felt the urge to act, to set off and exact what the new feelings told her to.

Another secret. She shook her head, throwing her legs over the edge of the bed, then stood. Without saying another word, she turned towards the exit, taking a moment to glance down at her great great grandmother, then strode the rest of the distance out the wooden doors, the excess blood coursing through her body as memories and emotions churned inside, pushing her towards her destiny.

Chapter 50: The Meeting in the Road to Gbinti

Kausha darted across the cobblestone back to her home, frightening the men inside as she swept aside the cloth barring her entrance, then bound up the stone steps two by two to the third floor. The blood inside pulsated throughout her body, driving her forward until she reached her wardrobe. She stood there, eyes sliding over the jumpsuits and robes therein, landing on a red and purple robe. She reached towards the sleeve and turned the front towards her to reveal the candle with its wax sliding down the side, freshly cleaned after her journey. *When did that happen?* she asked herself with a raised eyebrow.

She gripped the sleeve as rage filled her causing her to close her eyes and lean forward, throwing her other hand against the wardrobe to support her leaning body. As the rage subsided, she opened her eyes and looked down at the robe still held tight. She gathered herself, standing and releasing the robe from her grip, then proceeded to throw on the Bloodborn jumpsuit she had worn her entire life growing up. She removed the red and purple robe from the wardrobe, and with one final look at the candle, she threw one arm into it, then the other. *This is... right,* she realized, looking down.

The blood coursing throughout combined with the new emotions urged her legs to move, pushing her out of the room and retreating back down the steps. The men on the first floor huddled together, eyes wide, watching her as she crossed the main living space, shoving the cloth aside once again.

She froze. Her mother, grandmother, and great grandmother were there standing side by side, their faces flat. Kausha let the cloth fall behind her as she stepped out into the last of the full moon's light. None of them spoke, but their soft eyes and frowns on their mouths said all they needed to. *They went through this, too.* A cool ocean breeze shifted their robes. *Then they understand.*

Tearing her eyes from theirs, she stared east.

"Kausha, wait." Her mother stopped her in her tracks. She took two steps towards her holding out something in her hand. "She wanted me to give this to you after the passing."

Kausha looked down at something wrapped in a red cloth, not much smaller than the hand it sat in. She met her mother's eyes in the fading moonlight, a softness to them that Kausha did not recognize in such a stern woman, then she looked past her at her grandmother and great grandmother, both nodding in unison towards her. Looking down at the red cloth again, she reached for it, hesitating only an instant before taking it and pocketing it inside of her jumpsuit.

"Be safe," her mother wished before turning and retreating back to her place next to the other two women.

With a final nod to those that taught her so much, Kausha stared east once again, the blood inside feeling as if it were going to burst from her body at any moment, then set off in long strides down the cobblestone, through the main circle, then out the half-moon gate as the moon began to give way to the first hints of a new day in the distance. She paused just outside of the gate, something in the back of her mind telling her to take her shoes off. She did so, tossing them to the side, her feet digging into cool grass and dirt alike. That same something told, or guided, her to push blood from her toenails and coat the bottoms of her feet in a thick layer so her feet were almost floating off of the ground. She did so again, realizing she had plenty of blood to spare. Then all of a sudden she began to slide down the hill. Her arms flailed as she attempted to keep her balance, nearly falling backwards a time or two, until she leaned forward at her hips, balance solid again, gliding down the hill effortlessly as if the ground were solid ice beneath her. She looked down, the short grass folding beneath her feet, picking up speed, another thought popping into her head. *Run.* Looking towards the bottom of the hill, she bent her left leg behind her, shifting her weight above the right. She brought her left leg forward, landing in a slide that allowed her to pick up speed as she repeated the movement.

The landscape flew by in a blur once she hit the bottom of the long hill and continued East, gaining momentum, even on the flat parts of the countryside. Blood rushed through her legs, empowering her to continue forward. Wind buffeted her face causing tears to squeeze from the corners of her eyes and fly backwards with every blink.

The morning clouds exploded with oranges, reds, and yellows as the sun began to rise in the distance over The Forest. After gliding across the Veda River, she diverted southeast as to not run directly into The Forest, an imposing desert situated next to the lifeless Rulnarat Mountains jutting from the landscape off to her right.

Sweat caused her jumpsuit to stick to her skin, but curiously, neither her legs nor her lungs burned. *I'm not even breathing hard,* she realized while watching the final slivers of the sun rise above the trees, which grew larger with every stride. The bottom of her robe fluttered in the wind, and as she unconsciously pressed it down, she felt the item that her mother gave her before departing. She reached beneath her robe, digging the item from one of the many pockets on her jumpsuit, then pulled it out along with the red cloth it was wrapped in. She hadn't noticed in the dark, but it had the Bloodborn symbol embroidered into it in a dark red, nearly black, fiber. Her eyebrow rose as she rubbed the symbol, picturing her great great grandmother's purple eyes staring back at her. Glancing forward quickly to make sure the way was clear, she looked back down at the cloth and unfolded it to reveal a skinny hairpin made out of ujuntu. A memory popped into her head from her childhood when her great great grandmother tied her hair back in a bun, skewering it with the hairpin before releasing her to run around with the other kids. She turned it over lengthwise to look at the flattened end to reveal a single, red blood droplet - the Bloodborn symbol. She stuffed away the cloth once again, then stabbed the bun of her hair with the hairpin.

With the renewed reminder, Kausha squeezed her jaw tight, focused on what lay ahead, then forced even more blood through her legs causing them to swell with strength and increase her speed once again.

***

Olibtine watched in stunned silence as the thing lowered its long arms and began to float directly towards him and Daria while casually hovering a foot off of the ground. It stopped, then, for the first time since lowering itself to the ground, it looked down. Olibtine followed its eyes and saw that the Captain with a deep scowl on his face, blood squirting from the side of his head, held the creature's foot. The creature tilted its head as if curious, then let loose its fingers straight down into the Captain, his head tumbling from his lifeless body. But his grip held in some unnatural way, halting the creature's advancement. Its eyes grew brighter in anger as it let its fingers loose again, this time separating the Captain's hand from his arm, freeing itself. But the hand held as if the Captain was still alive.

The creature gazed back up, focusing on Olibtine, then slowly began to drift forward again, clearing the pile of lifeless soldiers. Olibtine tried to swallow, but found it impossible. His legs buckled watching the creature advance down the dirt road directly towards him. *This is it. The entire trip to the tower was worthless.* He envisioned Gbinti in ruins, people dead in the streets as buildings that burned crashed to the ground. *I failed them all.* Tears began forming in the bottom of his vision as his grip on the knife began to falter.

A tear dropped from his eyes with a blink. He squeezed them tight and when he opened them, Daria was in front of him, a flask in one hand, bow and arrow in the other. She glanced back at him with a smile on her face and a glisten in her eye. "We've been through worse," she realized, then turned towards the creature again.

Olibtine stared at her back, mouth open. *How can she...* He noticed movement at the bottom of his vision. His mouth closed while his eyes widened, noticing that her legs were shaking just as much as his were. *She's terrified! Moss, she's just as terrified as I am, but still, she moves forward.*

He gripped his knife tight once again, set his jaw, stood up straight, then sucked his tears in as he looked over the top of her head at the monster. *I haven't failed yet!*

"Why do you want us dead?!" Olibtine shouted, taking a step to the side and forward to get shoulder to shoulder with Daira again. She shot her head sideways, boring her eyes straight into the side of his face, but he stood strong, holding eye contact with the creature. *Moss. Those eyes.* They were like a whirlpool threatening to suck him in.

It tilted its head as if it were plain as day.

"Why," it started, in the odd double voice, "it is in the contract." A chill shot up Olibtine's spine, but he wasn't sure if it was due to the calm, yet mocking tone or the fact that there was a contract on his head.

"What contract?! Who gave it?" Olibtine demanded, forcing his voice steady. *I have to buy time... But for what?*

"Of that, we do not know. We received it before you even stepped foot inside of our tower."

Before? Olibtine's eyebrows scrunched. *No, that can't be.* He glanced left at Daria, noticing her face was pale beneath fur at the implication. He swallowed, then turned his eyes back to meet the creature's.

"We see you have connected the dots as well. We assumed as much, but your faces confirm it. No matter, you will be lying in your own blood and dirt soon enough, just as these others are."

It raised its right hand, but instead of its fingers breaking from the hand like before, it balled its hand into a fist, its fingers melding together in a smooth ball, then extended, curving up and then out to a sharp point with near-translucent red edges.

Olibtine looked on in horror as the creature's hand turned into a scythe the size of his body, sharp edges glistening in the backlit sunlight from far behind it in the distance. He gripped his knife so it wouldn't fall from his hand from the sweat dripping down his forearm. *Monsters!* He attempted to swallow again, but no spit was there to move down his throat.

Without taking its eyes from Olibtine, it crept forward, scythe aloft ready to strike.

"Olibtine, run!" Daria yelled, causing him to jump. He glanced left just in time to see her knock her arrow, the vial she held just a moment ago already half-way to the creature, glowing brighter as it flew, then let it loose. Without watching if the arrow connected, Daria had already turned to run, Olibtine taking her cue and doing the same.

The sound of glass shattering sounded behind him, creating a shadow in front of him as he ran, followed by a grunt. *It hit!*

"What now?" he asked, already breathing heavily after only a few steps.

"That's all I had! Think we can make it to Gbinti?"

He glanced back to see the creature already gliding after them. "Don't think so," he breathed between steps. *Think! Think!* he told himself as he ran.

***

With the desert sand of Baugroun underfoot and the sorcerer's black tower jutting into the sky to her right, Kausha felt an ominous feeling grow with every stride, which only increased when she saw a dense cloud in the distance on what was otherwise a clear day. The sun had reached its peak directly above, reflecting off of the sand below causing her to sweat through both layers of clothing as she continued.

What is that? She squinted at the cloud. With every stride, over every dune, she got closer and closer until she noticed the unnatural colors of red and black and gray within, swirling slowly like a whirlpool. A feeling of recognition in the back of her mind gave her pause. Not her recognition, but something else.

Nearly upon the cloud, she could see the desert's end underneath the shadow it cast upon the ground. Exiting the desert and with the ominous feeling at a crescendo, her eyes went wide and her breath caught as she turned her body sideways in an attempt to stop her momentum. She turned the slick blood on her feet into something rough, digging them into the dirt, skidding to a halt before a pile of bodies wearing blue and white over chainmail, covered in blood with helmets and pikes lying next to frightened faces.

***

"Olibtine, wait!" Daria yelled through breaths.

Olibtine skidded to a halt and pivoted while lifting his knife in front of him, ready to fight, only to find Daria standing still, bow down, staring back the way they came.

"It... stopped," she gulped, gathering her breath and wiping the fur on her brow.

"What?" he asked, standing up straight and lowering his knife. She was right, it wasn't even facing them any longer, it was facing the dead soldiers, scythe absent from its hand. *What the.*

He walked to stand side by side with Daria. "Why isn't it chasing us?"

She shook her head. "I'm not sure, but whatever it is, it's good for us. Should we run?"

He squinted through the long shadow, trying to make out what it was doing. *What is it looking at?* Curiosity got the better of him and he stepped off the road, stumbling down the short slope to short grass, attempting to see around it.

"Olibtine!" Daria shouted from the road. He ignored her, staring at the pile of blue and white corpses to see...

"Someone is there! Standing behind the soldiers!" he yelled back to Daria. She scrambled to his side and gasped.

"Is that a soldier?" she asked.

Olibtine shook his head. "No, I don't think so. It doesn't have blue or white on."

He watched on as they stood there, staring at one another. *They're talking.* "Let's get closer," he whispered to Nalia and started to creep forward without her waiting for a response.

***

Gbinti, Kausha recognized the colors. Her mind tore itself in two. *Senseless slaughter. Revenge.*

Her eyes wandered over the lifeless Gbinti soldiers, a headless soldier's body stretched out as if reaching for something catching her eyes. She looked in the direction its corpse pointed and froze, body stiffening at the thing in front of her down the road. Her insides shifted without thought, trying to find somewhere safe.

It was now clear to her what the ominous feeling was that pricked the back of her mind. Before she could move, the thing spoke.

"Ahh. The young Bloodborn comes again." Its voice sounded like two speaking at once as it hung suspended off of the ground.

Kausha glanced up and down its grotesque body. *The sorcerers. Blood magic.* A shiver ran down her spine.

"So you have chosen, we see."

Kausha's forehead furrowed.

"You still do not understand?" it asked before she could reply. "Do you not feel it pushing you into something you would not do alone? Do you not feel the pressure, the need, to act on things you yourself have not experienced? What is it you were moving towards if not false memories?"

A wave of pain shot from Kausha's hands to her feet as flashes of men with manic expressions on their faces, teeth bared with saliva running down the corners of their mouths, stabbed her in different places throughout her body. Her hands clenched as her head became even more jumbled. *They tortured us for our blood!*

"They tried to do the same to us, you know?"

Kausha shook herself in an attempt to clear her thoughts to stare at the thing in its deep, endless pits for eyes.

"You? But you betrayed us! You betrayed the Bloodborn!" It wasn't entirely her speaking then - the emotions raw and boiling up from somewhere deep inside.

"No!" it yelled as its glowing red eyes flamed brighter, the black void in the middle deepening. "It is the Bloodborn that betray *us*! Forcing us to do their bidding century after century, passing after passing. We are captives to grudges centuries old by those long forgotten. Time ticks by as their emotions hang on like a disease on the land. We refused to be used and were shunned from Bloodborn society for it. You can still stop this. Join us." it finished, holding out its unnaturally long arm and fingers.

Her eyes drooped to fall to her palms that hung level with the ground. *Great great grandmother? Great grandmother? Mother?*

Revenge! Blood coursed through her body urging her to act. Not think, act.

Before Kausha realized what she was doing, her body was flying through the air directly at the creature. Blood pumped into her arms as she squeezed the fingers on her right hand together, forcing blood from under her fingernails together to produce a straight, four foot long blood sword. The fingers on her left hand spread from one another, blood forcing its way from under her fingertips to produce blood daggers, which were immediately broken off and palmed, ready to be thrown.

The creature was ready for her though, gliding backwards effortlessly as soon as Kausha darted forward, producing a blood shield from its right hand.

Kausha twirled in mid-air, letting loose the blood daggers aimed directly at the creature's eyes. Blood shield raised, the daggers disappeared in ripples, blood being soaked up as if dropping water into water. Kausha landed, staring through the near-translucent red shield, right foot forward, blood sword in front of her body at the ready.

The creature spoke again, unphased by Kausha's attack. "What of your companions, then? They are from this land. Will you kill them as well?"

Kausha froze as Nalia's, Shaum's, Skirm's, Skip's, and Yaula's face popped into her head one by one. She shook herself again, half of her wanting to push forward, letting nothing get in her way, while the other half hesitated. *Great great grandmother, why?* She dug her back foot into the dirt road.

With blood enhanced legs, she shot forward again, closing the gap between her and the creature in a flash. She swiped the blood sword at its dangling feet, attempting to sever its limbs. Blood sword met blood scythe as the creature produced the weapon in a flash in its left hand, swinging it in an arch to deflect hers, still holding the form of a shield in its right. Kausha rolled with the momentum of the deflection as it drove her sword to the dirt, ending up on her right knee behind the creature. As she stood, she swung from below, attempting to catch it on its blindside. Before her sword could connect, the creature shot up into the air out of reach, spinning at the same time to face her once again.

***

Olibtine stood off to the side of the dirt road, jaw slack in awe while watching the monster and the newcomer, clearly a Bloodborn from how she formed a sword from her fingertips out of mid air, trading blows. *But that isn't the Bloodborn symbol,* he recognized, forehead scrunching, oblivious to the danger he was in just moments ago.

"Should we help?" Daria whispered to his left.

"Huh?" he started, blinking, only then realizing that his eyes were dry from staring for so long. "Oh. Um, help?" *Should we? Enemy of my enemy is my friend, right? Moss! How can we hope to help even if we wanted to?* His mind reeled watching the Bloodborn cut at the creature's feet.

"How would we?" he asked, keeping his eyes glued to the two as the Bloodborn rolled underneath the creature and swiped up with her sword only for the creature to rise further into the air as the sword missed its mark.

"We could distract it. I have one more vial in my pack."

It's better than gawking. "Okay," he nodded, tearing his eyes from the two. "Let's go get it."

***

Kausha caught movement from the corner of her eye as two figures crept by behind the creature, parallel to the dirt road. She couldn't afford to turn her head to get a better look at them, but she thought one was carrying a bow.

The creature struck first this time, diving at an angle directly towards her, scythe already slicing the air in a wide arch. Kausha flipped backwards, dodging the scythe while producing two daggers from under her fingernails, cutting the blood flow off and palming them. She landed with blood pooled throughout her legs, then dodged to the right as the creature swung backhanded, dirt flying up from the force of the swing in the place her feet were a second ago. She aimed at its shoulder this time, then let loose one of the daggers. The creature let the momentum of its upwards swing spin its body so the shield ended between them, absorbing the blood dagger.

Kausha bent her legs, pressing her feet into the ground, then jumped at an arch, aiming for the opposite side of the creature. She flew through the air, cloak flapping behind her, then reared back the second dagger, taking aim at its hollowed-out skull, then flung it with a blood-strengthened arm straight down from her jump's apex. It brought up its shield above its horns without even looking, absorbing the dagger once again, then began rearing back its arm scythe, its whirlpool eyes gazing up to meet hers as Kausha fell, unable to change her trajectory.

Kausha watched as the creature's scythe began cutting through the air, its arm fully extended, moving in a blur behind its head. At that moment, a calmness enveloped her from within. She felt her blood slow to a crawl as her heart, always beating steadily in her ear, ceased for the moment. With breath held, silence louder than any heartbeat enveloped her while she hung motionless in the air, the creature's arm scythe frozen behind its head.

What is this? She gazed down and noticed even the dirt seemed to freeze.

Thunk. As her heart beat, her body shifted a foot closer to the ground. The creature's arm scythe shifted up as well, now pointed straight behind its head as flecks of dirt all around shifted. She shifted her eyes off to the left to see the two from before frozen in time as well, mid run, at the edge of a line of tall grass.

Thunk. The scythe was in full view as it hovered over the creature's head, the translucent red threatening to slice her in half. *How am I so calm?* Kausha looked down to see that her feet were a foot off of the ground. Focusing on her arm with the blood sword, she strained, attempting to force her limb to move. It was like trying to move with every inch of your body wrapped in layers of thick cloth, then wrapped again in rope and tied down to a table. *MOVE!* she told her arm. It shifted an inch in slow motion, everything else in her vision still frozen in time.

Thunk. She saw dust that looked as if it was coming from below before she realized her feet were planted on the ground. She smirked, glancing up to see the scythe on its way down as the sun in the distance caught its edge throwing a reflection into her eye. *MOVE!* she told her entire body, legs first so they would squat into position to push off of, then her sword arm to thrust forward in preparation to stab the creature, and finally her free arm, straining to support her sword arm. Glancing again, her eyes grew wide as one of them had an arrow nocked and pulled to her cheek while the other, a man, had his arm pulled back as if to throw something. A feeling of anger shot through her mind as she saw the robes they wore. *Gbinti!*

Thunk. Whatever the thing the man had in his hand was flying through the air now, glowing, and on a direct path towards the creature. Kausha's eyebrows furrowed as she noticed the woman had let go of the arrow, barely clear of the bow string. She glanced back at the creature, the arm scythe two body lengths away, the red glow in its eyes intensifying with every heartbeat. *I can't just dive in at it, the scythe will hit me! Moss!* Her eyes darted up and down, left, then right, then back to the glowing object flying through the air.

Thunk. Her heart beat. The glowing object was nearly to the creature, the arrow less than a foot on its tail. *It's going to hit it!* Kausha realized, shifting her gaze back to the creature with its scythe arm fully extended, the fine, sharp edge a few feet from her face. *MOVE!* she told her legs, coiled like a spring, then pushed off with all the strength she could muster, legs and body fighting through frozen time parallel with the ground, no longer aiming for the creature, itself, but at...

Thunk. Dirt and chunks of rock spewed from the creature's scythe slamming into the road. Kausha snapped forward, the creature gone. *What the?!* She squinted as a bright light filled the air behind her. In that heartbeat, she heard what she thought was a grunt. Dark shadows from the creature and herself were cast against the road in front of her, completely overpowering the light from the sun in the distance. Her body moved before her mind could think, fighting through the thick space between heartbeats. She twisted towards the creature while shoving against the ground, her blood sword beginning to cut through the dirt and rocks alike, rising from below. She strained against frozen time, inch by inch, until the sword was directly beneath the creature.

Then, she breathed.

"Ahhhhhh!" Kausha yelled, hovering above the creature, a trail of blood flying through the air in an arc. Within an instant, she felt warmth on the back of her head as the spiraling cloud blinked out of existence. She stared down at the creature, its scythe and two halves of its body lost their shape in an instant, splashed to the ground, blood splattering and covering the road in every direction.

With the ominous feeling gone from her mind, she fell to the road in a crouch, eyes shut, blood sword held to her side. Then, redistributing the blood within, she stood, staring up at the two standing near the tall grass.

Chapter 51: Revenge

Kausha stood upon blood-soaked dirt with both hands at her side, one empty, one with the blood sword jutting out from her fingertips with its tip resting on the ground. *They're definitely from Gbinti,* she recognized, eyes flickering from one to the other, her mind struggling with what to do next.

Revenge.

She closed her eyes tight and tilted her head down as her free hand rose to her temple, rubbing it in small circles. *They helped me though.*

A warm breeze caught the bottom of her cloak, stirring it. She opened her eyes to gaze down at the Bloodborn assassin symbol on her chest, replaying what the creature said to her. *'We are captives to grudges centuries old by those long forgotten.'* They HAVE changed, I know it! The faces of Nalia, Shaum, Skirm, Skip, and Yaula flashed in her head. *Why did you do this to me, great great grandmother?* Tears began to fill the bottoms of her eyes causing her vision to go blurry.

Kausha sucked the tears in while lowering her hank back down to her side, then gazed up at the two again. She tilted her head sideways seeing one of them with a fresh arrow knocked. It wasn't cocked, but Kausha could see that she knew how to use it. The man beside her held a small knife in one of his hands now as well. Looking down at her right hand, she sucked her blood back in causing the sword to disappear, then glanced back up at the two, their jaws tight and their legs bent, ready to move.

She turned on her heel to face east, the warm breeze not doing anything for the sweat covering her forehead. Something pushed her in that direction. Taking a deep breath, she set her jaw, then...

"Wait!" she heard a man's voice behind her call out, instincts driving blood into her fingers before she could even take a step.

***

Olibtine stared at her standing there, her red and purple cloak fluttering in the breeze as she faced the road to Gbinti. The wind tossed around loose bits of dirt it could find between the gaps in the pooled blood coating the dirt. *Moss, I AM a fool,* he cursed, feeling Daria's eyes staring a hole into the side of his face.

"You don't have to do this! They're innocent citizens from all over Uradaria. We have no fight with you nor the Bloodborn."

What was it the creature said? False memories? His eyes grew wide upon recalling the book. His head darted to his pack then back to the Bloodborn.

"I have proof that... it..." he glanced at the blood trickling down the side of the road, swallowing, "...wasn't lying."

He startled as the Bloodborn shot a glance over her shoulder to stare directly at him. "Easy," he whispered from the corner of his mouth to Daria, feeling her tense up next to him.

"I have a book here that I took from the sorcerer's tower that describes a passing. And more importantly, what came after."

The Bloodborn turned the rest of her body to face him head-on, her face unreadable at the distance. Taking that as a good sign, he turned, crouching to dig into his pack to retrieve the book. He slowly turned back so as to not make any sudden movements, then raised it above his head. She stood unmoving as if rooted in place, only her cloak fluttering in the breeze giving any sign of life.

"It's here," he revealed, not wanting to make the first move. He tried to swallow again, but between the heat of the day and the scrutiny he faced under those eyes, he couldn't. Sweat slid down his arm under his cloak as he held the book aloft.

"Olibtine, I don't think this is a good idea," Daria whispered next to him. Without taking his eyes off of the Bloodborn, he responded, "It's the only way. It's not like we can stop her through force or even warn the city. This has to be done."

I can't give up yet. He narrowed his eyebrows, squeezing the book tighter.

***

A book? Kausha noticed, fighting the urge to charge them. *Who are these two and why did they go into the sorcerer's tower?*

Revenge.

Something in the back of her mind fought, taking in his cloak once more with the book and weight symbol on the front.

No! I must know! She clenched her jaw beneath narrowed eyes.

"Show me!" she yelled. The two flinched, but the one with the bow and arrow did not move to fully knock it. The man lowered the book, sparing a glance at the one next to him, then began walking up the low slope towards her.

***

Moss moss moss, Olibtine cursed, taking measured steps towards the road, making sure he didn't step in any of the blood that had run down the slope.

Reaching the dirt road, keeping a few body lengths apart from the Bloodborn as if it would do any good if she decided to attack, he finally caught a glimpse of her eyes. Purple and calm, not an ounce of malice in them, and then her face with dark skin and strikingly beautiful features that none in Uradarua could match. *A Bloodborn,* he awed, realizing he had held his gaze too long on her face, forcing his eyes to shift to the front of her cloak - a candle with wax sliding down its side. Feeling the weight of the book in his hand, he remembered why he met her face to face. He looked down as he lifted the book into both hands, then turned it to the page where the author had written about the ritual. He extended his arm while turning the book to face her, gazing up at her eyes again, then pointed, "It's here. She writes about seeing it herself, then, upon returning home, her village was burnt to the ground, everyone there, dead."

She stared down at the book, her face scrunching, eyebrows narrowing and jaw flexing, but she didn't take a step closer, nor did he.

"She says those that she came across were skewered through by means that weren't by normal convention. Limbs cleanly sliced off by similar means. She didn't see it happen, but she found survivors in the mountains nearby and each of them said the same thing: Bloodborn. It cannot be a coincidence," he finished, attempting to read her face.

***

It... was right. They... were right. Kausha's eyes stared past the book the man held into the dirt at nothing. *How could they do this? Why? For revenge?!*

Revenge, something said in the back of her head, forcing blood to course throughout her body, warming her skin and quickening her heart rate.

She squeezed her eyes shut, palming her face with her hands. *NO!* She fought back. *NO! This is not my fight!*

She pulled the blood from her feet and legs causing herself to fall to her knees. *You lied!* she screamed inside as tears began to fill her eyes.

Images flashed through her mind. Torture, manic faces, burning banners, bodies motionless in a street covered with blood coming up to her knees, a king with a crown, his eyes wide staring up at her crying, a king with a crown discarded, eyes wide with a blood sword through his heart. Passing after passing, a millennia of death, burning homes, screams. Oh, the screams. She squeezed her ears to block them out, but they filtered through anyway. *Stop. Stop. Stop. Stop. Stop!* she yelled inside, pushing down the voices that weren't hers. Humans change. Catsnif, dwarves, Marpets, Spearheads, Bloodborn, they all change. Holding on to past transgressions only prolongs the suffering. An endless cycle of fear and pain. *You will not have me perform your revenge!*

She could feel the blood inside pulsating from one spot to another, first through her arms down into her hands, then her chest, then her neck, back down to her stomach. Uncontrollable. Breathing heavy, focusing on her own blood, she willed it in the direction she wanted to go while the other blood, her ancestor's blood, flowed freely without control. Her mind focused inward, she knew this was something that had to be done. Following the old blood throughout her body, she poked and prodded at it, flashes of memories foreign to her causing emotions, both painful and joyous to bubble to the surface. Her body snarled at a particularly frightful event with a wild animal long swept from this land, but she discarded it, her focus inward. Frustration heightening, from her own or her ancestors, she wasn't sure, but she used it, pushing her own blood harder than she'd ever done before. Chasing it, prodding it, the memories flashed so fast in her head that they became a jumble until.

Snap.

She cornered the blood, and without slowing, snapped into it, a flood of warmth overwhelming her entire body as the blood merged and spread out in an instance.

The screams and flashes were replaced with the steady heat of a sun beating down in a cloudless sky and the smell of dirt. She opened her eyes to realize she was balled up on the dirt road, the man with the Gbinti colors kneeling next to her, eyebrows narrowed over gentle, green eyes, mouthing something.

"..Okay?" she heard. "Are you okay?" he repeated.

Kausha shook herself, sitting up as sweat dripped from her forehead to wet the dirt below.

The man held out the book towards her, nodding.

Kausha glanced down at the book, open to a page he fingered, then took it, reading the passage he indicated.

So it's true. Deep down, she always knew it was. She let the book slide from her fingers to her lap. *Everything the sorcerers said is true. But why?*

She waited for something to sound in the back of her mind as she squinted up at the man, who was standing patiently nearby, watching her with curious intent, but nothing did.

"Are you alright?" he asked in a soft tone.

Kausha nodded. "I am. Thank you for," she glanced at the book, "this."

Forcing blood back into her legs, she stood, swaying slightly until planting her feet shoulder-width apart. She wiped the dirt from her cloak, then held the book out to the man, who accepted it cautiously.

"You're... welcome," he replied hesitantly.

Kausha glanced back behind her, up the road towards Gbinti, no longer feeling the pull of revenge, then closed her eyes to tilt her head up to the sky to feel the warmth of the sun and the breeze enveloping her. After a few deep breaths, she glanced down at the symbol on her cloak, recognizing the taste of blood in her mouth, then took it off, tossing it to the side leaving her red and purple Bloodborn jumpsuit with the single teardrop symbol on the front. *It'll do for now.* She glanced up at the man, his eyebrow raised curiously.

"Kausha," she introduced, noticing his eyes expanding upon hearing that.

"Ol... Olibtine," he replied, nodding. He turned, nodding back down the road towards the woman who was now only a short distance behind. "That's Nalia." Kausha glanced towards her, nodding, a nod given in return, her bow and arrow still in hand.

So the Muddies were right. Her name is Kausha. Olibtine stared at Kausha's jumpsuit while palming the book, holding it flush against his leg. Her gaze shifted up over Daria, eyes squinting at the same time.

"Is Gbinti safe now?" he asked.

Kausha returned her eyes to his, nodding. "I think so. I have to fight the millennia of emotions running through my blood, but I believe I can do that." She turned sideways, glancing East, then back to meet his eyes. "I think I still might visit though," she finished.

Is she waiting on my approval? He held her eyes, trying to get a read on her intentions, then nodded. "I am sure the rest of the Council would like to speak to you."

Kausha's eyebrows furrowed. "The rest?" she asked.

Olibtine nodded. "I am the leader of the Minds."

Kausha's eyebrows rose, jaw dropping to the top of her jumpsuit collar. "But you're... you're so young," she exclaimed.

Olibtine smiled, giving a quiet chuckle while fingering the spine of the book. "I am compared to other Minds, but we are governed by intelligence, and anyone that takes the test and can prove their intelligence can join the Minds, no matter what age."

And mother said they haven't grown as a society, Kausha scoffed, nodding at Olibtine. "Okay then."

Olibtine nodded back, then narrowed his eyebrows while turning towards Nalia. "Let's grab our packs and relay what we saw here." She nodded, sparing a glance towards Kausha over his shoulder before walking off the road down the embankment and back to the tall grass, grabbing two packs, then returning to the road. Handing Olibtine one and shouldering the other, her bow and arrow still in hand, albeit with a looser grip than before, she waited.

After putting the book away, Olibtine threw his pack on, then stared at the pile of blue and white corpses of the Gbinti men in silence. He shook his head, his mouth turned down and his fists clenched. *Bjorgene. What is he up to?* He turned on his heel ahead of Kausha and Daria, leading the group towards Gbinti.

Chapter 52: A Reunion in Gbinti

Gbinti wasn't foreign to Kausha. She had traveled through the gates a number of times in the past, but approaching the city this time felt different than before. In the past, she'd venture through with her eyes turned town and hair hidden beneath an oversized hood so as to not attract any attention to herself. She stuck to the sparsely populated areas where inns were filled with diversity and the inebriated that wouldn't remember her even if she were to slip up and draw attention to herself, which she'd admit had happened every so often when she got swept up in the revelry.

Cresting the top of the final hill approaching Gbinti, Kausha gazed up at the familiar square, stone gate front lit by the sun setting behind her off to the west. The gate itself was the same as always; a square cut from a thick, flat wall with two gates, one on the outside of the wall, one on the inside, leaving a gap in between to trap any enemies that might try to enter or leave without permission. The walls themselves were a natural gray of the stone with a hint of yellow from the surrounding soil it was extracted from, tall enough to hide everything on the inside except stone guard towers jutting up like needles as tall as the largest trees in the middle of The Forest. The glistening water of the Binti off to the right caught Kausha's eye. It was one of the two main water sources that the city was built upon that flowed from the Surjant Mountains to provide fresh water to its citizens.

She stopped to stare at the blue and white banner with a book and scale upon it fluttering in the wind atop both sides of the gate's walls. The setting sun, drawing long shadows, caught the banner in a way that made it look as if it were burning, making Kausha catch her breath, instinctively sending blood into her fingertips. *No*, she told herself, averting her eyes down towards Olibtine and Daria ahead of her, their eyes studying her from the bottom of the hill.

She blinked, forcing the blood and the thoughts back where they belonged.

"Everything alright?" Olibtine asked when Kausha caught up to them. Daria studied her with squinting eyes, bow still in hand.

"Yeah, I'm okay, just forgot how the city looked. It's been a while," she replied, glancing up at the banners again, no longer looking as if they were burning.

Olibtine nodded. "Shall we, then?" he asked.

Kausha nodded, following him through the first gate past two guards, both outfitted in the same chainmail and helmet that the ones that fell to the creature on the road. They walked the span of the wall, rushing water growing louder with each step, then exited through the second gate and into the city proper. Only a dozen steps later, a wide wooden bridge with high sides spanned the Binti flowing through the city, which under the north wall, then back out underneath the south wall. It served two purposes: fresh water for the city and another obstacle for potential enemies to have to overcome to get into the city.

Once over the bridge, a stone street topped with sand welcomed them, which was wide enough for the populated city to feel sparse even during early evening where citizens hurried towards home and tavern alike. The street itself was lined with sturdy wooden homes and shops alike butted up against one another of varying levels. Some were a single story with a small front porch while others were four stories tall with goods hanging from strings on the first two levels, balconies jutting from the wall of the third and fourth levels where citizens stared below. The sound of rushing water was replaced with music and voices bellowing out from windows and doors on all sides. The city felt alive, unlike Purtghast where everyone was subdued and expected to express a quiet, dignified air.

Kausha couldn't help but smile at the passing children playing tag as music from passing taverns melded together upon leaving one puddle of light to the next, then shifted tempo as one overtook another after every few steps. The laughter and chatter from humans, Catsnif, Marpet, Muddy, dwarve, Spearhead, Juntu, and numerous other races, filled the moments between notes, creating music a city could only muster.

"Kausha!" she thought she heard between notes, swiveling her head back and forth from tavern to house to tavern. She shrugged, taking another step as the music crescendoed.

"Kaush!" she heard, pausing mid-stride. Olibtine and Daria paused ahead of her, glancing over their shoulders in search of her after realizing she was falling behind. Kausha caught a large shadow backlit by candlelight spilling from one of the taverns approaching from her right, laughter accompanying it. She turned towards it, squinting, to see Shaum and Skirm stumbling towards her, mugs in hand, the liquid inside slopping over their large hands onto the street.

"Shaum! Skirm!" Kausha exclaimed, tilting her head up as they approached. They stopped short of her then threw an arm around each other as they swayed back and forth attempting to keep their balance. Kausha's eyebrows rose, hoping they wouldn't fall on her.

"You two seem like you're having a good time," she smiled.

They glanced at each other, clinking their mugs, then took a gulp. Lowering their mugs, their toothy smiles stayed plastered on their faces.

"Ya made et ome.. *hick*.. ey see?" Shaum's eyes wandered as he looked her up and down.

Kausha glanced down at her jumpsuit, then back up to the two Spearheads nodding. "I did." She pivoted her weight to her right foot attempting to look around the two large bodies in front of her. "Are the others..."

"They're somewhere in.. *hick*.. there," Skirm interrupted, nodding his head in the direction they just came.

"Hey, you two Spearheads," came a voice behind them, "what are you doing out here?! They're asking for another..."

Shaum and Skirm parted ways, letting the candlelight shine through, illuminating Kausha's face for the voice to see.

"Well, I'll be." It was Skip, his red hair shifting to an orange from the light behind, string instrument strapped across his back holding a similar, but smaller, mug in one hand. "Kausha! How are ya?"

"Hey Skip. I'm good," Kausha replied with a smile on her face, glancing behind him towards the tavern he just exited.

"Hey Nalia! Kausha's here," he yelled behind him. Kausha saw a head turn towards them, ears fluttering about. A silhouette stood, face hidden by candlelight from behind, placed a mug down, then bound down the three steps to the street, running at her in stride.

"Kausha!" Nalia beamed as she threw her arms around Kausha in an embrace. Nalia pulled back, both hands resting on Kausha's shoulders, locking eyes as her furry ears twitched, casting odd shadows into Kausha's eyes. Kausha could smell the smoke and liquor on her breath as she spoke.

"You made it! Did you make it home?" Nalia asked. Kausha caught her sister, Roana, approaching from behind.

Kausha nodded, then looked left up the road at Olibtine and Daria, who were staring at her and her companions. "I did."

"Good," Nalia nodded, smiling. She shifted her eyes up the street to see what Kausha had looked at, smile fading as she removed her hands from her shoulders and took a step back to stand by her sister and the others in a line.

Fully adjusted to the shadows they cast, Kausha regarded her companions from left to right, starting with the two Spearheads leaning on each other, then Skip, then Nalia and Roana standing arm in arm, warmth flowing throughout her body. *They're safe,* she relaxed, only now feeling her cheeks beginning to ache from smiling for so long.

Kausha looked up the road again at Olibtine and Daria, the other's eyes following her gaze. *Maybe...* Kausha motioned the two towards her.

"This is Olibtine and Daria," Kausha started after her smile faded. "I ran into them on the way here and they are taking me to the Council of Minds." Olibtine and Daria entered the candlelight, nodding to the group. "Olibtine, I traveled with this group through The Forest and into Nortmund. If your Minds are as I've heard, they may not trust my word on who I am or my intentions. I would like these five to accompany us."

Olibtine and Daria shot a glance at Kausha, eyebrows furrowed in thought.

What is she up to? Olibtine thought.

Clothes and feet shuffled at the statement, both from Olibtine and the others alike as the grating sound of sand upon stone filled the space between music.

"Tha Council?!" Shaum exclaimed. "Moss! Tha means yer a Mind, too?!" he asked, nearly dropping his mug to the stone street.

Olibtine unfurrowed his eyebrows before turning towards Shaum and the others. "I am," he nodded. Shaum and Skirm stood taller at hearing that, only to return to their previous stances of leaning on each other a moment later.

Skip whistled. "Kausha, you just find yourself in the middle of everything, don't you? This tale just gets longer and longer," he finished, eyes wandering up at nothing in thought.

"So? What do you say?" Kausha asked, staring at Olibtine.

He nodded. "I would also like to hear this story. Let us be off. Their meeting should be ending soon."

Olibtine turned heel and began walking up the street, a new urgency to his pace, closely followed by Daria. As they entered the main square of the city, lit by dozens of candles hanging from tall stilts throughout, the noise from the taverns was replaced with tinks from blacksmiths, citizens haggling for food at small stalls littered throughout, and wooden carts rolling over stone streets carrying goods and citizens alike. The city buzzed with excitement and happiness everywhere Kausha looked.

Olibtine led them through the crowds, dodging carts and children alike, straight east towards the Palace of Minds that stood out from all the rest with its majestic white exterior trimmed with blue that sat at the end of the main street. Not only was the Palace larger than any others, seemingly taking up an entire block of the city, it was the only one made of stone, meant to ensure the longevity of the Minds and the relatively new way of governing Gbinti. A large oval dome jutted out the right side of the building where the Council Chamber was located, while the front of the Palace bore large pillars with a dozen steps leading from the street.

Kausha had seen the Palace from afar, but the closer she got, the more in awe she was. Purtghast took centuries to perfect, but Gbinti, while mostly wooden throughout the city, showed promise in its craftsmanship.

Approaching the steps, her head turned left and right, up and down, trying to take it all in.

"Wow," she whispered to herself, the others expressed the same reverence as she. Hearing the reverence behind him, Olibtine turned his head and smiled over his shoulder at them.

"I said the same not long ago." He took a moment to gaze up at the pillars as well. Daria, narrow eyed, simply glared at Kausha.

At least she put her bow away, Kausha smiled, feeling her eyes on her.

"As well as I think it would be nice to get cleaned up before heading to talk to the Minds, I do not think we can wait another minute before finding out what is going on here and why Bjorgene sent the soldiers and where they were heading." Olibtine's skull felt like it was going to explode with all of the implications.

"I would like to visit Guane." Daria tore her eyes from Kausha to meet Olibtine's. "I will find you after I tell him of our journey."

Olibtine nodded, then turned to Kausha and the others. "Shall we?"

Kausha nodded, then followed Olibtine with the others in tow. He gripped the handles of the darkly stained wooden double doors that could easily fit multiple Spearheads through standing shoulder to shoulder, then shoved them open. His robe was set alight from the numerous candles within, causing Kausha and the others to squint and shield their eyes.

The rough stone outside transitioned into polished, almost shining, tightly packed stone inside that reflected the countless candles lit upon the walls throughout the square entry that filled floor to ceiling. Between the candles hung mirrors and bright paintings of all shapes, styles, and sizes that drew the eye every which way. Leading from the main entry towards the rear and on either side were dark halls that lead to different parts of the Palace.

Sounds of awe escaped the group again as they stared up, open mouthed, at the picturesque entryway.

"Now this es somethin," Shaum admired slack-jawed.

Without waiting to see if they were following, Olibtine stalked off to the right towards the hall leading to the domed room Kausha saw from the outside. Picking up her jaw, she hurried after him, the others close behind echoing footsteps off the stone below and throughout the enormous entry room. He shoved open another set of wooden doors, leading the group into a stone hall ornamented with nothing but candles lining either wall. A pair of workers draped in the Gbiniti robe halted to the group, shoving themselves against the wall with eyes wide, mouths agape. Whispers of "He's alive?" followed by feet pattering against the polished stone underfoot echoed down the hall once they gathered their wits and ran off in the opposite way the odd group headed.

A large, polished white stone double door with the Gbinti symbols of a scale and book overlapping both doors in the middle marking the Council Chamber stood at the end of the hall, illuminated by candles on either side. Two guards draped in chainmail with a Gbinti robe overtop stood on either side of the doors, staring ahead with pikes in hand pointed directly at the oncomers. As soon as they noticed Olibtine, their mouths fell open. They looked at one another wide eyes, neither able to find their voice. In stride, Olibtine plucked out two books from his pack, discarding the rest with a muted clang as it hit the floor. He stopped short of the doors, glancing at either guard in turn as they gripped their pikes, boots scraping against the polished stone. They glanced at each other once again, seemingly coming to the same conclusion, nodded, then stood up straight, leaned their pikes against the walls, turned towards the doors, then shoved them open with both arms. A voice echoed into the hall.

"We are not to be distur..." the voice cut off as Olibtine stepped forward into the bright chamber.

Chapter 53: Arguments in the Council

Audible gasps combined with cloth rustling sounded from everywhere in the chamber as the Minds throughout turned or shuffled their positions to get a look at who disturbed the meeting.

"Olibtine!" a number of voices exclaimed, while others turned to their neighbor to whisper. Off to the left, Poreme jostled between Minds to get to him.

"Olibtine! We thought you were..." Poreme cut himself off noticing Kausha and the others standing in the doorway behind him, eyes widening in shock once he finally took in her jumpsuit.

Olibtine placed a hand on Poreme's shoulder, pulling his eyes back to his.

"I am fine, friend," he smiled. Poreme glanced at the bandages on his hand, then back to Olibtine's eyes, his forehead wrinkled from eyes practically popping out from his skull. "Well, for the most part," Olibtine shrugged, gripping Poreme's shoulder harder, forcing him to turn to face the inner Chamber with him.

"Council," Olibtine began, the room going still, voice boisterous and reverberating through the Chamber, "I apologize for the intrusion, but as you can see, I have returned whole from my expedition - no doubt to some's displeasure." He paused, glancing around at no one in particular, then lifted the two books in his left hand. "I have ven..."

Three loud taps echoed through the Chamber as wood slammed against stone, interrupting Olibtine. "You are not of the Mindsssss anymore," a cold, but firm voice growled from the bottom row. Cloth and feet rustling sounded throughout the Chamber as the Minds turned to look down at Bjorgene. "It hassss been voted on and you are no longer the Head, nor even of thissss Council." Arguments erupted, each expressing their opinion, both for and against, the Head.

So it's true, Olibtine glared at Bjorgene.

Three loud taps echoed through the Chamber again. Silence followed.

"Let us vote on it!" Poreme interrupted the silence before Bjorgene could begin again.

Shouts of "Yay!" and "Nay!" followed, prompting arguments to begin anew. All the while, Olibtine stood silently, staring down at Bjorgene, who gritted his teeth and tightened his grip on the armchair, unkempt eyebrows bobbing as he fixed his buggy eyeballs on him.

Bjorgene tore his eyes away from Olibtine's, then tapped wood on granite, the Mind's arguments cutting short.

"We are the Mindssss and we have wayssss of handling sssssuch issssuessss, do we not? We sssshall take this to a vote, assss Poreme ssssssuggessssted," Bjorgene announced, briefly glaring at Poreme before glancing around the room and standing. "Right handsss for allowing him to sssstay. Left hand for denying him. Begin."

Olibtine continued glaring at Bjorgene as right and left hands alike shot up throughout the chamber without discussion. Bjorgene fixed his eyes on Olibtine's once again, a smirk appearing on his lips momentarily, then he slowly raised his left hand.

"The motion hasss been..."

"Stop this foolery at once!" a booming, yet gentle voice echoed from behind Olibtine causing him to flinch at it unexpectedly. He turned to see Guane leaning on Daria, his arm draped over her shoulders. He met Daria's eyes, nodding, then looked to Guane, his heart aching as he looked him up and down. Guane, now a shell of what he was just a few moons ago with the skin on his face tight against his cheeks and jaw bones, his eyes sunken in with dark circles below as if he hadn't slept in ages. His robe hung from his body looking like there was nothing underneath.

What happened to you? Olibtine fought every urge to rush over to him and assist Daria in holding him up. He glanced back to meet Daria's eyes, an intensity to them as she shook her head slowly, for his eyes and his eyes alone. Olibtine nodded slowly, understanding the game that had to be played at this moment, even with the Minds.

He turned, glancing down to see Bjorgene's eyes narrow, his hand gripped on the chair's arm once again as he stared at Guane.

Guane planted his feet, removed his arm from around Daria, simply locking arms with her instead, then continued with chest high, his voice gentle and confident as always.

"Council. Are we not expected to use our Minds to pave a better tomorrow for Gbinti? Can we be so blind to information outside of the reach of our fingertips? If we turn our backs on new knowledge, even that which originates outside of this Council, how can we grow and adapt with the changing world? What was once foreign and impossible may become perfectly probably in time. Those just outside of this chamber going on with their lives without a care in the world are because of this Council. Take pride, but *do not* let that pride cloud your view on your continued duty to knowledge and using said knowledge to create a better life for everyone that calls Gbinti home." He paused, glancing to Olibtine for a moment, then back to the Minds.

"If you deny this man, a previous Head of Minds, for simply persevering through the task he set out to do, you deny Gbinti of new information and knowledge that we can use for the betterment of our citizenry. Will you, the smartest of all, turn your back on a chance to learn something new?! Even at my advancing age, I yearn for all that can be given! Uradaria is a magical place. Gbinti is a magical place. If you deny this, we will be no better off than all of the other cities dotting the landscape."

Guane met Olibtine's eyes once again while throwing his arm back around Daria's shoulder, then smiled that all too familiar smile. Olibtine returned it in kind, then faced the main part of the chamber while a light murmur grew, Minds whispering to one another.

"Friends," he began, holding up the two books in his hand and waiting for silence to return, "I have in my possession two books that we found while scouring the sorcerer's tower in Baugroun. One is a book of spells that they have been using these past centuries to assassinate and murder innocents. The other is a first hand written account of a Bloodborn's passing ritual."

Gasps broke through the silence alongside shuffling feet and wide eyes.

"Furthermore," he started, moving his body sideways and facing Kausha and the others, motioning for them to move forward. "To back up this account of the ritual is a Bloodborn herself, Kausha."

As Kausha and the others moved from the double doors further into the chamber to get into view for all the Minds to see. Olibtine glanced at Guane, who only smiled and nodded as if expecting everything as it unfolded.

Did he know who she was already? The Mind's gasped once again, shuffling their feet and shying back with every step Kausha took until she reached the edge of the top step next to him, her red and purple jumpsuit with the Bloodborn's teardrop of blood symbol in full view for all of the Minds to see.

"You have brought the enemy to our doorsssstep?!" Bjorgene yelled from the bottom of the chamber. "Guardsssss, arresssst thissss... creature!" he ordered. The discussions throughout grew to a fervent pitch.

Olibtine looked towards the two guards standing to either side of the double doors and moved to place himself between them and

Kausha's companions, spreading his arms wide, which gave pause to the guards as they glanced at each other with raised eyebrows.

"We are far from done here, Bjorgene!" Olibtine yelled over the ruckus without turning around. To his left, he noticed Guane turn and lift a hand in a shooing motion to the guards, who nodded, then took a step back to show that they would do as he said. Olibtine nodded a thanks to Guane, then he lowered his arms before turning and returned to stand side by side with Kausha, his dirty, blue and white cloak in stark contrast with the Bloodborn red and purple.

"I would also have you answer to why you sent those soldiers off. What irrefutable evidence do we have on hand that justifies sending a centuria of Gbinti men into battle, who all currently lie dead on the road leading from Gbinti? Do we not first rely on diplomacy? What steps were taken to ensure we did not have to cross swords with a possible enemy?" Olibtine asked, his voice rising with each question. The memory of a severed head surrounded by blue and white flashed into his head.

"Well, Bjorgene?!" he exclaimed, staring holes into the man. The Minds shuffled as each turned to face Bjorgene, who readjusted his stance underneath their gaze, his white eyebrows providing no hints at his intentions one way or another. He tore his eyes from Olibtine, moving them over the Minds nearby, then lifted a parchment by his head.

"Thissss issss the irrefutable proof you assssk for," he started with a smirk on the side of his mouth. "It issss a direct report from two of the sssssix themsssselvesss, both of which provided their housssse ssssealsss to confirm the claimssss within. Why, you asssk, did we deccccide to ssssend ssssssoldierssss to attack the Bloodborn?"

So they WERE heading towards Purtghast, Olibtine thought, scrunching his face.

"No lesssss than 30 Nortmund ssssoldiersssss and ccccitezenssss were brutally murdered by a young Bloodborn!" He then pointed at Kausha. "THAT Bloodborn!" he exclaimed.

Olibtine's face changed, his forehead scrunching as he looked to Kausha at his side. *What?!* He stared at the side of her face. Her eyes were turned down, face emotionless. *It's true...* His breath caught, his heart began to race, but he fought the urge to take a step back from her, parts of muffled conversations nearby breathing through his thoughts.

Shaum and Skirm's eyes narrowed as they stared at the back of Kausha's head. Nalia, standing right behind Kausha with her hand interlocked with her sister's, stared ahead as well, ears twitching as the conversations nearby increased in intensity. Skip, a sly smile on his lips, stood cross-armed, glancing from Mind to Mind, knowingly.

"Is it true?" Olibtine whispered, a slight quiver to his voice.

Kausha nodded softly, then tilted her head to meet Olibtine's eyes. "It was me."

"Oy. Twas us!" Shaum yelled over the commotion, staring over Kausha and the others, voice echoing throughout the chamber causing both Olibtine and the Minds to hold their breath while looking up at him. Eyes throughout darted between exits with hints of wanting to run away. "But thy wern't soldiers! Tell em, Kaush," he huffed, looking back down at the back of Kausha's head.

Olibtine's gaze returned to Kausha's, who was still staring at him, a softness to her eyes he hadn't expected. His eyebrows narrowed at the sight, a frown forming on his lips. *What is going on?* She nodded, then faced the council.

The truth, Kausha nodded. She took a deep breath, slowing her blood to calm herself, then spoke.

"It is true that I, we, were in Nortmund. It is also true that we killed a number of guards on our retreat out of the city. It is not true that we killed citizens. What that parchment no doubt fails to explain is that the entirety of the Nortmund guards were not themselves. They were under a Sorcerer's spell." Kausha noticed the man at the bottom level, Bjorgene, flinch at hearing that. The collectively held breaths of the Minds all exhaled at once as if a bubble burst while a buzzing of conversations replaced it as they turned towards one another to discuss. 'Sorcerers' and 'Spells' could clearly be heard among the chatter.

"This spell," Kausha began again, the chatter halting, "is one of nefarious means concocted by three sorcerers and three sorcerers alone. I do not know how it is done, but upon killing the final guard blocking our freedom, the sorcerers made their presence known. Each one of my companions can vouch for that."

Olibtine's eyes went wide remembering the books in his hand. *That spell!* He fumbled with the books, letting one fall to the floor as he moved the larger one he took from the top of tower to both hands, drawing Kausha's attention. He flipped through furiously to find the page he pictured in his head. *That spell. That spell!* His eyes darted from page to page until... He froze, swallowing.

"Here! It's that spell she speaks of - taken from the top of the sorcerer's tower while they were casting the spell over a large ujuntu basin! Proof that what she says is true!" Olibtine yelled, holding the book open towards the Minds. Kausha raised a single eyebrow towards him questioningly as Poreme leaned in to get a closer look, his mouth falling agape, then confirmed. "It's here! A drawing of the spell with... text... I cannot understand."

Conversations rose throughout the chamber, some turning into shouting matches up and down the different rows. Minds began to point at each other, then down to Bjorgene, their faces turning bright red with tempers flaring.

There are clear alliances now where there weren't before, Olibtine realized while scanning the Minds, lowering the book. *Has Bjorgene been drumming up support the entire time?*

A tap of wood on granite cut through the discussions, breaking Olibtine from his thoughts. The Minds hushed to turn towards the source - Bjorgene. He cleared his throat, gathered himself, then spoke.

"Why would the sssssix lie to ussss?" he asked, spreading his arms and slowly spinning to address all of the Minds, the parchment still in one hand while the other held a wooden cane - the Head's cane. "The quesssssstion isssss and important one - posssssibly the mosssst important. We rely on one another for trade, correct? We rely on one another to ssssussstain the ssssstability in Uradaria, correct? The sssssix have been a trussssted ally for more moonsssss than I can remember - no one can deny that!" He paused, lowering his hands to his side, then shaking his head while softening his eyes..

"Now," he started again, stopping his spin to stare at Olibtine and Kausha, "on the other hand, what might a Bloodborn gain by diverting the attention from her people? An iron grip on Uradaria, assss they have held for generatiossss, perhapssss? Sssssquasssssshing our ssssoccccieties and people into rubble asssss ssssson as we begin truly making progresssss? Or issss it that her people were the onessssss to provide the ssssspellsssss in that book to the ssssssorccccererssss for nefariousssss reassssons?!" Bjorgene exclaimed, spit shooting from his mouth with every other word, the veins on his neck jutting out as if they would burst from his pale skin.

"Aye!" a number of Minds called out. "Nay! an equal number of Minds grunted as if opposing every word brought forth.

Kausha heard Skirm mutter, "He can't be serious, can he?" behind her to their group. "Oy, ey think e es," Shaum replied, sounding flabbergasted.

Olibtine glanced over his shoulder, looking up at the Spearheads. "He's serious. We need more valid..."

Kausha cut him off with a step forward, her voice sharp and firm, cutting off fresh conversations that were beginning throughout the chamber.

"The Bloodborn do not care about your politics or your petty squabbles. Even standing here now, I could cut each and every last one of you down by barely lifting a finger."

The rustling of clothing sounded throughout the chamber as Minds shied back. From the looks on their faces, they would have ran if it wasn't for Kausha and the others barring their exit. Metal boots scraped on the granite floor behind as the two guards contemplated rushing at her, thoughts cut short as Shaum and Skirm turned and barred their sharp teeth at the two.

"While more than a few of my ancestors would do so," she continued, softening her eyes and tone while keeping her arms to her sides to show that she meant no harm, "I am not them. Even now, I am fighting back against millennia of wrongdoing that your ancestors enacted upon my great great grandmother, her great great grandmother, and more women from my bloodline. Images of torture at your ancestor's hands flash through my mind even as I speak. It is true that my ancestors gave into the feelings of revenge, killing populations and burning entire cities, but I will do no such thing. Thanks to Olibtine and his effort to retrieve those books from the sorcerer's tower, alongside my companions holding a place in my heart, I am fully aware of this now and will not give in to revenge. This is why Olibtine has brought me to meet with you all, the smartest of Gbinti, in hopes that you will listen and weigh reason and history alongside facts and logic to come to a conclusion."

Silence filled the chamber upon Kausha's finish, each Mind's face contorting as they thought everything over. She took a step back, glancing at Olibtine, his eyebrows narrow as he mulled over all possibilities. Then she looked back at her friends in turn, each nodding to her in acceptance. *Thank you.* She smiled briefly before looking to Guane, a smirk plastered on his face even before they locked eyes. She gathered herself before turning to face the Minds again.

Her eyebrows narrowed while scanning the bottom row. *He's gone!* Olitbine's eyebrows matched hers as his eyes darted, searching. He seemed to notice the same thing she had.

"Where is Bjorgene?" he said softly at first, causing Parjune and the others within earshot to perk up and glance down at the bottom row. "Where is Bjorgene?!" he repeated, loud enough to shake every Mind from their contemplation. The room exploded in movement as Minds looked every which way around the chamber.

"And Joran!" Porome exclaimed from off to Olibtine's left.

"And Manu!" another Mind sounded from across the room.

Moss! So it was coordinated. Olibtine felt like his heart was tearing apart. "Take a count of those that are missing that were previously here. No, take count of any that are not here right now and bring the names to me." He glanced back to Guane, noticing a frown upon his fragile face as if he'd seen all of this coming, then back to Kausha, holding her jaw clenched with eyebrows downturned.

Chapter 54: 8 Traitors

Eight, including Bjorgene, missing. Olibtine's forehead wrinkled as he read through the list of names once again while standing in Bjorgene's room with Porome, Kausha, and two guards. As soon as the names were brought forth, Minds were split between rooms to search for those missing, each accompanied by two guards, but so far coming up empty. Guane, Daria, and the rest of Kausha's companions stayed behind in the Mind's Chamber, for both protection as well as convenience. Once Olibtine finished searching Bjorgene's room, all would reconvene once more to discuss their findings, if any.

Bjorgene's room, unlike Olibtine's, was larger than most - a perk of Council seniority. Also unlike Olibtine's plain room, Bjorgene's had dark rugs covering all of the walls, windows included, from ceiling to floor, even covering the floor itself in multiple layers, throwing the room into pitch black without candlelight. Books and parchment were scattered throughout, covering tables and the bed alike.

Olibtine, Poreme, and Kausha each had a lit candle in hand as they made their way around the room, searching for signs of something, anything. Squatting, Olibtine flipped one of the books open on the low table at the foot of the bed that was stacked three high. *The Inexcusable Need of Nature,* it read on the opening page. Olibtine scrunched his eyebrows while closing it and putting it to the side. He rolled open a parchment nearby that had drawings of Gbinti before it was fully laid out in its current state, then placed that aside as well. He continued to flip open books, reading the title, sometimes flipping to the middle to read a sentence or two, then placing them in a stack to his left. After moving one called *Time Outside* into the stack, he sighed while glancing back to the unread pile, the candle he held casting a small shadow beneath a thick, leatherbound book. He shoved the large book to the side, then froze, his palms growing sweaty. *It's the book from before,* he recognized, wiping his hand on his robe before sliding his fingertips over the red and black cover feeling the cracks throughout. He glanced up at Kausha who held a candle in front of her, reading over the spines of books stacked vertically and horizontally on one of the bookshelves near the bed. He shifted his focus back to the book, grabbing it and pocketing it. *Later,* he promised, standing.

Moving his eyes to the opposite side of the room to Poreme, who was doing the same as Kausha, he had a thought. *Where would he have gone and why? If he's still in the city, he should be found quickly. He alone might be able to hide away, but eight Minds, possibly hiding together, would be hard to hide. Moss, Bjorgene.*

"Olibtine," Poreme interjected. He held open a book in one hand, candlelight illuminating the pages and the side of his frowning face. "You mentioned something about ujuntu, right? I found something about making a basin for communication at a distance."

Olibtine strode the few steps it took to reach Poreme while he started reading aloud. "It says that both users need to have basins made from ujuntu that are... dimensions here... and," he paused, eyes widening to Olibtine, then to Kausha. Olibtine reached him, taking the book from his hand.

"...Bloodborn blood," Olibtine finished reading, turning his head to look at Kausha, candlelight reflecting in her purple eyes as the wrinkles on her forehead deepened in thought.

This means that... Pain flashed through his hand, causing him to drop the candle he held. Poreme squealed as the candle splattered on the rugs, jumping to stamp out the fire before it could catch. Satisfied, he lifted his candle to light Olibtine's hand wrapped in cloth still. "Are you okay?" Porome asked, eyes wide in worry, shifting his gaze from his hand to his face to see Olibtine's downturned eyes.

Olibtine nodded, flexing his hand softly while staring at it, then closed the book with his other hand, squeezing it tight.

"Poreme, I think this means... It means Bjorgene, and possibly the others, tried to have me killed in the tower."

Kausha balked, lowering her hand from the shelf to stare at Olibtine. *Was it them, then that tried to have me killed as well?* She clenched her jaw as blood coursed through her fingers. Yaula's face, with her bright yellow eyes and fluffy ears, flashed in Kausha's head, anger driving blood throughout her body, urging her to act.

Revenge.

"We need to find the basin to make sure. Keep searching," Olibtine forced out between clenched teeth, whether through pain or anger, neither of the other two were sure. Poreme shuffled back to the bookshelf, leaving Olibtine in dim light from the hall, then began pulling books like levers, eyes darted wherever his light fell.

Kausha turned back to the bookshelf, a new goal in her mind as she haphazardly pulled books from the bookshelf, letting them fall to the rugs with a thunk. Upon emptying the shelves, leaving nothing but dust, she turned to the bed. Parchments and books lay open, strewn across most of the bed except for an outline just large enough for someone to lie down between. With an outstretched arm, the candlelight enveloped the bed, books, and parchments alike. *A Mind has nothing to fear in his own room.* She took a step back, then crouched while lifting the dark brown oversized blanket that draped over the side of the bed to the floor, crumpled on all sides. She extended the candle underneath the bed to illuminate it, revealing more books stacked one on top of another as if they were holding the bed up by themselves. She lifted the blanket further so it wouldn't fall back down, then moved a stack of books, then another, attempting to find the middle. She shifted one more, then saw something shining in the light. Her heart began racing as she reached in as far as she could, gripping something cold, then pulling it fully into the light.

Ujuntu, she recognizes, staring at the half-sphere basin with a square wooden base to hold it upright. Standing slowly, she whispered. "It's true."

"Wha..." Olibtine started, but cut himself off upon turning to see the ujuntu basin shining in Kausha's hand. His heart sank. *So, it's true. A Mind betrayed us. Possibly multiple.*

"It's the basin!" Poreme exclaimed, running around the bed to combine his candlelight with Kausha's, gawking the entire time. His mouth drew to a frown before looking at Olibtine. "This means..." he trailed off, realizing both Kausha and Olibtine's faces were scrunched tight, either in anger or disappointment, he couldn't tell.

"We need to take this to the Council immediately," Olibtine realized.

"Agreed," Poreme replied, looking at Kausha, then the basin in her hands, hesitating to reach out for it after noticing the intensity in her eyes. "Do you mind if I..." he asked softly.

Kausha shook herself, seeing Poreme standing in front of her with his free hand outstretched towards the basin. She nodded, pushing the basin into his hands. He accepted it, treating it as if it might bite him.

Chatter from the chamber echoed down the hall as Olibtine led Poreme and Kausha towards the Council of Minds. Upon Olibtine breaching the entryway, conversations quieted. He stepped to the right, allowing Poreme, who held the basin out in front of him, to be seen by everyone.

"My fellow Minds," Olibtine started looking around the room, then back to Kausha who was sweeping her eyes over Shaum, Skirm, Skip, Nalia, and Roana standing together, greeting her with smiles, "and new friends... It is with a heavy heart that I must relay this information to you all. Poreme holds an ujuntu basin. Something that is used for long-distance communication." He glanced at it, then back to Kausha, who nodded. He returned his eyes back to the Minds nearby and held up the book in his hand. "The instructions on creating, as well as using the device, are in this book, found close nearby the basin. The basin is one that is identical to two that I ran across in the sorcerer's tower."

Whispered conversations started sporadically, some putting the pieces together before Olibtine even voiced them.

"The book and the basin were both found... in Bjorgene's room."

Once whispered conversations grew to shouts and cries of "Traitor!" and "How could he?!" as Minds grappled with the fact that one of their own, one that had been a Mind for so long, betrayed them.

Kausha saw Nalia's ears twist, her head following. "What is it?" she whispered.

Nalia turned towards the hall, Kausha's eyes following, to see a guard running in a full sprint towards the chamber. Her eyebrows furrowed as she looked back to Nalia, who shrugged. "Olibtine," Kausha said over her shoulder, attempting to get his attention. "Olibtine," she repeated, a little louder for him to hear. He cut off what he was saying to glance over his shoulder, then noticed the runner out of the corner of his eye. "Sorito?"

The guard, Sorito, waved to Olibtine before halting just short of the double doors to the chamber, then put his hands on his hips, attempting to catch his breath. "We.." he started, "we.. found... one of the Minds, Lerician," he finished between breaths, pointing down the hall. "Found him... trying to leave the western gate. He... confessed... as soon as we identified him. He was headed to...

Nortmund," he finished, doubling over to place his hands on his knees, still attempting to catch his breath.

Olibtine gripped the book in hand until his knuckles were pure white. His eyebrows narrowed, drawing his head down towards the polished stone floor, staring at nothing. *Nortmund. The worst scenario comes true, then.*

Nortmund, Kausha thought, having to force blood away from her fingertips for fear of instinctively creating knives. *Those monsters!* She heard the others stiffen at hearing the city's name as well, Shaum and Skirm the most, as they rubbed their burly arms, shaking their heads.

"Did he say where the others are?" Kausha asked. Sorito turned his eyes up to meet hers, shaking his head. "No... um, Bloodborn. No, he only said he was to meet them in Nortmund."

Kausha nodded, then stared at Olibtine, his eyes glossed over, face scrunched in thought, jaw flexing all the while.

"We ave ta go after em," Shaum growled from behind, voice hard from remembering the mines. The others nodded in agreement.

"No," Olibtine broke in, a sharpness to his tone as he spoke through clenched teeth. "This is a decision for the Minds to take against their own. We have to weigh all of the options or we would be just like Bjorgene."

"But..." Shaum started, but before he could go on, Olibtine turned heel back into the heart of the Chamber, the Minds already quiet from trying to hear what Sorito said.

"What news?" one of the Minds asked.

Olibtine scanned the Minds from left to right. "Lerician has been caught attempting to flee the city," he announced, hushed whispers starting sporadically throughout. "He confessed that the others are heading to Nortmund as we speak - by way of which we cannot say. We are at a critical juncture currently and we must weigh our options together. Do we go after them with the possibility of all out war with the Nortmunders? Or do we leave them be, exiled to their failed ploy?" He paused, allowing the Minds a moment to contemplate, turning to the sound of two sets of feet shuffling into the chamber. He met Guane's tired eyes. *Your timing is impeccable as always.* He sent a quick smile towards Daria, who held him upright. *And thank you.*

A tap of wood on granite quieted the Minds.

A deep rumbling voice reverberated throughout the chamber as Wilbur spoke up. "I, like many of you here, have been deceived," he began, tugging his braided beard, glancing to his feet briefly before lifting his head to address the Minds, revealing a stern face and narrowed eyes. "For how long, I do not know, but my heart is split between anger and pain. If what Olibtine says is true, and I have no reason to believe it is not with all of the evidence, Bjorgene, and possibly others, have been using the sorcerers to further their plots for many moons. Ignoring the acid rains, ignoring the assassinations, and ignoring the possible countless other things they have done, if we look at this most recent betrayal in and by itself, we are justified in hunting them down and returning them to Gbinti to face their crimes."

A number of "Aye"'s sounded throughout as Wilbur tugged his beard once more, nodding.

A tap of wood on granite hushed the "Aye"'s as another Mind, the tallest in the Chamber with short-cut, deep black hair, a dark complexion, and bright blue eyes that seemed to glow against his skin, named Horunsup, cleared his throat and began speaking in a soft, silky voice.

"I would warn against fighting, no matter what the case. Bloodshed begets bloodshed, and we have already lost too many men, as Olibtine said. The dwarves of Nortmund are a practiced lot, sturdy and formidable, possibly the most formidable of all societies to grace Uradaria." He shook his head. "I would not want to see what they are fully capable of with the six driving them from behind. No, I would rather we continue using diplomacy and our intellect to continue working with the dwarves to better Gbinti and its citizens, forever banishing Bjorgene and the other Minds that were in cahoots with him. This may not seem enough a punishment to a number of you, but if we have a choice to fight or flight, I choose flight."

Horunsup met Olibtine's eyes, then nodded, the chamber around them going still, the air thick with contemplation.

Olibtine glanced at Kausha, noticing her hands were balled up in fists, knuckles white, her jaw flexed beneath a straight mouth and downturned eyes. *What is she thinking?*

He needs to pay, Kausha wanted to act - needing to act. She flinched, feeling a hand on her shoulder, looking over to find Nalia's large, yellow eyes staring into hers. Nalia shook her head, mouthing "Not yet," as if knowing what Kausha was thinking. Kausha relaxed her hands, unclenching them, then nodded, hearing another tap of wood on granite.

"Are there any other arguments?" Olibtine called out, sweeping the chamber with his eyes back and forth. He nodded. "Then we should..."

"Wait," Kausha interrupted.

Olibtine's head swiveled to see what she wanted, but he stumbled while caught under her gaze. He couldn't get a word out - it was like she froze him in place with just a look. She blinked and his body relaxed.

Kausha turned her body enough to sweep over Shaum, Skirm, Skip, and Roana, finally landing on Nalia. Each had their faces and eyebrows scrunched questioningly. She turned back to face Olibtine, the same expression on his face as the others. The Minds throughout the Chamber leaned forward, not wanting to miss a moment.

"You are right to not want to go to battle with the dwarves," she started, speaking up, glancing over the Minds. "If my brief times in Gbinti have shown me anything, it is that your way of governing is superior to anything before and you should hold that tight to your chest and never deviate. To deviate from your current ways would lead to the citizens getting the short end of goods and resources, ultimately causing your society to collapse. Take it from me, I've seen it first hand," *or at least those of the blood I've inherited have.* "I know personally just how formidable the dwarves are and believe it would be a futile effort in breaching their walls, traversing the towers, then locating Bjorgene and the other Minds with a Centuria, or any number of soldiers. There is only one course of action to take..."

"...Kausha..." she heard Skirm whisper behind her, but she continued on.

"I will go alone, acting on my own accord, and attempt to bring back Bjorgene," she finished, eyes forward, unblinking.

Revenge.

The air escaped the room as each Mind gasped. Olibtine's eyes went wide as soon as she finished. His mouth fell agape when shifting his eyes to Guane, whose face was soft, his eyes shut. *Of course he knew.* He snapped his mouth shut, then swept his sight over those behind Kausha, each with mouths in a line, their eyebrows turned down. *They thought the same, then?* Forcing a swallow, he finally returned his eyes to Kausha. Only then did he realize conversations were growing in tempo and pitch throughout the Chamber.

She's serious. He faltered, finally seeing it in her body language. A shiver crept up his spine. *How could she ever safely bring him back? Unless...*

Kausha turned to face Nalia and the others, scanning their faces, a mix of fright and worry on their brows.

"Ya can' go alone," Shaum pleaded.

"Yeah Kausha, we can help like we did before," Skirm added on, his mouth tightening upon finishing, his eyes growing distant from remembering his short, but brutal, time in the mines. Nalia and Skip nodded their heads in agreement.

Kausha shook her head. "No. It is far too dangerous for all of us to go together. I have to sneak in and out," *and I don't plan on coming back.*

Skirm opened his mouth to retort, but shut it before speaking a word, his mouth narrowing into a tight line as his oversized hands balled into tight fists.

The Mind's conversations grew louder once the groups grew in numbers to discuss their options. The occasional shout shot through the air accompanied by wild hand movements that looked as if things would come to blows. Kausha met Nalia's eyes, the only eyes of her companions that reflected a determination and understanding towards Kausha. They stared at one another for a moment before Nalia nodded.

"Do what you have to to get out of there alive."

"And please bring back the story of your adventure. I would very much like to wrap up this tale with a nice bow on top. Every bard's tale needs an ending, afterall." Skip flourished his hand, plastering a smile on his face.

"Wait." Olibtine stood up straight, causing her head to turn to meet his frantic eyes. "We haven't even voted on the choices."

"Then do so," Kausha pushed.

Olibtine swallowed hard, feeling the outcome of the vote obvious in the pit of his stomach. He nodded. "Alright." He tore his eyes away from Kausha to face the Minds. Conversations and arguments petered out as they noticed his intent to speak.

"We will take this to a vote," he announced. "Right hand will signal going to battle to retrieve Bjorgene and the other Minds, forcing them back to Gbinti to stand trial for their crimes. Left hand will signal exile for Bjorgene and the other Minds. Both hands clasped above your head will signal exile." He glanced to Kausha, then back to the Minds, "... with certain caveats."

The Minds shuffled, uncertainty straining their faces.

"Now, begin."

Right hands, left hands, and clasped hands shot up immediately, while others held off, their foreheads scrunched as they rubbed their chins in thought while mumbling inaudibly to themselves.

Slowly, more left hands went up, followed by clasped hands while, to Olibtine's delight, no other right hands rose. In fact, some even dropped, replaced by clasped hands.

Olibtine began to tally the votes in his head after nearly all the hands were up, scanning left to right, until he made it to Guane. To his shock, he held both hands clasped above his head, his eyes scanning the room and counting votes as well. *Guane? I thought you'd vote for the passive route. No wonder why other Minds are changing their votes.*

Olibtine shook himself, turning back to scan the Chamber once again. *All Minds have their votes. Moss, I sure hope you know what you're doing.* Then, he raised both hands, clasping them above his head.

"The third option wins out," he announced. "Exile with caveats."

No cheers or hisses sounded through the Chamber like a normal vote would have elicited. The weight of the situation overshadowed any sense of happiness or anger - all that was left in the Chamber was a quiet understanding of betrayal and what was to come.

Olibtine lowered his hands to his side, then turned to Kausha, her face passive and unreadable as she stared straight ahead, eyes focused on nothing.

Chapter 55: The Return to Nortmund

Kausha's blood-slicked feet guided her out of the west gate of Gbinti just after daybreak. She immediately turned north, hugging The Forest as wind roared past her ears, buffeting her Bloodborn jumpsuit. The Binti river reflected the morning sunlight to her right as she glided over rock and shrub alike. The Surjant Mountains broke the flat landscape in the distance, its snow capped peaks glistening in the sun like blood knives slicing through the sky, urging blood throughout her body. *Revenge.* The wind forced tears from the edges of her eyes. A long stretch of hills between the Surjant Mountains and the Uhlbrar Mountains changed the landscape, a constant rise and fall as trees, not even half the size of those found in The Forest, topped the hill crests in an attempt to reach the sun. Following The Forest's edge leading northwest with the sun warming her back, Kausha skidded to a halt at the top of a bare hill at the first sighting of the Uhlbrar Mountains with the white towers of Nortmund settled at its base. A cool, yet thick, gentle breeze carrying the smell of rain swept over the hilltops from behind, ruffling her jumpsuit and blowing a stray hair near her temple across her eyes.

She breathed deep, leveling her sights on the Nortmund towers, the excess blood from the passing still coursing through her veins. *Revenge,* something in the back of her mind whispered - and for once, she gave in to that thought.

Her legs pushed her down the hill, then up the next, more of the walls and spiraling towers coming into view with every crest. Dark clouds accompanied her overhead as the wind seemed to shove her blood-enhanced Bloodborn body forward. It wasn't long until the full height of the white-washed city walls appeared before her, hiding the atrocities that lie within. As she approached the giant moat, lightning streaked the sky overhead, followed closely by a crack of thunder. Following the moat towards the northern waterfall, she glanced at the top of the walls nearest her, the only movement that of the dark gray clouds streaking by above. The roar of the waterfall reached Kausha's ears as she reached the hidden path leading into the moat. She stepped down, then slowly made her way down the slope that hugs the wall, locking her eyes to the hidden cave behind the falling water. A crack of thunder cut through the roar as rain began to pellet her jumpsuit. She snuck behind the falling water, entering the hollowed-out cave, the roaring echo making it hard to even think.

Squinting into the darkened cave, Kausha scanned the far wall for the vines that covered the secret entrance. Her insides shifted, blood knives appearing immediately from beneath her fingernails as she noticed movement in the shadows.

Moss, did they expect me? She held her breath, staring at the spot of the movement a moment ago. Seeing nothing, she crept to the side, knives still at the ready, then shuffled closer, silently, then stood up straight. *Just the vines moving in the breeze.* She relaxed, retracting her blood knives.

Kausha parted the vines that lead into the tunnel, then suddenly the tip of a halbert flashed from the pitch black tunnel. Her organs and blood alike reacted without thought, shifting away as the point punctured her jumpsuit first, then the skin underneath. Her eyes grew wide as she stared down at the halbert, pain shooting through her body. Whoever was on the other end yanked it free, causing Kausha to stumble backwards and grab the side of her stomach without looking down. Gasping for breath between clenched teeth, she stared at the swinging vines. A dwarve, clad in full plated armor from feet to head wearing a white robe of the first, stepped from parted vines followed closely by two more wearing the same color. Holding halbert points towards Kausha, they spread themselves out along the back wall in shadows that made it impossible to see their faces.

Kausha felt the spot where she was stabbed with her fingertips, pulling up a dry hand to her face as the pain subsided, her wound closing slowly. Thunder rumbled through the cave from behind. *So much for any easy way in.*

With a sigh, Kausha created three blood daggers from her fingertips, then snapped them off to throw, one for each dwarve. *Should be enough.* The one on the right shuffled his feet. With a flash, she flicked her wrist, letting loose one of the daggers while aiming where she thought was an eye. These dwarves' eyes didn't glow, but the memory of the glowing red from the sorcerer's spell gave her a pretty good idea of where they were. A grunt, immediately followed by a crash of armor falling to the rough stone cut through the sound of water crashing behind. A flash of lightning lit the cave, confirming the dead dwarve crumpled on the stone. Out of the corner of her eye, she saw the other two dwarves looking towards their fallen companion as well. Before the flash subsided, Kausha darted forward while rearing back her hand with the blood knives in it, parting the two halberts pointed at her in an instant. The knives met their mark, the dwarves twitching and crumpling at her feet. Kausha breathed out slowly, then rolled up her sleeves as a roll of thunder sounded in the distance. Connecting her forearms together in front of her chest, one on top of the other, she forced blood through the pores in her forearms. The blood connected with itself as she pulled her forearms apart to create a thin, red blood shield that was the width of her body and covered her from hip to neck. She realized, unlike last time, that her body still felt strong as the blood from two Bloodborn coursed through her veins.

Should I? Kausha contemplated, looking at the shield, then at the pitch black passage hiding behind the vines. *Yes.* She rotated her arms slightly, a sharp *snap* coming from the top and bottom of the shield. Catching the blood shield in her right hand, she placed the back of her left hand in the middle of it. Releasing blood from the pores on the back of her hand, the connection solidified leaving her fingers free to move. A smile crossed her face as she lowered her arm and shield together to her side. Focusing on her right hand, she squeezed the fingers together, forcing blood from under her fingernails together to produce a straight, two foot long blood sword, perfect for close quarters combat. Lowering the sword to her side, she stared forward towards the vines as a flash of lightning set the cave alight, then, clearing the distance, she parted the vines once again. Her insides separated reflexively, leaving the middle section of her body void of blood and organs alike. In the distance, candles along the walls lit the passage in small pools, revealing nothing but rough stone walls and floors. She dropped the vines, leaving the roll of thunder and roar of the waterfall behind.

Focusing on the light towards the end of the tunnel, Kausha knelt in an attempt to see if any shapes obstructed the space between her and the candlelight. *Nothing.* She shifted her weight to both sides of the tunnel, nearly pressing herself against either wall. Satisfied, she stood and walked forward slowly with the blood shield in front, the stone cold and slick underfoot, the tunnel sucking in a cool breeze that struck her from behind, rustling her jumpsuit and wafting the smell of fresh rain around her.

Kausha approached the first candlelight, squinting and blinking in an attempt to acclimate her eyes. Seeing the corner turn ahead, she imagined the last visit through the tunnel. *There might be guards ahead.* With shield and sword at the ready, she turned to peek around the corner with one eye, seeing nothing but connected pools of candlelight the entire length of the tunnel. She stepped around the corner with narrowed eyebrows. *Why would they put three guards at the entrance to the tunnel only to leave this open?* Sweeping along the candles above, she noticed that all of the candles she had knocked down or put out were lit again. Cautiously, she walked forward, then glanced down to see gashes in the otherwise smooth stone floor. *They even cleaned all of this up. So, did they expect something or not? Maybe the soldiers were just there as a precautionary measure.*

She continued towards the dark patch at the end of the tunnel. *The stairwell,* she recalled, coming to a stop before reaching the corner. Shield held in front, parallel with the corner, she peeked into the dark landing, seeing nothing. Rounding the edge and leaving the candlelit hall behind, she entered the pitch-black stairwell. Memories flashed through her mind as she began the ascent, tip-toeing up each step so as to not alert those above, if there were any. *The room above is where the three dwarves stood guard.* Feint, flickering light welcomed her as she approached the landing. Sliding into the candlelight and pressing her back to the inner wall, she listened, hearing nothing but her own heart beat, then peeked around the corner until she had a full view of the nearly empty room, only crates in each corner occupying it now. Her eyebrows furrowed as she stepped into the room, blood shield and blood sword relaxed at her hips. *Empty?* She stepped over a jagged spot in the otherwise smooth stone floor where Skirm slammed the halbert through the dwarve and stone alike.

Kausha looked up at the entrance to the room. *Hallway and then stairs,* she recalled, lifting the shield on the back of her left hand in front of her chest, then began walking forward on her toes, listening for anything beyond her own heartbeat. Once again, she placed the shield parallel to the corner, complete darkness beyond, then peeked down the hall towards the candlelight at the base of the staircase. Nothing. She stuck the shield out, following it into the hall, her right hand with the blood sword placed just under the shield, pointed ahead. Her eyes darted left and right, searching with each step, using the light at the end as a guide. *Moss. Where are they?!* she cursed, standing in a puddle of candlelight at the bottom of the staircase. *It's too quiet.*

Listening for anything, but hearing nothing, Kausha turned into the stairway, hugging the inner wall while taking the steps two by two, shield up, angled above her head with the blood sword pointed to the side. The candlelight on the opposite side of the stairwell entrance spilled into the landing causing Kausha to slow and take the steps one at a time as she approached the hall that led to the back door of the tower. A quick peek around the corner and into the hall revealed only candles placed every few feet creating connected large pools of light on the floor.

Entering the main part of the tower, Kausha followed the halls towards the main kitchen, hearing and seeing nothing around each corner. That is, until she got to the walkway that overlooked the kitchen and main area nearby that led outside into the gardens. Kneeling, she sneaked forward and gazed over the railing to see two guards standing on either side of the doorway leading to the slave's floor. No one was moving in or out of the kitchen even though it was early evening. She crawled backwards to get out of the light. *So they were expecting something, which means most of the dwarves will be posted closer to the six or Bjorgene. They could all be together, as well, though. If all six and all of their guards...* she cut the thought off. Her eyebrows narrowed as she retracted the sword and hesitated before dropping the shield, replacing them with four daggers, two in each hand, then broke them off, readying them to be thrown. She squatted momentarily, then sprinted to the railing, lifting one foot to it while driving the other knee into the air, clearing the railing fully. One of the dwarves noticed her from the top of his vision, lifting his eyes and opening his mouth to say something, but it was too late. Kausha already let loose the daggers, aimed at their eyes, before the dwarves even raised their heads. Both corpses' grip slipped on the halberts as they tumbled backwards into the wall. Kausha landed on blood-filled legs, then darted forward the rest of the way to the falling halberts, snagging one, then the other, before they could come crashing down. The dwarves' armor made a muffled crash against the stone wall behind, their bodies soaking up most of the sound.

Kausha gently placed the halberts to the floor, then glanced down the stairwell to the slave's quarters, high-pitched voices reaching her ears for the first time. She pushed four blood knives from under her fingernails, keeping them connected for now, then started down the short steps to the quarters below. Before her toes breached the candlelight spilling from the slave's quarters, she paused, quickly glancing around the curve to see a guard standing next to the first door, a thick rope tied tight around the handle connected to a newly placed metal shaft jammed into the wall next to it. *There are six doors here, not including the bath,* she recalled, retrieving the daggers from her left hand, replacing them with a blood sword, then shortening the knives in her right hand into throwing daggers, adding two more from other fingers, then snapping them off. She glanced at her weapons, nodded, then measured the distance to the bottom of the steps. Pumping blood into her legs and working her organs to the left side of her body, she jumped, clearing the seven steps to the bottom while throwing a blood dagger at the wide-eyed dwarve guarding the first door. He didn't even have a chance to move. Kausha noticed at least three more in the hall, including one directly to the right of where she landed.

She shifted two of the daggers between her fingers, and spun, hurling them both at the dwarve to the right, one missing slightly and inserting itself into the wooden door next to his head with a thunk causing screeches to sound behind the door, the other finding its mark, slicing through skin and bone as it slammed into the dwarve's cheek sending a muffled *ting* through the air as it found metal helm.

Crouching between the two lifeless bodies, one dagger remaining and her sword in her left hand, she swept her gaze over the remaining four as they inched towards each other, creating a makeshift phalanx with halbert tips pointed directly at her. The dwarves shuffled a step back seeing Kausha stand straight up, their eyes darting between one another and the Bloodborn symbol on her chest. The candles from each wall seemed to have the same idea, their light barely reaching her.

"Drop your weapons, open the doors, and let these women out," Kausha demanded in a flat tone, glancing between the dead dwarves, then back to the four in front of her. "Or die," she finished, twisting the blood sword at her side, candlelight reflecting dark red, nearly black shadows from it. The dwarves shot glances at each other, their beards shaking while they nodded nervously. They tossed their halberts in unison, the sound of metal and wood connected with stone echoing through the hall and up the stairs. Silence followed as even the women locked inside each room listened for what came next, no doubt hearing what was said.

Kausha raised her eyebrows at the guards, each stuttering beneath her gaze before scrambling off to opposite doors and untying the thick rope from around the knobs. She looked to her left at the first door, took a few steps, then sliced the rope with one, smooth downward stroke of her sword. After doing the same to the other side, she glanced at the guards, their mouths wide as each stared at her, still holding the ropes in their hands. They quickly diverted their eyes back down to continue to fidget as the two doors that Kausha cut the rope from began to slowly open. Out popped an eyeball from one, slowly followed by a skinny, green middle section of a head and body, then another eyeball, seemingly attached to the same woman. Chef lumbered out next, a smile on her face accompanying a nod towards Kausha, followed closely by Linil. The old, hunched back, gray haired woman held her head as high as possible, meeting Kausha's eyes with her green ones. A smile spread ear to ear, revealing a completely wrinkled face causing Kausha to smile back with the corner of her mouth. The women inside filed out two by two to stand near the entrance to the stairs to face the dwarves, who were now dripping sweat from their foreheads as their eyes fidgeted between the group, Kausha, and the rope. The guards finished untying the ropes at the same time, then stumbled back into the far corner next to the bath door as if trying to hide. The remaining doors swung open and the rest of the women worked their way into the hall. Shock, fear, reverence, thanks, and a mix of other emotions shown on the faces of those that saw either the blood sword in hand or the Bloodborn jumpsuit Kausha wore, but none stared for long, for each had a similar enemy now.

The women parted, making room for Chef as she made her way to the guards, sparing a glance for Kausha before reaching the gap between women and guards, then pointing towards the room to the left with her thick hand. The guards followed her hand, then glanced at Kausha, then each other before lowering their eyes to their feet and walking into the room. Chef followed closely behind, closing the door after them, then tied the rope into a tight knot. She then turned to look directly at Kausha, all of the other women doing the same, creating a whoosh as their white slave cloaks turned in unison. Kausha swallowed under their gaze, the candlelight casting odd, dark shadows upon their faces as it grew in both heat and intensity. Kausha's blood instinctively filled her fingertips, her eyes darting from face to face in an attempt to read their intentions. Movement drew her eye as Chef and two others, hidden behind taller women, began making their way towards her. Linil, Chef, and Selene, the woman that showed Kausha her duties on her arrival, stood in front of her, faces flat as they looked her over, eyes landing on her sword.

"I see why you were so good with my knives," Chef chuckled. Linil and Selene nodded in agreement.

"I knew it," Linil smirked, "I knew it all along."

"Oh, you didn't," Selene scoffed with a sideways glance at Linil.

"I did, too! Didn't I tell you earlier, Chef? I said..."

Chef stared at the two, cutting them off. "Don't get me caught up in your arguments, Linil. You know I don't want any part of it." She glanced back to meet Kausha's eyes. "Anyways, thank you, Kausha. We were cattled into the rooms, then they were tied up like that without a reason as to why, but now I think I know what is going on," she finished, glancing at the symbol on her jumpsuit once more.

"So," Linil prodded, turning her attention to Kausha. "What's the plan?"

Kausha balked, her eyes widening beneath a scrunched forehead. "Me?" She pointed to herself. "What plan?"

Liniil shook her head. "We know you have a plan or at least a goal, now tell us so we can help."

Kausha bit her tongue, but upon reading the faces surrounding her again, she noticed that the women were indeed scarier than before. It wasn't just the candlelight playing tricks, it was written on their faces that they were ready to act. *They're all serious,* Kausha realized in awe.

She nodded, bringing her eyes back to the three in front of her. "Okay, the plan was to come here, find the Gbinti Minds that betrayed their city and tried to have me killed multiple times, then kill them."

The women's faces showed no sign of shock or worry, only the same serious nature as before. "Do you know where I might find them?" Kausha asked.

Linil touched the top of her head as if to hold up her hat that wasn't there while she looked up in contemplation. "If I had to guess, I would say the first's tower up above. As you know, they always congregate here, so why would they change that?" She lowered her head looking at Kausha again. "And why would the first ever voluntarily go to a lower tower?"

"Unless the first had nothing to do with anything Kausha is talking about," Selene countered.

"If anything happens, the first knows, Selene," Linil responded, rolling her eyes.

"Anyways," Chef barked, glancing at them both before returning to Kausha, "I would say the first's as well. You'll have to go through the dining room to get to the floors above, but if they were up there, it would be two floors above the dining room where personal meetings are held between the six."

"What about the women in the other towers? I can help free them first and then..." Kausha stopped as she saw all three women shaking their heads vigorously.

"This is something we need to do." Chef slammed a fist into her opposite, open hand. "They have held us and the others long enough. Who knows, we might even create a nice distraction for you," she shrugged.

"We aren't as strong as you, but we aren't helpless. Years and decades of hard slave work have us all ready to move. Don't worry, young Bloodborn, we can handle freeing the other towers," Linil ended with a smile and a flash in her green eyes that meant what Kausha felt. *Revenge.*

Kausha nodded. "Thank you."

All of the women throughout the large hall bowed, including Chef, Linil, and Selene, then stood straighter than before, parting the way like a wave towards the stairwell for her.

With a final nod, Kausha filled her legs with blood and took off running, blood sword in her left hand, a single blood dagger in her right. She reached the top of the stairs in a flash, the two dwarven guards dead to either side. Without hesitation, she darted diagonally to the far side of the corridor, aiming for the stairwell she had used to deliver food to the lavish dining room with the fluffy white rug. Forcing blood from her legs, she slid to a stop before the first stone step, then she looked up into the darkness. The pitter patter of rain hitting crops and the water they sat in urged her forward. Lightning from behind lit up the first few steps until the tight curve of the stairwell hid the rest from view. She looked down, turning the blood sword and opening her hand, revealing the blood dagger. Thunder from far away cracked through the air, echoing throughout the corridor and up the stairwell. Pocketing the blood dagger, she decided to create another blood sword to mirror the one in the left. She held her fingers together tightly, then pushed blood from under fingernails to create a skinny, sharp sword slightly longer than the other. Satisfied, she set her jaw, then began the ascent with both swords pointed forward and up, out in front.

In total darkness, another rumble of thunder sounded from below, bouncing off of the stone walls, following her along. Silence between claps. Only the beating of her heart in her ears kept her company with each step. The sight of light paused her ascent. Cautiously, she crept up the final five steps to the landing before the main hall leading to the dining room. She peeked around the corner into the bright candlelight, the familiar white, fluffy rug making the hall seem brighter than it really was. Following the rug, her eyebrows narrowed as she noticed the huge wooden double doors closed up ahead. Movement at the bottom of the door, back lit by the enormous fireplaces inside of the dining room, made her pause, her toes attempting to dig into the rug beneath. Whatever it was moved again, its shadow crossing the entirety of the door to the opposite side. She breathed slowly, not wanting to make a sound, then continued creeping forward, eyes darting between passing shadows beneath the door.

How can I get in without alerting those inside? She studied the door up and down to inspect the hinges, handles, and cracks. *Chef said that there is no other entrance to the floor above. I trust her. I guess I will just have to...*

Both doors slammed open at the same time causing Kausha to jump back or else get hit. Her heart raced, blood coursing throughout her body upon landing in a crouch. Her eyes shot wide seeing four dwarven guards in front, each with a long, braided beard, eyes squinted, staring at her beneath a metal helm. Their armor was similar to the rest of the dwarves she faced, except these wore different colored cloaks - purple, orange, green, white, yellow, and blue - showing which of the six they served. Halbert tips threatened in perfectly steady hands, something only possible from years of intense training. The phalanx they created in the doorway left no room for maneuvering, but what they lacked in that, they gained in sturdiness. Looking past the first row of dwarves, she saw two more, the first helping to finish the phalanx by holding their halberts between the two in front of them, creating eight shiny menacing points, while the second held their halberts tilted at an angle above those in front, blocking the rest of the doorway. *Moss,* Kausha cursed, finding no cracks in their defense.

Kausha's eyes darted between the dwarves, each still as a statue, then she measured the doorframe, the door, then the walls surrounding both, trying to find a way through. Returning to one of the thick double doors sitting slightly ajar, her eyebrows rose. *Maybe.* She stood, retracting the blood sword from her right hand and extending the one on her left causing the dwarves to shuffle their feet in anticipation, the sharp points of their halberts swaying ever so slightly. A smirk crossed Kausha's face before she darted with blood filled legs towards the right wall, then leapt, turning her body in mid-air and landing feet flush against the wall, her momentum pushing her down into a squatted position right next to the ajar door. In a split second, she placed her right hand on the door while shoving off of the wall with her legs, blood sword in her left hand extending past the edge of the door, pointed out. Grunting, she shoved the door closed with the aid of blood-filled legs, right back towards the dwarves. Armor clattered and voices yelled as they noticed what she was doing, but the phalanx with three rows of heavily armored, slow moving dwarves, made quick movements impossible. Kausha heard metal meet wood as the door slammed into halberts, pushing them together out in the open door. With one downward swoop of her blood sword, she severed the heads of eight of the halberts that were leveled towards her, the ones tilted up just out of reach as she dropped to the white rug. The door slammed all the way shut, hitting a few of the dwarves square in the chest creating a loud clang and crunch as they were squished between wood and bodies behind.

Leaving one side of the double doors open, Kausha dove into the dwarves, one with an orange cloak, one with a blue cloak, but both with eyes wide in fright as they stared down the wooden shafts of what were weapons just a moment ago. As they tried to retreat backwards, impossible with the two rows behind lost in confusion, Kausha stabbed her blood sword through the orange cloaked dwarve's mouth, his eyes growing even wider than before as the sword exited the back of his head, parting his metal helm behind, then inserting itself into the second row's dwarve through his cheek while he was looking towards his companions to his left. Kausha yanked the blood sword free in a spin, ending in a crouch before the dwarve in blue, whose mouth was agape after watching his companions fall so quickly. She shoved the sword upwards under the dwarve's chin, a muffled clang sounding throughout the room behind as the blood sword drove into the helmet, narrowly missing the dwarve behind. Pulling the sword free, the dwarve fell in a heap. *Three down,* Kausha counted, stepping forward, shortening the blood sword while creating five blood knives in her right hand.

Seeing the front row of their phalanx fail, the remaining dwarves that could still move spread out backwards into the dining room. Kausha peeked around the closed door, seeing four dwarves lying on the floor, three unmoving while the fourth, shadowed face staring up at her, lay trapped underneath two from the first row. Kausha stepped over the dead dwarves and entered the dining hall, white rug already stained with blood from dwarven wounds. The three giant fireplaces threw the entire dining hall and long dining table alight, the warmth noticeable even with stone ceilings and walls. The remaining dwarves spread out on opposite sides of the table, the ones with broken halberts discarding the useless wooden shafts on the white rug before pulling out two hidden one-handed axes from beneath their cloaks.

Five left, Kausha counted. The fireplace popped, setting their colorful cloaks alight from behind. She pushed her fingers together, connecting the blood knives, then pushed them out together to create another blood sword that almost seemed black in the dining hall. Shadows enveloping the dwarve's bearded faces made it impossible to see what they were thinking, but seeing their grip tighten on the wooden shafts gave Kausha an idea.

Suddenly, movement flashed from the right of the table forcing Kausha to slide to her left instinctively before the sound of splintering wood sounded behind her as an ax slammed into the door. As if that were a sign to attack, the five dwarves moved together, clanking plate armor echoing together, muffled only slightly by the rug underneath as cloaks flapped with the sudden surge of dwarven strength.

Kausha was forced to jump to her left again, closer to the three with intact halberts thrusting one after the other, attempting to keep her at bay until the two with axes could surround her. *Moss,* she cursed as a clang against the stone wall off to her left told her that an ax narrowly missed her head. She crossed her swords, diving forward into a roll under the tips of the halberts, ending with blood swords above her head in the shape of an X, then uncrossed them, slicing the metal ends from wooden shafts in an instant. With blood filled legs, she shoved off of the carpet while raising her swords, throwing herself between two of the dwarves, their eyes wide at the unexpected maneuver. She sliced through both necks at the same time, their heads toppling from their bodies next to her as she landed in a crouch. The third dwarve had his axes in hands, facing her before the bodies fell with a muffled crash. He jumped backwards to give himself space, ending up side by side with the two dwarves that were chasing her.

Three left. She felt sweat streak down her cheeks. A loud boom sounded at the opposite end of the hall, drawing her attention. Lightning flashed into the room through the newly opened door, throwing a dwarven-sized shadow into the room followed by a rumbling of heavy feet and armor as dwarves, one after another, filed into the hall in a quick march. The line split between rounding the table to reach the side she was on and turning immediately left upon entering to line the opposite side of the enormous table. Rather than the typical halberts, every dwarve, clad in their six's color, held a short ax in each hand. Kausha glanced back to the three behind, their smiling faces visible from the fires, twirling axes as they glanced between her and the dwarves filling the room on both sides.

Moss, Moss, Moss! Kausha cursed to herself as thunder and armor-clad feet mixed together to create a reverberating rumble that shook her bones as she watched the final dwarve enter the dining hall. The dwarves entering didn't attack, only stood staring silently with axes held casually to their sides.

"This is it, Bloodborn!" a gruff voice yelled nearby. Kausha's head swiveled to see one of the dwarves she had been fighting, one in white, standing tall. "Give up or die," he growled through gritted teeth, his eyes narrow beneath a red face. His jaw clenched as she turned to face him head-on.

Kausha dropped the blood swords to her sides, tips resting on the white rug, dripping blood, then she shrugged. "Give me the Minds that tried to have me killed and I will leave."

The dwarve turned to his left, then his right to look at his companions, then across the table to the numerous dwarves standing nearby, then back to meet Kausha's eyes. "You do not seriously think that you are in a position to negotiate, do you? Look around - you cannot defeat us all on this floor, let alone those above as well."

"We have something to say about that!" a female voice echoed from behind the three dwarves near the entry leading into the dining hall, causing them to twist their heads towards the voice. Kausha glanced around the dwarves towards the single open door to watch the second door open, Chef and another woman Kausha didn't recognize pushing it ajar to reveal dozens of women in the entrance hall in a rainbow of the six's colors. A closer look revealed that a number of women had blood stains on their cloaks and each held a weapon ranging from a knife to a wooden handle, a halbert, a pan, and more. Kausha smirked. *That was quick.* The three dwarves across the table turn towards them out of the corner of her eye.

"Ladies, charge!" Chef yelled, thrusting her knife over her head.

The three dwarves near Kausha darted their heads back to her, eyes wide, their feet shuffling trying to decide what to do. Kasha stood still, blood sword tips still rested on the carpet, then shrugged, tilting her head to the side while raising her eyebrows and frowning.

"Moss!" the dwarve in white cursed, fully turning towards the charging women, then running at them with his two companions.

Kausha turned to face the table, the dwarves on the near side of the table to her left shuffling now, the ones in back trying to get a glimpse of what was going on while the dwarves on the opposite side of the table started inching towards the skirmish, some even beginning to break off to join the fight.

Kausha raised her swords, leaping on top of the giant table, then turning to face the entire length, spreading her feet, the swords pointed out at her sides to cut off any further advancement of dwarves. The closest shuffled backwards two steps, raising their axes to their shoulders in preparation to fight. Grunts, yells, screams, and clangs of metal on metal or metal on wood met Kausha's ears as the fighting intensified behind her.

Looking down the length of the table, there were more dwarves as she thought there were initially, but the confines should make it an evenly matched fight. Fireplaces ahead and to her left and right, along with the one at the far end of the room, lit the dwarve's metal helms, axes, armor, and beards as they stared up at her. Their cloaks, mismatched from one another, shifted silently at even the smallest of movements or twitches of muscles underneath.

A twitch out of the corner of her eye set off a chain reaction inside, forcing blood away from her legs, moving her insides up into her chest, and extending the blood swords slightly in each hand. The dwarve's eyes close enough to see them lengthen, grew wide. *I think I have their attention,* she smirked. Without warning, she cartwheeled through the air to her right, stabbing both swords into the first dwarve's eyes, then pulling them out immediately, his axes dropping to the rug, blood and body falling in a heap. Landing in a squat, she darted forward, one sword pointed straight ahead in an outstretched arm at the next dwarve's chest, the other sword thrusting from below. The dwarve threw up both of his axes, deflecting the first sword, but failed to see the second as Kausha drove it up under his chin and through the metal helm, a nasty crunch following as she pulled it free, the dwarve's head snapping forward from the force, splattering the white rug in front of her feet.

Two clangs sounded on the wall to her right as soon as the dwarve fell. Kausha turned towards the table, diving into a roll over it. Her blood-filled legs slammed into the chests of two dwarves on the opposite side, throwing them off of their feet and landing with a muffled clang as the back of their chestplate toppled onto the rug. She planted her feet, bending over, then jumped forward, shorting her blood swords while raising them above her head. Landing between the fallen dwarves, she slammed the swords into either dwarve's face, stone crunching beneath as the sword sliced through bone, helm, and rug, into the floor below. Kneeling, she yanked the swords up, dwarven blood squirting into the air and splashing the sides of her jumpsuit. Instinctively, she spun on her knee towards the wall, glancing up to see two dwarves on the opposite side of the table ignoring her and running to join the other fight. Retracting the sword in her right hand and creating five blood daggers, she broke them off, then ran alongside the dwarves, palming three while placing two between her knuckles. With blood-filled legs, she pulled ahead of the two dwarves, their heads turning to see her, shocked, but it was too late. Kausha let loose two of the daggers in one quick motion, the blood causing them to flash red as they spun through the air before finding each of the dwarve's left eye, their bodies tumbling forward in a crash.

Kausha turned her body, skidding to a halt while shifting the remaining daggers between her knuckles, then stared back the way she just came. The remaining dwarves, unperturbed, repositioned to stand three by three on either side of the table, the firelight flickering across their beards as a hoarse, curdling yell sounded behind her, followed by silence. She afforded herself a glance back towards the entrance of the hall, a relief flowing through her as she saw Chef standing there, chest heaving, alongside a rainbow of colors backlit by the candles from the entry hall.

Kausha stood straight up, turning back towards the remaining dwarves in the middle of the dining hall, then stepped up onto the table once again. The dwarves repositioned slightly, keeping Kausha straight ahead as they held their axes in front. With sword to one side and daggers grasped between knuckles in the other, she began slowly walking down the middle of the table. Feeling the warmth from the fires and excess blood inside, she felt the urge to act while glancing from one dwarve to the next. The dwarves continued to shuffle, darting glances to their companions nearby, waiting to see who would act first.

Kausha stopped directly in between the two groups, facing neither. She breathed deep while staring at the giant fireplace at the end of the dining table, the fire dancing, urging her to act. The fireplaces behind the dwarves on either side of her cast shadows across the table to reach her legs, cooling them even with excess blood coursing throughout. Movement from her left - one of the dwarves in white lunged forward, sweeping his ax horizontally above the table, aiming for her knees. Kausha jumped, easily dodging the attack, then landed on top of the dwarve's hand with a crunch as feet met an armored hand beneath, throwing the dwarve off balance. His nose slamming into the side of the table with a crunch and a moan. Kausha raised her blood sword, then stabbed down through the top of the dwarve's helm, splitting helm and skull at the same time. She stepped off of the hand, the lifeless body falling and dragging the hand with it as it collapsed to the floor.

Footsteps vibrating the table from behind caused Kausha to spin and see all three of the dwarves from the first row climbing on top of the table with raised axes, their jaws flexing, faces alight with anger under metal helms. Without looking, Kausha threw the three daggers she held in her right hand behind her, hearing a satisfying grunt and two clangs as they met metal breastplates. Spinning towards them, she couldn't tell what hit. The dwarves stomped forward, swinging wildly, but ferociously with both axes as they advanced. Kausha attempted to fend off all six axes with one sword, but it was too much. A slice cut through her jumpsuit, piercing her skin as well in an attempt to dodge one of the blows. Another dwarve stabbed with the point of his ax, hitting her in the stomach, losing his hand in the process, but still he attacked. Neither of her wounds dripped blood and were healed almost instantly, but the dwarves kept on, not giving Kausha an opening to attack. Footsteps sounded behind her as she deflected another blow aimed at her neck while another caught her right leg, slicing her jumpsuit and nicking her leg at the same time.

Moss! she cursed as she breathed deep, then held it. Everything froze, even the fire's dance halting behind the dwarves in front of her. Scanning the dwarves in front, a blow was coming from below that was aimed to slice her in two from belly to head. Forcing blood into her neck, she turned slowly to look behind, movement coming easier this time than last when she fought the sorcerer's creature, to see an axe mere inches from the top of her head held by a dwarve with his mouth and eyes wide as if yelling a guttural cry. She pushed blood from her fingertips, creating a small blood sword - just large enough to block the axe above - while straining to move both arms, her left to block the blow coming from below, the right to block the once from above. She urged her body. *Move!*

Kausha let go of the breath, the dwarve's expected yell from behind sounding in her ear, mixing with two loud clangs, one above and one in front, as blood swords met axes. A mumbling of "How?!" could be heard from multiple dwarves as they froze, confused as to how their killing blows did not connect. Before they could regain their whits, Kausha cartwheeled to her left, spinning slightly, while extending the sword on her right hand to match the length of the one in her left, landing with feet wide and firm on the table, all of the dwarves now in front of her, still in shock.

That wasn't my best idea, she grimaced, looking down at her jumpsuit containing multiple slashes and holes as a roll of thunder met her ears from behind. Shrugging, she looked up and scanned the dwarves from left to right. Two on the left, five on the table, two on the right. *Nine left.* She separated her insides and moved them to either side of her body as training taught her. A pit formed in her stomach at the thought of home. *No.* She forced it away, clenching her jaw and narrowing her eyes towards the dwarves. *Not now.*

She drove her feet into the table, sprinting forward, both blood swords held above the right side of her head slanted down. The dwarves stood side by side, the previous confusion on their faces replaced with anger as they squatted, holding their axes ahead in preparation. Kausha leapt as they swung, flipping over the dwarve with the hand she severed, stabbing with both swords from directly above as he watched her sail overhead, his reaction too slow to block the swords. *Eight left.*

The four remaining on the table turned in unison, keeping their axes facing towards her. Landing with a thunk, she immediately changed direction and darted towards them, then leaned forward while shoving the swords ahead of her at the eyes of a dwarve in orange. He was ready for the attack and deflected the swords with a clang. Kausha recovered, spinning while crouching, swiping her swords at the legs of all four, slicing through the knees of the one in orange that just blocked her attack, a blood-curdling roar leaving his mouth as he dropped his axes to the table, his body falling to his right, crashing into a dwarve in purple next to him causing him to stagger and nearly fall. He dropped an ax in an attempt to support the dwarve in orange. Kausha's eyes went wide as she slipped on blood while stabbing upwards with her left hand at the face of the dwarve in purple, coming up short, but still drawing blood on his arm, the weight of the one in orange halting his movement, causing both dwarves to topple over into the one in white closest to the edge, all three falling off of the table in a heap.

Kausha pulled her right arm back, spinning to her back just as an ax slammed into the table beside her. The dwarve yanked at his axe above Kausha, face straining. She drove the sword in her left hand up into his neck, blood splattering her face and chest. She rolled twice, barely dodging the lifeless dwarve as it crashed into the table where she was just a moment ago. One more roll and she fell from the table, landing on one knee in a crouch. Driving blood into her legs, she leapt away from the table, scanning around to see where the remaining dwarves were. Two on the table, three on this side. *Five left,* she counted, watching two of the dwarves on her left kneeling down to help free the dwarve in white that was trapped between the dwarves in the purple and red. Ignoring the two on the table, Kausha sprinted towards the two kneeling. They both dropped the dwarve's trapped arms to face her and began swinging before she closed the gap, forcing Kausha to play their game, stabbing and slicing trying to find a gap. Metal on metal clangs, grunts, and yells sounded behind causing her to tense. *Moss, I should have taken care of...*

"We've got these two!" interrupted her thought. *Chef!* She trusted the woman to do as she said, returning her focus to the two dwarves in front, one in white and the other in blue. With teeth bare, they growled and spat with a ferocity Kausha had not seen before. *Seeing so many of your own die brings out an animal in anyone.* Her body vibrated from deflecting a wild slash from the one in blue. *Too far.* The slash carried the dwarve forward with his momentum. Kausha spun with the blow, following his arm while bringing both swords level with his neck. His eyes went wide once he saw it coming. The blood sword in her right hand cut right through his neck, severing it completely. Continuing the spin, she shoved the blood sword in her left hand forward, stabbing the dwarve in white through the side of his neck, a gurgling sound following as he gasped for air while shifting his wide eyes to look at her, the whites bright from the fireplace nearby. The first dwarve's head toppled over with a thunk, its body following as blood spurted from the second dwarve's neck upon removing the sword, coating Kausha's jumpsuit on her left side.

She glanced at the dwarve struggling with the two plated bodies on top. "No, please!" he pleaded with arms raised. Kausha took two steps, then drove both swords into his eyes. The dwarve twitched momentarily, then went motionless.

Kausha yanked the blood swords from the dwarve, then turned to find Chef and the other women staring at her, the fireplaces nearby lighting up their blood splattered faces to reveal a mix of reverence and horror all at once. She retracted the swords causing the women to jump, then stepped forward to make sure the dwarves they attacked were dead. Satisfied, she looked to Chef and the others, nodding. They nodded back, words unspoken. *I'm on my own here on out.* She turned, stepping over dwarven corpses and puddles of blood alike, then headed towards the fireplace at the end of the room. She turned to round the table towards the open door leading into the hallway, partially open to the elements.

Chapter 56: A Forgotten Enemy

A flash of lightning followed immediately by thunder blinded Kausha for a second as she approached a dark mid-section of the hall that was partially open to the elements. Glancing off into the night to her right, another flash of lightning arched through the sky in the distance through heavy rainfall. Wind gushed, smacking a handful of the droplets into the hall causing the bottom of her jumpsuit to become damp, her feet slick on the stones below. With eyes readjusting forward, she noticed two options; the first was to go straight, continuing through the partial hall, the second was a wide stairwell off to the left that seemed to curve back on itself. *Up,* she decided, looking up into the pitch-black stairwell. She connected her forearms to create a blood shield once again. Twisting her wrists, she broke the shield off, placing it flush with the back of her hand, connecting the two through blood. As white and black spots entered her vision, she slapped the wall above her head with her right hand, catching herself before falling over. *Moss, I'm using too much blood.* She glanced down at the blood shield and gritted her teeth. *Too late now.*

Gathering her footing and shaking her head to clear it, Kausha created three blood knives in her right hand and kept them attached for now, unsure what a full sword would do to her at this moment. Staring back up into the wide stairwell with a clenched jaw, her eyes narrowed before lifting the shield high enough to cover her head and chest. Step by step, she ascended into pitch black darkness, leaving the lights and the sounds from the storm below. She hugged the far wall, the outside of her right hand rested against it as a guide. She kept her eyes up and ahead, her feet sliding along cold, flat stone steps as it spiraled into itself. Placing her next step, her foot fell to the same level as the last. Scooting forward, no more steps stood in her way, the outer wall extending straight, but only pitch-black darkness appeared ahead. She blinked, shifting her eyes to try to catch any glimpse of light, but none appeared. Refusing to retrace her steps, she continued on, hand against the wall for guidance. Her toes hit solid wood with a quiet tap. Sliding her hand along the wall to where her foot was, she felt wood there too. Rubbing the side of her hand along its smooth, polished front, she searched for the handle, but found none on either side. Raising her eyebrow, she searched again, finding nothing. *What the...* She gave it a soft push. It budged, letting out a tiny sliver of light that seemingly set the entire hallway alight. She squinted and blinked hard as her eyes glossed over at the intensity.

Kausha moved her head to the sliver to peek inside, seeing a smooth, polished stone wall with a circular device set against it, which was putting off an intense, steady white-yellow light. Her eyebrows narrowed at the object as she continued to push the door slowly open, its hinges greased, giving off no hint at her entry, as solid, unflickering light enveloped her shield and body alike. Providing enough room for her to slide inside, she poked her head in first, seeing a straight hall with polished light gray stone walls, floors, and ceiling, just like that of the Minds entry hall, except the walls were lined with multiple white-yellow circular devices that left the hall, and the room ahead, lit without a hint of shadow anywhere. *What are those?* She stared while sliding the door shut behind her before scooting over to hug one of the walls.

Shaking her head, she regained her focus, staring down the bright hall into a room ahead seeing comfortable looking, high-backed wooden chairs with white cushions on opposite sides of a low wooden table sitting on top of a colorful circular rug that resembled a whirlpool that ended in a white point in the middle. On the wall directly opposite the hall she stood in was a large painting of what looked like a dwarven child in a pure white robe. *Is that the first?* She remembered the brief glimpse she got in the dining hall, but it wasn't long enough to match with the painting here. Creeping forward, her eyes darted left and right with every step, but the only thing she saw was furniture and more paintings along the walls. Nearing the end of the hall, the lavishness and size of the room came into full view.

"Moss." Kausha couldn't help but curse aloud as she gawked at the size - similar to the size of the room where the passing ritual had occurred except this one had no windows, just light gray stone. Her eyes shifted to the ujuntu-lined fireplace to her left, surrounded by ornate wooden chairs with footstools just as ornate next to tables with cups that shined in the firelight. Her eyes wandered above the fireplace to a shelf lined with ujuntu bowls of various sizes, then to the painting above both depicting the same dwarven child as the painting in the middle, but with two dwarves, both with perfectly kempt braided beards and hair, standing behind him with a hand on either shoulder.

"Hel-lo Blood-born," came a soft, melodic voice behind Kausha causing her to squat and spin, raising the blood shield between her and the voice, her right hand with the knives at the ready next to her head. Her eyes went wide upon seeing Parjune standing in front of a small stairwell on the opposite corner of the room she was looking at a moment ago. Draped in the same multicolored patched robe as before, the colors popping with an intensity from the white-yellow devices above. None of the colors she wore came close to the bright green, piercing eyes, though. Eyes set against her pure white skin staring at Kausha, seemingly pinning her to where she stood.

"We have been wait-ing for you." She glanced to the hallway, then back to Kausha. "I take it you dis-posed of the gu-ards we sent be-low."

Kausha forced her blood to flow into her legs, standing straight up while letting her arms fall to her side. Parjune's eyebrow rose, the slight movement enhanced by the unrelenting, steady lighting around the room.

"Where are the Minds?" Kausha asked, lowering her tone for emphasis.

"The Minds?" Parjune replied, lifting her skinny arms from inside her robe to scratch her chin in thought while looking up, then back to Kausha. "Ah, the pol-i-tic-ians from G-binti. Why, they are a-bove, just up this stair-well," she finished with a wave of her hand motioning behind her.

Kausha's eyebrows furrowed as she glanced to the ceiling above, then returned her sights on Parjune, nodding. She took a step towards Parjune.

"Tsk," Parjune waved one of her unnaturally long fingers at Kausha. "I can-not all-ow you to go any fur-ther."

Kausha raised an eyebrow. "Aren't you a scholar? Why would you stop me? I want nothing to do with your six, just the Minds that tried to have me killed."

Parjune lowered her arm back beneath her cloak before nodding, a smile crossing her face. "I am in-deed a scho-lar, but my race sees ma-ny things worth stu-dy-ing, in-clu-ding your kind."

Kausha's breath caught. *My kind?*

Parjune continued before Kausha could reply.

"We know that a pas-sing is the Blood-born's most cov-et-ed rit-u-al where tal-ents and mem-or-ies are pas-sed down through gen-er-a-tions, each spur-ring death and de-stru-ction in the form of old gru-dges in new bo-dies."

Revenge.

"We know that the sor-ce-rers are Blood-born them-selves, gi-ving in-to the dar-ker side of blood mag-ic. We know that you your-self are the on-ly Blood-born in re-cor-ded his-to-ry, what lit-tle there is th-anks to your kind, to fi-ght back the gru-dge of your an-ce-stors, and for that I app-laud you."

Kausha's blood coursed through her body as her heart pounded against her chest. *How does she know all of this?!*

"Tell me, if you were of G-bin-ti and had the me-ans to stop a to-tal de-stru-ction of your ci-ty, would you take the ne-ces-sary steps to do so?" Parjune asked, eyes leveled at Kausha.

Would I? Kausha imagined Purtghast burning, Bloodborn dead in the streets, her mother, grandmother, and great grandmother's eyes glossed over, dead to the world. Her eyebrows narrowed, nodding. "I would."

Parjune nodded. "Then how can you fault those that want you, their de-stru-ctor, dead?"

They could have contacted me. Contacted us... Kausha's thoughts trailed off knowing good and well that she wouldn't have believed them over her family. Her eyes fell to the polished stone floor, her smeared reflection staring back at her. *We're monsters. Without Bloodborn, how might civilizations grown if they had time, or even our help? Mother said that they were barbaric, but we're the ones laying entire cities to waste.* She shivered as flashes of Gbinti burning entered her mind. Her friends standing around Yaula's grave. Staring out over the Mind's chamber. Chef, Selene, and Linil smiling at her.

Kausha shook her head, then lifted her eyes to meet Parjune's again. "You're right," she admitted. Parjune's eyes narrowed for an instant before returning to their normal, calm state. "After everything my kind have put the entirety of Uradaria through, I can see why they would want me dead." Kausha paused, swallowing, her voice growing hard again. "But Bjorgene and the Minds he's with have also attempted to start a battle with the Bloodborn as well as assassinate the leader of the Minds. He fled here after being discovered and I have volunteered to take him back to Gbinti to stand trial."

Parjune stood there silently for a moment, not a hint of emotion given, not even a blink. "It is no doubt that op-en war-fare with the Blood-born would be... de-tri-men-tal to Nort-mund as well as G-bin-ti, but in-ter-nal squa-bbles are of no con-cern to the six. They have pro-sp-ered and been out of reach of the Blood-born for lon-ger than any ci-ty be-fore - this would have been the same."

Kausha tensed, her left hand squeezing into a fist beneath the blood shield as she clenched her jaw tight. "So that's it, then. Whatever happens outside of these walls is of no consequence to the six?! Who will refill the places of slaves that they work to death? Who will they trade with? Will they not exchange these few traitorous Minds for their continued way of life? What will they do with you once bodies stop coming through the gates?"

Parjune's eyes narrowed, mouth pursing as Kausha noticed a slight movement beneath the colorful cloak.

"This is as far as you go, Blood-born," Parjune threatened, a new bite to her words, as she undid her cloak from the inside. She let it fall to the floor, revealing her unnaturally skinny body that resembled a lone white sapling found on mountain peaks. A black, sleeveless, skin-tight jumpsuit covered her midsection from ankles to neck, the contrast between skin tone striking, causing Kausha's eyes to dart from cloth to skin and back again. *No weapons?* She searched Parjune from head to toe, seeing nothing.

Kausha's legs tensed, her insides constantly shifting every which way. *What the?!* The shifting intensified as Parjune took a step forward, clearing a distance that would have taken Kausha three steps to clear. Kausha took a step back, gulping, then threw her shield up in front to cover her face and chest while bringing her right hand up, knives, like long, sharp, red fingernails, next to her head. Parjune took another step forward, then sprang towards her, her large hands balling into fists as her green eyes narrowed. Using her length, she slammed her right fist into the blood shield with a grunt, shoving Kausha back in a skid, even with blood-strengthened legs.

Before Kausha could recover, another blow rained down on her shield causing her to grunt, driving her back again, Parjune's taller stature making it easy for her to aim at Kausha's head. Kausha only had time to focus on defense as Parjune twisted her body, supporting her weight with her left hand placed against the floor, then kicked with both feet, connecting with Kausha's legs, causing her feet to fly backwards at the force, body falling forward. *Moss!* Kausha cursed, having to retract the knives in her right hand as the blood shield crashed into the floor awkwardly. She quickly pushed off the floor with her right hand at an angle, rolling her body to the left right before wind buffeted her face, Parjune's large, white foot flashing before her eyes in a streak.

Kausha finished her roll, ending with her right arm bent against the floor, back towards Parjune, then lifted her knees to her chest while extending her arm and twisting her body to put the blood shield between her and Parjune. A loud snap sent Kausha twirling body over shield, slamming to a stop as she crashed into one of the big, ornate chairs near the fireplace.

"Oof," Kausha grunted as she went still, pain shooting through her left arm. She glanced up to see Parjune standing with her arms behind her back, staring at her with large, green eyes, shaking her head.

"I ex-pec-ted more from the Blood-born that es-caped this ci-ty," Parjune struggled, her voice returning to the soft, melodic normalcy. Kausha looked to her blood shield, eyes wide seeing a large section of the top right of it missing. *Did she?! How?* She returned her eyes to Parjune, placing one knee on the floor and using the chair for leverage to lift her other leg, staying in a kneel. She retracted the blood holding her shield in place, letting it drop to the floor with an echoed tink as she pulled her arm to her chest, squeezing her hand to get the feeling back. *How can I defeat her?* She breathed out slowly, slowing her blood flow while her insides still churned, then she forced herself to stand unaided, head swimming.

"And I underestimated you," Kausha replied, forcing a smile towards Parjune. "Something else your kind studies, I take it?"

Parjune smiled, nodding, the fire nearby flickering against her white skin. "In fact it is. Well..." she started, looking at her hand as she lifted it close to her face, squeezing it and twisting it a few times, then returning her eyes to Kausha's, "...with a few na-tu-ral ad-van-ta-ges."

The heat of the fire warmed Kausha's right side as she flexed her hand again, shaking it. *Think. Think.* An image of the Bloodborn hairpin in her hair flashed into her mind. *How would grandmother handle this? Something...new.* She closed her eyes, giving in to the blood and memories of her ancestors.

Buildings burning, dirt roads littered with bodies... *No!* Kausha forced those memories aside.

The sun setting behind her, feet solidly set in sand shoulder-width apart as she deflected flying daggers using blood-wrapped arms.

Rearing back and throwing a long spear attached to a blood chain connected to her hand, then waving it side to side to change its trajectory as it shot forward towards an unseen enemy.

Slamming a blood-spiked forearm into a rock, sending shards of rock flying everywhere.

She jerked her eyes open to see Parjune staring at her, her head tilted questioningly.

Kausha looked down at her arms, imagining how the blood-spiked forearms felt, then, pushing blood into her arms, she forced blood through the pores on the outside of her forearms and hands. Little, needle-like blood tips poked from every pore turning her arms blood red. Once each was roughly an inch long, Kausha forced the tips together, leaving dozens of sharp, dense, pyramid-shaped blood spikes along her arms and back of hands. Her vision wavered, head swimming from removing so much blood from her insides, but she stood strong, then narrowed her eyes while lifting her head, meeting Parjune's eyes once again.

The firelight fought against the steady light from the orbs throughout, casting half of Kausha's body in the warm, red glow while the other half felt cold, the lights providing no warmth at all. Parjune's green eyes, steady and unblinking, measured Kausha with a new curiosity, glancing at her hand and forearms as if taking notes in her head.

"This..." Parjune waved her hand, "...is from the ri-tu-al?" she asked.

Yes. Kausha narrowed her eyes at Parjune while clenching her fists.

"Ve-ry well," Parjune accepted with a twinkle in her eye before clearing the distance to Kausha in a flash. She planted her left foot, turned her body, then swept her right one back, aiming a kick at Kausha's head. Kausha squatted, bracing her legs while throwing up her left arm beside her head, blood spikes pointed outwards, meeting Parjune's kick with a loud thunk, a grunt escaping Parjune's lips. The force of the kick sent the loose strands of Kausha's hair fluttering, and although the kick vibrated throughout Kausha's arm and body, the blood spikes did not break. Parjune recovered with a grimace on her face, eyebrows narrowed as she gingerly placed her foot on the floor, green blood dripping down her shin to trickle down her foot.

Kausha flexed her left hand, pushing blood through it while studying the small pyramids. Parjune's green blood showed on a few of the tips. *So they held,* she admired, letting her blood course throughout where needed as she locked eyes with her adversary.

Go! She rushed forward, remembering her training. *Never.* She drove her foot into the floor. *Let.* Another step had her jumpsuit's looser parts fluttering backwards. *Your.* She reared back her right arm at the same time that Parjune spread her feet to turn sideways, rearing back her right arm as well. *Enemy.* Nearly clearing the gap to Parjune, Kausha drove her left arm across her body, causing her body to spin, catching the movement of Parjune's right arm streaking forward directly towards her face. *Recover.* Kausha pulled her right arm around like a whip, the back of her hand and forearm slamming spikes into the back of Parjune's fist, deflecting it with a loud crack while green blood flecks splattered into Kausha's face. The force of Parjune's punch, combined with an injured foot, drove her forward, throwing her off balance while Kausha squatted at Parjune's side. Parujune's eyes shot wide upon seeing Kausha whirling her left hand around, blood-spiked forearm flying at her midsection. Kausha jumped into Parjune, throwing her entire weight into her, blood spikes tearing through the black jumpsuit and skin alike causing green blood to squirt from multiple spikes. A high-pitched pained yell escaped from Parjune's lips as they both tumbled over each other to the polished stone.

Kausha rolled to her left off of Parjune, ending on her back, then slammed the back of her right hand into the spot she expected to meet flesh. A loud ting sounded throughout the room as blood spikes met stone, sending chips of stone flying. Kausha shot her eyes right to see Parjune rolling to her right, green blood trailing her injured body. She ended her roll, pressing off of the floor to a kneel, her chest heaving while she held her side with her left hand, green blood already covering her hand so only bits of white showed through. Her right arm dangled to the floor as green blood dripped from long fingertips and right leg alike.

Kausha rose slowly into a kneel, eyes fixed on Parjune, who, for the first time, was laboring to breathe with eyes tight and mouth clenched. Kausha stood, back-lit fire casting a shadow over Parjune. Aching all over, Kausha set her sights on the small stairwell on the opposite side of the room, then started walking, leaving Parjune in a pool of her own blood.

"You are right," Kausha heard from behind. "I am their... slave. They de-serve ev-er-y-thing com-ing to them."

Kausha glanced over her shoulder at Parjune, who gave no indication of fight left, then she turned back towards the stairs without saying a word.

Revenge.

Chapter 57: Revenge

Looking up at the well lit stairwell, one that ascended steeply, then turned sharply to its left, double backing on itself to the floor above, Kausha calmed her blood flow, spreading it out evenly within her body in a failing attempt to stave off the dizziness from discarding too much blood earlier. Each step felt as if her knees would buckle, sending her topping down, but still, she climbed. Nearing the middle landing where the stairs turned, Kausha could hear muffled voices above. She stopped and bent over for a moment to catch her breath, looking down at the spikes on the back of her forearms, then, deciding that she could repeat the same thing above, if needed, she retracted the blood, letting it flow freely. It helped clear her head for the most part, the dizziness fading, but a cloudy feeling lingered somewhere in her mind. Ignoring it, she listened closely, but the voices above quieted. Rightening herself, she followed the stairs up to a landing that ended straight, rather than in a curve like the one below. *Nearly there.* She urged herself to continue the climb. Her eyes breached the top step, providing a view into a short hall, floors, walls, and ceiling just as polished as the floor below, with a single circular light on the ceiling towards the center putting off an unwavering cold, white light.

Topping the landing, Kausha entered the short hall, the white light casting her shadow on the polished stone below. She turned her eyes forward, squinting into a dimly lit room. *Are those shadows?* An unseen fireplace sent long shadows of shifting heads along the distant wall. Stepping forward, she glanced in the direction of the source of the shadows to see...

"Hello again, Bloodborn. Or sssshould I sssssay Kaussssha?"

Bjorgene, twirling liquid in an ujuntu mug, stood in front of a large fireplace alongside six others, all draped in the Mind's blue and white cloaks, the intense fire behind them hiding the symbol of Gbinti. Kausha quickly scanned the room. *Only them?*

"I sssse you are even more resssourceful than initially thought," Bjorgene scoffed, walking a few steps to a high-backed wooden chair off to the side of the fire, placing one hand on it while taking a sip of something from the mug. Kausha glanced over the Minds in turn, their faces shadowed, their cloaks shifting from side to side in the firelight as if a wind buffeted them, but no wind was to be felt in the room.

"And you have come to take ussss back to Gbinti, I take it? Well," Bjorgene slurred, raising his arms in front, careful not to spill his drink, and putting his wrists together, "come take ussss."

A shuffling of feet came from the Minds before Bjorgene shot them a glance, half of his face visible in the firelight as he turned, a scowl appearing beneath white eyebrows. The Minds went still once again, Bjorgene returning his eyes to Kausha.

"Well? I know the Mindssss, Bloodborn, and I know they would have ussss sssit trial. I can picture poor Gaune in hissss frail ssssstate now; hissss head drooping, placccccing the blame on himsssself for not sssseeing it sssssoner. It'ssss a sssshame that he could not ssssee what we ssssse - the potential of it all." He looked down into his mug, shaking his head. "Olibtine," he blurted out through clenched teeth, raising his head, taking a swig.

"And you!" he yelled, spit flying, gripping the chair tight, lowering the mug, and pointing it at Kausha. "You were ssssssupposssssed to murder and burn like your ancessstorssss! Bloodborn after Bloodborn after Bloodborn and now thissss!?" Bjorgene lowered the mug to his side, then casually walked to a low table on the opposite side of the chair where he refilled his mug while Kausha and the other Minds looked on.

"So that's it, then?" Kausha started, glancing first at the Minds standing in front of the fireplace, none moving an inch, then at

Bjorgene. "You didn't mean to have me killed. You wanted me in enough of a rage at you and Gbinti to destroy your city? To what end? You would have been killed along with the others."

A coarse, hearty laugh filled the air as Bjorgene slammed his mug down on the table a few times, its contents spilling over the lip. Kausha's eyebrows narrowed at the reaction as Bjorgene recovered himself, refilling his mug back to the brim.

"You really think that we did not have a contingenccccy plan for when you came? How did we esssscape sssso quickly once found out? I figured your kind ssssmarter than thissss," he replied, walking casually towards the fireplace, placing his free hand against the mantle and staring into it, the lines on his face from age showing clearly under the bright flames.

"So you worked with the six in an attempt to... become just like them?" Kausha asked.

Bjorgene closed his eyes, pushed off of the mantle to stand unaided again, then strolled behind the Minds, taking a swig from his mug as he walked. "While they ssssit on their ujuntu thronessss, WE lay in boxessss. WE, the ssssame onessss that created a prossssperoussss ccccity, and for what?! A *feeling* of a job well done?!" His voice rose as he went on, the Minds in front following him with their eyes until he reached the final Mind to turn and stand next to him. Bjorgene tilted the mug back, gulping the liquid down, the other Minds following, then, mugs dry, they all tossed them into the fireplace behind.

Kausha raised an eyebrow at them curiously, then she watched them pull hidden knives from underneath their cloaks, the metal flashing in the firelight. Her insides shifted as blood filled her arms and legs, preparing for a fight.

Suddenly, she felt sharp pain as something struck her back, the pain instantly extending to her chest and stomach. Kausha looked down, wide eyed to see the tips of two red knives sticking out, the

Bloodborn symbol sliced into three pieces. She looked up to see the Minds all running at her in unison, their cloaks flapping as they charged with knives glistening in their hands above their heads.

"Now that you know the truth," came two soft voices next to her ears, one monotone, one rumbling, "join us in righting our wrongs. Break the cycle with us."

Kausha glanced down to see the two knives sliding back out of her stomach, pain forcing tears into her eyes. She looked up, the Minds now halfway across the room with knives held above their heads, faces now visible, eyes wide, mouths open as if yelling. But nothing reached her ears.

Flashes of Shaum, Skirm, Skip, Chef, Linil, Selene, Puid, Olibtine, Daria, Nalia, Yauna, Roana, and finally Yaula crossed her mind as pain turned to warmth, her blood returning to her stomach. The warmth bloomed into a fire inside. The pain returned more intensely causing Kausha to throw back her arms, her back arching in response.

Then, through blurry eyes, she watched as her blood shot forward through the holes in her stomach, fanning out towards the Minds. Their eyes grew wide, fear overtaking their clouded minds. They attempted to skid to a halt, but it was too late. The fanning blood sliced through cloth, skin, and bone alike, severing their bodies cleanly in two at the waist. As quickly as it shot from Kausha's body, it returned just as quickly, healing her wounds, then coursing throughout her body once again. She watched as blood and guts spewed from severed halves, splashing to the polished stone floor, puddles of blood expanding, crashing against her feet in waves. The final knife crashing to the floor sent a metal on stone clank into the air, then all was still, even the fire calming to a low flame.

Kausha took deep breaths as she scanned the corpses, sights ending on the horrified, lifeless face of Bjorgene. *Revenge.* She turned to the hall, leaving bloody footprints behind, descending the stairs into the opulent room, Parjune no longer there, only a trail of green blood leading from the room. Retracing her steps, silence enveloped the tower. Not a single soul in sight, only dead bodies and dying fireplaces.

Join us in righting our wrongs, Kausha repeated to herself as she stepped over corpses while walking across the white rug splotched with red all over, heading down the slave's stairwell. She felt through the jumpsuit where the knives sliced through, no wound to be found. *Did they know?* Making her way through the candlelit halls, down further into the lower levels, she wasn't sure what to make of it all. *Break the cycle with us.* Her legs carried her without thought.

Parting the vines, moonlight glistened through the waterfall sending the cave alight. Kausha made her way along the path hugging the wall, mist wetting her jumpsuit and cheeks, wiping away the accumulated blood and sweat from the night. She stepped on to the grass opposite the moat. Turning towards the moat, she sat, dangling her feet over the edge and looking up at the moon-lit towers beyond the walls, a number of them glowing from the inside from fires. A smile crossed her lips as she imagined Chef and the others freeing slaves throughout. She let herself collapse backwards for a moment, lingering puffs of clouds flying overhead, blocking the stars momentarily.

"Better get moving," she grumbled while struggling to her feet.. She shifted her insides with a passing thought, tightened the knot in her crimson hair like she had done thousands of times since her childhood, dusted off what wasn't already dried and crusted from the night's activities, then set off towards The Forest.

The End.

About the Author

Jackson Salzman is an advertiser by day, and a lover of games, reading, fitness, and food at night. All of the fun had in worlds created by the stroke of a pen is what has driven Jackson to often-times simply write. From poems to songs to novels, he finds that writing is the perfect way to find out things one already knows.

His goal in writing is for those reading to escape the realities of the world around.

www.ingramcontent.com/pod-product-compliance
Lightning Source LLC
Chambersburg PA
CBHW060804030726
47503CB00002B/326